Julie Caplin is addicted to travel and good food. Formerly a PR director, for many years she swanned around Europe taking top food and drink writers on press trips sampling the gastronomic delights of the continent. It was a tough job but someone had to do it. These trips have provided the inspiration and settings for her novels.

juleswake.co.uk

twitter.com/JulieCaplin
facebook.com/JulieCaplinAuthor

Also by Julie Caplin

Romantic Escapes

The Little Café in Copenhagen

The Little Brooklyn Bakery

The Little Paris Patisserie

The Northern Lights Lodge

The Secret Cove in Croatia

The Little Teashop in Tokyo

The Little Swiss Ski Chalet

THE COSY COTTAGE IN IRELAND

JULIE CAPLIN

One More Chapter
a division of HarperCollins*Publishers* Ltd
1 London Bridge Street
London SE1 9GF
www.harpercollins.co.uk

HarperCollins*Publishers*
1st Floor, Watermarque Building, Ringsend Road
Dublin 4, Ireland

This paperback edition 2021
9
First published in Great Britain in ebook format
by HarperCollins*Publishers* 2021

A catalogue record of this book is available from the British Library

ISBN: 978-0-00-839311-3

This novel is entirely a work of fiction. The names, characters and
incidents portrayed in it are the work of the author's imagination. Any
resemblance to actual persons, living or dead, events or localities is
entirely coincidental.

Printed and bound in the UK using 100% Renewable Electricity
by CPI Group (UK) Ltd

For Emily Yolland, one of the unsung heroes of publishing who always brightens my day by simply being a genuinely lovely person.

Chapter One

Wiping the rain from her face, Hannah pushed her way through the revolving door into the hotel lobby.

'A touch wet outdoors today, Miss Campbell,' commented the young male receptionist with a cheerful smile. 'There's a lovely fire in the bar if you'd like to warm up. It's not a day for sightseeing, I'm afraid.'

'No.' She laughed, pulling the hat from her head and shaking the raindrops from the ends of her curls. 'Although I did manage to see some of Trinity College.' Sadly, not the *Book of Kells* nor the Long Library, which had been top of her list, but the thought of being crammed in along with dozens of soggy tourists smelling of wet dog had put her off. They'd still be there tomorrow and every day of the next six weeks that she'd be in Ireland.

'Would you like me to take your coat? I can hang it up here in the cloakroom. It'll dry nicely and save you having to go up to your room.'

See, this was the bonus of staying in a small boutique hotel. She gave him a delighted smile, already accepting the implied suggestion that she should go toast her toes in front of the fire. While she was there she'd send a text to her sister, Mina, thanking her for recommending this place. It was definitely a Mina sort of place. Without her sister's intervention, Hannah would probably have booked a Travelodge or something, as it was only for one night, but Mina was the one who always managed to seek out the trendy, happening-right-now places.

Hannah handed over her dripping coat and walked through to the cosy bar with its lovely vintage feel. It was Victorian-brothel-meets-20s-speakeasy – quite a look to carry off but someone had done it rather well. Dimly lit, it offered a warm, cocoon-like welcome which, after the miserable wet weather outside, was extremely appealing. The long wooden bar with brass trimmings and accessories, which glinted in the low light, was presided over by another good-looking young man with a bright, open, friendly face. Like all the staff in the hotel he immediately swung around to greet her with sincere enthusiasm, as if she were the very person he wanted to see.

'Hello there. What can I get for you?' he asked, his smile tinged with a touch of masculine appreciation. She could get used to it. There were women at work, like Sadie Burns-Coutts, whom she tried very hard to like, with her svelte figure, swishy, straight hair, and flirty smiles, who got this sort of reaction all the time. Hannah had never quite mastered being that confident in her appearance or as playfully feminine. She'd been too focused on proving herself with her brains. But maybe now she could relax and enjoy herself, focus on the food and a new skill rather than being the smart one all the time? 'I've just opened a rather fine red wine, a Bordeaux, full of plum and cassis, just right for a dank day like today. Or I can offer you a very nice whiskey, our own Telling Small Batch, brewed right here in Dublin. That'll warm you up.' Again, he flashed her a wolfish grin.

Hannah wavered, struck by sudden, uncharacteristic indecision. Her intention had been to order a coffee. The temptation of something far more decadent brought about a brief internal debate. It was only four o'clock. But then, why shouldn't she? It wasn't as if she was going to make a habit of it. Time to live dangerously. Although really, was a glass of wine that dangerous? She almost laughed out loud. It was for her. Hannah always followed the rules. Coming to Ireland was the first out-of-character thing she'd ever done in her life. Her boss was still in shock at her asking to take a sabbatical and her family were bewildered. If it had been Mina, the impulsive, adventurous one, they wouldn't have been the least bit surprised.

'I'll have a glass of red wine.'

'Excellent choice. Would you like to take a seat and I'll bring it to you?'

Even more indulgent. Being waited on. Hannah nodded and turned to survey the room, which was empty apart from a family party over by the window; they were spread out around a long table full of empty glasses and plates and recently replenished pints and bottles of wine. Their lively chatter and laughter punctuated the calm atmosphere of the room, enveloping it with an aura of homeliness. With a smile she headed towards to the large open fireplace and one of a pair of wing-backed chairs that looked as if they might have been plucked from Sherlock Holmes's study. As soon as she sank into the plump velvet cushions, nestling back into the chair, she propped her feet up on the little footstool so she could warm them.

By the time the barman arrived with her glass, her feet were lovely and toasty and she'd kicked off her shoes to curl up in the generously sized chair with her warm toes under her bottom. It reminded her of being a little girl again when she could duck down into the sofa with a book and no one would know she was there.

'Thank you.'

'Enjoy. You've the best spot in the house here.'

She took a sip of the rich ruby wine and sighed with pleasure. This was heaven and she had just the thing to round off the experience perfectly: her Kindle. A book, a glass of wine, a fire, and nothing else to do. What was not to like? It was the first time in she didn't know how long that she'd not been working and striving towards the next thing: GSCEs, A levels, law degree, articles, and more recently meeting endless deadlines. Not that she was to be pitied – she loved her job; she was well paid and she was good at it. When she added it all up, taking this sabbatical was probably the craziest thing she'd ever done in her life and she still wasn't sure quite what had driven it. Not a mid-life crisis, a love affair gone wrong (chance would be a fine thing), or a temporary loss of sanity – all things that had been suggested to her in varying degrees of exasperation by her boss and colleagues. What had triggered her decision to give up work and come and do a residential course at one of the top cookery schools in Ireland was the most ridiculously minor event, but it had brought home the secret embarrassment that, even though she was nearing thirty, she still couldn't cook. Her sister was an absolute whizz in the kitchen and she'd accepted that she'd missed out on the cookery genes, but in recent years it had become a secret source of shame.

Since reading about the Killorgally cookery school in *The Sunday Times* magazine supplement, when she'd had a bout of flu, it had become a mild obsession, especially when she realised it wasn't that far from her best friends Aidan and Sorcha Fitzpatrick, whom she'd been promising to visit ever since they'd left Manchester to go back to Ireland. Surely it was meant to be? Going to cookery school and taking time out from her job was completely out of character, but their proximity was a definite bonus.

Part of her wondered if she'd avoided cooking because it was Mina's thing and she'd always tried to compensate for Mina's more impulsive personality by being the opposite to her sister.. The one who kept the family on an even keel and reassured their adopted parents that they weren't going to end up like their real parents.

Well, it was too late now to worry about whether she'd done the right thing. Tomorrow she'd be picking up a hire car and driving to County Kerry on the other side of Ireland to start the six-week course. And now she was set on this strange new path, she ought to just kick back and enjoy herself.

With that she took another good glug of wine and settled into the chair to read. The wine was so good that when the charming waiter came by to offer another glass – of course he was charming, he was trying to sell her wine – she accepted without a second thought. In the warmth of the fire, nestled into the comfortable chair, she felt delightfully cosy and was starting to have trouble keeping her eyes open. The lively family party were taking their rather lengthy and quite emotional leave and as their voices died away, she set her Kindle down on her lap and closed her eyes.

———

She was having the most delicious dream when something disturbed her. The quiet clip of glass on wood. Opening her eyes, she blinked her way up to the surface and found herself looking into the most gorgeous set of intense blue eyes. Without thinking and feeling ever so relaxed thanks to her surroundings, she gave their owner her most dazzling smile.

'Hello.' Her voice came out in some sort of sultry purr that was about as far removed from her usual vocal range as humanly possible.

'Hi, sorry, I didn't mean to disturb you.' The owner of the gorgeous eyes shot her a disarming grin as if he were used to disturbing females and it actually didn't bother him one iota. 'I didn't realise anyone was sitting here.'

Neither broke eye contact and something bright and sharp fizzed in the air between them.

Then he went and spoiled it when he glanced back over his shoulder at the sound of a carrying female voice and hurriedly dropped into the chair beside her. He was hiding.

She was still staring at him rather dreamily, wondering for a minute if she had conjured him up out of her imagination. With dark slashes of eyebrows over those vibrant blue eyes and dusky black stubble dotting his chin, he looked mad, bad, and dangerous to know, with a definite air of a pirate about him.

Hannah wanted to mentally slap herself. Talk about clichéd. Men did not look like pirates in anything but the movies and certainly not men of her acquaintance. See, this was what happened when you drank in the afternoon. Flights of fantasy were not Hannah Campbell's bag but she couldn't help smiling at him.

'I won't tell.' She could feel her eyes twinkling at him, teasing and flirting in a most un-Hannah-like way. 'If you put your feet up on the footstool no one will know you're here.'

His mouth curved in a very naughty smile as he put his feet up as she suggested. An aggrieved shrill voice began cross-examining the barman.

'Are you sure he's not here? It looked just like him! I do know him. He's a friend of mine.'

'I'm sure you are, but I've not seen him,' came the soft-voiced, unperturbed reply.

The man opposite Hannah smiled and mouthed a Heavenward, 'Thank you.'

But then heels began to tap towards them and he winced, pushing himself back into the chair.

Tap, tap, tap. There was a determined staccato to their beat and the man closed his eyes as if that might help hide him.

Hannah had no idea what impulse propelled her to act but act she did. Standing up quickly, she swapped seats. He let out a slight *ooof* as she plunked down into his lap, his eyes widening in shocked surprise. *Tap, tap, tap.* As the footsteps grew closer, she bent her head towards his so that her curtain of corkscrew curls hid his face.

With nowhere to turn, the two of them stared at each other as the high heels faltered. He pulled her a little closer so that now they were nose to nose. Her breath caught in her throat as she stared, mesmerised, at him.

'Oh, excuse me.'

The steps began to back away but both of them remained frozen until they receded out of earshot.

'I ought to thank you,' he whispered, still gazing at her, an engaging grin curving his lips.

'You ought to,' she replied.

'How do you suggest I do that?' His eyes dropped to her lips with blatant suggestion and she took an involuntary breath.

Don't do anything with your lips, Hannah. Don't draw attention to them. Don't even so much as move your mouth. But, of course, she did. She pressed her lips together and ever so slightly moistened them with her tongue in a silent invitation that had her hormones' fingerprints all over it.

And, of course, he followed right up on that invitation with the kiss that had been hovering in both their minds. His quick, gentle, teasing brush of the lips made her sigh into his mouth, without even thinking about it. And that, she told herself later, was her mistake. As she melted into the kiss with unexpected abandon – it had been a long time since she'd been kissed – she felt him pause momentarily and then he deepened the kiss, his mouth beginning a tentative but thorough exploration of hers. That was the point when everything changed. The hazy, dreamy, gentle kiss became something else entirely; every nerve ending went on alert as if several thousand volts had been switched on. He must have felt it too because he pressed forward and suddenly she was locked in the most delicious, passionate, wonderful kiss, giving back as much as was being given. It was like a firework burst on a dark, silent night. Shocking, thrilling, and totally out of character.

As she settled into his lap, the kiss became more leisurely and she certainly wasn't about to fight it. Why would she? She melted into him as he put his arms around her, one hand sliding into her hair, stroking her neck with feather-light touches. Apparently she'd taken leave of her senses when she stepped on the plane this morning and wasn't about to gather them up any time soon.

'Er, excuse me, Conor.'

They both jerked apart. Hannah felt the blush staining her cheek. She couldn't have been more mortified at being caught in such a public clinch.

'The young woman has gone.' The barman nodded and began to step away, but not before they both caught the wry smile on his face.

'Thanks, Niall,' called Conor, while Hannah closed her eyes. She was stuck. On a complete stranger's lap. At least she knew his name now. She couldn't bring herself to open her eyes and she had no idea what to do.

And now she was being ridiculous. What was she, six? Even so, she opened one cautious eye to find the man named Conor smiling at her.

'Perhaps we ought to introduce ourselves.'

She straightened and with as much dignity as she could gather somehow managed to slither from his lap and back into her own chair.

'Yes,' she squeaked. 'Although you're Conor.'

His smile faded a little. 'Of course, you have the advantage there.'

Slightly perplexed by the change in tone she said, 'That is your name, isn't it?'

'Don't you know?'

She frowned, feeling a little as if she were standing on the edge of a bog: one false step and she'd be up to her neck in it. A bit like being back at work confronted with a legal argument before she'd had the chance to check the precedents. 'Not unless I've developed some kind of psychic skills in the last few minutes, no. Did the barman make it up? I assumed he knows you.'

Conor, if that was his name, considered her for a moment and she could almost see him weighing things up. She knew she'd been found innocent of whatever crime he'd initially supposed when his face softened.

'Sorry, you're English. Yes Conor is my name. And now I've been churlish when you so charmingly came to my rescue.'

'Yes, you have,' said Hannah still feeling as if she'd

stepped into another dimension. 'Although I don't normally rescue people. Not like that anyway.'

'I'm glad to hear it.' Suddenly he was all smiles again and she felt back on solid ground, although she wasn't sure what to say now. What did you say when you'd just been kissed senseless?

'I'm Hannah.' She held out a formal hand as that seemed to be the only way she could regain some semblance of control.

'Conor.' He shook her hand. 'Can I get you another drink?' he asked with a gesture towards her empty glass.

'I'm not sure that's a good idea. I think that might have been what got me into this predicament in the first place.'

'Predicament.' He rolled the word around his mouth in his soft Irish accent and she found it gave her a little thrill somewhere in her solar plexus. 'I'm a predicament, am I?'

'Well.' She lifted her shoulders.

'I think I like being a predicament. What were you drinking?'

She couldn't resist.

'Red wine. The Bordeaux.'

'You know about wine?'

She laughed. 'No. Only that I liked that one.'

'With wine that's all you need to know.' He stood up and raised a hand at the barman, lifting Hannah's empty glass.

'And just like that. Does everyone do your bidding?'

Conor grinned, his eyes twinkling with a touch of devilment. 'Of course.'

'You're very sure of yourself.'

'If I'm not, who else will be looking out for me?'

'Good point,' Hannah acceded with a nod of her head.

'So what brings you to our fair city? Hen do? Stag do? Weekend break? Business?'

Hannah hesitated. Enough people at home thought she was crazy to just suddenly up sticks and go on a cookery course for six weeks, she didn't need a stranger concurring with them. 'Just a holiday.'

'I'm afraid you haven't had the weather for it today.'

'I've not heard that people come for the weather.'

He smiled. 'There is that. But when it's fine there's no place more beautiful.'

'Spoken like a true Irishman.'

'Whereabouts in England are you from?'

'Manchester.'

'Ah. I have cousins there.'

'Don't you have cousins everywhere?'

He laughed again. 'Pretty much. That's Catholic families for you. And we're big on emigrating. So what do you do in Manchester?'

'I'm a lawyer.'

He looked impressed.

'What do you do?'

'Me?' He paused. 'I… er manage an estate. Look after the repairs and maintenance, that sort of thing.'

She nodded, slightly surprised, which was wrong of her. Did his slight hesitation mean he was embarrassed? You shouldn't judge by appearances but he was wearing a well-tailored suit which even to her untrained eye looked expensive. Certainly not clothes to be doing repairs in.

'I've been to a business meeting,' he said, quickly catching her quizzical gaze. 'With my family's lawyer. You're much easier on the eye than him.'

Thankfully the barman appeared with her glass of wine so she didn't have to respond to the compliment. He was so sure of himself, and she suspected comments like that came easily without much substance to them but for all that, he was charming and entertaining. It wasn't as if she had any other plans for the rest of the day. The rain had put paid to those.

'Thank you,' she said to the barman as he handed her the red wine and gave a tumbler of amber liquid to Conor.

'*Sláinte*,' he said, lifting his glass.

'I always wondered how you say it. I've read it a score of times in books but never heard it said. *Sláinte*,' she said, trying to copy his pronunciation which sounded more like *slancha*.

'Not bad. Do you know what I like about you?'

Hannah jerked her head in surprise at the rather direct comment. 'No. As that wasn't a rhetorical question, I assume you're going to enlighten me.' Her mouth quirked in amusement as she realised she was rather enjoying this light sparring.

'You haven't looked at your phone once. So many people can't exist for five minutes without checking something. It's like some kind of addiction these days. We have a strict family rule at home: no phones at meal times or when we're all together. Mam won't have it.'

'My Aunt Miriam doesn't like phones much either but that's because she's a bit of a technophobe. My uncle loves a gadget, but he's rubbish with his phone. He usually has to get me or my sister to show him how to do everything and then he promptly forgets.' She laughed with a little pang as she thought of Miriam and Derek back home. Not her real parents, but the closest she and Mina had ever really had. Their birth parents had been the original daredevils, real thrill-seekers always on the lookout for the next adrenaline rush. But that was also the reason why they weren't in their lives. Hannah winced momentarily thinking about the crash that killed them. Her real mother, so like Mina, wouldn't have thought twice about giving up her job and going to a different country. Hannah had only managed to cross the Irish Sea and it felt like a giant leap. She often wondered whether, if her mother had lived, she would have been a disappointment to her.

'I have to admit I might have taken a couple of pictures if the weather had been more amenable.'

'That's the weather for you.' He lifted his glass in toast as he took a sip.

She stared a little curiously at the glass. 'I've never tried whiskey.'

'You've missed a treat and this is the good stuff. Want a taste?'

Normally it would have seemed far too familiar, but all her caution seemed to have been not just thrown to the wind but tossed into the Irish Sea.

'Yes please.'

He held out the glass. 'You have to smell it first.'

She took a cautious sniff and then a second.

'What do you smell?'

Oh no, she was rubbish at this sort of thing. Her sister was the foodie and Hannah felt a slight pang. She missed Mina's bubbly enthusiasm for anything relating to food and drink. But then that was why she was here – to learn. Taking a deep breath in, she closed her eyes and concentrated.

When she opened them, Conor was watching her. Darn it, he was into this stuff too. She hated getting things wrong. All she could smell was alcohol and matchsticks, and she was pretty sure neither was the correct answer but that's what she was getting, so she went with it.

To her surprise, he nodded eagerly. 'Matchsticks, yes. Exactly.' He gave her a delighted beam, which made her feel she'd aced a test. 'The whiskey is aged in oak barrels – that's where you get the woody aroma – the barrels have previously been used for Bourbon and then the whiskey is transferred to barrels that held American rum, which gives it that wonderful spiced characteristic.

'Now taste.'

Holding the cut-glass tumbler, she took a careful sip. She'd heard whiskey referred to as fire water before and she didn't want to make a complete fool of herself coughing and choking. To her surprise, notes of spice and even vanilla warmed on her tongue. Without thinking, she took a second sip, enjoying the slide of liquid down her throat, heating as it went.

'Wow, that's not what I was expecting at all.'

'Ah, that's because this is the good stuff. We keep it to ourselves.' He winked. 'May I?'

She realised she was clutching the glass to herself.

'Sorry. Yes.' As she thrust the glass towards him, her fingers brushed his and there it was again, that little sense of connection. Did he feel it too? Or had the wine and whiskey addled her brains?

'Have you any plans for this evening?' he asked before taking a smooth swallow from his glass. She eyed the column of his neck. God, he was sexy, that was for sure. Normally a man like this wouldn't look twice at her. She knew she could pull in a few admiring looks, but she was realistic enough to acknowledge she was no supermodel. It didn't matter to her. She'd always got by on her brains and work ethic, which were more important.

Oh God, he was still looking at her. Waiting for an answer to his question. *Be cool, Hannah.*

'No. I haven't.' She raised her chin, wondering what came next and ignoring the hopeful bump of her heart.

'I've got a table booked at a new restaurant. Would you like to join me? It's always better eating with company.'

Hannah laughed. That told her. 'That's a very practical approach.' But she liked practical.

He smiled. 'I'd also enjoy your company. Is that better?'

'It will do.' She gave him a prim nod which made him grin.

'I like you, Hannah. You don't take me too seriously.'

'Should I?'

'No. You shouldn't.' For a brief second his expression was unreadable. 'I ought to go. I've got some calls to make. How about we meet in the lobby at six forty-five? The table's booked for seven and, believe it or not, the rain is due to stop. It's a nice walk and I can show you a little bit of the city.'

'That would be great, thank you.'

He rose to his feet, tossed back the last of his whiskey and gave her a quick salute. 'Until later.'

Hannah sat perfectly still, not quite believing what had happened in the last hour. It looked like she'd got herself a date, although it had come with a clear warning. Charming as he was, he was not a man to be taken seriously.

Chapter Two

Packing for a six-week stay which took you from late summer to autumn was a tall order at the best of times, especially when someone was going somewhere so far out of their comfort zone. Mina's only recommendation had been trainers. 'There's a lot of standing in a kitchen. You'll be on your feet all day,' she'd said.

Hannah had tried to pack for every eventuality but going on a *sort of* date had not been in her original inventory. Thankfully she'd included a dress or two and a couple of nice tops and her perennially perfect, smart black trousers which had seen her through many a meeting at work. They'd cost a small fortune but, in hindsight, were worth every last penny.

After the soaking in the rain, her curls were wilder than ever, but today she decided she rather liked them; they were a differentiating feature – her only differentiating feature, it was fair to say. She tousled them with her fingers and gave herself a quick once-over in the mirror. 'You'll do,' she said out loud. 'It's just dinner.' But she couldn't help the sinuous little thought that slid into her brain. *What happens in Dublin, stays in Dublin.*

'Hannah Campbell!' She rolled her eyes at herself and shook her head before grabbing her coat and bag and crossing to the door of the hotel room.

Downstairs, she found Conor waiting for her and at the sight of him still wearing his suit, she was glad that she'd chosen the fancier chiffon and lace top and dressed it up with a fine silver chain and large hooped earrings.

'Perfect timing.' Outside, the sun had come out and had begun to dry the rain, leaving dappled patches of stone as the only clue of the day's earlier torrential downpour. 'Shall we?' He offered his arm with a charming, slightly tongue-in-cheek smile.

'How gallant,' she teased, her heart doing another one of those funny bunny hops, as she slid a hand into the crook of his arm.

'Always.'

They walked out into the warm, slightly humid evening, the air redolent of the earlier rain. Now Hannah looked around her with interest; earlier she'd had her head down, concentrating on not slipping on the wet cobbles.

'So this is the famous Temple Bar. It's lovely.'

'It is. Popular tourist hot spot. Lots of restaurants, bars and boutiques.' Despite the reference to tourists, there was a fondness in his voice. 'I love this pub here, The Temple Bar,' He pulled a comical face. 'When I was a student we had some big nights here. Not sure I could keep up with myself any more. But it's a great place for whiskey. Over 450 behind the bar. I've not worked my way through them all,' he laughed, 'although not for the want of trying.'

'Really? 450! I'm not sure I'd know where to begin.'

'You liked the Telling you had this afternoon. You should check out the distillery here. There are tours and tastings. It's very popular, especially the tasting.'

Hannah gave a non-committal nod. She was heading out of Dublin first thing and didn't want to spoil the evening by talking about real life. This all felt like a rather lovely fantasy and real life could butt out.

The narrow cobbled lanes were starting to liven up, boards outside pubs advertised live music, people spilled out onto the pavement, pints in hand, and there was a general air of jollity, almost as if a football match had been won.

Conor steered her down the lane and along another street until they came to a tall brick building with elegant arched windows situated high up in the walls through which glowed the currently fashionable bare lightbulbs hanging from black cables in the ceiling. Inside, there was a white marble staircase leading upwards.

'It used to be a bank,' explained Conor as he ushered her up the steps.

Upstairs, the restaurant, which was one large room with wooden floorboards, had a laid-back, mellow vibe. The relaxed decor held a touch of that not-trying-too-hard feel that had obviously cost a lot of money. Retro-style leather seats with metal legs were arranged around solid, not-quite rustic wooden circular tables, each of which was set with elegant glasses, silverware, and neat black linen napkins. A gentle hum of voices rose in the room which was packed.

'Conor, good to see you.' The casually dressed man at the front desk clapped Conor on the back with easy familiarity before turning to Hannah with a cheerful smile. 'Hello there, and welcome to Fintan's.'

'Gerard. Good to see you. Looks like you've got a hit on your hands. I had to beg for a table.'

'Sure, you did not. You and the family have always a welcome here. If it weren't for your mam I wouldn't be here. You know that.'

'She sends her love.'

'And well she might but when she's going to grace me with her presence?'

'You know her; it's almost impossible to winkle her out of her empire.'

'No surprise really. She's created a paradise there. Ah, Audrey,' Gerard called to a passing waitress. 'Will you show Conor and his friend to table one?'

'Sure,' she said and then as she looked at Conor properly, her eyes widened in sudden recognition. 'Good evening, sir. Gerard mentioned you were coming by. Nice to meet you.'

'Hi,' he said with his usual easy smile. She led the way through the tables and Hannah noticed a few heads turn as they passed but quickly forgot when they arrived at a corner table, right beside the window, with a fabulous view out over the River Liffey.

Hannah looked round with pleasure. 'We've got the best seat in the house. Gerard's a good friend I take it?'

'We go back a way.'

'Is it quite a new restaurant?'

'Yes. Opened two months ago and it's had rave reviews, but then it should do. He was taught by one of the best chefs in Ireland.'

'What's the food like?'

'Have you heard of the Slow Food Movement?'

Hannah shook her head. 'No.'

'It's about linking food back to the community, focusing on the ingredients and its provenance. Where it comes from and how it's been grown. That's a simplification, but there's a strong emphasis on preserving regional food traditions – good for the livestock and for the locals.'

'Wow,' said Hannah, for want of anything else to say. This was Mina's territory. Without her sister's influence she'd have been a strictly meat and two veg girl, but even so her knowledge of food was sketchy. Mina cooked it, she ate it. 'Sounds fascinating. So, what do they serve here?'

'Gerard has developed a menu that only uses seasonal ingredients that are available in Ireland. So it cuts down on the carbon footprint, instead of having things flown in from places like Peru and Kenya.'

'No avocados, then,' said Hannah, a touch flippantly.

'They don't grow so well in Ireland.' His eyes crinkled at her in a way that she was rapidly getting used to and was more than a little thrilled by. It had a way of making her feel like she was the centre of his attention that was both flattering and terrifying. Conor was a player who knew how to charm the ladies, but, for tonight, Hannah decided, why not join in the game?

When the waitress arrived to take their drinks orders and to hand over menus, Hannah picked hers up with no great expectation. What did they grow in Ireland? Sheep. Potatoes. Maybe fish. She'd heard of Dublin Bay prawns, so that might be something nice on the menu but she was expecting it to be fairly limited.

Which just went to prove that she knew nothing!

The menu, even to her own unsophisticated palate, sounded sublime, and when she ordered langoustine bisque followed by beef rib, with something called Roscoff onion, spinach, and pepper sauce, she knew she had a treat in store.

Conor insisted on ordering a half bottle of Chablis to go with their starters and a half of Malbec for the main course. It seemed a bit extravagant to ensure that they had the correct wine to go with seafood and beef, but she wasn't going to argue with an expert and when she took her first sip of the silky-smooth Chablis, she was pleased she'd left it up to him.

'This place is great. There's a real buzz.'

'Lots of hard work. Unsociable hours.' He grimaced. 'It's not for everyone.'

'Yes, there's a lot to be said for working nine to five.'

He raised an eyebrow. 'I always got the impression lawyers did their fair share of overtime. Isn't it all about billable hours?'

Hannah shrugged. She'd never minded the long hours. 'It's all right if you enjoy your job.'

'And do you?'

'Yes, I do. Occasionally, like everyone, I think I'd like a

change but I've no idea what else I'd do and I'm quite good at it.'

'Just because you're good at something doesn't mean you have to stick with it. Not if it doesn't make you happy.' She felt a raw nerve had been touched.

'True.' Hannah wondered if she'd made the right decision, taking time out from her job. *Stop it*, she told herself. *It's not forever. You wanted to do it. You can't get cold feet now you're actually here.*

Live in the moment. Enjoy yourself, especially when you're having dinner with a hot, twinkly-eyed Irishman who seems to be three steps ahead all the time.

Right on cue, he said, 'Are you all right? You look as if you're wrestling a personal demon.'

'No, not at all,' she lied, not wanting to tell him she'd taken a sabbatical or why. With his knowledge of food, he'd think she was a bit of boring and she was enjoying his flirty admiration. And if she was honest with herself, she was starting to feel a bit nervous. Work, her familiar routine and her little flat suddenly seemed a long way away. She thought about asking him what made him happy but decided that she didn't want some heavy, potentially philosophical discussion. She wanted to be Hannah the tourist, here for a fleeting moment. She wanted to enjoy some harmless flirtation. There was definitely a frisson between them and, what the hell, why not enjoy it? Why not be someone she wasn't for one evening?

She lifted her glass in toast. 'Thanks for inviting me for dinner.'

'Thank you for rescuing me.'

'I never asked. Who was she? And should I have been aiding and abetting you or standing up for sisterhood?'

'Aiding and abetting? Is that what they call it these days?' He raised a teasing eyebrow, clearly referring to their kiss.

She lifted her chin, hoping she wasn't blushing at the memory that was so indelibly printed on her brain it was still sizzling. 'I didn't see you complaining.'

'What's not to like? I enjoyed being rescued by a damsel.' His eyes flashed his approval. 'Are you always that quick-thinking?'

Hannah considered the question, unable to look away from his steady, interested gaze as his eyes danced with wicked amusement.

'No,' she said crisply. He was altogether too sure of himself and while she was enjoying herself enormously, she wasn't going to let him have the upper hand. 'Apparently the sight of you squirming in that chair upset my equilibrium.'

'Squirming?' He feigned outrage.

'Yes.' Relish tinged her words. 'Like a fish on a hook.'

'Is there no romance in your soul?'

She tilted her head to one side as if considering the question and then wrinkled her nose. 'It would appear not, and you still haven't answered the question.'

With a sigh he said, shaking his head, 'Spoken like a true lawyer. In my defence, it was a rather forthright young lady with, shall we say, a crush. I'd met her once before at a party and I had no mind to upset her by rejecting her as bluntly as I think I may have needed to. I was hoping to avoid a confrontation which, thanks to your noble actions, I was able to do.' He paused before adding, 'I am in your debt.'

'Don't worry, I won't hold you to it.' The thought didn't sit well with her, implying some kind of transaction was owed.

'That's a shame.' There was a definite challenge to his voice.

She rolled her eyes. 'You think a lot of yourself. Dinner will do fine.'

He grinned at her. 'If you're sure.'

'I'm sure.' Her severe tone didn't dampen the knowing look in his eyes. They were playing a game and it was up to her whether she decided to capitulate or not. At the moment the jury was out.

The food, when it arrived, was delicious; big on flavour and low on pretentiousness, which was a plus in Hannah's view.

'May I?' Conor had lifted his dessert spoon and dipped it into her soup before she could answer.

'Go ahead,' she said watching as he tasted the smooth pinky-orange bisque. She had to admit it smelled divine.

'Mm, that's good. Touch of tarragon in there, I think.'

'Excellent. I've never had an official food taster before.'

'Sorry, was that a bit rude? It runs in the family. We're always trying each other's food. Here, try a scallop.' He loaded a fork with a smear of bean puree, a piece of bacon, and a small creamy scallop and offered it to her.

The flavours burst in her mouth and she gave a greedy little moan. 'Mm, that is gorgeous.'

'Yes, the saltiness of the bacon and the flavour of the

garlic and cannellini bean mash sets the off the scallops to perfection. Gerard is a genius with seafood.'

God, she hoped he wasn't going to ask her to identify the ingredients of anything. She wouldn't know a cannellini bean if it came and spat in her face, let alone that you could make a mash with it.

'So what do you do when you're not working? Manchester's nightlife is great, isn't it?'

'It's also close to some glorious countryside. I like to unwind by getting outdoors at the weekends. There's nothing like fresh air and being in the Pennines to recharge after a manic week at work. I've got a bit of an addiction to canoeing. I love being out on the water.'

He raised an interested eyebrow as if she'd surprised him. To be honest, it surprised most people as she didn't strike anyone as the sporty type. 'Blame the children's book, *Swallows and Amazons*. I was obsessed with it as a child.'

'Fair enough. You ever done any sea kayaking? The coast here is perfect.'

'No, I stick to nice gentle rivers and canals.' What she really enjoyed was just being in the moment, enjoying the water without worrying about practical things like capsizing or crashing. Enjoying having the brain space to be fully present and aware of herself and her surroundings. She was quite happy pootling like a moorhen; she wasn't into the adrenaline rush of white water. 'Have you?'

'Not for ages. Too busy. I did quite a bit when I was younger. Where I grew up we weren't far from the beach. We had a little dinghy and would go out fishing, messing about on the water.'

'Sounds idyllic,' said Hannah, a touch enviously. Arthur Ransome's Lake District set books had been her favourites as a child and she'd hankered for that idyllic sort of outdoor life, having grown up on a very suburban street.

'Yes, there were four of us and we ran wild in the summer. You got any brothers or sisters?'

'A sister. She's just moved to Switzerland.'

'Have you been there?'

'Yes, in June for a long weekend. Where she lives is heavenly. Lots of wonderful walking, amazing views, clear air.'

'A long way from Manchester then.'

'Very.' She couldn't imagine ever moving to another country. It seemed such a leap into the unknown.

The tenderness and juiciness of the beef elicited another groan of pleasure which was quite unlike her, but it really was quite delicious. He insisted on her trying his meal and taking samples from her plate. It was a far cry from her aunt's plain cooking at home in a kitchen that was so out of date it was almost a museum piece. She had to admit that sharing was a lot of fun. There was a certain intimacy in focusing solely on one other person, waiting for them to elicit their pleasure and taking your own pleasure in theirs. Her sister, who was always keen to introduce people to new tastes and ingredients, would get along well with Conor.

'What are you smiling about?'

'I was thinking of my sister. She'd approve of you. I can never keep her away from my plate.'

'And what about you? Do you approve of me?'

'Definitely not.'

He laughed. It was a deep rumble that accompanied his eyes which flashed with an obvious delight that made Hannah feel slightly breathless. 'Probably a good idea, but I like you. You're not afraid to speak your mind.'

Not when it didn't matter. She was probably never going to see him again after this evening.

'And you're far too sure of yourself. That poor girl in the bar didn't know what she was getting herself into.'

Conor's smile faded. 'No, she didn't. She doesn't know me at all, she just thinks she does.'

'So I did everyone a good turn today. That makes me feel a lot better.' Hannah shot him a grin, wanting to lighten the atmosphere, which it appeared was easily done.

'You certainly made me feel a lot better.' His eyes strayed to her lips with a knowing grin which had her laughing out loud.

'You never give up do you?'

'Life's short. Why not enjoy yourself?'

There was a challenge in his words which lit a spark of rebellion in Hannah's chest. She'd always been the good girl, always done the right thing, but there was no doubt she was enjoying the flirty banter between them and as for that kiss…

Why not enjoy herself?

Chapter Three

It was one thing to enjoy yourself, which she undoubtedly had done, but it was a completely different kettle of frogs to wake up in a stranger's bed with absolutely no idea what etiquette dictated she do in these circumstances.

For a moment she lay quite still, the internal groan reverberating around her head. What had she done? Hannah Campbell did not go in for one-night stands, although her mortification was tinged with the tiniest touch of pride. Conor whatever his name was – God, she didn't even know his surname – well, whatever it was, he knew what he was doing. She still tingled all over at the memory of those kisses and the way his hands had touched her body. She wasn't a virgin by any stretch of the imagination, but after that...! Well, she'd clearly never had proper sex before. Sleeping with Conor had been a revelation.

She had no idea what time it was, but it was still dark outside. She picked out the shapes of the furniture in the room, trying to get her bearings. It was a different layout to the slightly smaller room she'd occupied – or rather, not occupied – on the next floor up. With a wince she tried to remember where her clothes might be. Scattered somewhere across the floor. Oh God, had they really snogged in the street? In the lift? Burst through his bedroom door in a desperate rush to strip off each other's clothes? She closed her eyes to shut out the starburst of images and the accompanying sensation of warmth in every last one of her lady parts. *Hannah Campbell, you tart.* She couldn't help smiling though – it had been bloody lovely.

Next to her, Conor shifted in his sleep and she froze again. How was she going to extricate herself from this? If she left now while he was still asleep, she wouldn't have to face him. She could get in the little hire car she'd picked up from the airport yesterday morning and drive away. He probably wouldn't mind. In fact, he'd probably be quite relieved. Let's face it, he was powered with the sort of Duracell-strength charm that would attract anyone he wanted. Yes, he'd be relieved to be spared her stuttering, gauche embarrassment. Last night's Hannah had been some weird aberration fuelled by Dutch courage. She would put it down to Ireland Hannah. Today saw the resumption of normal service and the return of England Hannah. Yes, the sensible thing would be to creep out now.

She slid out of bed and ducked to the floor with outstretched hands, trying to find her things. Creeping around an unfamiliar room trying to scramble into your clothes before you were caught was easier said than done. Ah, trousers! Where were her knickers? Inching her way across the soft carpet, her fingers scrabbled and by pure chance found them nestled into the skirting board. God, this was exactly why she didn't normally do this sort of thing. She was not cut out to be a ninja. With a cautious glance towards the bed, she wriggled into her knickers and trousers. When she found her top, she yanked it on quickly, praying she'd find her bra soon. And there it was. To save time, she stuffed it into her trouser pocket.

She quickly found her coat, handbag, and just one of her shoes. Where the hell was the other? Crisp cotton hotel sheets rustled as Conor turned over and she held her breath. *Please don't let him wake up.* It would be even more mortifying if he caught her trying to steal away. She listened, but his breathing remained steady and even. For a moment she was tempted to take a final peek at him but then she decided that was a) a bit pervy and b) too risky.

Where the heck was her dratted shoe? Cinderella she wasn't. Outside, the birds started up with a piping tweet here and a sweet whistle there. The dawn chorus. Strands of pink started to fill the sky through the window. In their haste last night, they hadn't bothered with curtains. Conor turned again and his breathing changed. Oh no, what if he woke up now?

Sod it. When was she going to wear heels again while she was here? Mina had told her she'd be on her feet all day. She'd have to leave it. On her hands and knees, she inched her way towards the door, grateful for the protection of the corridor which led to the bathroom. At last, she grasped the door handle and slipped out, so relieved that she'd made it she didn't care if there was anyone in the hallway to see her walk of shame.

―――――

Two hours later, she slipped into the driver's seat of the little Peugeot she'd hired, her head flopping back against the head rest as she went limp for a second. Phew. Mission accomplished. When she'd got back to her room, there was no way she could have gone back to sleep so she'd ordered a room service breakfast, and although her heart had hammered against her ribs when she was in reception checking out, she'd made it out to the car park without setting eyes on Conor. Now she was home free and could look forward to her next adventure. With a heartfelt sigh, she switched on the engine and steered the little Peugeot out of the hotel car park, following the directions of the map application on her phone.

It was eight o'clock and the roads were busy with people heading to work, but she navigated the ring road without too many problems and decided to take it steady. There was a four-hour drive ahead of her, crossing to the other side of Ireland to the county of Kerry. As she wasn't due until two, she had bags of time. She would stop for lunch; perhaps be brave and search out somewhere interesting en route.

She headed out of the city, her interest caught by unfamiliar places, Clondalkin, Rathcoole, Crookshane, The Curragh, Clonmullen. She said the names out loud as she passed the motorway signs, her mouth rolling around the consonants mimicking what she was convinced was an Irish accent. She decided, fancifully, that they were just begging to be spoken and amused herself by practising her accent in the privacy of her car.

As she drove, she noted that the fields on either side of the road were every bit as green and lush as reputed. The country deserved its other name, the Emerald Isle. Some landmarks like Tesco were familiar while others, like convenience store Centra and DIY wholesaler Woodies, were unfamiliar. In some ways the country felt familiar and in others, rather alien. She was really here after all this time.

After a few hours she pulled off the motorway into the services to grab a quick sandwich. She could almost hear her sister's voice in her ear telling her she was being boring and playing safe. Mina would have been off down a side road in search of local cafe faster than a lemming could throw itself off a cliff.

She peered at her roadmap as she unwrapped a cheese sandwich and then dropped her finger on the page in surprised delight. Tralee. Where Aidan and Sorcha lived. She hadn't realised it was quite *that* close to Kilorgally. With a grin she picked up her phone and texted her friends.

The Eagle has landed.

Yay. Hope you had a great journey. When can you come see us?

I'll give you a call when I'm settled and know a bit more about my routine. Can't wait to catch up and to see the bump. Had no idea you were so nearby. Xxx

Just a stone's throw by local standards. See you
soon. x

Once she left the motorway, it was easier to take in the scenery, and the roads grew smaller and quieter as they wound between lichen-dotted dry-stone walls. On either side, patchwork quilts of green fields draped the landscape with the cleanest sheep she'd ever seen dotted across them like embroidered knots of white. Above the final barrier of dry-stone walls, hills gathered along the horizon dappled with clouds of pale-purple heather interspersed with vivid green hillocks of grass. From memory, Hannah could picture the map of this part of Kerry, the land jutting out in a long, jagged finger that stretched out into the Atlantic. The coastline should be coming into view at any moment.

When the blue-green horizon finally came into view, an inner excitement compelled her to pull over and stop in the first small layby she saw, overlooking a craggy cove several feet below. It reminded her of her childhood holidays when the whole family competed to be the first to see the sea. Keen to see the view, she hopped out of the car. Normally her aim was to get from A to B as quickly and efficiently as possible without stopping, but there was something about Ireland that made her want to act out of character. A stiff breeze lifted and tossed her curls, bringing with it the tang of salt and the faint scent of the heather. This definitely beat looking out at a drizzly Manchester through her office window. White-headed waves churned and raced over the outcrop of rocks below, the oily green sea boiling and frothing into the nooks and crannies. There was something about the sea that made you feel alive, she thought as she watched the dancing ebb and flow of the water. She lifted her head to watch brilliant white clouds scudding across a cobalt sky as the wind plastered her hair across her face and she realised, with a blooming sense of wonder, that if she hadn't stopped she'd have missed this sense of exhilaration; the feeling of being alive and attuned to nature. Perhaps she ought to be a bit more adventurous instead of always taking the straight line. A punch of guilt hit her in the solar plexus. Maybe she shouldn't have crept out of that hotel room like that. Conor had been fun and he'd made it clear he wasn't expecting any great commitment or anything. She should have been braver and stayed to face him, like last night's Hannah would have done. Too late now, although the hotel staff had seemed to know him – the barman at least. Was she being silly for wondering if she might track him down? And do what? Apologise for leaving like a big fat coward?

With an irritated shake of her head, she climbed back into the car and checked her watch. It was only quarter to one. Oh well, she could sit and wait in the car if she arrived too early.

Setting off again, she came to the turning she needed to take, clearly signposted to Killorgally Cookery School. Making a split-second decision, she drove past the turning, staying on the main road. She'd be daft to sit in her car when it was so beautiful out here. This was a golden opportunity to do a bit of exploring. As the road curled around the coast, she spotted an intriguing spit of land stretching out into the sea closely followed by signs for somewhere called Inch Beach. That would be the perfect place to stop and take a walk.

She drove into a small hamlet, a collection of low rectangular white-washed cottages dotted to the right of the road overlooking the sea. On the side of the road was a small hotel, its wooden trim painted a deep royal blue, and opposite was a track leading down towards a car park and a wide expanse of sandy beach. Indicating, she pulled off the road and slowed to turn into the car park and stop the car. This time, when she got out, she went round to the boot, and dug out her walking boots and a windproof jacket. It might have been the tail end of August, but the wind was most definitely fresh.

There was a yellow-painted cafe doing a roaring trade in ice cream, and a surf hire shop on the edge of a wide, flat beach. To the left, a range of sand dunes covered in coarse grass stretched along the length of the beach out into the sea and opposite, across the narrow stretch of sea, hills rose as dark green shadows against the sunny sky. As she ambled along the beach she wondered at the name, Inch Beach – somewhat of a misnomer as the land extended for several miles. Although busy with surfers, walkers, and families enjoying windswept picnics, it didn't feel at all crowded. Stopping to breathe in long and deep, she watched a host of seabirds skittering backwards and forwards on spindly legs, synchronised in their busy searches with sudden changes of direction as they criss-crossed in and out of the wide shallows.

Fascinated by the birds, she watched and walked for a good twenty minutes, the peace seeping into every pore before she decided to turn back, grab an ice cream, and head to Killorgally. She smiled to herself as a little flutter of excitement danced low in her belly. Killorgally. Hopefully it would live up to her expectations, and hopefully the pictures in the Sunday supplement that had so entranced her had not been airbrushed and dressed to create a cosy farmhouse effect that didn't actually exist outside the pages of a glossy magazine. It would be such a disappointment. Now that she was here, having stepped out of her comfort zone, she wanted it to be every bit as good as she'd imagined. This was her adventure and she wanted to live every minute of it.

Chapter Four

'Welcome to Killorgally.'

The woman's effusive greeting reached Hannah before she'd even managed to pull her case over the threshold of the small stone-built office. She rose from behind an untidy desk, skirting it to hold out a hand.

'Hi, I'm Hannah Campbell. Here for the residential course.'

'Hello, Hannah. How lovely to have you here with us.' Her mellifluous words were filled with the sort of instant glowing warmth that suggested Hannah's arrival was the highlight of her day. 'I'm Adrienne Byrne.'

Hannah's eyes widened, suddenly a little starstruck at the sight of the glamourous woman in front of her. 'Hello. Gosh. Lovely to meet you too.' She hadn't expected the head honcho to greet her.

Adrienne smiled, her green eyes crinkling as if she was used to the effect she had. With her thick auburn hair curled around her face she looked more like a model than a cook.

She wore a long flowing burnt-orange linen dress that was saved from shapelessness by the brightly coloured apron covered in llamas that cinched it in at the waist. On her feet she wore jewelled flip-flops that flashed and glinted as she crossed the room to give Hannah a long and rather careful assessment, at the end of which she gave her a nod as if to say, 'You'll do'.

'Was your journey a good one? You found us all right?'

'Yes. It's beautiful around here.'

'That it is. We're blessed.'

She pointed to a framed photo on the wall behind her. 'It's taken a lot of love and care, but it's all ours.'

The photo showed a dilapidated, rundown collection of buildings around a small courtyard which Hannah recognised as the one she'd just crossed. Next to it was a large map with a boundary line picked out in yellow which she guessed was a map of the farm and its land.

'Now, I'd love you to come meet your fellow cooks. They're just treating themselves to a spot of tea and cake. We're waiting on a couple more arrivals and then I'll give you the guided tour of the farm and the gardens. If you leave your case here, I'll have someone take it to your cottage. You'll be sharing with one other person on the course.'

Hannah nodded. When she'd snagged the last place on the course, the choice of accommodation had been limited. A room in a two-bedroom cottage or a small single room sharing a bathroom in the hotel. Not that she minded – the description of the cottage, with two bedrooms, a lounge, and kitchen sounded delightful.

She followed Adrienne through a wooden-framed door at the back of the office into a big airy kitchen with Velux windows in the sloping roof, through which streamed bright sunlight. The centre of the room was dominated by long, solid farmhouse table around which several people were already seated.

'Everyone, this is Hannah. I'll leave you all to introduce yourselves. Hannah, help yourself to tea and there's barmbrack. Or tea cake, you would say.' With a wave she glided out of the room like a serene swan as if she had all the time in the world.

'Hi, Hannah, take a seat,' said a woman in front of her, pulling out one of the spindle-backed wooden chairs. 'I'm Meredith.' She grinned suddenly. 'Merry to my friends. Would you like a cup of tea? Have you come far? And you must try some of the cake; it is to die for.'

Hannah sat down in the seat with a plop, realising that the journey had tired her. 'I'd love a cup of tea. Thank you.'

Meredith picked up the pretty china teapot and poured the tea into a matching cup and saucer. Hannah couldn't remember the last time she'd drunk from anything but a mug. The delicate porcelain made it all seem rather genteel and more of an occasion.

'Here.' Meredith pushed a fat slab of cake towards her. 'I hope they're going to teach us how to cook this cake. It's blimmin' delicious.'

'Cake?' the young man across the table echoed with a distinct sense of horror on his face. 'If I've got to be here, I wanna learn to cook proper. Cakes is for mums and housewives.'

Meredith's friendly smile disappeared. 'And what's wrong with being a mum or a housewife, young man? Who brought you up? A robot? A dog?'

'Me mum. Sorry,' he said hastily, with a sudden cheeky smile. He lifted the handle of his cup of tea between finger and thumb and toasted her in quick apology. He glanced at Hannah. 'I'm Jason.'

'Hi.'

'And I'm Alan,' said the middle-aged man next to him. He seemed to be the only Irish person among them. Meredith had a distinct Scouse accent and Jason sounded like he was from the East End of London.

'Fliss,' added the girl across from her in a bored, posh voice, barely looking up from her phone.

'Hi, everyone.'

'Have you come far?' asked Meredith again.

'Manchester, but I flew to Dublin yesterday and drove up today.'

'I flew to Kerry. It's the sweetest little airport you've ever seen. Adrienne's son-in-law picked me up. He's the bread expert. I've seen him on the television sometimes with James Martin and Jamie Oliver. But he was lovely, not at all stuck up. And there I go again, running my mouth off. My daughters are always telling me I talk too much. It's nerves, that's all. This is the scariest thing I've ever done.'

Hannah realised that she could see lines of strain around the other woman's eyes.

'Me, too,' she volunteered, with a smile. 'Right out of my comfort zone.'

The woman patted her arm. 'We'll be in it together then.

Of course, I can cook. But it's the fancy stuff I want to learn. I mean, I watch *Great British Bake Off* and half the stuff they do I've never even heard of. Me and my friend are going to open a little cafe. Well, I say open. It's already open, but the current owners are selling up and have given us first refusal.' At Hannah's open mouth, she said, 'I'm doing it again, aren't I?'

She clapped a hand over her mouth and mumbled. 'Someone else talk. I'm not going to say another word.'

Alan took pity on her with a cheerful smile. 'That cake is grand. And now I'm feeling really nervous. I've had to do the cooking for the five years since my wife died. More recently I started experimenting. Moroccan food, Thai, Chinese – you name it, I've had a go. Anyway, my two daughters said I ought to come; one of them had heard of it. I took early retirement last year, read more about this place and thought, what the heck? Why not?' He looked pensive for a moment, before adding, 'You only live once, don't you?'

'I'm not nervous,' said Jason with a touch of scorn. 'My boss at the restaurant I work in wants me to learn posh stuff. He's payin' so why not?'

Fliss looked down her nose, her mouth curling. 'This is one of the best cookery schools in the world. Killorgally lit the beacon. Chefs from all over the world come here to teach and graduates from the programme have gone on to run Michelin-starred restaurants. You do realise it's not for the faint-hearted.'

'Well, that makes me feel a whole lot better,' said Meredith, rolling her eyes.

'I'm just pointing out the facts,' said Fliss a little stiffly. 'This is one of the best cookery schools in the world.'

'It is,' said Alan. 'Adrienne Byrne is a big name in Ireland and all over the world.'

'I ain't heard of her,' said Jason sulkily. 'She's not that big.'

Fliss gave a superior tut without looking at him, her thin lips compressing. 'In the bona fide cookery world she is.'

'Not in mine, she ain't.' Jason shot her a grin, almost as if he took pleasure in winding her up. He couldn't have been more than nineteen.

'It's certainly a beautiful place,' she chipped in. 'The small bit I've seen. It definitely lived up to expectation.'

'Yes. I'm dying to see the accommodation and the kitchens and the herb gardens,' said Meredith, clearly incapable of staying quiet for very long.

'I'm staying at the hotel,' announced Fliss.

'What 'otel?' asked Jason.

Fliss sighed as if he were too stupid for words. 'The Byrne family have owned this land for generations. Adrienne married into the family. Her in-laws had the original farmhouse and turned it into a hotel. Adrienne and her husband – before he died – moved into this farmhouse and turned the outbuildings into the kitchens, the demonstration rooms, and the cafe. They turned the barns into living quarters for the workers and a few of the cottages in the grounds into accommodation for guests and students. It's been a twenty-year project. Surely everyone knows that.'

'Well, I didn't,' said Jason, glaring at her.

'How lovely,' said Meredith with a sigh. 'Keeping it in the family. I miss my daughters something rotten. They both left home last year. The house feels so empty without them.'

'I'm dreading mine leaving home,' said Alan, shooting her a sympathetic smile. 'Although I wouldn't mind the peace and quiet now and then. How many daughters have you got?'

'Two, but there were always a dozen friends about. Lots of laughter and noise. I sometimes think I miss their friends nearly as much as them. We always had an open house.'

Alan laughed. 'I don't think there's much choice, is there, when you have daughters.'

Jason rolled his eyes. 'Like a bunch of hyenas round ours when my sisters have their mates over. Honestly, I'm the only bloke. It's effin' tough.'

'Ah.' Adrienne appeared silently like a glamorous wraith. 'That gives me the perfect opening. There's no swearing in my kitchen. I've no patience with these foul-mouthed chefs, cursing and cussing at their colleagues. Mutual respect is what I expect. So I don't tolerate swearing. A cuss word slips out of your mouth and you'll be fined. It's a euro in the jar every time.' She gave Jason a benign smile. 'I'll let you off the first one.'

'Bloody hell,' muttered Jason.

'But not that one. One euro in the jar.' With a sweet smile, she added, 'I'd hate to bankrupt you. Now, the house rules. I was waiting on more, but as they've yet to arrive I'll not hold the rest of you up. I expect punctuality. There is a certificate at the end of the course and it requires full attendance to every session, no matter what went on the night before.'

'Sounds ominous,' said Alan.

'Of course, you'll get the most out of this course if you throw yourself in and so we ask you to join in the chores. Everything from feeding the animals, collecting the hens' eggs, and bringing in the cows, to picking the fruit and sweeping out the barns. There are also other things you can get involved in if you want to. You can do as little or as much as you want. Breakfast, lunch, and dinner are provided throughout the week but at the weekends you have to fend for yourself unless you're staying in the hotel. But you'll be given provisions to cook with and there are some excellent restaurants in Dingle about twenty kilometres away which I'd urge you to check out, and there are also lots of pubs roundabout here.

'Towards the end of the course, we'll be having our annual autumn Orchard Party which you'll be welcome to join. I'll tell you more about that in time.'

Fliss clapped her hands. 'I've heard all about the orchard party – it's famous. I'm so glad I'm going to be here for it.' Her face held the smugness of knowing that no one else had a clue what it was.

'Suck-up,' muttered Jason beneath his breath.

Adrienne ignored him, favoured Fliss with a brief, approving, if slightly shrewd smile and continued. 'While you're here, you're free to roam over all of our land. We own everything from here down to the sea and there's a path down to the main road that takes you to the beach. Just make sure you shut any gates behind you if you're out walking. Any questions?'

It seemed pretty comprehensive and Hannah couldn't think of anything in response.

'What time do we start in the mornings?' asked Jason warily.

'Breakfast is at seven-thirty. We start at nine, but if you've chores like feeding the hens, you'll have to be up and away a bit earlier.'

'I've never fed hens,' said Meredith, her eyes shining with enthusiasm. 'Or collected fresh eggs.'

'There's nothing quite like a fresh organic free-range egg.' Adrienne beamed. 'Once you've had one, you'll never taste another like it.'

Hannah wasn't about to rock the boat but she was pretty sure there was an awful lot of hype in Adrienne's words. An egg was an egg at the end of the day.

'I didn't know we were here to work.' Fliss's nostrils flared.

'Me neither,' grumbled Jason and the two of them glared at each other, as if horrified that they agreed about anything.

'It's not work,' chided Adrienne. 'It's all about appreciating and understanding where our food comes from. Come on, I'll show you around.'

Suddenly there was a skittering of feet as someone came bursting into the room framed by a halo of flying red hair. 'So sorry I'm late,' she said in a Scottish accent. 'Sheep on the road. I had to stop and help and when I said I was due here, the farmer said to say hello.'

Adrienne's mouth quirked with wry amusement. 'And here I was talking about punctuality. I'm betting that was Pádraig O'Brien – he's a menace that man. Those sheep are always on the road but he's enough charm to feed the birds from his hands. You must be Isabel McBride.'

'Oh, please call me Izzy. My mother's the only person that calls me Isabel and she's quite dotty.'

'Welcome to Killorgally, Izzy. I'll let the others introduce themselves as we do the tour. Leave your case here. Would you like some cake and a cup of tea?'

'No, it's fine. I've held you up already,' said Izzy, shooting a quick look of longing at the table.

'Here, love.' Meredith was already cutting a slab of cake. 'And have a quick sip of tea to whet your whistle. We don't mind waiting a minute or two, do we?'

Poor Izzy looked mortified. 'I'll bring my cake with me and just have a quick slurp.'

'No, no,' said Adrienne. 'I just didn't want to keep everyone waiting, but if they don't mind it's fine. We're still waiting on one more and, besides, cake should never be rushed.' She sank gracefully into one of the chairs. 'I was just explaining some of the rules.' As Izzy munched her cake, Adrienne reiterated her earlier words.

'One thing I forgot to say. No mobile phones in the kitchen or at the table.'

'What?' Fliss's eyes bulged. 'You don't mean that?'

'Oh but I do. How can you concentrate when your mind is half a world away, floating off all over the internet? Unless someone is sending you life-saving instructions to enable you to perform emergency brain surgery, I can't think of a single reason as to why you would need your phone on during a meal or while cooking. All agreed?' She looked around with a calm, no-nonsense, implacable smile. Hannah decided that Adrienne was as terrifying as she was charming. Everything would be fine as long as you did things her way.

The smell of rosemary, as they brushed along the neat hedge skirting the stone path that ran through the herb garden, was wonderful. Every now and then Adrienne would stop beside another plant, pluck a leaf, rub it between her fingers and offer it around to encourage them to smell and try to identify it. Hannah managed sage, mint, parsley, and basil, while Meredith identified tarragon, chives, lemon verbena, oregano, and thyme but Alan was the standout winner naming borage, feverfew, chervil, and sorrel. Jason hung at the back, his hands in his pockets and an impatient expression on his face, making it clear this wasn't his bag.

Bees abounded in the immaculately planted gardens, buzzing busily from flower to flower. Neat stone paths weaved in and out of the different beds and as the group walked through, brushing against the different plants, the air was perfumed with bursts of herbal scents.

From the pretty enclosed herb garden, Adrienne shepherded them through an arch towards a vast vegetable garden, although she had to double back and collect Meredith, who had her head buried in a patch of Thai basil.

'Sorry, it's just such a fragrant smell. It's wonderful.'

Adrienne nodded, delighted with her enthusiasm. 'This is our vegetable garden.' She swept out an arm. As far as the eye could see, there were neatly tended raised beds, patches of earth with tender shoots, towering canes loaded with greenery and a huge arched polytunnel which stretched away into the distance. 'We grow a large proportion of our ingredients here. Everything from courgettes, aubergines, potatoes, and tomatoes, to peas, beans, cucumbers, and lettuce. We also grow our own fruit. Over to the west,' she pointed, 'we've got an orchard where we grow apples and pears. At the back there, we have our fruit canes where we grow soft fruit.'

A woman with long, dark hair and milky skin, looking rather romantic in her long summer dress and wearing a large, brimmed hat was wandering along with an older man with slightly bandy legs who wore a smart panama. As they ambled between the beds they picked this and that, putting their harvest into the large trugs they carried. They made an idyllic picture.

'Whatever they collect, we'll be eating for dinner,' said Adrienne as she saw Hannah's gaze stray their way. 'Part of my philosophy is to eat seasonally. So whatever is in season is served in the restaurant for dinner and each menu is prepared weekly, or sometimes monthly, according to what is available.'

'Sounds like a lot of work to me,' muttered Jason.

Fliss gave him a disparaging sneer. 'What sort of restaurant do you work in? A burger bar?'

Adrienne chose to ignore them both and turned to everyone with her sunshine smile. 'Now I'm going to get on my hobby horse.' She crossed over to the nearest bed and plucked a couple of pea pods from the plants trailing up cones of intertwined canes. She handed them around.

'Open them up. Taste.'

Everyone did as they were told – they wouldn't have dared otherwise. Adrienne had a certain commanding presence about her that made you want to please her. Hannah popped open the bright-green shiny pod. Immediately, the fragrant grassy scent burst out and when she popped one tiny pea into her mouth to taste its sweet, clean flavour, an involuntary 'mmm' escaped.

'Good?' Adrienne asked her.

'Yes,' she replied, surprised by just how good it tasted. 'I've never eaten a raw pea before. Absolutely delicious. They're my favourite vegetable anyway.'

'There's none better, I promise you. You can't beat fresh just-picked produce.'

She turned to everyone else, the group having arranged itself into a natural semi-circle around her, and then bent and dug a hand in the soil, letting the grains trickle through her fingers.

'This is where the magic happens.'

Obediently, Hannah, like everyone else, stared down at the dark soil.

'Everything we eat comes from the soil; the plants we grow to feed our animals, that we harvest to eat, all of it is dependent on looking after our soil. The quality of the soil determines the quality of our food. Looking after the soil, the animals, the plants in the most sustainable, environmentally friendly way is important for the planet.

'I believe that we have a part to play, encouraging

biodiversity, organic farming, and sustainability. People have become too used to cheap food that is not being grown or produced to proper standards. Here at Killorgally we use seasonal and locally grown produce wherever we can, and when we can't we aim to buy from sustainable and ethical sources. For example, all our spices come from a family supplier in India; in fact, the owner came here on a cookery course ten years ago and was inspired to set up his spice company.

'Everything we grow is organic and aimed at increasing biodiversity. For example,' she turned to Meredith with a smile, 'you know we grow basil. There are approximately 150 varieties of basil. We have fifty-five. Still a way to go, but we're trying to do our bit for biodiversity. Among our pigs, sheep, cattle, and hens, we keep a number of rare breeds.'

She grinned at them. 'You'll find I bang on about it quite a lot. It's been said by some of my beloved family that I'm a bit of bore, but once you work with these ingredients, I tell you, you'll never look back. Now, come meet Daisy and Co.'

The next hour was spent touring the farm, meeting the docile-looking Kerry cows, big and black with large brown liquid eyes, noisy, friendly goats who pushed each other out of the way nosing for food, and plump bustling hens, which Adrienne pointed out. 'Rhode Island Reds, Silver Grey Dorkings, and Partridge Chanteclers.'

Hannah decided the latter with their russet-patterned feathers were her favourites as they scurried about pecking at the ground. The whole place looked immaculate – even the wooden hen houses were beautiful, painted in duck-egg blue with little ramps leading up to each one. It was just as wonderful as she'd hoped it would be.

From there they walked across a paddock through to a large quadrangle.

'On your left are the kitchens and that's where we'll assemble at nine o'clock tomorrow. This evening we'll have dinner at the hotel in a private dining room. Breakfast is in the farm kitchen, where you had tea and cake. And now we'll go back there to the office to get keys and such.'

As she led them back to where they'd started, Hannah realised that they'd done a huge loop of the farm.

'Your luggage has all been delivered to your rooms. Now, Fliss, you're in the hotel. Alan and Jason, you're sharing the flat in Larkspur Cottage, just across the way.' She pointed out of the window towards a pair of pastel-painted terraced cottages, one blue and one pink. 'Meredith and Isabel, you're next door in Rose Cottage in the second-floor flat. And, Hannah, you're in Marigold Cottage and you'll be sharing, although they haven't turned up yet. My son will show you down there if you don't mind waiting here while I take the others.'

'No, that's fine,' said Hannah with a touch of excitement.

No sooner had the others departed than the door behind her opened. She turned around to find a pair of blue eyes studying her. For the briefest of moments they looked familiar but then the memory danced out of reach.

'Hi.'

'Hello there. You for Marigold Cottage?'

'That's right. I'm Hannah.'

'Fergus. I'm the youngest one so I'm the put-upon one. I get all the crappy jobs.' He slapped a hand over his mouth. 'Not that you're a crappy job, of course.' His white freckled skin flushed bright red. 'Sorry, I'm an eejit.'

Hannah laughed. He was probably only about eighteen or so. 'It's fine. I know about being the youngest. You always have to go to bed earlier than everyone else.'

'And that's just the start. Honest to God, they all think they're the boss of me. I never have a minute's peace. Fergus do this, Fergus do that. I tell you, my life's a trial.' He said it with a comically mournful long-suffering sigh that made Hannah laugh again.

'You poor wee soul.'

'You see, you understand. I am a poor wee soul.'

They set off across the quadrangle and turned left down a small, gravelled track.

'This is the best cottage, I think, because you're away on your own and you've got a fabulous view of the sea. And you've only got to share it with one other, although the mammy said she'd missed her ferry or something. She's coming from Liverpool.'

Hannah grimaced. There was nothing worse than missing transport or being late. That would be her worst nightmare.

They picked their way down the path, Fergus hefting her huge wheeled suitcase over the ruts and pits of the track with ease.

With its golden-yellow painted walls, Marigold Cottage looked like a burst of sunshine, tucked as it was into the rolling green hillside.

'Oh it's so pretty.'

'Mm, most people think so,' said Fergus with a non-committal shrug, clearly a young man who didn't do pretty.

Hannah definitely thought so. It had a tiny porch with white-painted wooden trim, windows on either side of the front door, both up and down, and a dark tiled roof with a gentle pitch. Honeysuckle trailed up one side of the porch bushing out over its roof in a cloud of green and yellow. Window boxes filled the downstairs sills with a profusion of the cottage's namesake in autumn ochre, sunshine yellow and bright orange, their heads bobbing in the breeze in welcome, and below them in wide semi-circular beds the jewel-bright coloured flowers of tall black-eyed Susans, bronze and gold coreopsis and deep-orange crocosmia. Hannah's heart lifted at the picturesque sight. This place was more than pretty; it was gorgeous and offered the perfect spot to enjoy the sea view from the little patio set just in front of one of the windows.

Fergus led the way and unlocked the little wooden door.

'Home sweet home.'

Eagerly, Hannah glanced round. The hallway was a generous size with a neat wooden staircase climbing upwards and on either side were sage-green wooden doors. The first led into a good-sized kitchen-diner with solid oak units arranged at one end. At the other end by the window was a round pine table on which sat a large glass jam jar filled with wild flowers and two pretty table settings of a cereal bowl, floral napkin and chunky green glass tumbler.

On the other side of the hallway was a sitting room containing a large L-shaped sofa in pale-grey linen which

Hannah could guarantee would be perfect for sinking into at the end of a long day; opposite was an open fireplace with a small grate, already laid with kindling ready to be lit. Thank goodness for that. She'd never lit an open fire in her life and despite her thorough reading of the *Swallows and Amazons* books, she wasn't sure she actually knew how it was done.

The walls were wainscoted and painted in the same sage green and there was another vase of wild flowers tucked into what must have once been a window nook. The colour scheme felt restful and relaxing, and there were several pale green and cream cable-knit throws folded over the back of the sofa.

'There are a few provisions in the fridge,' said Fergus. 'To keep you going. You don't have to eat with everyone if you don't want to. Some people like to have breakfast by themselves. It gets a bit intense being with everyone all day every day. Especially if you've got some aul fecker on the course.' He stopped with a guilty expression. 'You didn't hear me say that. Everyone's always grand.' With a roll of his eyes, he grimaced. 'Don't tell anyone.'

'I won't.' Hannah shot him a conspiratorial grin. 'I'm sure everyone will be lovely.' Although she had her doubts about Jason and Fliss.

She looked around again at the cosy little sitting room, imagining snuggling down on the sofa, tucked up in a throw with the fire burning, a good book, and a glass of something. She wondered if provisions included wine but at least she had her transport – she could go off and do her own shopping if need be.

'I'll take your bag upstairs. As you're first here, you get first dibs on the bedroom. One has the en suite, the other, the main bathroom. The choice is yours.'

Upstairs, the two bedrooms faced each other over the small hallway. One had a large double bed, the other two singles. Hannah ummed and ahhed for a minute, her natural decency feeling that it wasn't fair to choose when the poor woman had missed her ferry. Swings and roundabouts. The twin room had the en suite with a rather impressive shower with a magic button by the bathroom door which you could use to set the shower going before you even set foot in the room. Although she was taken with the idea of not having to wait for the shower to warm up, she also liked the light airy double room with its big wooden bed, plump pillows, and soft cotton-clad feather duvet. Perhaps if they got on well, her new housemate might let her use the shower occasionally.

'If you just leave my case here, we'll toss for it when the other lady gets here.'

Fergus stared at her with a touch of teenage scorn. 'I'd have bagged the big bed.'

Hannah lifted her shoulders. 'I have to live with her.'

He grinned. 'Every man for himself.'

She laughed. 'I'd rather live in harmony, thank you very much.'

'You don't come from a big family, do you?'

'No,' she acceded, thinking of her gentle aunt and uncle who had brought her up. Hannah often wondered what sort of childhood she'd have had if she and her sister had grown up with their real parents.

As soon as Fergus left, Hannah went down and wandered around her little domain, like a dog or a cat laying claim to new territory, feeling a little frisson of proprietorship as she opened drawers and cupboards in the kitchen. On a painted dresser there was a ceramic egg holder with half a dozen fresh eggs in varying shades of brown and pale cream, a domed glass cake stand with a couple of scones and slices of brownies, and a selection of rustic earthenware, pottery plates in the plate rack, and mugs hanging from hooks underneath. It really was quite perfect. She opened the compact under-the-counter fridge, finding to her delight a pat of greaseproof-wrapped butter – was it home-made? – as well as a bottle of white wine, some raspberries, small wedges of cheese and an earthenware dish of stuffed olives. In the bread bin beside the kettle was a large country loaf. Hannah's stomach rumbled. Unable to resist, she carved herself a slice of bread, slathered on a generous helping of the pale-gold butter and added a few slices of the creamy cheese.

Munching happily, she took herself outside and sat at the little table and chairs, tipping her face up to the sunshine and listening to the birdsong and the distant shush of the sea. This was her idea of Heaven. For the first time since she'd set foot in Ireland, the nerves that had been fretting at the back of her mind eased. She'd done the right thing. This place was beautiful. She was going to make the most of her time and enjoy herself. How could she not? Izzy, Merry, and Alan all seemed very nice. Jason was just young and maybe Fliss was just as nervous and hiding it in a different way.

She leaned back in her chair and closed her eyes, smiling to herself. This was absolutely perfect.

'What the hell are you doing here?' The voice came from nowhere and she sat up with a start, opening her eyes and squinting in the sunshine. She blinked and sat up, her head shooting up with sudden sharpness. It couldn't be. Those blue eyes. The pirate's stubble. *Conor?* Was she hallucinating? She had to be. But no, it was him, standing in front of her, his arms folded and glaring at her.

'I might have known.'

'What?' She blinked again in confusion, her cheeks flushing as she stared at him, still not quite able to believe that it really was him. What on earth was he doing here? Oh no, was he on the cookery course, too? Please, no! He couldn't be. What were the chances? She swallowed. Maybe he'd followed her to give her a piece of his mind. If the shoe were on the other foot, she'd have been furious if someone treated her like that. Shoe! Had he followed her to bring her shoe back?

'Conor,' she croaked, wanting to die of embarrassment. This couldn't be happening. Gone was the flirtatious charmer; instead, an angry dark-eyed tornado stood over her, his eyes full of fury and his mouth curled in disgust.

The clichéd words danced on the tip of her tongue: *I can explain.* What, that she was a complete coward and hadn't been grown up enough to own her first one-night stand? *Pitiful, Hannah, pitiful.*

'I'm s-sorry. I—'

'You're not the first, you know.' His eyes narrowed as he glared at her.

Despite the mortification flooding through her, his sharp anger pricked at her. It wasn't as if she'd committed the crime of the century – what did he have to be so cross about? It was her right to leave if she wanted to. If she wasn't mistaken, he knew the score – he'd probably written the damn thing – but something inside her refused to be cowed. 'I'm well aware of that. No one could doubt that you know what you're doing.'

Clearly taken aback, he opened his mouth and shut it with pleasing incoherence as if lost for words. She couldn't help grinning, proud of herself for scoring that little hit. Where had this new Hannah come from? Talk about sticking your whole arm right into the mouth of the lion. No prizes for guessing he hadn't taken too kindly to be being abandoned in the middle of the night – which she might have apologised for if he hadn't come steaming in, all guns blazing, with a bug up his butt.

His scowl darkened. 'You really had me fooled with that wide-eyed, innocent act. I suppose you think you're clever.'

'A few people have remarked upon it.' And there she went again. It was as if she had no control over her mouth around Conor. Maybe it was because he was so far out of her league that she had absolutely nothing to lose.

'Well, it won't get you very far. I know what your game is. I never sleep with the guests.'

'I wasn't aware that I'd asked you to.' Cheeky so and so, although she did wonder what guests he was referring to. It hadn't stopped him when she was a hotel guest. 'It was good but not quite in the sex-god category. Must try harder.'

He gaped at her and she had to bite back a smile at the grimness of his expression, although the tightening of his features emphasised his dark good looks. Today he was channelling 'angry pirate', especially with that five o'clock shadow dusting his jaw.

Big mistake. For a moment she allowed herself to remember the feel of those bristles across her skin and it brought back a flood of sensation that made her knees wobble. OK, it had been quite a night but not so mind-blowing that she'd lost her wits and come chasing after him as he seemed to assume. God, the man had some ego.

As she tried to steady her stupid noodle legs, another thought suddenly crossed her mind. What if Fergus had got it wrong? What if the *she* who missed the ferry was a *he*? *Please God don't let him be my housemate.* That would be a nightmare.

'What are you doing here?' she asked, her voice cracking a little in anticipation of the answer. It would be an absolute disaster if they had to share this gorgeous little cottage.

'Funny, very funny. You know damn well I live here.'

'What? Here, here?' She glanced over her shoulder.

'Don't be facetious. You know what I mean.'

No, she didn't, but she refused to give him the satisfaction of admitting as much. She had absolutely no idea what he was talking about. Her mind raced a mile a minute. How the heck could she have possibly known he lived here? And what were the chances? It was the coincidence from hell. Things like this just didn't happen in real life. She gave him a bland smile. 'If you say so. Did you want something?'

His lip curled as he looked at her. 'No, I don't.'

Ouch, that stung. He didn't need to make his dislike that obvious. Clearly she'd been a safe bet as a one-night stand but now he was embarrassed by her showing up on his doorstep, wherever that was.

'I brought you a message. The guest due to be sharing with you had to turn back. The next ferry crossing was cancelled and she had a call to say her father had been taken ill.'

Hannah's stomach clenched. 'You're not moving in here, are you?'

'Why would I want to do that?' The horror on his face made his feelings quite plain.

She shrugged, a wash of heat rinsing her cheeks.

'Unfortunately for you and your plans, you won't see very much of me at all. Sorry about that, but your scheme has backfired big time.' With that he turned on his heel, leaving her wondering if she'd just fallen down a rabbit hole. She still didn't know who he was or why he had this peculiar idea that she'd followed him here.

Chapter Five

With a certain amount of trepidation, Hannah approached the hotel entrance and was immediately entranced by the beautiful stone building. It was softened by a trailing Virginia creeper that was just starting to adopt its autumn hues, turning from rich green to burgundy, as it trailed around neatly painted windows with bright-red sills.

However, it only took her mind off things for a moment. The unexpected meeting with Conor had completely unnerved her. What were the chances of running into him again? And how mortifying after doing a runner on him. Her heart had only just resumed normal service after her pulse rate had risen so high she could feel it thudding in her veins.

'Hello there, welcome to Killorgally Hotel. You must be Hannah. I'm Bridget Byrne.'

'Hello. Yes, I've come up for dinner. Sorry I'm a little late.'

'Ach, you're not late at all. My daughter-in-law needs to relax a little. She's always on the go, that girl, and much as I love her for it, she could take a little time to smell the roses. Come on through. Dinner's not for another fifteen minutes. We like to have a glass of something to celebrate the day before we eat.'

Hannah immediately warmed to the woman with her lively eyes and ready smile. Despite her age – she had to be everyone's favourite granny – in a pink gingham pinny tied over well-worn jeans and a bright fuchsia-pink sweatshirt with matching lipstick, she looked like a mischievous pixie about to bounce into action.

When Hannah followed Bridget through to a small dining room, she found the others already assembled in one corner with a bay window overlooking a cobbled courtyard.

'Ah, there you are, Hannah.' Adrienne greeted her with a warm smile, this evening wearing a glamourous emerald-green silk tea dress which wafted around her slim figure. It made Hannah doubly glad she'd changed into a pretty floral dress with a flouncy tiered skirt for dinner. She felt the need of armour after the bruising encounter with Conor. 'Conor gave you the message. Will you be all right on your own out there? I don't want you to feel lonely or anything.'

'I'm fine. The cottage is absolutely gorgeous. I'll be quite happy there, especially with that lovely view out over the sea.'

'Yes, Conor's done a grand job on that one. He did all the renovation.'

He had? Damn, she didn't want to admire what he'd done but there was no doubting the man had an eye.

'Erm, can I ask? Who *is* Conor? I mean, does he work here? Is he your handyman?'

Fliss tutted loudly. 'You are kidding me. You haven't heard of *Good Enough to Eat*?'

Even Meredith and Alan gave her slightly shocked glances and Meredith added, 'Or *Good Enough to Eat Again*?'

Bridget and Adrienne both began to laugh and Bridget said with a naughty grin, 'Well that'll bring the boy down a peg or two.'

'Conor's my son. The second of my four children.'

'Y-your son.' Hannah could barely get the words out. She'd slept with Adrienne's son. Could this get any worse?

'Yes. Conor Byrne?' Adrienne raised her eyebrows.

The way she said his full name made it obvious that Hannah should have heard of him. Was he famous? Given the reaction of the others, they knew something she didn't.

'Can I get you a drink, Hannah?' Adrienne continued. 'Wine? Sherry? Gin? Beer?'

'I'd love a glass of white wine if you have one.'

'We certainly do.'

As Adrienne disappeared to the sideboard which was stocked with a fine selection of spirits and bottles, Meredith came to her side.

'Conor Byrne is a celebrity chef here in Ireland. He's huge. He's had his own TV shows, run his own restaurants all over the place and written lots of cookery books. He's the Irish equivalent of Jamie Oliver.'

'Oh.' Hannah swallowed. Now she felt a complete fool. No wonder they'd all been fawning over him at the restaurant and the hotel in Dublin.

'But now he works here managing the estate for his mother.'

Now it came back to her, she remembered him telling her exactly that. He'd just omitted the celebrity chef bit.

'He does the design and renovation work on the cottages. Handy with his hands, I hear. I wouldn't mind finding out how handy he is.' Meredith lifted her eyebrows in comic lasciviousness. 'Although I'm almost old enough to be his mother. He's what we called in my day *hot stuff*.'

'He is very good-looking,' said Izzy. 'No wonder he did so well on the telly.'

'Is he still on the telly?' Now the waitress' reaction to him, and Gerard's, made sense. They all knew who he was – that girl looking for him in the bar too.

'No, he's given it all up,' replied Izzy.

'And no one knows why,' said Meredith in a sepulchral whisper, her eyes wide with mock-dramatic effect.

'Is he really that famous?' Hannah asked just to make sure, even though it all made sense now.

'Yup,' said Izzy. 'The whole family are cookery royalty. Adrienne used to have her own show, her daughter and son-in-law write cookery books, and the other daughter is married to some top chef in the US.'

Hannah felt woefully ignorant, which wasn't like her at all. At work she was renowned for being well prepared and thorough in her research but that was different; that was serious stuff. For a starter, she'd seriously underestimated the prestige of Killorgally. Part of her had been sold by the fact it was close to Aidan and Sorcha and she thought it would be fun to see them. Clearly bloody Conor Byrne had assumed she knew who he was. Did he think that was why she'd kissed him? Flip. Of course he flaming well did.

Adrienne breezed up with a glass of wine, thrusting it into her hand before turning to address some comment to Jason.

'You all right, Hannah?' asked Izzy kindly. 'You look a bit...'

'I'm fine.' Apart from dying of embarrassment inside. 'I think travelling always takes it out of you. Where did you come from today?'

'Oh I had quite the journey. A drive to Edinburgh to catch a flight to Luton and then a flight to Kerry. And then I picked up a hire car. I'm cream crackered. I'll be taking to my bed not long after dinner if we've got to be up early tomorrow.'

'No chores tomorrow,' Adrienne piped up, turning again from her conversation with Jason. 'We'll sort out who's doing what later and we'll take it easy on your first day. It's going to get intense though.' She beamed at them. 'I can't wait to knock you all into shape.'

Hannah and Izzy exchanged a quick glance and when Adrienne moved on to talk to Alan, Izzy whispered. 'God, sounds like cookery boot camp. I might have bitten off more than I can chew but I need to learn to cook really well, really fast and this seemed the best option.'

'I'm sure it will be fine,' said Hannah, wondering at Izzy's need for urgency.

'It's going to be fun,' said Meredith. 'Feeding people and making them happy. What could be better? It will be a joy. Trust me.'

'You sound like my sister. She loves feeding people. Now, she can cook. She runs a cafe in Switzerland and does the cooking for a small ski chalet.'

'That sounds wonderful. Have you been?'

'Only for a long weekend but it was fabulous. The scenery was incredible and Swiss cakes... who knew? Some of them are amazing.'

'Ooh. I'm looking for cake recipes for my cafe. I want to create some real signature pieces that people can't get elsewhere.'

'I'll have to put you in touch with Mina, although chocolate is her real passion.'

'Sounds heavenly. Chocolate cake.'

'And don't forget the cheese,' added Meredith.

'That's one of the things I'm really interested in,' said Izzy with sudden enthusiasm. 'You know you can have a go at making cheese here. We've got goats in Scotland; I'm wondering if making goat's cheese would be a goer.'

Hannah was starting to think that maybe she'd also bitten off more than she could chew. When she'd signed up she'd liked the idea of being away from home and seeing her friends as much as learning to cook, but it hadn't occurred to her that perhaps she needed a basic level of expertise to start with.

'Dinner is served,' called Bridget. 'Come sit.'

Hannah was pleased to find herself between Meredith and Izzy who were both easy company but then she realised that there were a few extra place settings at the table, one bang opposite her.

Oh no, please don't let Conor Byrne be coming for dinner.

To her relief, Fergus entered the room at that moment and slid his lanky form into the seat opposite and he was followed by the woman and man Hannah had seen harvesting the vegetables.

'I'm famished. I could eat a small cow.'

'Everyone, this is my youngest son, Fergus. He's permanently hungry,' Adrienne said with a fond smile at him. 'And my father-in-law, Franklin Byrne, and my daughter, Mairead, who is married to Eamon Buchanan.' They both nodded with warm smiles. Hannah had heard of Eamon Buchanan, the cookery school's bread expert.

'Welcome to Killorgally,' said Franklin, his eyes twinkling from beneath bushy white eyebrows.

'And here's Conor,' Adrienne added as he strode in, 'who needs no introduction.' Even Jason, it seemed, had heard of him and gave him a quick salute. Thankfully, Conor slipped into the seat next to Fliss, whose face brightened immediately; blossoming like a flower finding the sunshine.

Izzy nudged Hannah in the ribs. 'Someone's happy. Although I'm not surprised. Like Meredith said, he's a hottie. Even better in the flesh.'

'Fliss is welcome to him,' muttered Hannah.

'Doesn't float your boat?'

'No! Too full of himself by half,' said Hannah, scowling as he looked across the table at her. He shot her a mocking glare as if he knew exactly what she'd said and she wished she dared glare back at him but she didn't want to draw unwanted attention to herself. Instead, she ignored him and studiously addressed herself to her food, except it was impossible. She couldn't help herself sneaking the odd look his way and every damn time he caught her.

Mind you, Fliss seemed to be having a lovely time, tossing her blonde hair and shooting him lots of flirtatious smiles. Conor, of course, lapped it up. But then he would – Hannah knew now what he was like. An arrogant so and so. He'd clearly assumed she was another groupie – the big-headed idiot – who knew he was famous.

The first course was a chilled tomato soup with a light hint of spice and a trace of sharpness, served with lovely rustic bread with large, glossy holes in it. Hannah had to admit, given the choice, she wouldn't have chosen cold soup in a million years, but it was delicious.

'This gazpacho is to die for,' said Meredith with loud enthusiasm that made everyone around the table break off conversation and look up.

'I adore gazpacho and this is as good as any I've tasted in Barcelona,' agreed Fliss.

Hannah had never tasted gazpacho before and she was quite surprised by how good it tasted for cold tomato soup.

'I can taste garlic and—' Alan started to say, holding up a spoonful of his soup and sniffing.

'Tomatoes?' suggested Jason with a snigger.

'It's a lovely, simple recipe. One of Conor's.' Adrienne nodded to her son. 'Perhaps you can share the ingredients.'

'Tomatoes, of course,' Conor inclined his head towards Jason, 'garlic, olive oil, red wine vinegar, seasoning all blended together and then I add very finely chopped green pepper.'

'Ah, it's the green pepper I can taste,' said Alan. 'I knew

there was something.'

'And that piquancy comes from the red wine vinegar,' said Meredith happily. 'It's just lovely.'

They all cast admiring glances his way as each of them took another mouthful of the soup, pulling careful tasting faces. Hannah almost laughed out loud. Unfortunately, she couldn't deny that his soup was sublime – not that she'd have given him the satisfaction. There was no way she was feeding Conor Byrne's massive ego any more.

The next course was brought in by Bridget and Mairead: medallions of pork in a cream and apple-brandy sauce served on a big oval platter followed by tureens of jewel-bright vegetables, peas, broccoli, kale, and an enamel tray of deliciously crisp roast potatoes.

Everyone fell upon the tender pork with sighs of delight and approval. Hannah thought if they were going to eat like this every night, once the course was over she was going to have to live on salad until Christmas.

'This is the best pork I've ever tasted,' said Jason, waving his fork in the air.

Adrienne smiled. 'This is one of our Large Blacks. They're a heritage breed which we farm here. When we cover pork on the course we'll talk more about breeds.'

Jason frowned and looked thoughtful. 'Does it really make much difference?'

Adrienne looked at his plate. 'What do you think?'

'It's blood— dead good.'

She nodded as if she'd made her point. Hannah realised that Adrienne was a born teacher with a real passion for food, a bit like Mina. There was an authenticity about her.

She really believed in all this stuff. Hannah still wasn't convinced, but Adrienne certainly knew a lot; hopefully Hannah might absorb some of her teaching and knowledge by osmosis.

As everyone relaxed during the meal, the conversation began to flow along with the wine but Hannah, mindful of Adrienne's admonishment that hangovers were no excuse for lateness, decided to swap to water. After not a lot of sleep the night before, she was starting to flag.

Was it really this time last night that she'd been having dinner with Conor? Was it only this morning she'd snuck out of his bed? It felt like a lifetime ago and as if it had happened to another person. Now she regretted it with all her heart. What on earth had she been thinking?

A little voice inside her reminded her that she hadn't been thinking at all – she'd been feeling and going with it. *And it was rather nice, if you recall*, the voice reminded her with ill-disguised glee.

Stupidly she looked up and over at Conor, who caught her. He raised a brow and she blushed as X-rated memories of last night flooded into her head. Conor kissing her, Conor removing her bra with smooth expertise, Conor making her... nope not going there. She clamped down on the thoughts and glared at him. He glared back and she uttered a quick prayer that the summons to these family meals didn't happen very regularly. If he was out working on the estate and she was in the kitchen all day, she could pretend that what happened in Dublin had stayed there.

As far as she was concerned, she never wanted to see him again.

Chapter Six

'Oh what a lovely touch,' cried Meredith the following morning, immediately tugging her apron over her head. Her name was embroidered in shocking pink on the dark-blue bib.

'Hmm,' said Fliss, looking with displeasure at the word *Felicity*, picked out in lime green on orange cotton.

'Bit poncy, if you ask me,' muttered Jason, but he looked relieved that his name was featured in white on black.

Hannah unfolded the apron on the stool in front of her; it was a pretty duck-egg blue and her name was sewn in cream.

It was day one in the kitchen and they were all as excitable as a litter of puppies – even Fliss who actually smiled when they first walked into the high-beamed kitchen which had once been an old barn. Light spilled in from a wall of bifold windows on one side and high Velux windows built into the sloping roof. The view took in sweeping green hills topped by distant clouds of heather, and between them a vee-shaped shadowy glimpse of the sea, where the cool grey of the horizon almost merged with the water.

Four long work benches ran parallel to a demonstration kitchen area which had a bank of built-in ovens to the right and a whiteboard and TV screen on the back wall. On each bench there was a sink in the middle and a good few metres of counter space on either side. Orderly piles of utensils, including measuring jugs, scales, bowls, as well as wooden spoons and spatulas in tall pottery jars, were arranged at seven stations, two to each bench with one solo one at the back bench, to which Jason immediately gravitated. If there ever was someone who wanted to be at the back of the class it was him.

Earlier, Hannah had woken in the big double bed to bright sunshine spilling in through the dormer window and had rather chicken-heartedly opted to have toast and jam in her own kitchen instead of visiting the main house again. Last night's dinner had been quite enough for her, thank you.

'Morning, Hannah. We missed you at breakfast,' said Izzy, coming to stand beside her. 'Although if I eat a breakfast like that every day, I'll be the size of a house. Honestly, the bacon was to die for. I think there might be something in all this organic rare breed stuff.'

'Do you think so? I mean, can food really taste that different?'

Izzy shrugged. 'I don't know. I'm willing to be persuaded.'

'I just came to learn to cook.'

'Me too.' Izzy caught her bottom lip between her teeth. 'I've got a lot riding on it.'

Before Hannah could ask any more, Adrienne swanned in, looking as glamorous and gorgeous as ever, her skin positively glowing with good health and wellbeing. This morning her glorious auburn hair was tied back and she had a white hat on. She was followed by Mairead, another woman, and a tiny girl with a very fierce, determined face, all of whom wore green aprons with the cookery school logo and white headbands keeping their hair from their faces.

'Good morning, everyone. I hope you slept well. Welcome to the cookery school. I'd like to introduce you to Bronagh, my deputy, and Niamh, my granddaughter, who along with Mairead are our kitchen assistants this week. If you need anything, they're here to help you.'

She ran through a few basic house rules. Hannah knew from the schedule that week one was all about flour. They'd be making bread, pastry, cakes, biscuits, and scones during the week. Which all seemed quite straightforward.

'First of all, today we're going to be talking about bread, namely traditional Irish soda bread and sourdough. Does anyone know what makes these two different from other kinds of bread?'

Alan raised a hand. 'Neither are made using yeast.'

'Don't you need a starter?' suggested Meredith.

Adrienne beamed at them. Clearly they were going to be the class swots, thought Hannah rather uncharitably, given that for most of her life she'd been exactly that.

'Thank you. Yes. Soda bread is the easiest bread you'll

ever make but no less tasty for it. The joy of soda bread is that you can make it quickly and eat it fresh when you want it. Whereas sourdough is a little more complicated because you need a starter. That's a natural fermentation of yeast found in flour that you make with flour and water, and that's what we'll be *starting* with today.' She beamed at the small pun and went on to explain the processes that were involved. 'Basically it's like having a pet. You have to feed it each day and look after it. And,' she paused, 'you have to give it a name.'

Behind her, Hannah heard Jason swear, while Meredith and Alan were already discussing names.

'That'll be a euro in the jar.' Adrienne picked up an empty Kilner jar from the front bench and shook it at Jason. Clearly she had bat ears. Although Jason rolled his eyes, he dug in his pocket and sauntered to the front to drop the coin with a clink into the glass jar.

Then they were off and by ten-thirty, the first coffee break, they had mixed up their sourdough starters, all duly named. Hannah had settled on Herbert as she sealed the jar with the unprepossessing mixture. Didn't you make glue from flour and water?

They'd also made a soda bread with buttermilk and, as Adrienne had promised, it really was very easy and seemed a lot more practical than the seven days of faffing with flour and water that the sourdough required. After that they made a white loaf with yeast. Who knew that kneading bread dough was such hard work?

'When I knead dough, I like to really take any frustrations of the day out on it. The harder you work it, the more you release, warm, and stretch the gluten to give you a nice elastic, springy dough. I always think it's a great way of balancing out any negativity.'

'I always imagine it's my ex's head,' announced Meredith with gleeful venom.

'Yes. Me too,' said Fliss. 'Why are men – present company excluded of course – such bastards?'

'We're not all bad,' protested Alan.

'Oh, I don't know,' piped up Jason with an evil leer that made them all burst out laughing.

Never having kneaded anything in her life, Hannah found it hard to get into the natural rocking rhythm that the others all seemed to have. Luckily Bronagh, her kitchen assistant, was on hand to show her the technique. It was a relief when the required ten minutes was up and she could relinquish the dough to prove.

At lunchtime they all congregated at a scarred oak table for a buffet lunch of salads and large glasses of home-made elderflower cordial. Hannah made a mental note to text her sister to thank her for the tip about comfortable shoes. Being on your feet for a whole morning certainly took its toll. Goodness only knows what her poor tootsies would feel like by the end of the week – and her shoulders were killing her from all that kneading.

'Right. Chores,' announced Adrienne as they were eating. 'I'll allocate them now but if at the end of the week you want to try something else, just let me know. It's good if you can try everything while you're here. Hannah, you'll be on feeding the chickens and collecting the eggs. Meredith, you'll be helping Mairead harvest and pick the fruit and vegetables for dinner. Jason, you'll be feeding the pigs. Alan, if you could help bring in the cows – easy job, it's just a question of opening the gates. They know the way. Fliss, if you can help Franklin in the greenhouse, opening up and closing the windows and operating the sprinkler system. Izzy, you'll be in the herb garden collecting herbs in the mornings and using the dehydrator to dry herbs, mushrooms, and chillies.'

'Wow, that sounds interesting,' said Izzy, with an enthusiastic grin. 'Izzy The Dehydrator – better than The Terminator.' Hannah and Meredith giggled while Jason muttered under his breath. 'Bit of a cheek getting us to do the work.'

Fliss nodded her head, her mouth curving downwards in disgruntlement, although she didn't acknowledge him. Hannah hid a smile. Fliss didn't want to be seen to be agreeing with Jason.

Adrienne looked at him over the top of her glass, taking a slow sip before saying with her usual serenity. 'It's important to understand the relationship we have to the land and our food. When you see where things come from, you'll have more appreciation.'

'Hmmph,' replied Jason, ducking his head and applying himself to a mound of potato salad on his plate.

'This salad is amazing,' said Meredith, who'd already assumed the role of peacekeeper. 'What leaves are these and the little flowers? They're delicious.'

'The flowers are from white and blue borage. And there's golden marjoram and chervil in among the lambs lettuce and watercress.'

Hannah's head buzzed. There was so much to learn. She needed a notebook to write all this stuff down.

As if by magic, Adrienne rose from the table and crossed to one of the cupboards on the side.

'I completely forgot. Does anyone want a notebook and pencil?' she asked as she pulled out a stack of spiral-bound notebooks in the green livery of the cookery school, along with a handful of matching pencils. Before Hannah could say a word, she handed her one of each.

'Thank you,' she said, a little bemused. She was starting to think that perhaps Adrienne was psychic.

When the final loaves came out of the ovens at half past three and they were lined up on the counter on cooling trays, Adrienne went through the merits and failures of each one. Alan and Meredith's loaves had risen well, Izzy and Fliss's were a little lumpen but had risen. Jason's was an absolute triumph – golden, well-risen, and a perfect shape. In contrast, Hannah's attempts had the density of house bricks and weren't dissimilar in shape.

Adrienne gave her a kind smile. 'It comes with practice. A lot of it is in the kneading. Jason's got good strong muscles.'

In response he flexed his arms in a Popeye pose. 'Ef—great guns, me.' He shot the swear jar a look of loathing. He'd contributed seven euros already today.

'Well, that's a wrap for today. Well done, everyone. Dinner is at seven, if you want to come up. It'll just be the six of you. See you all tomorrow, bright and early.'

She exited the room, leaving the three kitchen assistants tidying up and setting out utensils for the following day as the six of them peeled off their aprons and hung them on their designated hooks.

'Phew, that was intense,' said Izzy as she and Hannah walked out into the fresh air.

'Yes. My head's spinning.'

'Mine too. I think I'm going to have a lie-down before dinner. My feet are killing me.'

Hannah looked down at her white memory-foam-lined tennis shoes and smiled to herself.

'See you at dinner.'

It was such a lovely fresh afternoon and, as there were a couple of hours before dinner, Hannah decided that her feet could stand a little more exercise. She dropped her bag off at the cottage, grabbed a sweater and a bottle of water from the fridge as well as an apple from the fruit bowl and set off down the hill to see if she could find a path down over the headland to the road and the beach.

The wind had dropped today and her feet crunched on the flint-dotted path that led west towards the sea. Above her a couple of seabirds wheeled on the thermals, their harsh cries echoing across the open fields. She followed a path along a dry-stone wall, the sharp-edged slanting stones packed like haphazard library books, taking in the soft-eyed Kerry cattle that occasionally lifted their heads to watch her progress. Her hamstrings pulled as she walked up the hill but once at the top the view was worth it. Ahead of her she could see the golden sandy spit of Inch Beach sticking out into the sea, surrounded by the rolling hills of Kerry over the water. Energised by the breeze and the sight of the dancing white waves rushing into shore, having been inside for most of the day, she picked up her pace and began to stride down the hill to the road she could see at the bottom. Away to the right she could see the gravelly stone track leading from the road down to the beach and was delighted with her navigating skills.

Unfortunately, just ahead of her was a fence blocking the path. She studied it, wondering if she should climb it. The wooden posts and rails edged an area no wider than two lanes of the motorway and cut into the field like a dogleg. There seemed to be no rhyme or reason for it and she stared down at the ground wondering if there were something planted there that she shouldn't walk on; beyond the fence she could see that the path carried on until the next section of fence only a few metres further on. To walk round the fence wasn't so far out of her way but she'd have to turn left for a few hundred metres and plough across the uneven field before going straight and then she'd have to come back the same distance to join the path that she could see led quite clearly straight through the field. Adrienne had said earlier, quite unequivocally, that the land from the farm down to the beach belonged to the Byrne family.

She hoisted herself up over the sturdy fence which looked brand new and set off along the clearly discernible path which followed the dry-stone wall. Further along, built into the wall, was a half-ruined structure that had seen better days, it looked like some kind of animal shelter.

'Stop!'

A man stepped out of the shelter, his face contorted in sudden fury as he spotted her, but what stopped Hannah dead in her tracks was the shotgun he raised and pointed it straight at her.

She'd never even seen a gun before, let alone one this close, and he was advancing on her, the gun held high.

'You're trespassing.' He stopped a few feet in front of her, a squat solid man in a tweedy cap wearing a filthy waxed coat that had seen better days.

'I... er...'

Didn't you see the fence? You stupid or something?'

Hannah's mouth dried.

'I'm staying at Killorgally.'

'You're still trespassing.'

He gestured with the gun and came forward until the barrel actually touched her chest. An unpleasant smirk twisted his mouth.

'I... I thought this was Killorgally land.'

'Well, it's not and this is my fence you're climbing all over,' he spat in his thick accent. 'You'd better not have damaged it.'

'I'm sorry.' Her heart banged hard against her ribs. She could feel the press of metal against her stomach but she didn't dare grasp the long stem of the barrel; the adrenaline that was sending her pulse racing also brought with it an outraged sense of indignation. 'There's no need to point a gun at me.' Her voice came out considerably stronger and more authoritative than she felt and it made her a touch braver. She lifted her chin and said with a haughty stare, 'I'm hardly a poacher or anything. I'm just going for a walk. I don't think you have any right to threaten me.' Actually, she had no idea. Was the law in Ireland the same as at home? She knew that landlords were allowed to ask people to leave but they weren't allowed to use excessive force. A shotgun was definitely excessive. But maybe it was different here.

'I'm a lawyer,' she said more confidently than she sounded.

'A lawyer?' The expression on his face changed for a moment, his eyes sharpening. 'Good for you. Law or no law, I can do what I like on my land.' With that he pushed at her with the gun, a hard, sharp shove that had her involuntarily stepping back as much in fear as in surprise. Her heel caught on a tussock of grass and she went straight down onto her bottom, leaving her staring up at the two dark holes of the barrel of the gun. Fear gripped her stomach and her grazed hands grappled with the gravelly soil, trying to gain purchase.

The man smiled, grim and satisfied.

'Get out of here.' He waved the gun and she scrabbled backwards until she was able to get onto her feet, too scared to turn her back on him.

She held up both hands, desperately hoping a show of submission might make him lower the gun. 'OK, OK, I'm going.'

Slowly she turned. Her breath caught painfully in her lungs and she walked on shaking legs back to the fence. It took all her strength to haul herself up over the top rail with wobbly arms and stinging hands. Virtually falling over the fence, she managed to stay upright, pressing her feet firmly into the ground with each step to reassure herself she could still move. She walked slowly and steadily up the slope, determined not to look back over her shoulder. Every nerve ending was hyper aware and had switched to red alert, and her heart banged so hard in her chest she feared she might be sick at any minute. Still she walked until she reached the lee of the hill, hating the fact that he stood watching her defeat.

At the top, sickened by her fear, fury boiling up that he'd had the power to do this to her, she turned. The man had gone. She took in a sharp, harsh breath. Thank God. The relief made her almost crumple as every part of her began to shake. For a moment she couldn't do anything. Her teeth started to chatter so hard, and then some instinct made her run. Run to the safety of the cottage. Like some scarecrow with scant control over her limbs, she tore across the field to the little yellow building that shouted sanctuary.

She half ran and half stumbled through the gate, throwing herself through the front door and slamming it behind her. Shelter. Safety. She bolted it top and bottom and then sank to the floor, her back sliding down the door, her legs completely giving out. Hot, fast tears came as she rested her forehead on one knee and all the fear that she'd tried to contain came flooding out in one horrible rush of sobs and gasps. Reaction, that's all it was. But even as she tried to tell herself it was a logical response, she relived the awful memory of being so powerless and the tears ran faster.

'Hannah?'

Her heart tripped at the sound of the voice and when she lifted her head, through the blur of tears, she saw the outline of someone coming towards her.

Chapter Seven

She shrank back against the door as the lilting voice filled with gentle concern murmured her name again.

Oh no, not Conor. What was he doing here? She closed her eyes and dropped her head back on her knees.

'Hey, hey.'

He sat down next to her, slid an arm along her shoulders, and pulled her into his chest. 'Hey. It's OK. You're OK.'

A soothing hand rubbed circles along her shoulder blade, grounding strokes that brought her back up from the terror that had clouded everything, and with her limbs still shaken and rubbery, even though it went against the grain, she sank into the comfort he offered.

Concentrating on her breathing, she fought the sobs into submission and was able to lift her head to find him studying her with a bemused frown.

'Come on, let's get you up.' He rose and gently pulled her up, leading her into the sitting room to sit on the sofa where he tugged one of the throws loose and tucked it around her, coming back to sit down next to her. She breathed in the subtle scent of his lemony aftershave, the smell of him familiar and comforting. Instinctively her body relaxed.

'Want to tell me what's wrong?'

'What are you doing here?' she asked, still trying to gather her scrambled thoughts.

'Leaking tap.' He paused. 'And an apology.'

She jerked her head up to look at him.

'Mam told me that you had no idea who I was. With great satisfaction, I might add. And Granny Bridget did the same. And then my sister joined in. They all think it's hilarious, although they don't know what a dick I was.'

Hannah nodded, taking it all in.

'I know who you are now. No wonder you were so pleased with yourself.'

'I'm not so pleased with myself now. When you knew my name I just assumed…'

'I told you, the barman called you Conor. To be honest, you're not going to like this, but I've never even heard of you.'

'To be honest, I do quite like that. You slept with *me*. Not Conor Byrne.'

'I'm pretty sure I slept with Conor Byrne.'

'So why did you run out on me?'

She creased her face. 'Did you have to ask that, right now?'

'Hmm, sorry. So what's happened? You looked terrified

when you came running up the hill. I saw you from the window upstairs.'

'Your neighbour.' She sighed, still not quite believing it had turned so nasty. She'd heard of farmers shooting dogs that attacked their sheep but pointing a shotgun and prodding someone with it seemed excessive.

'Moss Murphy. What's he been doing now? He's a mad aul coot but harmless.'

'Harmless! He threatened me with a shotgun because I was trespassing.'

'Trespassing? Where were you?'

'On the path down to the sea but I climbed a fence. I knew I shouldn't – stupid really – but the path went straight through and I couldn't see any reason not to.'

'It's all our land. You weren't trespassing. Murphy gets his knickers in a twist because the farm here has done so well. He's a curmudgeon. Way back he put that rickety old fence up as a protest about something. To be honest, Niamh had just been born and was a bit poorly in the hospital. It was the last thing on all our minds and we just let it go. Humoured the daft eejit. He's always complaining about something and doing his best to cause trouble. Last week it was a new shed we put up that upset him. He wanted to know if we'd got a hold of planning permission. Wanted to measure the height to make sure it was within the regulations. I tell you, he's a mad old bird.'

'He didn't look daft to me, or old,' said Hannah hotly, anger suddenly dousing her fear. 'He was really menacing.'

Conor frowned. 'What did he look like?'

'About thirty or forty, dark hair. Quite stocky and big dark eyebrows. Small piggy eyes.'

'That's not Moss Murphy. Ah, I bet it's that nephew of his. I heard he was a hothead. Throwing his weight around down the pub. Sorry for that. I'll go see Murphy in the morning and have a word with him. Are you feeling better now?'

Hannah nodded although there was still a definite tremor to her limbs. 'Oh God, what time is it?'

'Six-thirty.'

She rose to her feet. 'I'm supposed to be going up to the house for dinner.'

'That's probably a good idea. Help you forget about what's happened.' He stood up and took a step back and she felt both the physical and metaphorical distance fall between them. 'I'll just finish that tap and get out of your hair. Sorry to intrude. I saw you go out for a walk and thought you'd be longer and the tap quicker. Enjoy your stay here.'

She gave him a wan smile, realising that he'd been trying to avoid her and was giving her a clear message that he wouldn't be seeking her out anytime soon.

It was a shame that the Conor she'd been out to dinner with in Dublin was no longer present and that the Hannah she'd been that night had vanished too. Although, even if he had been in the market for one, she wasn't the sort to have a holiday fling… or not usually.

Chapter Eight

H annah approached the hen house with a fair amount of trepidation. She knew nothing about chickens and couldn't decide whether to be relieved or nervous to find Adrienne waiting for her with a serene smile.

A noisy dinner with the other cookery school students had taken her mind off the unpleasantness of her run-in with shotgun man, although the adrenaline hangover had given her one doozy of a headache. Thankfully this had gone with a good night's sleep.

'Morning.'

'Hello, lovely girl. How are you this morning? I'm so upset for you. How are you feeling?'

'You heard then?'

'Conor told me. Honestly, if it's not one thing, it's another with that man. I've put a call into the guard and I've phoned Murphy myself and Conor has been round there. It'll not happen again.'

'The police?'

'Yes. I'll not have him terrorising our guests like that.'

'I'm sure if you've spoken to your neighbour, that's enough.' Hannah didn't want to have to start giving interviews to the police. She'd spent enough time in police stations in her early career when she'd been a duty solicitor. 'Please don't bother the police.'

'I'm not sure, Hannah, it's a serious matter.'

'I'd rather put it behind me. Honestly.'

Adrienne studied her and must have seen the implacable lift of her chin. Hannah could be very stubborn when she wanted to be.

'Well, if you're sure.' She shook her head. 'I hope you don't think that everyone round here is like that. Now, for something a lot more pleasant. Let me show you one of the very best bits of Killorgally. My ladies. There's nothing like the chickens. Their eggs are nature's bounty and a boon to cooks.'

'Mmm,' said Hannah, bemused by the fervent light shining in her eyes.

'Don't worry, I'm not mad.'

Clearly Conor got his mind-reading abilities from his mother.

'I didn't… It's just I've never been anywhere near a chicken before.'

'Gosh, that is sad,' she said and then beamed. 'All that is about to change. You'll never look back. I just know you're going to fall in love with the girls. You're in for a treat, Hannah. Difficult to believe that you really have never come across a chook before.'

Her words once again reinforced the realisation that Killorgally was a world apart from her life in the city.

'Not many chickens in suburban Manchester, or certainly not round where I live.'

'You'll have to move,' declared Adrienne with calm certainty. 'Come on, they're foostering to be out.'

'Foostering?'

'Good Irish word.' She linked her arm through Hannah's. 'It means fussing, fidgeting. It's perfectly apt. The way they walk, you know, all fussy, bustly, and madam-y. They're like the village gossips, all desperate to be out. We have to shut them away at night because of the foxes. Beautiful creatures but destructive; they have an unpleasant habit of slaughtering the whole coop if they get in.'

She picked up an empty bucket and over the next quarter of an hour showed Hannah the barn where they filled the buckets with the grain and pellet mix that made up the hens' main diet, and chatted away, explaining everything she did. Then she led Hannah to the large fenced enclosure where they poured the mix into a big circular trough. Next, Adrienne showed her the tap that supplied fresh water to the bird feeders.

When they finally let the hens out, they came bustling and squawking down a wooden ramp, furious bundles of feathers as if indignant at being cooped up for the night. Adrienne laughed with delight.

'Morning, ladies, welcome to the day. This is Hannah. She'll be keeping an eye on you for the next few weeks.' She turned to Hannah. 'I'll tell you their names later when you get to know them; you'll not take it all in today and once you know their characters it's easier to remember them all.'

Most made a beeline for the feeder but a couple were more canny and loitered near Adrienne and Hannah, as if they knew that the tin buckets they held contained the juicy kitchen scraps of broccoli, cauliflower, raspberries, and potatoes.

'They'll eat most things but we only give them organic stuff,' explained Adrienne as she scattered the scraps across the ground to the delight of the hangers-back who immediately began pecking with comical staccato jabs. Hannah laughed and watched as one came right up to her feet, nosing quite happily around her. She'd never thought of chickens as cute before but she was quite taken with them.

'Watch this one. I said I'd give you their names once you'd got to know them. This one, I call Attila.'

Hannah laughed. 'Of course, she's the leader of the pack.'

'Exactly. She's very bossy and convinced that she's queen bee. There's a pecking order, as you've probably seen.'

'Is that really where the phrase comes from?'

'Oh yes. Bottom of the order here is Henrietta.' She pointed to a lone white chicken loitering at the back. 'So I always save the best scraps for her.' Adrienne gave her a pixie-like grin which was reminiscent of her mother-in-law, Bridget, and quite at odds with her usual slightly scary business-like manner. 'She's a sweetheart. And that's Elsie, she's got attitude, and that one is Audrey. Don't you think she's got a bit of Hepburn about her?'

Hannah stared at the little black and white chicken who strutted along with quite a sassy wiggle and couldn't help laughing again. 'You're right.'

Adrienne lifted her shoulders in a casual of-course-I-am shrug that made Hannah grin.

'And that one is Princess Lay-a. She used to be quite garrulous, but for some reason she likes to keep herself to herself these days.' Adrienne grimaced. 'A bit like my son.' She shook her head.

Intrigued Hannah ventured, 'Conor?'

'Yes.' There was a droop to Adrienne's mouth. 'I suppose you know he used to be quite the big deal. And now he's content to play maintenance man and builder. He doesn't want anything to do with the cookery side of the things. Won't even teach. He'll help out when we need him to, but he won't take up a proper role. Breaks my heart. And he won't talk to me about it.' She sighed. 'All that talent.' Then she smoothed her hair back and said, 'Well, all this talk won't bring the eggs in, will it?

She darted off to the barn, leaving Hannah wondering what all that had been about.

She came back a moment later with a pair of straw-lined baskets and handed one of them over. With it tucked on the crook of her arm, Hannah felt like something out of *Little House on the Prairie*.

Finding her first egg brought with it the joy of discovering treasure and Hannah grinned with an odd sense of triumph. How amazing that one of those busy strutting and pecking ladies had laid this. It was still warm to the touch. She tucked it into the straw in her basket and carried on looking for more. It didn't take long to discover that with fifty hens there was an abundance of eggs. After she'd found fifteen she stopped counting, but it was still a thrill each time she gently added another one to her basket.

'I'll leave you to it. Take them to the kitchen when you think you've found them all. I'll see you later.' Adrienne clamped a wide-brimmed straw hat on her head and walked away, her voluminous – pale blue today – linen dress wafting about her, making her look as if she'd stepped out of a pre-Raphaelite painting. Hefting the now heavy basket, with a ridiculously overblown sense of achievement, Hannah bore the eggs over to the big farmhouse kitchen where Bridget, presiding over a large range oven, greeted her with a friendly smile.

'Good morning to ye, Hannah. Eggscellent timing,' she said with a mischievous grin. 'Come grab a drink. Tea. Coffee. Help yourself.' She inclined her head to the side where a selection of mugs and a large cafetière of coffee were arranged around the kettle.

Meredith and Alan were already seated at the table, chatting away over large mugs of coffee with empty plates in front of them.

'Morning.'

'Hiya, Hannah. I've been out harvesting the vegetables.' Meredith's words tumbled out in her usual runaway fashion. 'Honestly, it's heaven. Everything is just so fresh. I can't wait to cook with them later. When I get home to Liverpool, I'm going to get myself an allotment. You have to come work in the garden.'

Hannah smiled at her enthusiasm. 'I don't know, I've been collecting eggs and there's something rather magical about finding each one.' She'd surprised herself saying that out loud, especially as she wasn't one for fanciful turns of phrases.

Meredith sighed. 'That sounds so romantic. Collecting eggs.'

Bridget smiled at both of them and wiped her hands on her apron. 'And would you like one for breakfast? How would you like it?'

Hannah didn't normally eat more than toast, and that was usually as she was halfway out of the door on her way to work. However, this morning she felt she deserved one, especially as she was going to be on her feet all day rather than on her bottom in an office. 'Can I have a boiled egg?'

'Hard or soft?'

'Soft, please.' She turned to Alan. 'How were the cows?'

'Bovine,' said Alan. 'And big. I tell you, I was a bit anxious but all I had to do was open the gates. The old dears know where they're going.'

Jason stomped in wearing Darth Vader socks, closely followed by Izzy and Fliss, as Hannah sliced off the top of her boiled egg. The golden yolk inside stopped her for a moment. It was almost orange in colour, unlike the pale yellow she was used to.

Jason threw himself into a chair and moodily helped himself to some toast from the rack on the table.

'Fancy some bacon and eggs, dearie?' asked Bridget, turning from her post at the gas rings, that same mischievous smile playing at her mouth.

'Those pigs stink!' He did not look impressed. 'And I've got shit all over my trainers.'

'Don't let Adrienne hear you,' said Fliss with a smirk.

He glared at her and shot up two fingers. 'I don't give a—'

'Children,' said Meredith, shaking her head with an exasperated huff. 'How old are the pair of you?'

Fliss stuck her nose up in the air and flounced over to the coffee pot.

'I'd bloody love some bacon,' said Jason with sudden gleeful relish and everyone burst out laughing as Bridget put several rashers into a big cast-iron skillet.

'Oh my goodness. This is the best egg I've ever eaten.' Hannah stared down at the egg cup, not quite able to believe it. 'It really does taste amazing.' Obviously because it was so fresh but there was also a funny little sense of satisfaction that she'd collected it and that she'd met the hen – well sort of – that had laid it.

Meredith and Alan both nodded as if it were something they'd known all along. 'Wait until you try the bacon.'

'You left dinner early last night. Were you all right?'

'Yes, just had a bit of a headache.'

'I was pooped,' said Izzy. 'Nearly fell asleep in dessert.'

'You did fall asleep in your dessert,' pointed out Fliss. 'You had cream in your hair.'

Izzy gave her a bright smile and ignored the sharp triumph in Fliss's tone, instead turning to Meredith. 'The smell of those herbs is just divine. As soon as I get home I'm going to plant a herb bed. I feel so inspired.'

'Having tasted this egg, I'm tempted to say I'll get some

chickens but I live in a second-floor flat, so I'm not sure they'd be very happy on the balcony.'

'You could move,' suggested Izzy.

'Yeah. Right. Of course I could,' said Hannah with a laugh. She couldn't imagine ever moving out of Manchester, let alone to somewhere where she'd keep chickens. It had taken her forever to choose her particular apartment because she'd been so worried about making a mistake. Her parents' chaotic lives and the way they had died made her all too aware of the consequences of jumping into things without thinking them through carefully.

After breakfast they all headed to the kitchen, falling into pairs: Hannah and Izzy, Meredith and Alan and a silent Fliss and Jason.

Adrienne welcomed them with a sunny smile and her boundless energy. 'How are we all today? Raring to go? As I said before, this week is all about flour. It's the most basic of our foodstuffs but one of the most universally used around the world. Today we're going to be making pastry. Shortcrust, puff, and suet. And you'll be eating the fruits of your labour tonight. Chicken and leek pie, steak pudding, and raspberry puff pastry tarts.

'Oooh, I harvested the leeks and the raspberries and pulled up onions,' said Meredith, her voice rising with sudden excitement as she pointed to the trugs on the counter.

'And my herbs are right there,' said Izzy, pointing to the jam jars filled with greenery.

'Bully for you,' muttered Fliss, clearly not impressed with her job in the greenhouse.

Adrienne's superpower hearing picked it up. 'You'll all get a turn at everything, if you want to. I want you all to feel in touch with the land and the food. Which reminds me, Jason, is it one or two euro in the pot this morning?'

He scratched his head but her steady look had him walking to the front and putting in two euros. Hannah heard him mutter, 'Swear she's a witch.'

The kitchen assistants filed in carrying trays of flour and butter which they deposited at each station.

'We're going to start with shortcrust pastry. Nice and simple. What's the most important thing with pastry?'

'Not to overwork it,' suggested Alan.

'Yes.'

'And keep the fat as cool as possible,' said Meredith.

'Excellent.' Adrienne gave a quick explanation as to why and then they were on their own.

Hannah read the recipe. She'd made pastry once in domestic science class at secondary school in Year 8, which was a million years ago.

She watched as Meredith chopped her block of butter into chunks then slid them into the bowl of flour she'd already weighed. Hannah, keeping a wary eye on the others, copied Meredith and plonked the butter into the flour, letting loose a cloud that almost choked her. She had to blink furiously to get it out of her eyes. She saw Fliss roll her eyes.

Hannah began to rub the cool flour into the butter and found herself thinking of other things, wondering why the man with the shotgun had been so irate when it turned out it wasn't his land at all. There was something odd about his complete overreaction, even if she had been trespassing. Surely it hadn't warranted that much anger. There was definitely more going on between the two families than she realised. Maybe she should have asked Conor. With a sigh she remembered how kind he'd been the night before. Which was a mistake because now she couldn't stop the memories sneaking through her mind. His body over hers, those kisses. And, heaven help her, her response to him. *Stop*, she told herself. She had to stop. Just because it had been the best sex ever didn't mean anything. Yes, she fancied him. And even more so when he'd been so kind last night, but he'd made it quite clear that he didn't want anything more to do with her. He didn't get involved with guests. Besides, Hannah told herself, men like Conor Byrne didn't date the likes of her – guest or not.

'Hannah,' Adrienne's voice beside her interrupted her thoughts. 'You're giving that butter a thorough workout. You need to be gentler with it. Treat it like a lover.'

Hannah blushed. Her last lover had been Adrienne's son. God, it would be so embarrassing if that came out. What would Adrienne think of her?

'It should look like fine breadcrumbs.'

She looked down at the mangled butter and grimaced. 'Sorry. I wasn't concentrating.'

Adrienne's expression was a touch sorrowful. 'Love. It needs love.'

Hannah winced. It hadn't been love she'd been thinking about at all. Following the recipe, she added the water and mixed it to a rather lumpy dough and left it to cool in the fridge while they all crowded around Adrienne to watch her roll out, line, and trim her pastry to fit a pie dish. Hannah watched her skilful, deft movements, knowing that her pie was never going to look like that in a million years.

'Right, now I'm going to demonstrate the filling. First of all, your meat is important and you should go for quality, although you always want a pair of good-sized, plump breasts.' There was a ripple of amusement through her students, but Adrienne seemed oblivious and carried on talking. 'I like these ones; they're from a local butcher who specialises in rare breeds. This one is Plymouth Rocks.'

Once she'd finished the demonstration, they all returned to their own workstations to make the chicken and leek filling. At least this didn't require much skill, thought Hannah in relief as she carefully chopped her leeks. Behind her, Jason was demonstrating admirable knife skills as he sliced his vegetables at top speed.

'Impressive,' she said, watching in envy.

'Misspent youth,' he said with a grin, lifting the knife and spinning it with dextrous fingers.

'Careful. You'll chop your fingers off.' She winced in alarm.

'Nah, got to live dangerously.' Jason flipped the knife, caught it, and began chopping again.

'This isn't a circus.' Adrienne's reproving voice had Jason giving her a cheeky grin. 'But excellent knife skills, Jason.'

To Hannah's surprise he blushed with pleasure and ducked his head shyly. It was rather sweet and the opposite to his usual cocksure confidence.

'Idiot,' said Fliss, who was chopping with neat and speedy precision at the bench in front of him.

For once he ignored her and carried on working.

'Hannah,' Adrienne grabbed her hand, 'you want to slice through vegetables with a good hard thrust, slicing down and forwards. It's all in the wrist movement and the way you handle it.'

She heard Jason sniggering again and even Fliss glanced up with a smirk, but once again Adrienne appeared completely oblivious to her double entendres.

By the time it came to the morning break, they'd all made chicken pies of varying standards. Meredith's was decorated with pastry leaves, Jason's had beautiful, fluted edges, Alan and Fliss's were both neat and workmanlike, Izzy's a bit wonky and Hannah's... well, the less said the better. She'd worked hard but her pastry had been a bit slippery and shiny and she certainly didn't have any decorating skill. When it had cooked, the pastry had shrunk away from the edges and sunk onto the top of the filling. It wasn't quite a disaster but it didn't compare to the others. Thank goodness it wasn't like the *Bake Off*, otherwise she'd definitely be going home.

When Adrienne looked at her pie, she smiled kindly. 'I think you know where you went wrong.'

No, Hannah didn't. She'd followed the recipe, the same as everyone else. Thankfully Adrienne moved on down along the line. 'How long have you been cooking, Jason?' she asked. The others had obviously been cooking for a long time.

'About a month. I... er... I got a job in a restaurant. This geezer... well it's a long story but basically I ended up cooking. I quite like it. He decided to send me here. Fu— knows why.' He looked over at Adrienne whose lips twitched ever so slightly. He dug his hand in his pocket and held up a euro and waved it at her. 'Anyway, here I am, might as well give it a go. Not like I've got anything else to do.' Adrienne gave a regal nod and moved on to Meredith.

Jason glanced down at Hannah's pie. 'Why are you here?' To be fair, he made an effort not to laugh, pressing his lips together.

Hannah sighed. 'I'm not very good at cooking.'

'Tell me something I don't know.'

'Thanks, Jason.'

'Sorry, just joking. It looks edible.'

'That's about all you can say.' She sighed. 'I came because I wanted to learn to cook properly.'

'What do you mean properly?' Jason drew his brows together, intrigued.

'You know in those cookery programmes when they use words like braise, broil, sauté, dauphinois, bain marie, or they talk about a shoulder of meat or a knuckle, I just want to know what it all is.'

Now he stared at her. 'Why?'

That was a good question but Hannah shrugged, almost too embarrassed to admit the real reason. She wasn't about to admit that she didn't like not being good at something so basic, especially when Jason clearly had some kind of natural talent. It went a bit deeper than that. She knew she was good at her job; everyone at work knew her as dynamic and brilliant and that had kept her going until the arrival of

Sadie Burns-Coutts at work. Blonde, beautiful, a first from Oxford, and a brilliant cook. There was just something about her that brought Hannah's deeply buried insecurities to the surface. Sadie was posh, had a plum-in-the-mouth voice, dressed like a model, and had flair, style, and charisma. Hannah knew that intellectually she was Sadie's equal, but Sadie was immediately super popular, a bit like Mina had always been. Hannah had friends, but it took her longer to make them; she liked to be sure of them before she committed. If she was honest she had always been a little envious of Mina's ability to make friends so easily and bring them all together.

Hannah might have got over her initial feelings had Sadie not suggested a company-wide bake off for Comic Relief. When Hannah produced her Victoria sponge, made to a recipe her aunt had taught her when she was thirteen, she had been proud of the rise of the sponge, the even shape, and the perfectly sprinkled icing sugar on top. It looked professional and competent... until she saw Sadie's magnificent three-tiered raspberry mousse and chocolate cake that looked as if it could have been served at The Ritz for tea. For some reason it made Hannah feel safe and dull. She was still plodding the same safe furrow that had guided her since childhood. Still using the same recipe. Still working for the same company. Still the same, sensible person. Stupid that something like a cake had brought her up short, but it had. She'd always stuck to the easy things, never made herself do things out of her comfort zone. When she'd seen the article in the Sunday supplement about Adrienne, something inside her had taken it as a sign.

That competitive part of her didn't like being bad at something.

Jason was still looking at her and she realised he was still expecting an answer. 'I saw an article about Adrienne and the school. I thought it would be a good thing to learn to cook properly.'

Jason snorted.

'What about you? What did you do before you worked in the restaurant?'

'Bit o' this, bit o' that. You know. What do you do?'

'I'm a lawyer.'

Jason's eyes widened with comical instant horror. 'The law.' He shuddered, making Hannah laugh.

'Don't worry. These days I don't do criminal law.'

'You mean you don't do the police station jobs then.'

'I did once. Not anymore.' He nodded and turned around as if he couldn't get away fast enough.

The challenge in the afternoon was puff pastry, which turned out to be a right old faff. Each time it came to turning it to fold it again, Hannah couldn't remember if she'd turned it the right way.

'The other way,' whispered Bronagh at her elbow. The girl was assisting her and Fliss, buzzing between them as she removed dirty dishes, brought over more supplies, and wiped up spillages.

'Whoops, thanks.' After the shrinking pastry of the morning, she'd resolved to do better and had been more focused, following Adrienne's instructions more carefully, running her hands under cold water, taking care when she rubbed the butter into the pastry, taking her time with each step. But once again, her mind had drifted. It was a puzzle. Why had the man with the shotgun been so irate? And while she'd been working the pastry, something else had also come to mind. Conor had said something about a rickety old fence. The fence she'd climbed had been brand new. It had that freshly sawn wood smell. That blond colour. She might not be a country mouse, but she knew unweathered wood when she saw it.

'Hannah.' Bronagh nudged her.

Oops. This time she focused on her pastry and when it came to the final stage, she even used a ruler to score the pastry in neat lines, rather than attempt it by freehand in the confident way Alan and Meredith were doing. When she came to lay out her rectangular tart cases with their neatly pricked bottoms, she was pleased to see that they looked quite acceptable, and by the end of the day she felt she'd achieved something, even if her finished raspberry tarts didn't look as professional as Jason's. For her they were actually quite good.

'Better, Hannah,' said Adrienne as she did her rounds.

'Thank you.' She beamed with satisfaction.

'Just imagine how good they could be, if you put some love in.'

Chapter Nine

The rest of the week fell into an easy pattern. Hannah quickly grew to love the chickens and their individual personalities, and each night she collapsed into bed with aching feet and her brain whirling with all that she was learning. By Friday night she was more than ready for the trip to the pub proposed by Jason, who was living up to her suspicion that he was a born ringleader of trouble.

At his first suggestion, Fliss had been the only one who'd seemed reluctant but Jason's teasing, 'Too posh for you,' had clearly needled her into responding.

It was arranged that they'd meet outside Larkspur Cottage, but fifteen minutes after the appointed time they were still waiting for Fliss.

'Where is the daft cow?' muttered Jason, pacing up and down. 'We're missing drinking time.'

He paced another length of the cobbled courtyard before saying. 'Let's just go without her.'

'She'll be here soon,' said Meredith, who'd already carved out her role as the placating mother hen.

'At last. What kept you? Didn't have enough Polyfilla?' asked Jason, grinning at Fliss, who looked immaculate with freshly blow-dried hair and perfect makeup that highlighted her high cheekbones and almond-shaped eyes.

'Very funny, but don't give up the day job. I don't think stand-up is for you.'

They moved off with Jason leading the way.

'Honestly, those two are like brother and sister, bickering all the time.' Meredith pursed her lips.

'From opposite sides of the tracks,' observed Alan. 'They don't come much posher than Fliss, and young Jason has a rough side to him – although I think under the bravado he's a nice kid.'

'They seem to enjoy rubbing each other up the wrong way, that's for sure. But hopefully they'll enjoy a change of scenery and the pub sounds just the thing.'

Jason, with that unerring ability young men had when it came to beer, had sussed out the most direct route to the pub via a footpath from the back of the farmhouse that led up over the hill and down to the pub. Hannah followed, enjoying not being in charge or having to make any decisions. Following the herd, every now and then, was rather relaxing, especially on a warm summer's evening, crossing the green hillside with a view of the sea and the mountains away over on the horizon. Birds chattered in warning from the trees as they set across the field to reach the path, down which they walked in twos alongside one of the dry-stone walls.

'Oh fuck me! What is that smell?' asked Jason, suddenly halting and putting an arm out to pull Alan up short.

'That's awful,' wailed Fliss, pulling the scarf around her neck up over her nose.

The stench was so strong that Hannah's eyes watered.

On the other side of the wall was a huge pile of manure running parallel to the wall for almost the whole length of the field.

'Ugh.' Izzy pulled an I'm-about-to-be-sick face as Hannah blinked rapidly.

'That's gross,' said Jason, pulling his sweatshirt up over half of his face. 'Quick. Let's get past this stinking pile of shit. Why would you leave it there?'

None of them answered; they were all too busy pinching their noses and hurrying past the offending piles of manure. For a moment Hannah wondered if this was more of Moss Murphy's doing. It seemed like exactly the sort of thing a troublemaker would do.

'And that's why I don't live in the country,' said Jason, as they made the final descent down the path.

There was no missing the pub that nestled at the side of the road just along from the track they'd come down. Its walls were sunshine yellow with a pair of toucans rather incongruously painted on either side of the door.

'The Guinness toucan,' exclaimed Alan. 'There's an Irish pub in Soho called The Toucan.'

'What?'

'Iconic advertising from the 1930s which has survived. Incredible.'

'I can't see what on earth a toucan has to do with Irish beer,' sniffed Fliss as they all trooped into the pub.

'I think that was the point,' explained Alan. 'So it stuck in people's minds and was used for years afterwards. As an aside, the crime writer Dorothy L. Sayers was a copywriter on the Toucan Guinness ad copy.'

'How on earth did you know that?' Meredith asked, her eyes crinkling with approval.

'I'm a mine of useless information,' he said with a grin, looking rather pleased with her obvious admiration.

Inside the low-ceilinged pub, photos lined the walls and behind the bar, an eclectic mix of commemorative plates, brewery glasses, and memorabilia including yellow Australian road signs, models of camper vans, and old calendars was displayed. In pride of place was pinned a big black T-shirt featuring the capital letters FBI in yellow with smaller text beneath that read: Foley's Bar, Inch.

Hannah couldn't help smiling as they slid through the Friday-night released-from-work crowd towards the bar. There was that universal sense of relief that tomorrow was Saturday and a comfortable noise of rising chatter enveloped her. There wasn't a sound like it, she decided; that mid-level buzz of voices, punctuated with laughter and happiness. Tourists and locals rubbed shoulders in casual shirts and jeans, drinking and talking with no one vying for attention or the limelight like they might do at one of the trendy bars in Manchester. The barman hailed them as they approached. There was an altogether more laid-back atmosphere without the familiar trying-too-hard-to-have-fun overtones that she'd noticed back home. The Irish, it seemed, knew how to kick back and enjoy themselves.

'Evening, folks. What'll you have?' And there was the universally friendly welcome that she'd noticed everywhere she'd been so far.

'You have to have a Guinness,' announced Alan, taking a rare lead. He was a quiet, watchful man, gentle and attentive. Hannah had noticed that he was always ready to help everyone else in the kitchen but wasn't pushy about it. 'It's always better in Ireland.'

'Ugh, I once tried it,' said Meredith. 'Tastes like earwax.'

'And how do you know what earwax tastes like?' asked Alan with genuine curiosity.

'Well, you know,' Meredith with a half-laugh. 'I haven't tried it again and it was a long time ago.' She scrunched up her face under his smiling gaze. 'Tell you what, I'll have a half to show willing.'

Izzy and Hannah both chose to have a half as well, but in response to Jason's teasing that she wouldn't like it, Fliss ordered a full pint.

'Bet you can't down it in one,' said Jason.

Fliss looked down her nose, a sudden twinkle in her eye. 'How much?'

'Ten euros.'

'I'd have thought you'd want to keep your money. You're putting enough in the swear jar at the moment.'

'Tenner.'

'Children,' interjected Meredith but they were like a pair of cowboys staring each other down.

'Bet you I can down it faster than you,' said Fliss picking up her glass and tossing her hair over her shoulder.

'You're on.'

The two of them lifted their glasses while the others looked on. To everyone's amazement, Fliss drank hers down in several smooth swallows without any sign of discomfort or difficulty, slamming her empty glass down before Jason had spluttered his way through a third of a pint.

'Bloody 'ell, girl.' He thrust a hand out to her. 'Fair play.' They shook hands and then he slapped a ten-euro note down on the table.

'It's all right. I don't need to take your money.'

Jason insisted, pushing the euro note into her hand. 'Flaming hell. Where'd you learn to do that?'

'I've got brothers who always think girls can't do anything. It's my life's mission to prove them wrong.' Her smile was smug.

Guinness, Hannah decided, was all right. She enjoyed the smooth bitterness as it slipped down her throat. With the six of them gathered around the table, Fliss and Jason in rare accord, it was a convivial evening. All of them were tired but mellow and the drinks went down well as they talked about the first week's experiences. It was funny, thought Hannah, how quickly they'd all bonded into a united group, even though they were all so different.

Hannah's brain reeled with all the new information and her feet were still complaining, but the atmosphere of the pub and the novelty of being somewhere different began to perk them all up. Jason and Alan wandered off to the dartboard followed by Fliss who, it turned out, was a dab hand with the arrows and soon she and Jason were betting each other again as to who could score the highest.

Hannah was quite happy relaxing and listening to Meredith talking about her daughters.

'I realised that I'm in danger of being left behind. I came on the course because I wanted something for me. I've been a wife and mother and I don't want to be a nothing when they go off to lead their own lives.'

Izzy rolled her eyes. 'Lucky you. I don't think my mother could cope without me. She's absolutely hopeless. Leaving her for this long is a bit of a gamble. She'll probably burn the place down, which would be a blessing because at least then we'd have the insurance.'

'Check your policy,' said Hannah. 'If something happens for which someone is at fault, you might not get a payout.'

'And aren't you a regular ray of sunbeams,' Izzy said, taking a swig of Guinness.

'Sorry, force of habit. I had clients who took their insurers to court because they wouldn't pay out when their house burned down. They'd left a hairdryer on while they'd had a power cut. Went out for dinner and the power came back on. Half the house went up in flames. The insurers said they were responsible. Took quite a battle to agree that it was accidental.'

'I bet you're the sort that always reads the policy, aren't you?' teased Izzy.

'Yes. Always,' admitted Hannah. 'It's just being careful. No point taking risks, if you can help it.'

'Huh! That's no way to live life,' said Meredith with

surprising animation. 'You can't allow for everything. When I got married, it never occurred to me that my husband would run off with another woman and leave me with two small children. And if you'd have told me that would happen I might have run a mile, but do you know what? Now I wouldn't change a thing. Yes it was tough, but I'm so close to my girls that I'm grateful to the old git.'

As Meredith spoke, Hannah looked up, some sixth sense drawing her attention to the arrival of Conor coming through the door with Fergus. She immediately dropped her gaze and picked up the damp beer mat on the table in front of her, but not before she'd managed to register that in a navy-blue T-shirt that fitted his lean frame rather nicely along with thigh-hugging, faded jeans, he looked rather hot. Something stirred low in her belly but that might have been because she could remember what his chest looked like under the blue jersey fabric. She reminded herself sharply that he might be handsome and he'd been kind to her the other night, but he was still far too full of himself.

'Did you see who just walked in?' asked Izzy. 'Mr Hottie himself.'

'I'm old enough to be his grandmother, but he has a certain something,' said Meredith. 'They handed sex appeal out in sack loads where he's concerned. No wonder he was so popular. Bit of a lothario by all accounts. Always in the paper with some actress or model. Do you know he was engaged to Polly Daventree? Actress-turned-chef. She's gorgeous. I bet they made a stunning couple.'

'What happened? You said *was*.' Izzy asked the very question that Hannah longed to. She'd heard of Polly

Daventree – she'd won *Celebrity Masterchef* a year or so ago, which Hannah might not have watched but couldn't have not known because it had been in all the tabloid newspapers.

'No one knows. One minute wedding bells were on the horizon, the next she's taken up with someone else. Not that it bothered Conor. He's had a succession of arm candy ever since. Been playing the field – he's got more mileage in him than a hire car. I don't think he's the sort to settle down. He's got what my mother would call a roving eye. And look at him. He has to beat them off with a stick.'

That girl in the bar in Dublin was a case in point, thought Hannah. No wonder he wasn't interested in her, no one would mistake her for a celebrity. He could have anyone he wanted and probably had.

'You don't look so impressed, Hannah,' observed Izzy. 'Not your type?'

She gave a half-laugh. 'No, I'm not keen on people who think so much of themselves.'

'Sensible girl,' said Meredith in stout support. 'Far too good for him. Have you got a boyfriend at home?'

'No,' said Hannah.

'Whyever not? Attractive girl like you.'

Hannah shrugged. 'I've had a few, but…' She lifted her shoulders. 'Not met the right one.'

Most of the men she met were work colleagues who were already taken or men who tried to pick her up with lame chat-up lines that revealed the gulf between them. She wanted someone smart and driven with ambition; they didn't need to be wealthy, but they needed to have something about them. It wasn't that much to ask, was it?

'What about you, Izzy?'

Izzy laughed as well. 'Nope. Spectacularly single. Although I've had a few offers, but more because they think I'm rich, which I'm not.'

'Sounds interesting.'

'Not really. It's a bit of a disaster, actually. My great uncle left me his stately pile. And can I leave it at that?' Izzy slumped a little and drained her glass. 'Who's for another?'

'Let me get them,' said Hannah, jumping to her feet, part of her wanting to prove to herself and to Conor that she was indifferent to him.

'What would you like, Merry?' She looked over to the bar. Conor was there chatting to the barman.

'I'll have a wine this time. Less volume. I'll be peeing all night if I drink any more Guinness. To be honest, I'm not that keen. Still think it tastes like earwax.' She nodded at her almost-full glass. 'I'll offer Jason the rest. He doesn't seem the sort to be too fussy.'

As Hannah approached the bar, butterflies taking ridiculously over-enthusiastic flight in her stomach, she tried to school her face into a casual, fancy-seeing-you-here expression, as if she hadn't noticed him before.

'Hello, Hannah.'

'Conor.' She ignored the sudden tightening in her stomach. She could be civilised towards him. As far as she was concerned, they seemed to have come to an unspoken agreement that they would forget what had happened in Dublin, which suited her just fine.

'Welcome to the hot spot of Inch. Night out?' He looked beyond her and nodded to Meredith and Izzy.

She nodded. Suddenly tongue-tied, she couldn't do more than look at his black-bristled chin. She saw his mouth curve into a knowing smile and wanted to sink through the floor. God, she was an idiot. Why hadn't she let Izzy get the drinks? She was so obvious and then she was annoyed with herself. Straightening, she looked him in the eye, determined to show him she wasn't the least bit bothered by his presence, even though her pulse was tripping the light fantastic at that very moment. What was it about him that sent her system haywire?

Honestly, she was barking up the wrong tree here; he couldn't have made it plainer. She lifted her chin. 'I guess this is the Friday night place to be, round here.'

'It certainly is. Great craic.'

'Seems it.' She took the opportunity to look away from him and those piercing blue eyes that seemed to see everything. 'Busy.'

'Another couple of weeks and it'll thin out. The kids all go back to school next week and then everything starts to wind down.'

'Ah, I wondered about Niamh helping out at the school.'

'My niece? She just works in the summer. She'll be back to getting the bus to Tralee every morning.'

She smiled at his pronunciation.

'What's the matter?'

'Nothing, just the way you say it. It sounds different to the way I read it and I didn't realise it was so close. Friends of mine from university lives there.' And she really ought to give them a ring.

'Yes, you Brits mangle our language. It's quite amusing.'

'I'm sure it is. Do you speak Irish?' She'd been surprised by all the dual language signs.

'Sadly not as well as I should. I'm a bit rusty, but Granny Bridget is the real *gaeilgeoir*. Irish speaker.'

'What are you having?' the barman interrupted.

'Can I have three glasses of white wine?'

'Sure you can. Anything for a fine thing like yourself. Where've you been all my life?'

Conor shook his head. 'Barra O'Toole, can the blarney. She's a guest up at the house and she's not so foolish as to fall for your carry-on.'

'Jaysus, you big spoilsport, Conor. Keeping her for yourself I'll mind and when you already have a stream of women panting after you.' He tutted with a good-natured roll of his eyes. 'Honest to God, he's just plain greedy.' He grinned at Hannah. 'Three glasses of white wine, coming up. How long are you here for?'

'Six weeks. This is my first week.'

'Plenty of time to get to know you then.' He winked and moved to the back of the bar to grab three glasses.

'Ignore him,' said Conor. 'He's a player.'

Hannah raised an eyebrow and she was pleased to see it disconcerted him very briefly.

Barra returned with the glasses and poured three.

'I'll give you a hand with those,' said Conor, taking two of the glasses while she pulled out her purse to pay.

'Er, thanks,' she said as he grabbed them, along with his

own pint glass, and began walking to the table where Merry and Izzy had been covertly watching them – and then he went and sat down to join them.

'Great,' she said under her breath as she followed with her own glass.

'Thanks, Hannah.' Izzy and Merry lifted their glasses.

'To a wonderful course,' said Merry. 'I'm already enjoying it. I've learned so much.'

'Oh God, me too,' said Izzy fervently. 'It's all a bit mind-boggling, but fantastic.'

'How 'bout you Hannah? Enjoying it?' Conor turned to her.

'Mmm,' said Hannah, non-committally. 'It's hard work though.'

'Oh, yes. Mam is a hard taskmaster.'

'She makes it all look so easy and she's so inspirational. Those herb flowers she uses in the salads. So many ideas. I've been writing notes like crazy.' Meredith stopped. 'And listen to me rattle on. I think I've got a bit of a crush on her. She's so wonderful.'

'That's quite normal,' said Conor a touch dryly. 'I've never known anyone not develop a crush on her. She's still in touch with students from all over the world. They often come back to teach. You never quite know who will be at the table. Life at Killorgally is always an adventure.'

'Must have been wonderful growing up here.'

'Mmm.' Now Conor was the non-committal one, the perfunctory smile not reaching his eyes. Hannah gave a sharp glance at that impassive face. 'Mealtimes were always entertaining. We didn't just eat the food, it always had to be discussed and debated.'

Conor's upbringing sounded erratic, unconventional, and uncomfortable. Imagine not knowing who was coming at any time. Sharing your house with lots of strangers. It sounded far too disorganised for comfort.

'But living here...' Merry waved her hand towards the glorious view through the window down to the sea.

Conor nodded, his mouth curving upwards, and Hannah noticed that this time the smile lit up his face. 'Sure, it was mighty. We'd be happy out. Especially when we had the whole beach at our disposal. In the holidays, once we'd done all the chores, my sisters and me with Fergus tagging along would go down to the beach and spend the whole day down there.'

'I haven't been to the beach yet,' said Izzy. 'Is it far?'

'There's a path down from the farm. Just past Hannah's cottage.' Conor exchanged a quick look with Hannah. 'Just follow the path straight down to the main road and go a little way along the road and the track to the beach is right there. You can't miss it.' He looked at Hannah again. 'And ignore the fence that cuts across the path, although it's probably on its last legs.'

'Actually,' Hannah butted in, 'the fence looked brand new to me.'

'New?' His eyebrows furrowed in scepticism. 'I wouldn't have thought so. Moss Murphy's not going to waste good money on new fencing.' He gave her a patronising smile. 'You must be mistaken.'

Hannah narrowed her eyes at him. 'About the fence, what with being a townie?'

'You were a little shaken. Not surprisingly. I've been to Moss Murphy's house and had a word with him. I warned him the guard will be involved if anything like this happens again, even though he claims not to know anything about it.'

Merry and Izzy watched both of them, with sudden, avid interest.

'Shaken? What happened?' Merry, not one for subtlety, was straight onto this snippet.

Hannah glared at Conor. 'I had a run-in with one of the neighbours who told me off for trespassing. And, shaken or not, I think I can tell the difference between a rickety old fence down on the sea path and a brand-new one.'

'Maybe we're talking at cross purposes and you were on a different path.'

'How far is it down to the sea?' asked Meredith, ever the peacekeeper.

'A couple of kilometres. Not far.' Conor flashed his charming smile at the older woman while Hannah gave him a sour glance. She wasn't wrong. She knew she wasn't, but if he didn't believe her that was his problem.

'Well I hope it's not as pungent as the walk here,' said Meredith.

Conor winced. 'Yes. I'm sorry about that. Murphy again. His latest protest is an unwelcome manure pile right on the boundary, but at least it's not outside the main gateway to the farm like it was last time. He's like a stone in our shoes. He's not happy that I'm completely rebuilding one of the cottages, though he knows full well it's not for renting out. I'll be living there.'

'Why wouldn't he be happy about it?' asked Izzy with a puzzled frown.

'Success breeds envy,' said Conor, his mouth turning down at one corner in sympathy. 'It's not easy to make money just from sheep farming and it's hard work. He sees Mam attracting people from all over the world. We hold food festivals, the Orchard Dinner and famous chefs visit, all of which get covered in the local paper. He's none too happy about it happening right next door to him, even though it doesn't really impact on him. We have shared access on the road up from the main road and at least once a month his tractor breaks down in the middle of it.'

'But your mum works really hard,' objected Meredith.

'He doesn't see that,' replied Conor dryly.

The strains of violin started and a duo of a guitarist and violinist, one standing, one seated in the small corner near the bar, began to play a folksong. Almost everyone in the pub seemed to know it as they stopped talking when the young man on the guitar began to sing, his floppy curls bouncing in time to the music. The girl playing the violin next to him had the same dark hair and well-defined features and they shared the same pointed chin and dreamy smiles as they played.

Soon people began to clap in time and quite a few began to sing along. When the song came to an end, there were a few shouts and whoops before they launched into the more familiar 'Wild Rover'.

'They're good,' said Izzy.

'They've been playing for years. Brother and sister, although they're just home for the summer break. They're both at Trinity in Dublin.'

'Do they have a name?'

Conor laughed. 'Rory and Roisin. The Two Rs. That's what they call themselves. They've been playing here since they were youngsters. Barra's their cousin.'

'Does Barra own the pub? asked Hannah.

'Yes, well, he took it over from his granda a while back. His da died. He was a fisherman out of Dingle. Swept overboard in a storm in '97.'

'Do you know everyone round here?' asked Meredith.

'Pretty much.'

'That must be nice,' said Hannah, thinking of her apartment block where she knew a few people by sight but no one ever said hello.

'It has its downsides. Mrs Clonnarty, who runs the post office, still remembers catching me and Rona McPhail skinny-dipping when we were fourteen and loves to remind me, especially when she's got an audience of tourists in the shop.' He gave a rueful grin. 'Rona's now married with four girls and has the loudest laugh you ever heard. She's a great girl but I could do without Mrs C remembering my misspent youth every time I put a letter in the mail.'

They all laughed and Hannah had to give him a brownie point for poking fun at himself. Though clearly, once a player always a player. And why was she telling herself something she already knew?

When the darts players re-joined them, she had to squish

up on the bench with Conor next to her. His proximity was both heaven and hell. She could feel the warmth of his thigh through the jeans he wore and every time he leaned forward to grasp his pint, she got a waft of his lemony aftershave which brought memories back in wave after wave of sensation. She had to think hard to stop herself from remembering all that had happened in that hotel room.

She tried instead to focus on the atmosphere in the pub. Everyone had relaxed into the weekend and that good-natured vibe of being off duty seemed to have been reinforced by the music. Everywhere she looked, people to a man were smiling, nodding, and toe-tapping as the young couple continued to play a mix of songs, all with an Irish flavour from U2, The Cranberries, Damien Rice and a couple of haunting more folky melodies that she didn't know.

'Hey, Conor Byrne,' called Barra from the bar. 'Give us a song with your brother.'

There was a shout of approval from the young lads surrounding Fergus, who began pushing him forward.

Conor rose with a grin. 'If I must.' He and his brother conferred for a moment with Rory and Roisin and then she handed over her violin to Fergus who tapped the bow and counted to three as Rory burst into a rousing and vaguely familiar tune.

'One of my favourites,' said Alan with a broad smile, tapping his hand on the table in time.

'What is it?' whispered Hannah, not quite being able to place it.

'One of the greats. "Fisherman's Blues" by The Waterboys.'

With a loud whoop, Conor began singing while Fergus played violin with great panache, dancing as he did. Conor had a husky, deep voice which he belted out to the obvious delight of the regulars. The two of them were clearly old hands as they played to the crowd, singing to different people and receiving enthusiastic applause and shouts of approval. Together they had that stage presence that some people seemed to be blessed with and Hannah couldn't help smiling and clapping. Most of the crowd began to sing along. The joy of the music and the simple pleasure of being among happy people was infectious and soon the whole table was joining in the chorus. Quite a few people were up and dancing.

As soon as the song finished, they segued straight into 'The Whole of the Moon', much to the delight of the entire pub who joined in with the words. Conor moved around the pub, a real showman, dancing with some of the girls and serenading them, with a big smile on his face. He was clearly in his element. Hannah ignored the quick pang of jealousy. She had no reason to feel anything towards Conor. They'd had an ill-advised night and it was over and done with. Determined to enjoy herself and not think about him, she gave into the infectious atmosphere and tugged on Izzy's hand to pull her up to dance. Then Alan asked Meredith and soon the whole pub was on its feet, dancing and singing. At one dizzying point she danced into Conor's orbit. He caught her eye and she couldn't look away. There was a gentle tilt to his mouth as he smiled at her and in that moment she could have sworn he was singing the line, *the whole of the moon*, to her… or maybe it was wishful thinking.

When the song finished to riotous applause, Conor took a bow, clapped his hands towards Rory, and shouldered his way through the crowd back to Hannah's table. Everyone wanted to stop him and pat him on the back. When he sat down, draining his pint in one, his eyes shone and his grin was as wide as ever.

'Well, that was a bit of fun.'

'It was brilliant,' said Hannah, beaming at him, still buoyed up by the wonderful atmosphere. 'It's like being at a party.' She glanced around the busy pub at the animated, happy faces, everyone united by the music. It was a rare moment and her heart burst with joy. She could see exactly why people fell in love with Ireland.

'That's the craic for you. We love a song and a dance. There's nowhere quite like a pub on a Friday night in Ireland.'

Barra appeared with a pint of Guinness and put it in front of Conor. 'Good job, boyo. Any time you want a slot, you let me know. You'll have to get Mairead along too.'

Conor lifted his pint with a grateful nod at Barra 'Cheers but we're not The Corrs just yet.'

'Give it time. Young Niamh can hold a tune, I hear.'

'Granny Bridget will have us all singing at the Orchard Party, don't you worry.' Conor rolled his eyes. 'And she'll dance the night away with more energy than anyone else.'

'Your granny's a legend. There's no better woman on the fiddle.' Barra picked up a few empty glasses and made his way back to the bar.

'Would you look at the time!' said Meredith, putting down her glass and blinking a little woozily. 'Where's the night gone? It's half past eleven and it's pitch black out there. How will we find our way home?'

'Don't worry,' said Conor. 'I'll guide you up the path. The moon's out so you'll be able to see where you're going.'

There was some low-level grumbling from Jason about leaving so early but Fliss gave him short shrift for being a selfish bugger. After the busy week they'd had, they were all pretty tired and Hannah, for one, had had more than enough to drink.

Stepping outside from the warm, fuggy, noisy pub into the cool night air, the silence was quite a contrast. It didn't quite sober Hannah up, but it certainly brought her to her senses.

'Look at the stars,' she said.

'Bloody 'ell,' said Jason. 'Is that for real?'

'No light pollution. Isn't it glorious? It's like this in the place I've just moved to. I'm thinking about offering stargazing breaks,' said Izzy.

'Where the 'ell do you live? The middle of nowhere?' asked Jason as he, Hannah, and Izzy walked three abreast following the others. Alan had made a beeline for Meredith and, no surprise, Fliss had moved in on Conor. Hannah could see her tossing her long blonde hair with coquettish flips and laughing obligingly and loudly in the night.

'I live in the Highlands, in Scotland. In a castle.'

'Seriously. I live in a two-up, two-down council house with my mum and sisters in Bethnal Green.'

'Don't be too impressed. The whole place is falling down and I've got to save it somehow. It was left to me by my mad great-uncle, but my mum is desperate to stay. She always thought it would come to her. And that's a whole other story. The whole place is one ginormous money pit.' She let out a loud sigh. 'I really don't want to think about it right now.'

Poor Izzy sounded quite depressed.

'I bet she lives in a palace or something, that Fliss. Right stuck-up tart she is.'

While Fliss's sharp tongue hadn't endeared her to Hannah, she didn't like the idea of bitching about the other girl. None of them knew each other that well.

'Give her a chance, Jason. We're all different. And we're stuck with each other for the next few weeks.'

'S'pose you're right. Mind you, she's a laugh down the pub. We're going to play pool next time. Probably thrash me again. Bet she's got her own billiard room or something, like in Cluedo.'

They followed Conor and Fliss to a gap in the hedge and thanks to the nearly full moon, they were able to pick their way up the hill. An owl hooted away in a thicket over to the left and a few birds chirped in alarm. Across the field there were occasional flashes of a rabbit's tail darting away to safety.

After several glasses of wine, Hannah felt pleasantly woozy and extremely grateful she didn't have to get up in the morning. She and Izzy had made tentative plans to go down to the beach at lunchtime, but she was going to take it easy for most of the day. Who knew that cooking all week would be so exhausting? She was quite grateful that at the weekends they were left to fend for themselves. They could help themselves to herbs and vegetables from the garden and there were plenty of eggs, bacon, ham, and bread on offer in the cookery kitchen early that afternoon. Hannah had already decided that she would probably eat sandwiches and salad all weekend rather than bother cooking anything for herself.

'This is us, Hannah,' said Izzy as they crossed into the farmyard, pointing to the row of cottages opposite the cookery kitchen. She and Meredith were sharing a cottage which was next door to the one that Jason and Alan shared.

'Night, everyone,' said Hannah.

'Wait,' called Conor. 'Just let me see Fliss to the hotel and then I'll come down with you.'

'You don't need to do that. I'll be fine.' She wasn't afraid of the dark or the walk on her own, but a sudden unexpected frisson of excitement fizzed through her at the idea of spending time alone with him.

'I know,' his voice was as dry as dust, 'but I was brought up to make sure ladies get home safely.'

She waited in the courtyard, listening to the others calling good night, the rattling of keys in doors and the murmured inaudible conversation between Conor and Fliss, who sounded disgruntled.

'Ready?' he asked her when he re-joined her.

'Yes, but you really don't need to do this.'

The snap of a twig over to her left stopped Hannah in

her tracks. Was that the scuff of a footstep? She put an arm on Conor's to stop him. 'Did you hear that?'

'Hear what?'

'I thought I heard someone,' she whispered.

Conor let out a small half laugh. 'You're a proper townie. Probably just an animal – we have them out here in the country.'

'Very funny,' said Hannah in a quiet voice, some instinct making her tense. Even though there was no sound, the hairs on the back of her neck stood proud. Logic told her there was nothing there but that funny sixth sense argued back. She glanced around but in the moonlight it was difficult to see anything but shadows.

She was grateful that Conor had accompanied her even though he was shaking his head with patronising exasperation.

'Promise you, whatever it is, is no bigger than a weasel or a fox. If it was anything bigger like a deer you'd hear it crashing through the undergrowth.'

He set off again and she hurried after him up to the front door.

'Here you go, madam. Have you got your key?'

There was an electric silence between them and she made the mistake of glancing at his lips, remembering in a sudden rush the last time they'd been outside a door together. His mouth twitched. Oh God, he remembered too. The two of them kissing furiously, his hand tugging at her top, her fingers undoing buttons, as he fumbled with the key card.

They stood in awkward but very-aware-of-each-other

silence in the tiny porch as she delved into her bag for her key. Her uncooperative fingers scrabbled about like fat sausages as she tried to gain purchase on the stupid thing nestled at the bottom of her handbag.

Conor leaned back against the oak post, his arms folded and a smile on his face as Hannah felt her face heat up. At last, she found it.

'Got it.' She held the key up in triumph, gripped between finger and thumb, and then the dratted thing pinged out of her hand and bounced on the floor with a metallic clink.

They both ducked to their knees on the floor to find it, her fingers brushing over the wooden planks in the darkness. His warm hand nudged and covered hers for a brief second and they both pulled back with the shock of the touch as if they'd been zapped with a brief burst of electricity.

'Here, let me,' snapped Conor, pulling out his phone and switching on the torch function.

The light cast dark shadows on the grim set of his face. He really didn't want to be here and Hannah felt embarrassed by her continuing response to him. The camaraderie of the pub had made her forget that for her own self-preservation she was supposed to be keeping her distance from him.

It was a relief when the torch beam glinted on the silver key in one corner and she leaped forward to grab it, unfortunately at the very moment Conor did. They collided, shoulders crashing into each other. He grabbed her forearms to steady her, his phone falling from his grasp.

Face to face, she could see his eyes glinting in the moonlight and feel his warm breath on her cheek. She could feel the magnetic pull between them, just like the first time she'd met him, sitting on his lap. The memory brought with it a sudden flush of heat and she moistened her lips. Conor watched the movement with dark, brooding eyes, giving nothing away. Her heart thudded in her chest as her eyes met his and she was convinced he must be able to hear it. His head dipped towards her and she held her breath, their eyes holding each other's gaze.

She wasn't sure who made the first move, what she did know beyond the thudding of her pulse in her ears, was that any second she might just burst into flames. The moment his lips touched hers, an explosion of lust and longing went off consuming her in desire. Without hesitation she wound an arm around his neck to pull him closer, as thankfully his hands dug into her waist anchoring her to him.

When his hand slid inside her blouse to graze her breast, she had to stifle a whimper of desperation. With his tongue duelling with hers, each of them fought to take control. Everything inside felt taut and tense. With the rising heat between her legs and the spiralling tension, she squirmed against his fingers teasing the soft skin around her nipple with dangerous and thorough intent. She hung on tight, feeling as if she could be swept away by a rip tide at any moment. There was no doubt, they had chemistry between them. Conor groaned, sending a thrill of power through her, as he adjusted the angle of his kiss, his lips. A moan escaped her. 'Conor.' Driving need made her want to writhe shamelessly against him. She was a complete hussy and she absolutely did not give a flying fig. Her body was making all the demands and her hormones had taken full control.

They got a nasty shock when Conor suddenly wrenched himself away, pulling back as if he'd come face to face with an anaconda or something equally nasty. The rejection was like a bucket of ice water thrown straight into her face.

'Buggering hell,' snapped Conor. 'That's not supposed to happen.'

'Well, it did,' she said, masking a touch of triumph. Despite the sudden withdrawal, Conor wasn't as averse to her as he'd claimed.

He drew in a ragged breath and pushed his hand through his hair. 'It can't happen again. I told you. I don't get involved with guests.'

'I didn't ask you to kiss me.'

'You didn't fight me off.'

She shrugged 'Was I supposed to?' Where it came from, she didn't know, probably those pesky hormones again. 'I quite liked it.' Ireland Hannah was back. 'We're both adults.'

Conor scowled at her. 'I've already told you. Dublin was a one-off. It can't happen again.'

He ducked down, snatched up his phone from the floor and shone it on the key lying in the corner of the porch. 'Don't move. I'll get the key,' muttered Conor.

He rose with the key in his hand and took a step back as he held it out to her as if determined to keep his distance. She eyed him, about to take it from his outstretched hand. 'Thank you.'

'My pleasure,' he said smoothly before adding, 'The key, I mean.'

'Of course, I didn't think you meant anything else,' she purred with an insincere smile.

'Hannah.' He sighed and then thought better of what he was about to say, slotting the key into the lock as if to make sure he was seeing her in. Opening the door, he held out an arm ushering her in. 'Goodnight.'

As soon as she stepped over the threshold, she turned but he was already walking down the path with brisk strides as if he couldn't wait to get away from her.

Chapter Ten

'I reckon we just have to run in,' said Izzy, looking at the sea rippling over the sand in wide, shallow waves.

'It's going to be cold.' Hannah shielded her eyes from the sun and peered out across the water. 'Next stop is America. This is the North Atlantic.'

'I'm from Scotland – I'm used to being cold. There are plenty of people already in.'

'Yes and half of them are wearing wetsuits.'

'Don't be such a Jessie.'

'Who are you calling a Jessie?' said Hannah, taking off at a run and shouting over her shoulder, 'Last one in buys lunch.'

Izzy tore after her and the two of them ploughed into the sea, shrieking with the shock of the cold but both determined not to let the other beat them.

As soon as it was deep enough, Hannah threw herself in, gasping as she struck out with a strong breaststroke. 'Flip it's cold,' she shouted to Izzy who'd followed suit.

'Good for the soul,' yelled Izzy, doing a clumsy crawl alongside her.

Gradually Hannah's body acclimatised to the temperature and she swam out a little further, glad that she'd taken the plunge. Thank goodness she'd shoved her bikini in her suitcase at the last minute.

As it was such a gorgeous day, she and Izzy had agreed to put their cossies on and take towels down to the beach. They'd set up camp halfway along the beach, which was much quieter, away from the families and quite a few cars that were actually parked on the sand itself just in front of the dunes.

'This is Heaven,' said Izzy, floating on her back, her feet pointing up out of the sea. 'No responsibilities, no worries. God, I wish I could stay here.'

'Would you really want to stay here?' Hannah surveyed the hills around them and the beautiful view with the houses dotted on the hillside.

'Only in as much as it's away from home. I lived in Edinburgh until three months ago. I miss it, although I do like living in the country. It's just all the hassle that comes with living in a crumbling pile with my batty mother who is adamant we have to stay.'

'Do you have to stay with her?'

'I wasn't exaggerating when I said she might burn the house down.'

'Oh, is she a bit forgetful?'

'Something like that. She's not got Alzheimer's or anything. There's not a speck of common sense in her body. Flipping liability, she is.'

Hannah shook her head. She couldn't imagine living with someone like that. 'I've got the opposite. My rellies have too much common sense. It takes them forever to make a decision because they have to weigh up all the odds. They were horrified when I took a sabbatical to come out here.'

'Why? It's your life, isn't it?'

'They worry. My mother and father were complete adrenaline junkies. I think they've always had the slight worry that my sister and I might turn out like them. Mina is quite impulsive, so I'm the sensible one. I've always been at pains not to worry them. To try and do the right thing. The sensible thing. I thought learning to cook properly was being quite sensible but it sent my boss, my aunt and uncle, and half my colleagues into a complete tailspin. I almost chickened out.'

'Glad you didn't. It's nice to have someone the same age who isn't a shit-hot cook.'

Hannah laughed. 'You mean I'm a bit crap.'

Izzy winced and grinned. 'Oops. I didn't mean it like that but you're not perfect and neither am I. The others all seem to know what they're doing. I mean, Meredith's lovely but she's about the same age as my mum and Fliss... she's so flipping posh she terrifies me. And I don't think I've got much in common with Jason. He sounds a bit wild.'

'That still leaves Alan.'

'He's a sweetie but I think he's got his eye on Meredith. Wouldn't that be lovely? They've both been on their own for years.'

'They probably like it that way.'

'Do you have any romance in your body, Hannah?' grumbled Izzy with a good-natured frown.

'Not much, no. Far too practical. What about you?'

'I live in hope that the man of my dreams will come and sweep my off my feet, but sadly the only men in my dreams are building surveyors, tax inspectors, and local historians, none of whom are my idea of Regé-Jean Page.'

'Who?'

'Lord, girl. The Duke of Hastings. Have you not watched *Bridgerton*?'

Hannah shook her head. She'd heard of the Netflix hit but had not seen it.

'You really aren't a romantic, are you?'

''Fraid not.'

'Ah well. I thought there might be something going on with you and Conor.'

'Huh, you must be joking. He's not my type at all.' Even as she said the words she wondered if she was protesting too much. It was more a case that she wasn't his type, as he'd made so abundantly clear last night, although judging from that kiss, there was something there. But she wasn't going to make a complete fool of herself by giving into the floaty butterfly feelings he gave her whenever he came into the vicinity.

'Shame.' She grinned. 'He seems to like you.'

'What makes you think that?' Her words almost fell over themselves and she realised she sounded horribly defensive or was that horribly hopeful?

'I've seen him watching you a couple of times, like he was trying to figure you out. I wouldn't mind a man who looks like that looking at me the way he was looking at you.'

'I'm sure you're imagining it.'

'Yeah, yeah, if you say so, Hannah. Come on, don't you think he's just a little easy on the eye?'

'He's OK. But way out of my league. You said yourself he goes out with models and actresses.'

'Don't do yourself down. Besides, not all men are stupid enough to believe that all there is to a woman is looks. Conor strikes me as quite intelligent and,' she grinned, 'very charming.'

'Hmm,' said Hannah, thinking he wasn't always charming. Striding off after kissing her senseless hadn't been charming at all. Conor might be intelligent, but he was also used to picking and choosing women and, from what she'd gathered, she was nothing like his usual conquests.

After twenty minutes in the sea, they returned to their pile of towels and wrapped themselves up, then sat chatting as the sea breeze whipped at their hair, drying it slightly stiff with salt.

'It is beautiful here,' said Hannah, gazing up at the rolling hills around them. It might be hard going back to work after enjoying all this.'

'I don't know about you, but I'm starving. Fancy grabbing some lunch at the cafe? After all that posh food, I could murder some unhealthy, unorganic chips and a greasy burger.'

Hannah laughed. 'You're on. Let's go.'

'Yum. Heaven,' said Izzy, nibbling at one of the big, fat crispy chips. 'Why do fish and chips always taste better outside and by the sea?'

'Are you expecting an answer to that?' Hannah laughed. They were sitting on wooden benches at one of the tables outside Sammy's beach cafe. The place was busy and they'd snagged one of the last empty tables.

'Oh, look who it is.' Izzy nodded and Hannah turned round.

Hannah caught her lip between her teeth. Conor. So much for avoiding him. There was a funny catch in her throat as she remembered that sizzling kiss last night.

She sneaked a glance towards him. He was with his brother, Fergus, and the two of them were in wetsuits with damp, tousled hair and carrying surf boards under their arms. No prizes for guessing where they'd spent the last few hours.

'Hey!' Fergus spotted them, waved and, without waiting for Conor, came over. 'Hi, guys, do you mind if we join you?' Without waiting for an answer, he plonked his board down and called over to his brother. 'The usual. I'll get it,' and then he dashed off inside the cafe.

Conor nodded and Hannah saw his mouth tighten as he wandered over.

'Afternoon. Been on the beach?'

'Yes,' Izzy gave him an enthusiastic smile, shunting up along the bench to allow him to sit down. 'We went for a dip. Flipping freezing. I deduce from the boards that you've been surfing.'

'Well done, Sherlock.' Conor loosened up enough to give

her one of his flashing grins. 'Lovely morning for it. Don't let me stop you eating.' He nodded to the tins of chips in front of them.

'Oops,' said Izzy. 'Caught.'

'I'm not going to judge you.'

'I feel guilty, but there's just something about a big, fat greasy chip.'

'Don't let Adrienne hear you say that,' teased Hannah.

'No,' said Conor, giving her a quick smile.

Izzy said. 'Although you have to say, just look at her, she positively glows with health. She's one hell of an advert for good living. Like, she could be a model or something even though she must be, what, in her fifties?'

'I'm far too much of a gentleman to reveal my mother's age.'

'She's like the original earth mother,' continued Izzy. 'Just gorgeous.'

'I'd like to be like that when I grow up,' said Hannah wistfully, thinking of Adrienne's effortless elegance.

Conor raised one eyebrow as if to say, Really?

She would have asked him what was wrong with that if it hadn't been for the arrival of his brother with two steaming cups.

'Here you go.' Fergus passed one over to him. 'Ah, chips. The Devil's food.' He looked longingly at them.

'Here, have one, help yourself. I can't eat all of them. Not with this huge piece of fish as well,' said Izzy.

Fergus dived straight in and moaned, pulling a comic blissed-out face. 'Don't tell the mammy, whatever you do.'

They all laughed, but Hannah wondered at Conor's unspoken cynicism about his mother.

'Do you want one, Conor?' Hannah offered him her plate.

For a moment he considered it and then with a quick grin took one from the plate and popped it whole into his mouth.

'Our secret,' she said and then immediately regretted her choice of words as his eyes met hers.

'So what is there to do in Inch of a weekend?' she asked hurriedly.

Thankfully Fergus jumped in, while Conor continued to eye her thoughtfully, making her heart skip a little in her chest. She was never going to live that one-night stand down, was she?

'Conor likes to escape to Dublin when he can. I reckon he's got a fancy lady tucked away.'

Conor's mouth twitched ever so slightly and Hannah dropped her eyes, focusing hard on munching through her fish.

'I go into Dingle with the boys. There are a couple of good pubs there and quite a few the other way in Tralee. Both are great to go out on the lash.'

'You'll have to give us some recommendations,' said Izzy.

'Bear in mind, he's eighteen,' drawled Conor. 'His idea of good craic is significantly different from mine.'

'You're just an aul stick in the mud, so you are,' said Fergus with a mocking grin, which took the sting out of his words. 'We had great craic at Foley's last night.'

'Less of the aul, young fella.' The brothers, despite the significant age gap were obviously close.

'Ever tried surfing?' asked Fergus.

'I've always wanted to, but it looks far too difficult,' said Hannah, looking down towards the beach where there were quite a few surfers.

'Just takes practice and a bit of balance.'

'Ha! That's me out then,' said Izzy. 'I have no sense of balance. I couldn't even stand up on a skateboard.'

Hannah hadn't ever been on a skateboard, another thing that had looked a bit too scary when she was a child. She'd always preferred to play it safe. Her adventures came through her books.

'You ought to have a go. The board hire here is pretty reasonable.'

'I might,' said Izzy and suddenly laughed, turning to Hannah. 'I bet Jason and Fliss would be up for it, can you imagine?'

'Oh yes. Those two would turn it into a duel to the death. They're fiercely competitive. Our very own Lady and The Tramp, though with maybe more of a sibling vibe.'

It was a blessed relief when Fergus suddenly swallowed down the last of his coffee. 'Back to the sea. Coming, aul man?' He kicked his brother under the table.

'Nice chatting with you ladies.'

They picked up their boards and headed back down to the beach, Hannah watching Conor's wetsuit-clad form. Even in neoprene he looked something else.

They climbed the path back up to the farm after another swim and hour on the beach.

'You lucked out with this place,' said Izzy when they came to her cottage. 'Having it all to yourself. I couldn't afford one of these, even sharing. Right, I'd best be off. See you later. I think Jason was talking about a return trip to the pub tonight. Not sure I'm up for that. I'm going to see what Meredith's planning. I'll text you if there's a plan.'

'Why don't the two of you come down here? There's plenty of room and I could nip out and get some wine or something.'

'That sounds like a great idea. Let me find out what Meredith is up to.'

Izzy walked away up to the path to the main farmhouse and Hannah stood and admired the cottage for a moment. She liked living on her own, but she'd enjoy the company tonight. As she walked up to the front door, she frowned. The bed of flowers under the sitting room window looked trampled upon as if some animal had sat down in them. What a shame. She crossed to the patch and picked a few of the less-mangled flowers, deciding she'd pop them in one of the many vases of flowers inside. Determined to forget about Conor Bloody Byrne, a girls' night was just what she needed.

Chapter Eleven

'Oooh, isn't this lovely. And haven't you got a great view!' exclaimed Meredith as she and Izzy came through the front door at half past seven. It was still a lovely evening but the breeze had picked up and rather than sit in the garden as she'd originally planned, Hannah was glad she'd decided to lay everything out in the sitting room. She was still miffed about the desecration of the flowers outside the window and looking at it would have irked her.

'Come in,' she said and led the way into the kitchen. 'Would you like a glass of Prosecco?'

'Yes,' said Meredith with delight. 'Who doesn't love a bit of fizz? Where did you find that, then? There wasn't any in our fridge.'

Hannah laughed. 'I popped into Tralee earlier and found an Aldi on the outskirts of the town.' If she'd had more time she would have phoned Aidan and Sorcha's and popped in to see them. How could she have been here a week and not called them yet?

She'd had a lovely soak in the bath, come down and got some nice glasses out of the cupboard, arranged some dips in bowls on the coffee table, lit the candles on the mantlepiece and put out the crisps. It was funny how quickly she become quite proprietorial towards the cottage and how excited she was about welcoming her first guests to come and enjoy its hospitality. At home, she rarely invited people round to her apartment. Most people if they were coming into the city preferred to meet at a restaurant or bar.

'That's the downside of not having a car here,' said Meredith. 'I hadn't thought about it before, although to be honest I'm not much of a driver. The thought of driving in a strange country put me off too.'

'Thankfully, they drive on the same side of the road as us, although some of the road signs are quite different. But it's pretty quiet round here. I'll take you anywhere you want to go,' offered Hannah. 'I've got a hire car and I'm paying for it, so I might as well make use of it.'

'That's kind. Alan's offered as well. He knows Kerry quite well. In fact, we're going for a drive tomorrow.'

'Are you now?' Izzy's arch teasing brought an exasperated sigh from Meredith as Hannah eased the cork out of the bottle and poured the gently fizzing wine into three glasses.

'Don't you go getting ideas. You're as bad as my girls. I'm far too old for all that nonsense. Besides, he's only asked me because I've more in common with him. Similar age. Two daughters.'

'Both single,' said Izzy mischievously as she took a glass from Hannah.

'I doubt very much he'd be interested in a dull, frumpy old bat like me. Cheers, girls. Thanks for inviting me, even thought I could be old enough to be mother to the both of you.'

Hannah led the way into the other room, shaking her head at Meredith's unflattering view of herself.

'You're not old,' said Izzy. 'Not in attitude, that's for sure.'

'Definitely not,' agreed Hannah. 'And you're not a frumpy old bat, either.'

'That's what my girls keep telling me.' Meredith took the far side of the sofa, putting her glass on the table and taking a handful of crisps. 'They've been trying to smarten me up and get me to do that online dating. Don't tell them, but I tried it once. It was awful. I got myself into such a state I couldn't even go through with it. I got all dressed up, stood outside the restaurant for half an hour, and I couldn't go in.'

'Oh Merry. Why not? Was he awful?'

'I never found out. I mean, look at me. Two stone overweight.' She pulled a face at one of the crisps as she put it in her mouth. 'Bags under my eyes. Grey hairs everywhere. And I mean *everywhere*. Good lord, there's no way I could ever get naked with anyone again, that's for sure. Everything has gone south.'

'That's nonsense,' said Izzy. 'You've just lost your confidence.'

It was nonsense. In fact, with her rosy smiling face, clear, guileless blue eyes and soft cloud of sandy hair, she was pretty; she went in and out in all the right places and had the most wonderful curvy figure. She did, however, have appalling taste in clothes – the shapeless sweaters and baggy trousers didn't do her any favours. Hannah was no expert but she knew Meredith would look fabulous in the right sort of dress.

'I'm not sure I ever had any confidence. The girls' dad, well it took me a while to see what he was really like. I was so grateful that someone was interested, I ignored the warnings. My mum, bless her, kept asking if I was sure. I tell you, by the time he cheated on me for the third time, I was sure. Sure I'd made the biggest mistake of my life but by then I had two under two, no job, and nowhere to go. I stuck it out for another couple of years but then he started getting mean. I wasn't going to stand for that. Told my eldest Bethany that she was stupid and ugly. That was it. He might put me down but I wasn't having him do it to the girls. And I've been on my own ever since. Good riddance. I don't need a man around. I'm fine as I am.'

She took a defiant sip of Prosecco.

'Me too,' said Izzy, her mouth turned down. 'I hung on waiting for someone for years. We were friends, occasionally with benefits. Stupid me, I was convinced he'd see the light one day. He did. And married a girl he'd met six months before.'

'Ouch,' said Hannah.

'Yeah, left me heartbroken for a while. Now I can't believe how stupid I was. Like Meredith said, everyone else could see it but would I listen? I thought because I loved him, he must feel like that about me really. He just didn't realise it. Talk about deluded. Unrequited love, eh? No wonder *Persuasion* is my favourite Jane Austen book. Except my Captain Wentworth turned out to be Captain Knobhead.'

Hannah and Meredith burst out laughing at Izzy's disgruntled tone.

'I'm quite glad I'm not a romantic in that case,' said Hannah. 'I haven't been out with anyone for ages and I certainly haven't ever been heartbroken.' Was that because she was too practical and sensible? She finished with most blokes before they were able to inflict any emotional damage; she didn't gave them the chance. If they didn't measure up quite quickly she didn't see the point of keeping on seeing them. 'I can't see the point of going out with someone if you know they're not right.'

'How long do you give them?' asked Meredith, with interest.

Hannah lifted her shoulders. 'You can usually tell after one date.'

'Hannah! You've got to give them a chance,' protested Meredith, which was somewhat ironic given what she'd said about her ex-husband. 'What's the longest you've been out with someone?'

'What, properly?'

'What's not properly?'

'Well, you know, when you're a teenager. I went out with Richard Bradley in the sixth form for nearly six months but only because we all ran around in the same crowd.'

'No one longer than that?' asked Meredith with round eyes. 'How old are you?'

'Twenty-seven.'

'So what is the longest you've been out with anyone since then?'

'Five months.'

'And what happened to him?'

'I quite liked him but he got a transfer to London and… well, there didn't seem much point starting a long-distance relationship.'

'You didn't fancy going to London?'

'It just seemed like a big step. What if it hadn't worked out?'

'If it hadn't worked out, you pick yourself up and you make the best of things,' said Meredith. 'I knew in my heart of hearts that I was taking a risk marrying Darren, but if I hadn't I wouldn't have my two girls and they definitely were worth the risk.'

'Yeah,' agreed Izzy. 'Sometimes you have to go for it. If I hadn't followed Philip to Edinburgh, I wouldn't have ended up living there and working at the Festival which was the best job ever, and I made so many brilliant friends and I loved living in the city. It's one of the best in the world. So although it didn't turn out the way I wanted it to, it was still worth taking the chance.'

Hannah nodded, not believing either of them. Look what had happened in Dublin. If she'd played it safe, she wouldn't be in this horribly awkward situation with Conor where every time she saw him she wanted to die of mortification.

'Is that your phone, Hannah?' asked Izzy suddenly as a mobile began to ring.

'Yes.' Hannah picked up the phone but didn't recognise the number. Curiosity won over manners. 'Sorry, will you excuse me?' she said to Meredith and Izzy. Unknown numbers freaked her out a little. She knew that there was a strong chance it was some sales call but at the same time, it could be a policeman or a hospital.

'Hello, Hannah Campbell speaking.'

'Hannah!' She grinned at the sound of her old university friend's familiar bellow. 'It's Aidan. When are we seeing you?'

'Aidan,' her tone warmed with the delight of hearing his voice. 'How are you? I'm so sorry I haven't called yet, it's been so busy.'

'Don't you fret. I've got you now,' he replied. 'What are you doing tomorrow? Come for lunch.'

She laughed. Same old Aidan. 'I'd love to. Text me your address.'

'I will. Twelve-thirty? See you then.' With that Aidan disconnected the phone and found Meredith and Izzy staring at her, full of curiosity.

'He's an old university friend and colleague. We worked together in Manchester and then he came back to Tralee to take over his father's practice.'

'Oh, that's lovely,' said Meredith. 'An old flame?'

'Huh! No. Just a very good friend. He's married to another friend of ours from uni.'

'That'll do you good. It's a long stretch to be away from home,' said Meredith. 'Although I'm quite enjoying being with other people. It gets quite lonely on your own when you've been used to a house full of people for so long.'

Meredith gave them a sad smile and then perked up a little. 'Although as much fun as it was to spend the evening with you, I'm going to have to head up the hill to bed. I agreed I'd meet Alan at nine and... well, I'd rather not look like too knackered. I do have some pride.'

'Atta girl,' said Izzy. 'I'll come with you. Thanks so much for having us, Hannah. To be honest I *was* feeling a little bit homesick, and this was just what I needed. Not that I am missing home'– she pulled a face and Hannah knew she was referring to her mother – 'but I just felt a bit... lonely isn't the word but a long way from home. Does that make sense?'

Hannah smiled at her and then realised she didn't agree. The homely cottage with its restful coloured walls, the little vases of flowers and votives of candles, cushions, and throws, and charming pictures of contemporary watercolour landscapes was a world away from her own apartment and she fallen in love with her new surroundings. Her furnishings were strictly utilitarian – in fact, the only cushion she owned – a bright-pink one with a beaming pug on the front – had been a gift from her sister.

Meredith gave Hannah a big hug at the door. 'Thank you for this and for including me. It was a lovely evening.' With a cheeky grin, she added, 'I hope we can do it again, if it's not too forward. I'm inviting myself but you've got that beautiful garden.'

'You're welcome anytime,' said Hannah, feeling an unexpected glow of warmth towards both Meredith and Izzy. 'It's been fun.'

With a happy smile on her face, she closed the door

behind them and sat down on the sofa to finish her glass of Prosecco. She'd enjoyed their company; they hadn't stopped talking and laughing all evening and they'd managed to get through two bottles of Prosecco. It was one of the best nights she'd had for a while – well, Dublin excepted, and that was best forgotten. With a sigh, she realised she'd become a little too used to and resigned to the loneliness of living on her own. When had it become the norm? She kept herself busy, going walking and kayaking, but now she realised that they were coping mechanisms. Since her sister had moved to Switzerland, her social life had dwindled to nothing. Had coming here been a subconscious hankering for change?

She thought about it for a while as she sipped her wine. An unfamiliar noise made her glance up out of the window. It was dark out there now. A little prickle of unease ran down her spine. She was being daft – see, she was lonely now the others had gone. Time for bed. She'd read for a while on her Kindle. Rising to her feet, she gathered up the bowls and glasses and carried them through to the kitchen. Washing up quickly, she left everything to drain and then went back into the sitting room to turn out the lamps and collect the empty bottles.

As she turned out the last lamp, two bottles in hand, she glanced up.

A face stared at her through the window. For a brief moment she thought it must be Meredith or Izzy coming back. But the face moved back out of sight. Startled, the bottles slipped out her hand with a crash and she looked down as they clattered and rolled across the stone floor, the loud noise in tandem with her hammering heart.

Frozen for a moment, she stood in the dark, realising that whoever it was couldn't see her now, and then hurriedly drew the curtains, bolted the door, and switched off all the downstairs lights.

Chapter Twelve

The next morning, with the sun shining brightly through the window, she lay there feeling stupid. Last night, still jittery, she'd put a chair up against her bedroom door. Now, with sunbeams lighting up dancing dust motes in the air, she wondered why she'd been so scared. All those thrillers she'd read, no doubt, along with an overactive imagination. It could have been any number of things: Fergus coming back from the pub, someone checking on the animals, or... well, there were probably plenty of explanations. Whoever it was had probably been just as startled as her.

As it was so gorgeous, she decided to take her breakfast and a book outside and sit at the little bistro table in the front garden, and, after a quick shower, with tea and toast on a tray, she stepped out into the glorious morning. Clear blue sky stretching as far as the eye could see greeted her, the colour so pure it made her heart sing. There wouldn't be many more days like this. September began tomorrow, and already there was a slight chill in the morning air.

As she admired the day, her eyes strayed to the window and she frowned at the sight of the mangled flowers. They seemed worse today. Picking up her tea, she walked over to the bed, that prickling sense of unease trickling back.

She stared down at the bed, her eyes focusing on the solid outline indented into the soil. Footprints. Right in front of the window. A hand squeezed her heart.

'Don't be daft, Hannah.' She said the words out loud to emphasis her stupidity, as if saying them made them true. She was being over dramatic and neurotic.

'Talking to yourself.'

She jumped, throwing her cup up in the air, and hot tea slopped over her wrist.

'Bloody hell, Conor! What are you doing here?' She shook her arm and rubbed at it before wiping it on her jeans.

'I'm on my way down to the beach, if that's all right with you.' He indicated the surfboard under his arm.

'Well, you shouldn't have crept up on me.'

'I wasn't creeping. You seem a bit jumpy this morning. Besides, you were absorbed in communing with nature. My mother's teaching is obviously rubbing off already.' There was a slightly sarcastic tone to his voice. He looked down at the battered crocosmia and frowned. 'Didn't you like the flowers?'

'It wasn't me! Someone stood here.' She hadn't planned on making a fuss about it because she was still trying to convince herself that there was a sensible explanation, but the accusation in his words made her blurt out, 'I saw someone looking in my window last night.'

Conor raised an eyebrow, put down his board and came over.

Now she felt a bit foolish. To justify herself, she pointed to the footprints and said a little belligerently, 'See.'

Conor studied the scene in silence for a few seconds and then bent down to touch the damp soil before turning and looking up at her. 'You saw someone looking in through the window?'

'Yes. Just a face. Only a glimpse, but there was definitely someone there, and then this morning I thought I was being silly but then…' She waved a hand at the flowers, her stomach turning over with the realisation that there really had been someone there. She couldn't help an involuntary shiver.

'When was this?'

'Last night at about half-ten. At the time, I thought maybe it was… I don't know, someone larking about coming back from the pub or something.'

'We were all at home last night. Family dinner celebrating Mairead and Eamon's wedding anniversary.'

'Maybe someone was out locking up the animals or something.'

Conor's eyes narrowed as he rose to his feet still studying the trampled flowers and the clear footprints. 'Maybe.' Even he didn't sound convinced.

It didn't take a detective to see that whoever had stood here had been right up against the window. That wasn't just someone walking past.

Hannah took a hasty gulp of what was left of her tea, her hand shaking. Then another thought struck her.

'The flowers. They were like this the day before.'

'One of the pigs got out. Porker. It might have been him.'

'I suppose, but does he wear size-ten boots?'

Conor huffed out a sigh. 'No.'

Together they stood staring down at the untidy flower bed with the torn petals and squashed flower heads.

'Let me have a think. We can move you somewhere else, although I'm not sure where. I'm mid-renovation on the other two cottages we have. There'll be a room in the hotel, I think.'

Hannah pinched her lips together. 'Don't be silly. It was probably a one-off. I'll draw the curtains at night.' The cottage was so lovely she was loathe to leave it and now, on such a gorgeous day, it felt as if she were overreacting. 'I've read too many thrillers. I'm sure you don't have that many serial killers round here.'

'None that I'm aware of. There are very few strangers round here. We know everyone and tourists don't tend to stray this way. Do you get a phone signal here?'

'Yes.'

'Let me give you my mobile number so at least you can call if you're worried. You all right?'

'I'm fine. Feeling a bit foolish now. Especially when it's such a gorgeous sunny day. Looks a perfect beach day.'

'It is.' He picked up his board but didn't move.

'It's lovely here,' said Hannah at last, giving into the urge to prolong the conversation, that flicker of attraction licking inside her. She shouldn't do it to herself. He was used to red carpets, Michelin restaurants, five-star hotels, and designer-clad women in the sort of heels she couldn't stand up in, let alone walk in.

'Yes, it's not difficult to come back to.'

'Where were you before?'

'Dublin. LA. New York.'

Hannah raised her eyebrows and her mouth twisted as she bit back a grin. 'You really were a big cheese.'

'You really didn't know?' His voice held note of puzzlement.

'No, I didn't. I'm not that interested in celebrities and I'm not a foodie. Or rather, I wasn't. Your mother is amazing.'

He rolled his eyes. 'Everyone thinks that. She is amazing but I also think Killorgally works its own magic as well.'

She smiled at him. 'It certainly does. It's beautiful here. I love it.'

'Despite people peering in your windows at night.'

Hannah shrugged but looked uneasily at the trampled flowers, wondering if perhaps it hadn't been the first time. 'Maybe I scared him off last night.' Hannah really hated making a fuss and she'd settled in the cottage. It was her little domain. The last thing she wanted to do was move to another cottage elsewhere. 'And I love this cottage. I'm not moving.' She took so much pleasure in the pretty, stylish interior.

'Did you choose the colours and the design?'

'What do you mean?'

'In the cottage, I love the woodwork in the lounge, the

painted wood. It's such a gorgeous sage green and the built-in cupboard is gorgeous.'

Conor nodded, but he didn't smile back at her. 'Thanks. I like doing that sort of stuff, without anyone breathing down your neck until its finished. And it's mine. No one else in the family is interested. They leave me to it. When it's food, everyone has an opinion – or at least in this family they do.'

'Well, it's beautiful.' Envy tinged her words as she thought of her square-walled, contemporary flat. Work always seemed to come first, so she hadn't done much decorating and she'd chosen the flat because it was practical and easy to maintain but it lacked the ingredient of character, which the cottage had in abundance with its fireplace, wooden floorboards, and sash windows with the lovely chapel-style frames.

'I like working with my hands.' He grinned and she pursed her lips. 'I'm away then, if you're sure you don't want to move.'

'I don't want to move,' she said with sudden resolution. No one was going to chase her out of this place. And whoever it was had probably been just as startled as she was and wouldn't be back.

'OK, then.' He gave her a brief salute and headed down the track to the beach. She was struck by a sudden thought. He and Fergus must have gone that way yesterday.

'Conor!' she called.

'What?'

'The fence over the path. It's been bothering me. You said it was rickety.'

He frowned as if wondering why on earth she was asking and, for a moment, she thought he might think she was deliberately trying to keep him. Then he shrugged. 'Seems Moss Murphy decided to update it. Daft aul fool. Everyone knows it's our land. I don't know why he's wasting good money but that's his problem. Why?'

'Don't you think it's odd?'

'No. Moss Murphy is a law unto himself.' He suddenly grinned. 'Murphy's Law. And he takes great delight in causing trouble. That manure by the wall was no accident.'

'Could it have been him looking in the window?'

Conor shook his head. 'No, not his style. He tends to be bloody-minded and difficult rather than creep about. Putting up another fence to be difficult is him all over. It's nothing for you to worry about.'

'But it is. By putting a fence up he's claiming that land.' She knew in law that after a period of time, if a land grab went unchallenged, the claimant could keep it. What was it, eleven or twelve years? She couldn't remember the exact details and maybe it was different in Ireland. Maybe that's why Conor seemed so unconcerned.

'Have you seen the size of it? A pocket handkerchief. Why would he want to do that? It's of no use to man nor beast, I promise you.'

Hannah shook her head. It might not make sense but the principle of it niggled. It wasn't right. But as Conor had so clearly indicated, it wasn't her problem.

When she knocked at the door of a tidy Georgian terrace an hour later, it was thrown open with an almighty crash and a red-haired bearded bear of a man appeared, as if he'd been lurking behind it waiting for her. He threw open his arms and snatched her into a hug.

'Mother of God, Aidan, put the poor girl down,' said a small blonde girl, wriggling and working her way into the hug as Hannah found her nose buried in a tweedy jacket and the soft silk of Sorcha's blouse across her neck.

Sudden tears pricked at Hannah's eyes at their enthusiastic welcome. Aidan and Sorcha had been two of her best friends, and she hadn't realised until now how much she'd missed them.

'By all that is holy. Hannah Campbell, just look at you.' Aidan released her and stepped back to give her a quick inspection. 'How the bloody hell are you? Apart from being very wet,' he boomed in the rich baritone he'd been famed for, stepping back and brushing down his front. At university he'd been renowned for his ability to spot friends at the front of the bar and yelling in his powerful voice, 'Get us a pint'.

'It wasn't raining when I left,' grumbled Hannah, despite the big smile on her face.

'That's the weather here for you,' said Sorcha. 'Come in. Come in. Come in.'

Aidan hooked an arm around her shoulder and dragged her unceremoniously into the large hallway.

'It's so good to see you, Hannah,' said Sorcha, leading the way into a big farmhouse-style kitchen with an Aga built into a large inglenook. It looked as if they were doing very well for themselves, but then Aidan had always been a brilliant lawyer with a serious work ethic. 'Tea. Builders? Same as always?' She lifted a mischievous brow and Hannah immediately remembered how the two of them had got through pints of the stuff when they were revising for their finals in the house the three of them had shared. In some ways it seemed like yesterday.

'Of course.'

As the tea was made they caught up on mutual friends, family, and all the latest news in a rapid three-way conversation with Aidan and Sorcha constantly interrupting each other.

'Honest, moving back here was the best thing,' said Aidan.

'It was. Lovely to be near family.'

'And we could afford to buy this place.'

'If we'd realised how easy it was to practice—'

'All you need is a certificate from the—'

'It helped that you had a guaranteed job at your da's practice.'

'And the experience at Ingrams. I can't believe you're still there, Hannah.'

'I can't believe you're here,' said Sorcha for about the fifth time, patting her wrist. 'It's so good to see you.'

'And you,' said Hannah. 'And still sane after working with Aidan for all this time.'

Sorcha rolled her eyes. 'He's a trial and no mistake. But not for much longer.' She gave a sudden grin and patted her stomach.

'No!' Hannah's eyes widened in delight.

'Yes, another Fitzpatrick blessing the world.' Sorcha sat back in her chair with a satisfied beam on her face. 'It's due next March.'

'That's wonderful news. Oh congratulations.' Hannah felt tears welling up again. Her friends seemed so happy and settled, and for a moment a tiny nudge of envy pushed at her. Not that she was unhappy with her life but there was a difference between contentment and this shining happiness that exuded from both of them.

'You're the first we've told, so don't go telling anyone just yet. Oh and look, now I'm crying too.'

'You do that all the time,' said Aidan, leaning away from his wife as if well aware that he was risking a poke in the ribs from her.

'Pregnancy hormones are pure shite,' said Sorcha with feeling, taking her third chocolate biscuit from the plate in the middle of the table. 'I had a hard time not crying when one of our clients said she wanted to get a divorce.'

Aidan shook his head in mock despair. 'And she comes in once a month wanting a divorce. Keeps her husband out of the pub for a couple of weeks.'

'That's true. Herself and Kenny love a good fight. And she's as glad to have him back in the pub most of the time.'

Hannah laughed.

'Sure, it's a madhouse round here,' said Aidan, 'but I wouldn't change it. If I thought you'd move, I'd offer you a partnership, like, yesterday. Business is growing and with Sorcha off on maternity leave, I'm going to be swamped.'

'You know me,' said Hannah, shaking her head vehemently.

'Indeed I do. The only way you'll leave Ingrams is in a coffin,' he observed, with a mournful twist to his mouth. 'You know it would be dead easy for you to come here.'

'I don't know anything about the Irish law system.'

'Ah but that's the good thing. It's very similar to the UK; all you need is a certificate of admission.' He turned puppy dog eyes on her. 'They're easy to get.'

Hannah laughed. 'Not buying. I'm happy where I am.'

'You'll find someone,' said Sorcha patting his hand and exchanging a wry smile with Hannah. 'He's almost as bad as you are. Wanting everything to stay the same.'

'I just want someone I know I can work with.' Aidan pulled a face. 'That won't let me down and knows how to make a decent cup of tea.'

'Not worried about their legal qualifications then?' teased Hannah.

'Lord, no. As long as they can read my writing and make tea, they'll be grand.'

They all laughed. Hannah knew for a fact that Aidan, like Sorcha, was extremely meticulous and methodical in his work, which was why the three of them had always got on so well.

'So how's your dad?' asked Hannah with a deliberate change of subject.

'He's a new man. In fact if I hadn't seen him all grey and wizened in the hospital, I'd a thought he was faking it, just to get me to come home but he was fierce poorly. He says retiring is the best thing he's ever done.'

'That's because he spends all his time on the golf course,' chipped in Sorcha. 'You'll need to find someone in the office soon otherwise you won't be having your Friday golf days with your daddy.'

'They're business strategy meetings,' said Aidan with a cocky wink.

'Sure they are.' Sorcha said peaceably. 'That'll all stop when the baby comes.'

'No, I'll get one of those pouch things. For sure, you can still swing a golf club. I'll be super dad and you can take the day off.' He stood up, stuffed a tea towel in a bundle down his shirt and mimed taking a shot.

'I think you'll probably decapitate the baby,' said Hannah, trying to hold back her laugh. 'I've just realised how much I missed you guys. It *is* so good to see you.'

'You, too.'

'Now tell us what's the famous Conor Byrne like. Have you met him? He's a handsome devil,' Sorcha held up her hand as Aidan began a mock protest. 'Nearly as handsome as you, my darlin'.'

Hannah huffed out a breath. 'He might be handsome but he knows it.' Her face creased in a naughty smile, 'Although I didn't have a clue who he was. I don't think that did his ego much good.'

'Honest to God, Hannah. What are you like? He's proper famous.' Sorcha patted her hand pityingly.

'You know me.' Hannah shrugged. 'I've never been into all that celebrity stuff.'

'Jesus, even I've heard of the man,' said Aidan. 'Without the aid of Google. They all talk about him round here.'

Hannah resolved as soon as she got back to the cottage

to Google him to find out just what the big deal was. Was he really that famous?

'An' what's your sister up to these days?' asked Sorcha. 'Still throwing the best parties?'

Hannah shot them both a grin and began to tell them exactly what Mina had been up to in the last year.

By the time she left the house, promising to come back very soon, her stomach ached from so much laughter. It was amazing; with true friends it didn't matter how long ago it was since you'd seen them, you could always pick straight up where you left off. She might not have seen Aidan or Sorcha for three years but it hadn't stopped them talking non-stop for the last three hours. With a pang she realised how much she'd missed them. There was nothing like being with people who really knew you. Funny that it had taken her coming here to see them again. They seemed so settled and happy, especially Sorcha who, despite the Irish name, was Kent born and bred. Hannah couldn't imagine moving to a different country, even though her own sister had made the move to Switzerland. Hannah had never even considered it. She'd always thought she was quite content with her life the way it was. Now she was beginning to wonder.

Chapter Thirteen

As soon as she got back from Aidan and Sorcha's, she opened up her laptop and, leaning back in the comfortable sofa, she typed Conor's name into the search engine, expecting to find a succinct Wikipedia biography which would give her a some background on what he'd done to make him such a local celebrity.

Oh my God to the power five thousand and ten. Dozens and dozens of photos of Conor immediately appeared and her jaw dropped. Conor was very much the man about town. Man about the world.

She winced as she scrolled through the images, glad she'd not done it before. Big cheese didn't begin to describe it. He was pictured on red carpets in Manhattan, London, Cannes, Sydney, and Paris, in smart Michelin-starred restaurants all over the globe, at gallery openings, fundraisers, charity golf days, and always with a different red-carpet-ready woman on his arm.

Now she wished she hadn't succumbed to her curiosity.

Talk about feeling foolish. Conor, it appeared, belonged in the A-list category of celebrities. The real deal. Actresses, models, newscasters decorated his arm at numerous events, all suitably gorgeous, making her ask why he had gone out with her that night in Dublin? His standards were usually much higher. Hannah didn't lack self-confidence but on a practical level she knew who she was and there was no way she compared, or even wanted to, with these glamazons. They reminded her a lot of Sadie Burns-Coutts. He might have slept with her once and kissed her since, but Conor Byrne was used to the Sadies of this world, brimming with style and sophistication. It felt like he'd been slumming it with her.

What would Mina say if she told her what had happened? She'd be shocked Hannah had done anything so wild, let alone with someone like Conor. Her sister constantly teased her about always playing safe. It would appear there were good reasons for doing so and if she had, she wouldn't have ended up being quite so mortified. Thankfully it should be easy enough to stay out of his way.

Almost as if she'd challenged providence, an unexpected knock at the door made her slam the laptop shut like a guilty schoolgirl caught out stalking a crush. When she opened the door, her heart sank. It was almost as if she'd conjured him up but at least his mother was with him, her face not quite obscured by an enormous arrangement of flowers, while he glowered behind her with a dark scowl on his face.

'Adrienne. Conor.'

'Hello, lovely. These are for you.' Adrienne thrust the

flowers into Hannah's hands and somehow managed to sweep Hannah along into the kitchen as if she were the hostess, which, to be fair, she was. As much as Hannah loved this cottage, it wasn't hers. Conor walked in behind her and didn't even so much as look at her as he put a bottle of wine on the table.

'Conor, do the honours, darling.' She turned to Hannah, her eyes scanning the room with bright satisfaction. 'I think this is my favourite cottage. My son did an excellent job on this one.'

Hannah dredged up a smile. The last thing she felt like was loading Conor's ego with any more praise.

'I'm so sorry to barge in on you but Conor told me about the trouble you've had and... please let me tell you how horrified I am. Not to mention mortified. Are you all right?'

Hannah nodded. 'Yes I'm—'

'I've spoken to everyone who works on the farm.' Adrienne paced up and down the kitchen, rubbing at the worry lines on her forehead. 'I don't understand it. No one has been anywhere near here. They've no reason and Porker the pig was found in the herb garden, so he's not the culprit. Not for the squished flowers at any rate. I've been racking my brains as to who you might have seen.' Her mouth crumpled and Hannah thought she might cry.

'It's OK,' said Hannah, wanting to soothe her. 'It's not your fault.'

'But it is,' Adrienne wailed.

Hannah glanced over at a tight-lipped Conor, who was busy with a corkscrew, completely focused on his task. She guessed he'd heard a lot of this already.

'I take full responsibility for the health and wellbeing of all my guests and after the incident with Moss Murphy's nephew and his shotgun and now this... It would be terrible for the reputation of the cookery school if anything happened.' Her eyes glistened with tears as she fidgeted from foot to foot with agitation, and Hannah found herself wanting to give Adrienne a hug, it was discomforting to see her in distress.

Conor had opened the wine and poured three glasses, handing one to Adrienne and one to Hannah. 'Here you go, Mam, and don't be fretting yourself.' He turned to Hannah. 'I've been telling her that it's probably nothing. You probably overreacted.' He narrowed his eyes as if willing her to agree with him.

'Darling, that's not the point. Someone was out there. We've discussed this.' She gave him a steely look, before chinking her glass against Hannah's. 'Do you mind if we take a seat?' She gestured towards the pine kitchen table.

Once they were seated, Adrienne took a breath and tasted the wine. 'Ah. Sorry, I need to calm down.' She took a couple more deep breaths. 'This wine. This makes me happy. It's a great one but even better for knowing that it comes from an ex-student of mine. He and his wife bought the vineyard in France. They come back every year to do food and wine pairings for us. It's things like that which make me remember everything we've achieved here.' She glanced at Conor with an encouraging smile before turning back to Hannah. 'I've been worrying about you all day, ever since Conor phoned me this morning but,' she emphasised the final consonant with a note of triumph, 'I've come up with the ideal solution. At first I thought about asking Izzy or Meredith to move in with you but I don't want them in danger either. I ummed and ahhed about it and then I came up with the perfect solution.'

Hannah's eyes widened as behind Adrienne, still on his feet, Conor raised his eyes Heavenward and then knocked his glass back and drained it in one go.

She stared at him. That was drastic.

'Conor is going to move in.'

No wonder he drained his glass. His eyes met hers.

'C-Conor.' Hannah's mind went blank, she put her wine down with a clumsy thud. 'H-here?'

'Yes.' Adrienne beamed as if she'd just solved the all the mysteries of the universe in one go. 'It's the perfect solution, isn't it?'

'B-but... but... er...' Hannah took a quick slug of wine herself, trying to fortify herself but all words seemed to have deserted her. Conor living here. In this house. With her. Oh Lord, how would she cope? It was a terrible idea. At least, judging by the expression on his face, he agreed.

'Don't worry, lovely. Honest to God, it makes no difference to Conor. He's away at work all day. He only needs to be here to keep an eye on things in the evenings. I can see you're worried but I promise you he's quite well house trained. He might even cook for you, if you're lucky.' Although she flashed a quick grin, it didn't hide her incipient worry.

'I am here, just in case you'd forgotten,' he said frostily.

'You are indeed, and isn't it lucky for us all.' Adrienne was crisp now, back in charge. 'She'll probably be glad of the company. You're not a complete neanderthal.' She turned back to Hannah. 'And you were expecting to share with someone.'

'Yes, but—' Hannah looked desperately at Conor for support.

'I insist,' said Adrienne, and from the set of her jaw Hannah knew that there would be no changing her mind. 'I would be devastated if anything happened to you.'

'But…' Her mind darted in different directions, trying to find an answer. 'I've been using the shower in the other bedroom.'

'Oh, don't be worrying about that. I'm sure you can come to some arrangement. Conor is an early riser. He won't give you any bother.'

Conor didn't even look her way, giving her the clear impression that he couldn't care less what she did.

'Besides, he's fully occupied with his cottage. Not that I'm allowed to see it.' Although she said it with a light smile, Hannah got the impression that it irked her slightly. She liked to be in control.

'Are you sure he's… you're not too busy? I'd hate to disrupt your work.'

'I'll be so much happier knowing he's here with you,' said Adrienne. 'We've never had any trouble like this before but I'm sorry to say by the looks of those footprints we might have ourselves a peeping Tom and I want to reassure everyone that we're taking it seriously. I'd like to think it's Moss Murphy up to his usual tricks but, as Conor says, it's just not his style. I've called the guard again but there's nothing they can do. I've no idea who it could have been;

it's not someone local that's for sure and that's what really worries me.' She clasped her hands together over her chest, not quite wringing them but close enough and Hannah realised that she was genuinely anxious.

With that realisation came the memory of last night when she'd been alone in the cottage knowing there was someone outside. In daylight it was easy to dismiss that heart-thumping moment and how scared she'd been, but how would she feel tonight after dark? She glanced at Conor's face, reluctantly deciding that, on balance, he was the lesser of two evils. Having him there would at least make her feel... not safe, but secure. That was it. There was nothing safe about Conor, which was a salutary reminder to keep her distance from him. She was going to have to accede to Adrienne's wishes.

Conor was drumming his fingers on the table very lightly. She noticed he wasn't saying anything.

Swallowing down her pride and a touch of resentment she carefully focused on Adrienne, not looking at him. 'If you really think it's necessary...' She let the words drift away, not willing to completely accede.

'I do,' said Adrienne firmly and dusted her hands together as if to seal the deal. 'Right, I'm away. We'll see you at seven for dinner.' She gave Hannah a quick hug. 'Don't worry, sweetheart, we'll make sure you're all right.' She darted towards the door without looking back as if leaving the two of them to talk.

'Apparently it's my job now to rescue the damsel in distress.' Conor favoured her with a reluctant smile.

'I thought that was my job,' she quipped before she

could stop herself and immediately realised she'd said the wrong thing. 'It doesn't change anything,' said Conor quietly.

'I never thought it did,' she said. 'I'll do my best not to throw myself at you.'

He turned and left, pulling the door closed behind him.

'Grrr,' she said to herself. The last person she wanted staying with her was Conor, she thought as she flounced up the stairs to get ready for dinner. Bloomin' Adrienne and her determination to protect Killorgally at all costs.

'Underestimate her at your peril,' the newspaper article she'd read had said. 'There's some that believe she has the touch of the fae about her. She's certainly weaved considerable magic at Killorgally.'

Hannah might not believe in magical powers but there was no denying Adrienne had a certain charismatic aura about her. How else had she managed to bring about the last thing she and Conor wanted?

Chapter Fourteen

'Just so you know. This was all my mother's idea.' Conor met her after dinner on the path outside the farmhouse, a holdall in his hand.

Their feet crunched on the gravel path that led through the herb garden and wound down around the back of the house. Thyme and rosemary perfumed the air as they walked past the knot garden edges and the quiet evening was filled with the somnolent buzz of the bees hovering in and out of the tall sprigs of lavender. In the dying warmth of the day, it should have been tranquil and relaxing but instead Hannah's nerves sizzled with tension.

'I think you made that quite obvious. I wish you'd put up more of a fight.'

'How could I? Tears were involved. For some reason she seems to like you.'

'Quite a lot of people do. Even you, the first time you met me.'

'That was before I knew you were going to be living with me.'

'I'm not overjoyed about it.' She'd enjoyed having the cottage to herself this last week. Having Conor underfoot would be dangerously distracting. It was good to know that *he* was impervious to her charms. There was no knowing where things would lead if she acted on the attraction that she harboured. He wasn't the comfortable, safe sort of man she was used to.

'I guess your mother did say you were housetrained.'

'To a point. Do we need some house rules?'

'I don't know. Have you any bad habits?'

'No one's complained so far.'

'Of course they haven't,' she muttered, more to herself than him.

'I've got a request.'

'Oh, isn't it my space you're invading? I'm not sure you should be laying down the law. After all, I don't even want you there.'

'And I don't want to be there. Blame my mother, not me. I'm just the bodyguard.'

She was about to say she didn't need a bodyguard but she had been unnerved by the face at the window and now it appeared that there was no obvious explanation, she was *almost* glad that Conor would be there.

'So what's this request?'

'That you don't walk around half-naked. And perhaps avoid wearing those shorts you had on yesterday around the house.'

'What's wrong with my shorts?' her voice rose in

pique. They were her favourites. Who was he to dictate what she wore? He could go sing. From now on, she'd wear them all the time in the house, no matter what the weather.

'There's nothing wrong with the shorts. It's the legs.'

'What's wrong with my legs?' That stung; if there was one part of her body she liked, it was most definitely her legs. Her sister had got the womanly curves and Hannah had got longish legs and a disappointingly flat chest. She'd have thought their genes could have been a bit more fairly shared out but apparently not.

'Oh mother of God, woman. I've told you I don't sleep with guests ever.'

'I think you might have said that before but that doesn't explain what's wrong my legs.'

'You're being deliberately thick. I'm trying to tell you I'm only human.'

She frowned. 'I still have no idea what you're talking about.'

'Jaysus, woman. They're indecent. Nobody wants to see all that leg.'

'What?' She frowned.

'Those little shorts. On the beach. Very little. You've got fine legs. And I do have a very good memory. I've seen them up close.'

She blushed, remembering some of the things that had gone on in his bed and then couldn't help a little smirk.

'And you can take that look off your face.'

'What look?' she said with a demure raise of her eyebrows.

'The very-pleased-with-yourself, cat-that-got-the-cream-*and*-the-chocolate-cake-*and*-drank-the-Guinness look.'

She grinned at him. 'If you've got it, aren't you supposed to flaunt it?'

He laughed. 'You've a quick, clever mind, Hannah Campbell.'

'And I thought it was just my legs.'

'There's much more.' His eyes rested on her face. 'But I'll be looking not touching. I know I've said it before but you're a guest.'

'Just out of interest, what's your deal with guests? Been burnt before?'

'It's not real. Everyone falls in love with Killorgally. With my mam, the place, the idea of it. The scales fell off my last girlfriend's eyes pretty quickly when she came to live out here.'

Disappointment twinged low in Hannah's gut, she'd have liked to think that she was a bit more self-aware than that but it made sense now.

She gave him a teasing smile to soften the words.

'I think I got the message loud and clear. I don't suppose it occurs to you that I never thought I'd see you again and that what happened in Dublin was supposed to stay in Dublin. It certainly wasn't meant to travel.'

'Grand. So we're on the same page.'

'Yes. We can both be grown up about it and move on.'

'That sounds like a good idea given we've got to share a home for the next week or so. Truce.' He held out his hand. She took it deliberately, making her handshake firm and business-like, ignoring the persistent thought that these very hands had roved all over her body.

'Fresh start,' she agreed. 'Dublin never happened.'

'Dublin never happened.' Conor nodded, putting the subject to bed once and for all.

When both of them exhaled a relieved sigh, they glanced at each other. Conor rolled his eyes and Hannah laughed at him.

They walked in silence until the cottage came into view, the yellow walls glowing in the evening sunshine.

'Lovely night,' she said wistfully, looking at the golden-tipped clouds strewn across the pearly-blue sky. For some reason she didn't want to go inside just yet.

'There'll be a great sunset on the beach. Want to go down?'

'Yes.' Hannah said quickly, realising that she was delaying the moment they had to go inside. Perhaps spending time outside with Conor first might help her acclimatise to him being around.

'Just let me drop my bag off.'

He let himself into the cottage – with his own key, she noticed – and left the holdall in the hallway, and then together they strolled down the path to the beach. Two birds took flight, their haunting plaintive cries echoing over the quiet fields.

'Curlews,' said Conor as she lifted her head to watch them, fascinated. 'See the very distinctive long, curved beak.'

'I'm impressed.'

'Don't be. I've just picked it up living here over the years.'

'Do you know what the birds on the beach are, the little long-legged ones that seem to run in and out with the tide?'

'Probably redshanks. Funny things, you can watch them for hours.'

She nodded with a jolt of recognition; she loved their antics and had indeed watched them for a long time the other day on the beach with Izzy.

'Did you miss all this' – she waved her hand at the view – 'when you were away? It's a long way from New York.' She wanted to ask if that was why he'd come back but it felt a bit too nosy and intrusive. She couldn't imagine giving up somewhere like that to come back here to what seemed like... nothing. It was so quiet and she was guessing there wasn't a 24/7 for miles.

'Always. I loved the buzz of New York. It's frenetic but I had to do it at the time to establish myself and there's a love of the Irish in New York; they just hear the accent and they want to know you.' He paused as he hauled himself over the fence and then waited to make sure she got over safely. 'Then I moved to LA. In some ways it was more laidback, but I never really felt I fitted in. That was a means to an end and I didn't feel at home there, not at all. And then I came back to Dublin, having made my name, and I got a backer who opened the restaurant. RTE asked me to do a cookery show for them which I thought would be great publicity for the restaurant, so I couldn't say no and' – he lifted his shoulders – 'it all went wild.' A musing smile touched his lips. 'And I thought I could do anything. Have anything. But sometimes even that isn't enough.'

'Sounds a bit cryptic.' She lifted her head, hearing the wash and rush of the sea as they came down to the road.

'It's all I'm saying.'

'Do you miss it?'

'What, cooking? Fame? Being a' – he held up fingers in quote marks as they crossed to the track down to the beach – '"celebrity"? No. I love it here. And what about you? What's your story? What's a lawyer doing at a cookery school? Burnt out too?'

'No. I've worked since I left school. I fancied a sabbatical.'

'There must have been something that made you decide.'

She laughed. 'It's boring.'

They stopped on the edge of the beach. The tide was a long way out leaving a wide expanse of beach striated with patterns of shell fragments and darker sand. Shallow water rippled and undulated across the surface, sparkling with fractured sunlight.

'Come on. Let's walk as far as we can. We'll head back as the sun starts to set.'

She nodded, pulling the pashmina she'd grabbed from her car around her shoulders. Although the sun had unexpectedly come out on her drive home, it was a little cooler outside after spending the afternoon in the cosy warmth of Sorcha and Aidan's kitchen. No wonder she'd been loath to leave.

'So try me.'

She turned to him, puzzled.

'What prompted you to take a sabbatical? I'm pretty sure you said in Dublin you liked your job and you're good at it.'

'I am and I do but... well, it's all I've ever done and it's safe. I've never even changed companies. I was worried... I was worried about... being stale. I like it there but it's all I've ever known. So I'd been thinking about whether I ought to make a change but it felt like change for change's sake. And this is the stupid bit.'

'I promise I won't judge.'

She laughed. 'You probably will when you hear.

'There was a bake-off competition at work. You know, *The Great British Bake Off*.'

'I think I've heard of it,' he said dryly.

'Well,' she huffed out a sigh. 'It's so embarrassing. I don't even know why I'm telling you. Basically, everyone took it really seriously and when I rocked up with my very dull cake, I realised I'd been seriously outclassed and it annoyed me.' She was not going to tell him about Sadie Burns-Coutts, who was probably exactly Conor's type of woman.

'Annoyed you?'

'Yes. At work I'm the smart one, the practical go-to-for-solutions one. I always have the answers. I hate not being competent at something. And it's such an easy thing. Everyone can cook. It's not rocket science.'

'It's not, but there is quite a lot of science involved.'

She shot him a dirty look. 'Not if you follow a recipe. Anyone can follow a recipe. Or at least I thought so. It really bugged me that I couldn't cook. My sister is brilliant – not that I'm trying to compete with her. We're so different; we don't even worry about that sort of thing, but I should at least be competent. And it just so happened that I read an article in a Sunday supplement about Killorgally and I've friends near here, so I began to think about coming here and the idea wouldn't let go. Weird. It just gnawed away at me.'

'So you took a sabbatical from your job. Because you wanted to be competent.' He raised a sceptical eyebrow.

'Sounds stupid, doesn't it? But I figured if I was going to do it, I was going to do it properly.' Her thinking being that by doing it properly it was less risky. Less chance of failure. And more of a certainty of being better in the future. She liked to know what the outcome of things would be. She wasn't one for surprises.

'There's a lot to be said for doing things properly.' His mouth quirked.

'That's what I thought. And you're laughing at me.'

'When you do things properly, you really go big, don't you? People come from all over the world to do this cookery course. It's one of the most intense courses you can do.'

'I told you, I wanted to do it properly. Leave nothing to chance.'

'And now?'

She glowered at him. 'You heard what your mother said. I'm finding it hard. Really hard. Everyone else – well, apart from Izzy – they seem to know what they're doing whereas I'm a rank beginner.' She'd made it all sound funny to Aidan and Sorcha, recounting her various disasters, but they knew her, and knew that she was fantastically competent in other areas. It was easy to be self-deprecating in front of them. With a pout she said, 'I can't even chop vegetables. I'm always miles behind everyone else. And Herbert has died.'

He stopped, a look of consternation on his face. 'Oh Jesus, I'm so sorry. He's your...?'

'Herbert?'

'Yes, boss, brother, boyfriend.' With a stricken expression he added, 'Father?'

Hannah sniggered and shook her head as laughter bubbled up in her throat. It took her a few seconds before she caught her lip between her teeth and collected herself.

'My sourdough starter.'

'Of course it is,' murmured Conor dryly.

'Although mine's more of a non-starter. How could I get that wrong? It's just flour and water, for goodness' sake.'

Conor shook his head. 'Don't ever say that in front of Eamon or Mam. Where are you keeping it?'

'In the kitchen.'

'And what are you feeding it on?'

'Seventy-five grams of flour and seventy-five millilitres of water, like the recipe said. It's supposed to have bubbles. Lots of them. Mine just looks like thick milk.'

'How about I take a look when we get back?'

'If you like,' Hannah said grudgingly. She couldn't imagine what he could do differently. According to the others, their starters had doubled in size and Jason's had foamed out of the top of the jar.

While they'd been walking, the sun had gradually sunk,

tingeing the grey clouds with a pinky-peach glow and spreading a golden shadow across the sea that rippled into the shore. Now, as it dipped behind the roller coaster horizon of the hills, they stopped to watch the final shimmer of light disappear, leaving the shadows to deepen and lengthen, changing the outlines of the rocks and altering the colour of the sea as the sparkle on its surface faded away.

They sat on the dunes, each in quiet contemplation. A few persistent surfers rode into shore and picked up their boards, their dark shapes silhouetted by the twilight.

'Until tomorrow,' murmured Conor, 'when we start all over again. A fresh start and a clean slate.'

'That's a lovely thought.' Hannah gazed around her, at the redshanks dipping in and out of the water, at the white surf rolling and frothing, at the wheeling seagulls gliding away out to sea on thermals as if packing up and leaving for the day, at her fingers running through the damp sand, catching at the spiky, coarse grass of the dunes. The simple, stark beauty almost stopped her heart. She couldn't remember the last time she'd felt this content. Just to be.

Chapter Fifteen

As the water trickled into the bath, she looked again at the time on her phone and sighed. Having a bath in the morning really slowed things down. There'd been no sound from behind Conor's door this morning and she wasn't about to wake him up to ask to use his shower.

At eight she was due back on chicken duty and, funnily enough, was looking forward to seeing her new feathered friends. What she wasn't looking forward to was a flipping bath. She was a shower-in-the-morning girl. Baths seemed too wallowy and decadent for this time of the day when there was stuff to be done. With bad grace she bathed and dried herself, the itch of grumpiness scratching at her. OK, she wasn't a morning person either, which normally didn't matter as she had solitude. Everything was perfect before Conor moved in.

'Did you want something?' She jumped as his door opened and he found her standing there talking to herself –

admittedly inside her head, but all the same she must have looked like a mad one.

'Er, no. Just going downstairs.'

He followed her down. 'Nice bath.'

'Now you mention it, no. I much prefer a shower in the mornings. I was using the one in your room.'

'You're welcome to use it when I'm not here.'

'That's not going to work is it, given we're both heading out at the same time.'

'Can't do anything about this week as I'm playing kitchen assistant. Bronagh has a week's holiday and Niamh is back to school, so I've been drafted in for washing and cleaning-up duties.'

'What, in our kitchen?'

'That'll be the one. Don't look so worried. I'll not be marking you out of ten or anything.'

That was exactly what she was worried about. It was bad enough making a hash of things, but doing it in front of him seemed so much worse. Disconsolately she followed him into the kitchen where he immediately took charge of the kettle and the counter area, busying himself making coffee.

Not wanting to get into his personal space, she loitered by the table, feeling like a spare part. This was her kitchen – how had she been relegated to bystander?

'Do you want coffee?' he asked, spooning coffee grounds into a large cafetière.

Sharing coffee with him felt too cosy. 'No thanks, I prefer tea in the mornings.' She didn't want him making coffee for her, it might make her imagine things that were out of reach. It was too dangerous to fall for Conor, where would it lead?

'Are you having breakfast here or up at the house?'

'You're kidding. Miss out on freshly collected eggs?'

'That's one of my earliest memories – going out with Granny and collecting the eggs, and then she'd boil them and make us dippy soldiers.'

'Mm, you're making me hungry.'

'How do you take your tea?'

'Er, milk. No sugar.'

'You might as well take a seat. You look awkward standing there.'

'Funny that, being in my own kitchen.'

'Sorry, have I taken over? Force of habit.'

He handed her a mug of tea.

'So how are the cottages coming along?' She sat down at the table, nursing the hot mug between both hands.

'They're coming; some of them need more work than others. A couple were done up when Mam and Da first set this place up back when they had no money. They're long overdue for a refurb. Guests expect much more these days and the plan is to Airbnb one of them and I'll be moving into the other one.'

'Built to your own specifications?'

'Yes. The kitchen will be bigger than this and I'm extending it so that it's a big kitchen-diner and more bedrooms upstairs. Best of all there'll be a great view, out over the sea.'

It sounded wonderful and he spoke with a gleam of passion shining in his eyes.

'You still like cooking, then.'

'Now that the pressure's off, yes. What about you? Are you missing your work?'

Hannah shook her head. 'I'm still in holiday mode.' Although if she were honest, she missed knowing what she was doing and not feeling like an incompetent twit half the time.

When Hannah arrived in the kitchen with her basket of eggs, everyone was already there, bar Izzy. Once she'd put in her order of boiled egg and coffee to Bridget, she sat down at the table next to Alan.

'How was the trip?' she asked.

'Excellent,' said Meredith. 'We drove to Kilorgan Castle and did part of the Ring of Kerry and had a lovely lunch at Moll's Gap. And I bought the most gorgeous jumper in one of the mill shops. I'd wear it today but as a woman of a certain age, I don't think I can cook in it, not unless people don't mind a quick striptease every five minutes.'

Hannah caught Alan suddenly studying the leavings on his plate. If he was interested in Meredith he'd have to get used to her outspoken, open ways. As Hannah had discovered on Saturday evening, there was no filter there; Meredith wasn't about to spare his blushes, perhaps because she'd lived in an all-female household for so long, but then again, Alan must be used to that if he had daughters too.

'It was Alan that made me buy it. I'd never normally go for such a bold colour. I'm a navy girl.'

'I didn't make you buy it,' he said with a sudden twinkle in his eye, 'I just told you that you suited that colour. It looked lovely on you.'

Hannah caught Fliss giving Alan a stony stare and an impatient yawn. He caught it too and blushed.

'What colour is it?' asked Hannah, ignoring the sulky woman, who seemed to like sucking the joy out of things.

'It's the most gorgeous cherry-red. I'd never have picked it in a thousand years but Alan suggested I try it on. I was all for buying another navy jumper. I wasn't going to buy it but he persuaded me.'

'She was dithering,' he said, although there was a shy smile lurking in his eyes. 'I just wanted out of the shop. I've done my time in H&M. Now my girls are older, I can leave them to get on with it. Thank goodness. Besides, I needed a coffee. Lovely little town though. Kenmare.'

'And we found a funny little place for coffee. The girl's accent almost sounded Scandinavian rather than Irish.'

'I spent most of the weekend down the pub, after I'd had a good lie-in. Didn't get up until two on Saturday or on Sunday,' said Jason. 'Mind you there's bug— not much else to do round here.'

Fliss tutted.

'We went to the beach, didn't we, Hannah,' said Izzy. 'It's amazing.'

'What beach?' asked Jason.

Everyone turned and stared at him. He put both hands up. 'What?'

Fliss looked over at him as if she were peering over the top of a pair of glasses. 'Don't you know anything? Philistine. Inch beach is one of the longest beaches in Europe.'

Jason shrugged, indifferent to her rudeness. 'Never heard of it.'

'Don't suppose you've ever been surfing?' asked Fliss with a curl of her lip, but her eyes were watchful.

'Nope. Not much call in Bethnal Green.'

She studied him for a moment and then with a quick regal assent of her head said, 'I'll take you next Saturday.'

'You're on.' Jason raised a hand for a high five. Fliss gave him a withering look and he lowered his hand with nonchalant grin.

The hands of the clock crept closer to nine o'clock and one by one they finished their breakfast and sauntered through to the kitchen. Izzy was already there pulling on her clean, neatly pressed apron.

'Look, they've all been washed over the weekend. Isn't that a nice touch?

'I like to start the week clean, fresh, and ready to go,' said Adrienne, appearing behind her like a silent cat and making Izzy jump. How on earth did she manage that in those jewelled flip-flops that she wore?

The kitchen had been set up in readiness with various bowls and implements and by the central counter were several tiered baskets of vegetables filled with carrots, onions, potatoes, broccoli, and a couple of leafy greens that Hannah wasn't familiar with. Conor and Mairead appeared, carrying another two baskets of vegetables.

'Morning all. I hope you've had a lovely weekend. The weather was certainly fine.'

Everyone chorused 'Morning' like primary school children in assembly.

'This week we're focusing on vegetables, although I'm going to start with making a stock. A really good stock is the foundation of lots of so many dishes and once you've got this learned, you'll never use another stock cube again. Or I certainly hope you won't.'

Hannah heard Jason snicker while Alan and Meredith both dutifully nodded. 'Today we're going to make a simple beef stock. Easy to keep in the freezer.'

They were dispatched to their stations and Hannah smiled to herself. Making stock didn't sound too challenging. A nice easy start to Monday.

Following Adrienne's instructions – which were given via a microphone clipped to the top of her shirt collar and a camera filming what she was doing in close-up relayed on the screen on the wall behind her – they chopped beef scraps using a terrifying-looking knife that was so sharp, Hannah was worried she might lose a finger. Unfortunately, that was the least of her worries; the whole day turned into a complete disaster and by the end of the day she was definitely wondering why on earth she was putting herself through the cookery course.

'Hey, Hannah, how's it going?'

Mina had answered on the first ring, her voice full of her usual enthusiasm.

'I bet you're having a brilliant time. What's Adrienne Byrne like? Is she gorgeous? She always looked it.'

Hannah held in her forlorn sigh instead saying, 'It's... it's good.'

'Good?' Mina's voice held a query.

The sigh escaped. 'Today was terrible.'

'How could it be terrible? I've seen pictures of Killorgally.'

'I burnt the stock. How was I supposed to know that a splash of olive oil is like a good old glug? So my bones didn't caramelise with the veg. And how is a sprinkle of herbs actually a flipping great big handful?'

'You'll learn,' sympathised Mina.

'Huh! I'm not so sure. It seems I can't chop vegetables – certainly nowhere near as quickly as everyone else – and my dauphinoise potatoes were raw because I hadn't sliced the potatoes thinly enough. Everyone else seems to know what they're doing. I feel like a complete dunce.' And it didn't sit well with her. 'And I was so far behind everyone else at one point that Conor had to rescue me and chop up my vegetables for the coleslaw.'

'Ooh, Conor Byrne. What's he like?'

Hannah winced, hearing the hero worship in her voice.

'Fine.'

'Fine. He's flipping gorgeous in the pictures I've seen. Honestly, Han, did you even look at him? What are you like? I bet you were too busy concentrating on the instructions, weren't you? It doesn't matter if you get things wrong, you know. Unless you use the wrong mushrooms, no one is going to die.'

'I know,' she said, grateful for Mina's assumptions. She really didn't want to think about that night in Dublin. Her sister truly would be amazed if Hannah told her she'd had a one-night stand with him.

'Just give it time. It's just practice. You have to go with the flow a bit. Relax. I bet you're wanting precise instructions all the time, aren't you?'

'Yes,' said Hannah grumpily, 'And what's wrong with that?'

'When you're cooking, it's about the flavours and the tastes and the love.'

'Oh don't you start. Adrienne has a bit of that new-age rubbish going on.'

Mina laughed. 'You do sound cranky. Why don't you run yourself a nice bath, pour a glass of wine, and chill? Tomorrow is another day.'

When Hannah finally pulled herself from the bath, her spirits had not improved so she decided to stay put and not go up to the farmhouse for dinner. As she crossed the landing to her room, she heard the door open downstairs. Great. Now she had to face Conor to add to her humiliation. She listened for a while, hoping that he might come upstairs to his room so she could nip into the kitchen to grab a glass of wine and a bowl of crisps. She couldn't face cooking anything. They were welcome to take anything back to their own kitchens but she was sick of the sight of the whole lot of today's cooking, especially since hers had all been disasters.

She listened but Conor seemed to have stayed put downstairs. Just great. She was going to have face him. Reluctantly, she trailed down the stairs to find him in the kitchen with a glass of wine, sitting with his laptop on the table.

'Staying in tonight?'

She nodded. He must think she was a complete loser.

'Thanks for rescuing me today.' She sighed.

'Hey, don't worry. You came to learn, remember.' He poured her a glass of wine and handed it to her.

'Yes, but everyone else seems to know what they're doing.' She shuddered, thinking of the smoking bones.

'You just need to improve your chopping technique.'

'Do you say that to all the girls?' she joked.

He looked up, considering her for a moment. 'Knife skills. That's what you need.'

'I'm not in training to be a serial killer.'

From beneath the table, he pulled out a briefcase and opened it up to reveal a set of rather terrifying-looking knives. 'Chef's best friend and his most essential tools.'

Hannah frowned, examining the blackish surface of most of the knives. She'd have expected chef's knives to be gleaming silver instead of the slightly dull appearance of these ones. 'They don't look very…' She was about to say *clean* and then thought better of it.

Conor picked up one of the knives. 'These are made of

carbon steel, so they tend to discolour but I prefer using them. Easier to sharpen and they stay sharp for longer.'

He stood up, picking up one of the knives. 'Come on. I'll give you your first lesson.' Crossing to the kitchen counter, she noticed there was a wicker basket containing a miscellaneous selection of past-their-best and misshapen fruit and vegetables.

'That's nice of you,' said Hannah warily, following him.

'I'm a nice guy.' He flashed her one of his brilliant smiles before adding, 'Purely selfish reasons. I haven't got time to rush you off to Accident and Emergency with a finger in a bag of peas.' He shuddered. 'I'm not sure my nerves can stand another day wondering which of your fingers you're going to chop off.'

In spite of herself Hannah laughed. 'I wasn't that bad.'

He raised an eyebrow.

'OK, I was.'

'Which is why I'm going to give you a lesson.'

He opened one of the kitchen drawers and pulled out a knife. 'This will do – not perhaps as sharp as mine.'

'I could use one of yours.' She indicated the briefcase on the table.

'Over my dead and buried body. You'll not be touching them.'

'Why? Have they got diamond-encrusted handles or something?'

'No.' He shook his head in mild disbelief as if he couldn't believe she really didn't know. 'But chefs are very territorial about their knives. We always use our own and rarely let anyone touch them. At least I don't. You don't want some ham-fisted eejit dulling your blade.'

Hannah rolled her eyes. *Talk about precious.* Although, admittedly, she had a special fountain pen she used at work to annotate things, so perhaps there was a similarity.

'I saw that.'

'You were supposed to.'

'Now, watch.' He took an onion from the basket and sliced it in two, deftly peeling off the skin. 'Keep the point on the board and lift and slice.'

She watched as he demonstrated with a swift seesawing action, while using the middle joints of his fingers as a guide for the knife. Of course he made it look effortless.

'Now you try. Take it slow.'

She picked up the knife and tentatively arranged her hand like his around the onion, trying to copy his slicing motion. Getting confident, she forgot to keep her hand crabbed over the onion and took a chunk out of her thumbnail.

'Eek!' she squeaked.

'Keep it slow to start with.'

'I thought this was supposed to help me speed up.'

'Even at this speed you're more effective than you were. Economy of movement is what you're after.'

She had another go, this time more slowly.

'No, like this.' Stepping behind her, he put his arm parallel to her arm and a warm, firm hand over hers to guide the movement. 'Here.' He gently gripped her hand and steered the knife with a steady seesawing motion backwards and forwards. Conscious of his closeness, she tried to relax at his touch but all she could think of was the smell of him and feel of his big, solid body up against hers. Her breath caught in her chest and she did her best to ease it out slowly so he wouldn't notice. Every nerve ending was aware of him, standing to attention, breathlessly waiting for any movement from him.

'Thank you,' she said as his breath fluttered against her neck. Instinctively she inhaled, leaning back just the barest centimetre as the sharp punch of desire bathed her.

The silence in the room weighed heavy for a moment. 'No problem.' He dropped her hand and stepped back smartly, as if she were contaminated all of a sudden.

Hannah wanted to roll her eyes. Instead, she said lightly as if it were of no account, 'I'm not going to bite you.'

'That wasn't what I was worried about.' She turned to face him finding his eyes straying to her lips.

'I wasn't going to kiss you either,' she said, unable to help the twitch of her lips.

Now he rolled his eyes and snatched up a carrot and tossed it on the chopping board.

This time it was her turn to raise an eyebrow. 'Unfortunate choice.' They both looked at the rather obscenely shaped vegetable and with one quick swipe of devilment, she chopped it clean in it two.

Conor sniggered and quick amusement danced in his eyes as he winced dramatically. 'Ouch, that's me told.' He laughed, shaking his head. 'What was it you were saying about serial killers?'

It was hard to resist his spontaneous grin.

'Sorry, couldn't resist.'

'That poor carrot, whatever had it done to you. I've unleashed a monster.'

There was altogether too much of that smiley eye contact going on and Hannah could feel herself growing warm. Relaxed, amused Conor made her heart beat that little bit faster and it needed to back right off. He'd made his feelings quite clear. With a force of will she hadn't known she was capable of, she turned back to the chopping board, steadied her hand, and began slicing the poor savaged carrot into equal slices. Already, using this technique she had more control of the knife and could chop in even pieces.

'That's much better,' said Conor, who had stepped right back and was now leaning onto the corner of the counter as far from her as was possible in the small space.

'Thank you.' She kept her head down, not wanting him to see her flushed face and bright eyes. Why did he have such a damn effect on her? Honestly it was worse than being a teenager all over again.

'Have you got any plans for dinner?' he asked.

'No, I was just going to have a quick sandwich.' She wasn't about to admit that she couldn't face cooking and especially not when he was around. It was bad enough that he'd witnessed today's incompetence; she didn't need to give him a repeat performance. 'And then I was planning, if you don't mind, to put my feet up and read a book this evening or watch some rubbish television.'

'I don't mind at all. I was planning to do some work, so I can work right here. You can have the lounge all to yourself.'

'Great,' she said, giving him a perfunctory smile. She couldn't decide whether she was relieved or slightly put out that he didn't want her company. *Come on, Hannah. How many times does he have to make it obvious that he's under sufferance and doesn't want your company?*

'Sorry. It must be a pain for you to have to be here.' Despite that, she wasn't about to offer to read up in her bedroom. She'd paid extra to have a cottage.

'It's fine.' His mouth twisted with wry cynicism. 'Guests come first. Talking of which, I'm cooking for myself and it would be a shame to waste these vegetables. How do you fancy a sweet potato and haddock stew?'

She had no idea what that would be like; in fact, she'd never bought a sweet potato in her life but when someone was offering to cook for her – a famous chef at that – she wasn't about to turn it down.

'Done,' she said. 'Thank you.'

'You can peel and chop for your supper. Get some practice in, although without the violence this time.'

She grinned. 'I promise I'll behave with the vegetables.'

'Good to hear it.'

Watching Conor cook was a real pleasure. He had an economy of movement and a calm, steady approach, always one step ahead of himself. He also explained each step and why he was doing things, which she found fascinating. He was a good teacher.

'Why don't you teach here?' she asked on impulse.

'There are too many cooks in this family. I want something of my own and the rest of them are absolutely bloody useless at anything DIY or practical. The only one who has any non-culinary skills is Fergus, who's handy with a computer. He built the school's website and does all the social media posting, although Mam and Mairead write all the copy and take all the pictures. Make it look idyllic.'

'It *is* idyllic,' said Hannah, remembering what he'd said on the beach. 'You came back.'

'Yes, but beware snakes in the garden of Eden.'

'That's very cryptic.'

'And that's all you're getting.' He shot her a thoughtful look. 'There's something about you that always makes me say more than I should.'

'Like what?' asked Hannah, slightly pleased at this accomplishment.

'You don't back off, do you?'

'I like to get answers. Always have done.'

'Yes, I think that's what it is. You sit there waiting with that patient expression on your face without overtly pushing. It's almost as if you expect an answer so you get one.'

Hannah laughed. 'Well that's all new.'

'I'm used to people asking questions for the sake of them, prying, wanting to know more about the surface stuff.' He rolled his eyes. 'Every sodding interview I ever did, they always wanted to know about my flaming love life. I only had to be pictured with someone and there'd be a whole load of speculation. And there were lots of pictures and the more well known I became…' He shrugged. 'Poor little rich boy, eh? Complaining about the accoutrements of wealth and celebrity. That's why I gave it up.'

Hannah frowned, not following. 'What do you mean?'

'If you can't stand the heat, get out of the kitchen, to use a well-worn but extremely apt cliché.'

'Was it really that bad?'

'No, it wasn't. I had a ball. I enjoyed the attention. Enjoyed being able to do what I wanted.' He grinned. 'Back in the day, I became an arrogant shite for a wee while. Mam soon knocked that on the head. So then I settled down. Found a nice girl. A really nice girl. Polly Daventree. You might have heard of her.'

Hannah nodded, remembering her conversation with Izzy.

'She's now my ex. Ex-fiancée no less. But now she's the new rising star, Adrienne Byrne's natural replacement.'

There was a bitter tone to his words and she gave him a perplexed look.

'I'm sure there's a subtext to all this, Conor, but you'll have to humour me. I'm completely oblivious.'

'Oh God, do I have to? Explaining all my angst makes me look like a right eejit.' He laughed. 'I can't take myself and my woes so seriously if I have to do that.'

'That sounds like a good thing,' said Hannah, suddenly pleased that they could have this back and forth without any awkwardness. She could be friends with him, she realised with a jolt of pleasure. Perhaps that would be enough? It had to be, he came from a different world to her.

'Polly was an actress. When she won *Celebrity Masterchef* in the UK, she and her agent decided that they'd reinvent her as a cookery expert. Didn't take her long to decide that she could become the next Adrienne Byrne – history repeating itself by marrying into the family. We got engaged but then I realised I was a means to an end... That sounds arrogant, doesn't it? She met someone else but didn't want to give up the gig with Mam, so it was all very civilised. She stayed here and became Mam's latest protégée.' He gave a twisted smile. 'Polly moved into the farmhouse.'

Hannah's mouth dropped open. 'That's...' She wanted to say *brutal*.

'Yeah, but Polly was a new disciple, a convert. There's nothing my mam likes so much as people spreading the word, reinforcing the Killorgally success story. It's all good PR and I let the side down by giving it all up.'

'But surely your mum understood how you felt...' Hannah, shocked at his harsh tone, couldn't believe Adrienne would be so impartial where her own son was concerned. Her aunt might not be Hannah's biological mother but in every other way she *was* her mother, and would have been the fiercest in protection of her chicks.

Conor lifted his chin and gazed over her head out of the window but she could see the hurt in his taut jawline.

'Anyway, all water under the bridge now and I've no idea why I'm spilling my guts like this to you.'

'Because you can?' suggested Hannah.

'Something like that. You've no preconceived notions of me and I don't feel I have to explain too much, you're sharp. Like a good knife. You cut away through the crap to the nub of things.'

For some reason being compared to one of his stock-in-trade tools felt like a high compliment.

'Now, can you boil that kettle for me and make some stock?' He slid a stock cube along the counter towards her.

She picked up the foil-wrapped cube. 'Stock cube? I thought we were supposed to caramelise bones in the oven and boil them and all that malarky.'

'And sometimes a common stock cube will do.' He winked.

'Thank God for that,' said Hannah, with a heartfelt tone that made him smile.

Chapter Sixteen

The rest of the week passed rather amicably between her and Conor which was just as well because there was just no way of getting away from him; he worked in the kitchen every day and was at home in the cottage every evening.

He had a fund of funny, self-deprecating stories about his days in New York and LA, about celebrities and famous people behaving badly, and he shared them with wicked humour. Despite the growing awareness that he was a lot more down to earth than she'd first thought, she still knew that she had to keep her distance. It was getting harder and harder, especially when he was so easy to be with. However, the same thought kept coming back to her, if something more did happen between them where could it possibly lead? A broken heart? She couldn't take that risk.

One night after dinner at the farmhouse with the others, she came home to find him in the kitchen frowning over a set of plans. The sight of the unfurled rolls of paper piqued her interest and she tried to squint at them without appearing to.

'You look fed up or cross or something,' she observed.

'Just trying to solve a knotty problem. I've got to put a dirty great RSJ in, to extend the kitchen, but I'm trying to work out if I need to get a crane in.'

'Oh,' said Hannah, none the wiser.

He lifted his head from the plans. 'See here.' She walked round to stand beside him.

'Looks impressive.'

'It will be when it's finished. See, this is the kitchen.'

He talked through the plans with a passion that surprised her. 'There'll be a breakfast bar here but it will be two levels. The lower level will have a sink in it, so that whoever is in the kitchen and is working doesn't have their back to their guests.'

Hannah nodded. 'Good call. You're right. When you're washing up, you sort of become invisible.'

'Exactly, and if you're the host you should be the star of the show.'

'Not sure about that one,' said Hannah. Maybe that was why she'd never been one for cooking. She preferred to stay in the background, unlike her more extrovert sister.

'And this will be a big bifold window that will fold right back so that the patio in front becomes an extension of the house. But then,' he grinned at her, 'there'll be a wood burner here because the weather isn't always that kind.'

'It's been gorgeous this week. I'm starting to think it's always like this here.' Every day this week had been a golden last hurrah of summer but there was a definite smell of autumn in the air and the temperature in the evening held a distinct chill. The apples in the orchard were ripening to a rosy hue, the raspberry canes were bare, and hay bales in the fields opposite had been gathered in.

'Enjoy it while it lasts, this Indian summer.' He glanced around the kitchen. 'I remodelled this place so that you could enjoy the view of the sea but still feel snug and warm. Everyone thought a wood burner in here as well as an open fireplace in the lounge was overkill.'

'It's very homely.' She pulled a face, thinking of her own bland apartment. 'I ought to make more effort. My place is somewhere to sleep. I don't spend much time there.' Or rather, she didn't spend much *quality* time there.

'Where do you spend time then?'

'Well, it always used to be round at my sister's place. She knows how to throw a party or a get-together. Now she's gone, my social life has taken a bit of a nose dive. I mean, I go out after work with friends from the office but… well, it's not quite the same without Mina. I miss her, I guess. God, she would love it here. She'd be in her element. Although I think she might drive your mum mad as she does like to experiment and doesn't stick to a recipe.' She glanced around the room. 'You have a good eye. Especially for a bloke.'

'Sexist!'

'Well, it's cosy. Not quite feminine but it's not all leather and taupe.' She pointed to the sage-green painted cupboards and the pale linen-grey sofa with printed cushions in naïve Scandinavian designs of pale yellow and the same sage green, as well as the cashmere throw tossed over the back. On the floor were a couple of tall jugs with elegant looped handles filled with dried reeds, and a set of striking prints hung on the wall featuring sea birds, picked out with bold black slashes and elements of colour in the background.

'I spent a lot of time in hotels and rented accommodation feeling homesick. One thing I always want to do is make sure that people feel at home. I can't bear those stark places where everything is nailed down because they're worried people are going to steal it. I want people to have those little creature comforts that they would have in their own place.'

Hannah wrinkled her nose. 'I need to take a leaf out of your book. My place isn't very homely.'

'Maybe it's not home.'

'Of course it's home.'

'Always so pragmatic. You don't have much romance in your soul.'

'You're the second person who's said that to me recently. My mother had plenty of romance and it didn't get her very far. Or rather, it took her too far.'

Conor didn't say anything and for a moment it was as if the tables from the other night had been reversed. 'My mother and father died when I was a toddler. They were adrenaline junkies – skiing, white-water rafting, you name it. They would leave us with my aunt and uncle for the weekend while they went off for an adventure. One weekend they didn't come back.'

'That's… rough.'

'Yeah, and selfish. And foolish. And a whole load of

other things. But luckily for me and my sister, we stayed with my aunt and uncle who are the opposite.' And she'd made sure she never worried them or put a foot wrong. As she'd grown older, a deep, dark hidden part of her had been cross that her parents had put their adventures ahead of their daughters and she had determined that she would never act in such a foolhardy way. Mina was the impulsive one, so it was up to Hannah to be the sensible one and it hadn't been so hard to fall into that mould. Hannah liked to know where she was, what she'd be doing next, and what her plans for the future were. Coming to Ireland had been the riskiest thing she'd ever done in her life and now she was paying for it, because she was starting to question her view of herself. Why should she let herself be defined by her parents? They were long gone. They'd made their own decisions. Perhaps she should start doing the things that she really wanted to do instead of always erring on the side of caution to reassure herself and others that she wasn't like them.

The more time she spent with Conor, the more she liked him. Genuinely liked him. This close proximity helped to make him less of a fable and less out of reach. When she'd met him in Dublin he'd been a person from another world – sophisticated, smart, and good looking... and way out of her league. Now she'd got to know him, he was very human and down to earth and he seemed to enjoy her company, and would often come and sit in the lounge with her in the evenings. He'd fallen into a routine of making coffee for her in the mornings and as she drank it would settle into the sofa by the wood burner for a quick chat, which invariably meant that they walked up to the kitchen together.

It was almost as if he were determined to prove that they were just good friends. What if she didn't play safe, could she handle the fall out in the long term? Somehow she didn't think she could.

After a quiet weekend when she'd visited Aidan and Sorcha and walked the entire length of the beach with Izzy, Hannah was all set for week three of the course and headed up to the hen houses to start the day.

'Morning, Hannah.'

Adrienne's low-toned greeting made Hannah jump.

'M-morning,' she said, trying to sound bright and breezy. She'd actually been lost in thought, pondering what to wear when she went kayaking with Conor. He'd issued the invitation, almost a challenge, over coffee this morning after expressing disappointment that she'd not done more exploring at the weekend. When she'd explained that she was exhausted after a week on her feet, he teased her that she needed to man up and that kayaking would be easy on her feet.

'And how are our fine ladies, this morning?' She knelt in front of one of the hens who immediately bustled up, feathery breeches swaying with busy intent, to check out the food situation. Adrienne laughed and petted her before throwing down a handful of potato peelings and pea pods.

'They're all good,' said Hannah with a fond smile. It

might be cupboard love but there was something satisfying about being greeted with so much enthusiasm on a morning.

'Grand. I see you've a real fondness for the ladies.'

'I've got used to them. They're all so funny and they have such distinct personalities. It's like the school playground.' She paused. 'Those two are too cool for school and keep themselves to themselves. That one likes to be in the thick of everything, like the queen bee of gossip. That one is the attention-seeking, naughty one and that little gaggle over there are the giggling herd that follow the leader and she' – Hannah pointed to a pure white hen– 'fusses over everyone.'

'Ah, that's Agnetha.'

Hanna gave her a questioning look.

'After the blonde one in Abba, because of her colouring. We don't name all of them, only the ones who really stand out. She's always been the bossy, mother-hen one.'

Hannah grinned with sudden awareness.

Adrienne narrowed her eyes in mock offence. 'And yes, Conor and Fergus said she ought to be called Adrienne.'

'I didn't say a word.'

'You didn't need to. It was written all over your face. Hannah, darlin', you're an open book.'

Behind her back, Hannah crossed her fingers. She really hoped she wasn't.

After gathering up the haul of eggs, which still gave her a thrill, she headed towards the big farmhouse kitchen.

'I'll see you in the kitchen. This week we'll be focusing on cooking with eggs. It's going to be so much fun.'

Hannah nodded while remembering this week's schedule. It sounded by far the most full-on and quite intimidating. They'd be tackling a huge range of dishes and sauces which included learning to make hollandaise sauce, mayonnaise, sabayon (and she had no idea what that even was), crème anglaise (again, not sure), soufflé, mousse, meringue, custard omelette, and quiche. Half of those sounded horribly complicated. And why? You could buy perfectly good mayonnaise and custard in the supermarket and Tesco did those lovely little six packs of chocolate mousses. She scrunched up her nose; she'd never so much as considered buying hollandaise.

Now that they'd moved into the third week of the cookery school programme, everyone had settled into a routine at breakfast, much of which, it seemed, had been set on that very first morning. Meredith and Alan were always first in and by the time Hannah arrived, were sitting companionably chatting over coffee. Izzy usually burst in not long after, piling her plate high, always ravenous. Fliss would saunter in with that slightly bored expression on her face as if this homely scene was somehow rather beneath her while Jason would stomp in complaining vociferously to anyone who would listen – although these days no one listened – about the pigs.

'I'm really looking forward to this week,' said Meredith. 'Learning how to do the fancy stuff.'

'So am I. Proper cooking at last,' said Fliss. 'My last sabayon curdled.'

'Oh, that is annoying,' sympathised Meredith. 'It's not something I've made before. Although I tried to make those gorgeous Portuguese nata and my custard was more like very fine scrambled egg. Tasted delicious but the texture was awful.'

Hannah listened, bemused. They might as well be talking another language as far as she was concerned. Thankfully Izzy caught her eye and pulled a face. Clearly she wasn't the only one.

'It's all a load of bollocks,' said Jason. 'You can buy a litre of Hollandaise for a fiver from the cash and carry.' At Fliss's blank look, he added, 'Delivered and all. And I bet you punters can't tell the difference.' Everyone suddenly became very interested in the plates in front of them. Jason with his back to the door continued, 'Life's too short to be faffing about separating eggs every five bloody minutes.'

Hannah winced at the prune-mouthed expression on Adrienne's face.

'That'll be two euros in the jar, I believe, Jason,' she said, adopting a benign smile, which Hannah could tell, despite its apparent benevolence, promised later retribution. Meredith drew in a quick gasp and Fliss's eyes sharpened with quick amusement. Like Alan and Izzy, Hannah slid down her chair trying to pretend she wasn't there.

He flinched, mouthing, 'Oh fuck,' and then turned round. 'All right there, Adrienne.' He nodded with his usual insouciance. Hannah pressed her lips together. It wouldn't have been appropriate to laugh, no matter how much she wanted to. The two of them reminded her of a pair of cats facing off.

'And that'll be another euro in the jar,' she added sweetly before turning to smile at everyone else. 'All set? I'll see you in the kitchen in five minutes.' With that she glided out of the room, leaving Jason shaking his head.

'How does she do that?'

'She just knows what an idiot you are,' sniped Fliss.

'Better than being a toffee-nosed—'

'Jason,' Meredith rose and took his arm, leading him away to the cookery school. 'How was the...?'

'Oops,' said Izzy as Meredith's voice died away through the doorway.

'Huh, he's such a berk,' said Fliss. 'I've no idea what he's doing here.'

'He's pretty good,' said Izzy.

'You think? He can use a knife, but that doesn't make you a chef. Probably got that with his ASBO. You have to have a certain aesthetic when you're cooking.'

'And what's that when it's at home?' asked Izzy.

'An appreciation of the art of cooking. It's not just food—'

'It's Marks and Spencer's food,' chipped in Hannah, recalling the store's famous advertising campaign, and received a frosty glare for her trouble. Fliss tossed her hair over her shoulder and muttered, 'Philistines, the lot of you,' as she marched out of the kitchen.

'And then there were three,' said Izzy with a quick grin.

'Three who'll be in the doghouse, if we don't shake a

leg,' said Alan. 'Come on, lasses. Let's get this party started.'

They trooped into the kitchen and donned their aprons. Hannah glanced around quickly. There was Conor but Adrienne was whispering in his ear, and, with a look of surprise he stepped back from her. She gave him a gentle push on his shoulder and, shaking his head, he left the room, already putting his phone up to his ear with a disgruntled frown.

The six of them crowded around Adrienne's bench where she began whipping up a hollandaise sauce, explaining what she was doing and why. Meredith chipped in with knowledgeable questions while Alan exclaimed over the explanations that Adrienne gave. He loved his science and always wanted to know how the mechanics of things worked. Fliss seemed happy to listen and learn, while Jason barely paid attention, unlike her and Izzy who hung on every word, terrified they were going to miss something.

After that they were sent back to their own benches to make their own sauce. Thankfully it looked pretty easy and Hannah started following the recipe without too many qualms, feeling quite confident, even though she did have to fish some of the egg shell out of the bowl. For once she managed to separate the eggs without breaking a single yolk. Happy with this positive start, she carefully measured out all the ingredients. As always, she was a good few minutes behind the others when she began to whisk them together but luckily she'd had the foresight to set a pan to boil on the gas ring. When she popped the bowl over the boiling water, she was only a minute after everyone else. She carried on whisking the mix and checked the recipe. What was it? Three to five minutes? She watched hopefully as the golden yolks began to pale. She'd got this. A few minutes later she examined the sauce, realising there were lots of orangey lumps in it that weren't supposed to be there. It didn't look anything like the smooth, pale, creamy sauce that Adrienne's had made. If anything, it looked rather spotty. She pulled a face and poked at one of the slightly rubbery lumps.

What had she done wrong? She'd done exactly what Adrienne had told them to do and followed the recipe. She glanced around the room. The others were all lifting their bowls from the hot water and none of them seemed to be poking at lumps. Maybe she could strain it before Adrienne came this way. Bending down, she pulled out one of the utensil drawers and rooted around for a sieve. She found a fancy stainless steel conical one that looked just the job. Unfortunately, when she strained the sauce through it, most of the lumps stuck in the holes and stopped the sauce dripping through, so then she had to stir it to give it a helping hand which just forced the yellow orange blobs through.

'You all right there, Hannah?' called Jason.

'Yes. Yes. Fine,' she said, pushing her hair from her sweaty forehead and glancing quickly at Adrienne, hoping she wasn't heading her way. Of course she was.

'Oh dear,' she said.

Hannah gave her a weak smile. 'I'm not sure what I did wrong.'

Adrienne looked at the pan of water still furiously bubbling because Hannah had forgotten to turn it off. She leaned over and turned the temperature down. 'It should be barely simmering. What's happened is the egg has started to cook too quickly – that's what the little lumps are. The cooked yolk.'

Hannah sighed.

'Not to worry,' said Adrienne, patting her arm. 'You only learn by making mistakes. I always say you have to get it wrong to know what right looks like.'

Hannah frowned. Adrienne was just being kind, but as usual with her mind-reading trick she said, 'Have you ever watched *Bake Off*?'

With a sputtered laugh, remembering her own cake-making disaster at work, Hannah said, 'Yes.'

'And do you think it's the first time those folk have baked a cake?'

'Well, no.'

'No, they've been practising their little socks off. I promise you, the more you cook, the better you get. You'll know next time. You won't make that mistake again.' She shot Hannah a brilliant, encouraging smile and, at that moment, Hannah would have followed her to the ends of the earth.

'Come on. Let's have another go.'

Patiently, she stood watching as Hannah started over, her hands shaking slightly under the personal tuition. It was especially nerve-racking as all the others had finished now and were leaning back against their benches observing. She could feel the sweaty patches under her arms growing as she concentrated on every aspect. At least this time she wasn't worrying about being last – she *was* last! And, miraculously, when she whisked her hollandaise sauce over the low, barely simmering water, it thickened into a beautiful, soft lemon-coloured thick sauce.

'Right, now season it, just a tiny bit at a time and then a taste. Then add more.'

After her second pinch of cayenne and a couple of drips of lemon juice, she nodded. 'I think that's it.'

Adrienne dipped in a spoon and tasted. 'Spot on. That is fabulous. Well done, Hannah.' She beamed at her, as Hannah wilted with relief on the spot. 'Now, let's try everyone else's.' She walked from bench to bench tasting everyone's sauce, encouraging them to all try each other's.

'Mm, good job, Fliss, perhaps a wee bit more seasoning. Excellent, Meredith. Very nice, Alan. Not bad at all, Izzy, although I can't taste any seasoning at all and, Jason, go steady on the cayenne but very nice consistency. Ah, and Conor is back.'

They all looked up to see him carrying what looked like a juice carton. Adrienne smiled, with an unnerving combination of mischief and Machiavellian cunning.

'Right, we're going to do a blind tasting. All of you bring your sauces to the front and then line up and turn around.'

Like obedient children they all walked up with their identical glass bowls and popped them down one by one and then lined up as instructed. Izzy shot Hannah a what-is-she-up-to grimace, while Fliss rolled her eyes and muttered, 'Enough with the drama already,' and Jason yawned. He looked as if he'd spent the last night few nights down at the pub.

There was a lot of tapping and chinking in the background until Adrienne invited them to turn around and approach the bench. Conor handed out clipboards and pens. Adrienne filled a tumbler full of teaspoons and motioned to two bowls on the counter top.

'Right. I want you to taste each one and then mark it out of five. On the sheets you'll see that there are five categories. Consistency. Depth of flavour. Colour. Smell. And how much you like it. This is bowl A and this is bowl B. I would suggest you taste both, then, before you mark them, taste them again. Off you go.'

They all crowded forward. Hannah didn't feel so confident about this task. What if she got it wrong? She reached for a teaspoon, keeping her eyes down, conscious of Conor in his Killorgally polo shirt and black jeans.

Even in colour, the two sauces looked very different. In fact, if she hadn't known they were supposed to be the same thing, she might not have realised. Gingerly, she dipped a teaspoon in the paler, thinner sauce and tasted it, watching as Fliss closed her eyes, her nose pointing up in the air slightly. Hannah wanted to laugh at what she imagined was a wine-snob pose, but concentrated instead on the flavour of the sauce. Sweet, zingy, and quite pleasant. She'd only had eggs Benedict a couple of times, but it tasted familiar. She took a second taste, closing her eyes to concentrate, licking her lips to get one last taste. When she opened them, she found Conor watching her. Clumsily, she grabbed a second spoon, to move onto the second dish,

Sauce B. This time she focused on the sauce, ignoring her awareness of Conor. This was a little more golden with a creamy thickness and… oh my goodness, the taste! It was like a firework going off on her tongue and her eyes widened as she savoured the delicious flavours. She could taste the cayenne, the lemon, and it just felt so much nicer on her tongue, if that were a real thing. Inadvertently she turned to Conor, remembering him talking her through that first taste of whiskey. 'Wow,' she said. 'What a difference.'

'Thoughts?' Adrienne's expression held a touch of smugness, as she turned to Jason. 'What do you think?'

He gave her a cheerful grin. 'Sauce B.'

'And why is that?' she pressed.

'Mouthfeel, flavour, colour and, it's blo— delicious.'

She raised an imperious eyebrow but didn't comment on his near slip of the tongue. 'Hannah?'

Hannah started and stared for a second. 'Er… yes. Definitely B.' She could almost see the I-rest-my-case gleam in Adrienne's eyes.

'And why?'

'It just…' Oh God, everyone was looking at her. She hated not knowing the right answer.

'How does it make you feel?'

Adrienne wasn't going to let her off the hook, was she?

'It's…' There was as strong temptation to look at her feet. 'It's…' She caught Conor's eye again. As if he'd read her mind, he gave her a tiny encouraging smile. 'It's like a firework going on your tongue compared to a damp squib,' she said in a rush.

'Ah!' Adrienne threw back her head, auburn curls

tumbling down her back. 'What a wonderful description. We'll make a chef of you yet, Hannah.' Her gorgeous green eyes glowed and for a minute it was easy to believe that she might actually be one of the fae, but Hannah felt as if she'd snapped up the best prize in the world. She'd got it right in the circle of cooks.

Still beaming, Adrienne addressed the whole group. 'Sauce A is from a well-known wholesaler in Tralee, and Sauce B is actually the second one Hannah made.'

Surprised but also delighted, Hannah blushed with sheer pleasure. It was a complete revelation. She'd genuinely never before believed that there could be such a distinction. If she were honest, she'd always thought her sister made a bit of a fuss about sourcing authentic ingredients and cooking everything from scratch. No wonder everything Mina made always tasted so good. She always went the extra mile because she cared and it had puzzled Hannah because cooking from scratch was potentially dangerous – look at her first attempt at hollandaise with grainy orange lumps. So many things could go wrong and you might end up with a roomful of starving guests or looking useless. That wasn't in Hannah's DNA. She was the reliable one. But maybe, just maybe, it was worth the risk.

'I think you can tell the difference and how easy it is to make, when you take the time and the trouble for something that tastes so much better. Using the freshest, most wholesome ingredients makes all the difference.' She straightened, her face softened, and she added with a wink, 'And there ends today's lecture.'

'OK, I get the message,' said Jason with a good-natured thumbs-up.

Adrienne patted him on the shoulder. 'Don't think that gets you out of the fine. That'll be another euro in the jar.'

'Fairy nuff,' said Jason, cheerfully dropping the coin into the jar.

'OK. Now with the egg whites, we're going to make meringues.'

Alan groaned. 'Oh no, my nemesis.'

Fliss winced. 'Mine too. They always crack and fall apart.'

'Hurrah!' crowed Izzy, rubbing her hands together. 'Something you're not good at. Meringues are the only pudding I can make. If you ever come to my house, it's the only pudding you'll get.'

When Hannah approached her bench, Conor was drying up the utensils ready for the next round of cooking.

'Thank you,' she said, not looking up. England Hannah was back in charge. She felt almost schizophrenic around Conor, flopping between being completely wet and useless, and being overtly brash and taking charge. She much preferred it when Ireland Hannah was in the house.

Chapter Seventeen

'Are you set?' asked Conor, closing the front door behind them.

'Let me just check,' she said, delving into her rucksack. Phone, purse, tissues, paracetamols, spare socks, extra T-shirt.

'What have you got in there?' he asked.

'Essentials, and a few extras, just in case.'

'In case of what?' He peered into the top of the bag. 'What do you need the torch for?'

'Well, a torch is always handy.'

'Cable ties?'

'They're useful; you never know when you might need one.'

'When you're a serial killer possibly. And what's that?'

'A candle.' She pulled a face. 'In case of power cuts and things. Overkill?'

'Possibly, but I like that you're prepared for anything.'

'I like to call it organised,' she said, zipping up her fleece and letting loose a big sigh. Now that she was sure she'd got everything she needed she could relax. How lovely to be spending the day outdoors and even better that the weather had decided to be on their side. It was a warm, bright morning and although it was probably heresy round these parts to say it, she was looking forward to a whole day away from the kitchen. A week of cooking with eggs, which seemed to be a delicate balance between science and natural flare, had left her wrung out and she wasn't sure she ever wanted to see another egg yolk again. She'd had more than her share of disasters, although she was quite pleased she wasn't on her own. Even Meredith's soufflé had collapsed and Alan's sabayon had curdled. Fliss had put her first euro in the jar, although Fliss being Fliss had managed to make the f-word sound posh.

'Where are we going?'

'To Dingle. Dingle Bay. It's quite sheltered there and there's… well I think I'll leave it as a surprise.'

'I'm not sure I like surprises.' In fact, Hannah didn't like surprises at all, but saying it out loud always made her sound like a bit of a killjoy. Surprises snuck up on you, you couldn't prepare for them, and you didn't know how to school your face to deal with them.

'Live a little.' He nudged her with his elbow, setting light to a funny little spark in the bottom of her belly.

Ignoring the fluttery, butterfly wing sensation, she climbed into his big four-wheel drive, determined to enjoy the day. As they set off, rumbling down the track to the main road, she sank into the seat, glad that there was no one around to see them leave. She had a feeling that there'd be a few comments, especially as the two of them were sharing the cottage, and she felt sure she'd blush wildly because they had no idea what she and Conor had got up to the first time they met.

The road wound along the coast and Hannah gazed out of the window, watching the sea that appeared here and there, white surf frothing on the dark, rocky crags below until they turned inland, crossing through wide valleys fringed with rolling hills that were dotted with sheep grazing with contended placidity. Conor drove at a steady speed as they passed the odd car here and there. The pace of life was so much slower than she was used to and she found herself imagining what it would be like to live here. Driving, as she'd already discovered, was a pleasure, instead of the stressful stop-start of the rush hour in Manchester and the manic aggression on the motorways as everyone tried to get home of an evening. It had become an inescapable fact of life and until now she'd never considered that you didn't have to put up with it.

'Do you ever get traffic jams here?' she asked.

'Yes, when Pádraig O'Brien's sheep get out on the road. And the summer can be murder, all the coaches touring the Ring of Kerry – they block the roads entirely. There's an unwritten rule that they drive the route clockwise so you don't have the coaches trying to pass each other on the boreens. Although some of those drivers drive like fecking eejits.'

'Boreens?'

'You know, the smaller roads.'

'Not heard that one before and can you explain? What is the Ring of Kerry?'

'It's a circular drive, a hundred and eleven miles, that takes in some grand sights like Killorglin, Gap of Dunloe, Kenmare, Skellig Michael, and Ross Castle.'

Hannah sighed, enjoying listening to his rolling accent. 'They all sound wonderful.'

'Well, I'm biased but I do think you see some of the best Ireland has to offer. Maybe I'll take you to see a few parts. In Irish it's *Mórchuaird Chiarraí*.'

An unexpected shiver ran across her skin at the deep register of his voice. The words sounded like a caress and his accompanying smile held a touch of seduction, as if he knew exactly how they'd affected her. Cross that he could read her so well and uncomfortable that he knew it, she said, 'That sounds like it's from Tolkien, a place in Middle Earth or something.'

'Some of us call it the Kingdom of Kerry. There's no place finer.' He glanced across at her. 'I didn't have you for a *Lord of the Rings* fan.'

'I read all the books as a teenager and of course I've seen the films.' She shot him a quick grin, feeling like she was back on steadier ground. 'Big Aragorn fan, although that might have something to do with Viggo Mortensen.'

'I'm more of an Eowyn fan myself. Can't beat a Shieldmaiden of Rohan.'

'Not Liv Tyler?'

'No, a bit too ethereal for me. I like a woman who goes into battle. There are lots of warrior goddesses in Irish folklore: Badb, who took the form of a crow, Morrígan, the phantom queen, and their sister, Macha.'

'I thought Irish folklore had fairies rather than goddesses.'

'Not fairies originally. Irish mythology includes the Tuatha Dé Danann, supernatural beings who originally lived in the Otherworld but freely interacted with humans. They were eventually driven underground, and the survivors, the Sidhe, or fairies, now live in the mounds that you see all over Ireland. You have to take care that you don't anger or insult them. They guard their abodes fiercely.'

'Really?' She raised sceptical eyebrows, amused by the seriousness of his expression.

'Oh yes. There are certain places, fairy rings, mounds, particular trees or woods that you trespass upon at your peril.'

'Trespass upon?' she teased. 'That sounds far too much like legal terminology.'

'Or ancient terminology. They're stories passed down.' His face lightened. 'We're great ones for storytelling. My da had a wealth of old stories. They're great tales of woe and suffering. You've heard of changelings stealing human children and replacing them with their own in retaliation against those who trespass on Sidhe land. We tease Fergus that he's a changeling because of his computer skills and lack of interest in cooking.'

'I'm not sure I buy that one. He looks just like Adrienne,' said Hannah, amused.

'Ha, but we tease her that she's a descendent of Morrígan.'

'I can see that. She's pretty queen-like.'

Conor grinned. 'So you're another falling under her spell.'

For some reason Hannah felt the need to defend herself. She wasn't the sort of person to be easily influenced or swayed by an argument, and she prided herself on always being able to see both sides of the story.

'That's very cynical for someone who's been talking about fairies and folklore. She's very inspirational and this is all new to me. There are lots of things she talks about that I've never considered before. She's very passionate and that's interesting.'

'Hmm, she certainly is,' he said with a wry smile.

'Aren't you proud of her?'

'Of course I'm proud of her. She's incredible.' Conor straightened suddenly as if he'd received a sharp prod in the ribs. 'What she's achieved is brilliant. Killorgally is renowned the world over. She's created a real legacy. I can't complain. I've fame and fortune as a result.'

'But…' pressed Hannah.

Conor wrinkled his nose, patting the steering wheel before he finally spoke. 'Being a Byrne comes with a price. Ma's put her heart and soul into the place, but…' He left the words hanging in the small space in the front of the car.

'There's nothing left for anyone else?' Hannah understood that. Her own parents had forgone building a secure future for their daughters in favour of adrenaline highs.

He shot her a sharp look but didn't say anything.

'It must be hard sharing your mother with everyone else all the time.'

He shrugged. 'Occasionally. You tend to get used to the media attention and step around the fan girls at her feet.'

'I can imagine.' His indifferent response suggested he didn't want to talk about himself. 'Families, eh? I told you about my parents. I've often wondered why me and my sister weren't enough for them. Why they had to go on adventures all the time and leave us.'

She could see a parallel. Adrienne might be there, geographically, but her time was compromised. There were so many demands upon it and she could see how Conor might feel that her work came first.

'First World problems, eh?' Conor patted the steering wheel again.

Hannah felt he was being a little hard on himself and she laid a hand on his arm, stopping the irritated movement of his hand. 'No, we can't help how we feel, but we can choose how we react.'

It was a mantra that she stuck by. Her reactions were logical and sensible, weighing up both sides; it was what made her so good at her job. Some people came into law because they felt a burning need to balance justice and pursued that at all costs. She wanted to tread the path between, finding solutions that suited both sides – or at least provided the right outcome according to the law.

'We choose how we react?'

'Yes. You can choose to be pissed off and angry at things, but if you do that the only person who's upset is you, or you can choose to move on and ignore those things. Focus on the positives.'

'You make it sound easy.'

'Ha!' She gave a mirthless laugh. 'I didn't say it was easy or that I was able to do it. It was something I read once and it… well I think about it a lot. I've got a colleague at work who spills the coffee grounds all over the counter every single morning. It pisses me off big time. I'm not sure I choose to be pissed off but I can't help myself, and I've definitely not got it nailed when I think about my parents.'

'Hmm.' For the rest of the journey, Conor said very little.

When they pulled into Dingle harbour, parking in one of the side streets, Conor led the way to the hire shop on the quay.

'Conor Byrne. What's the craic? Got fed up with the telly business, did you now?'

'Sure, you know yourself,' Conor agreed as the grizzled man behind the counter inspected him with slow care.

'Kayaks, is it you're after? For you and the young lady?' He gave Hannah a quick but thorough inspection.

'That's right. How's Margaret and the baby?' He turned to Hannah. 'Danny and I were at school together, although he was a few years above.'

'Not that many years, but thanks for asking. They're both grand. Another on the way.'

'Congratulations. Who'd a thought? Danny Kielty, father of two.' He turned to Hannah. 'Back in the day, he was quite the hell-raiser in Dingle.'

'Go on with you.' Danny rapped Conor's knuckles with the Biro in his hand. 'And you were an angel.' He gave

Hannah a conspiratorial wink. 'If you're wanting the dirt on Con here, you just come chat to me. I can tell you a tale or two. He wasn't always so fancy, you know.'

'Go on out of that, Danny. Two kids doesn't make you a saint either.'

Danny punched him on the arm and laughed. 'Nor more it does. How long do you want the boats for?'

'An hour or two should do it.'

'Well, you picked a fine day. And it's quiet – you might have some fun with Fungie.'

If Hannah hadn't been so aware of Conor she might have missed that almost infinitesimal shake of his head.

'Fungie?'

'Local joke,' said Conor. 'Now, Danny, how much do I owe you?'

'Mates rates for you.' He grinned. 'A hundred euro an hour because you're a rich telly bastard now.'

'Very funny. I'm just the odd job man, these days.'

'Rumour is that Moss Murphy's about to hit the jackpot. He says his land is worth a fortune.'

'Murphy? What, don't tell me there's gold in them there hills of his? He's drilling for oil?'

Danny shrugged. 'No idea, but he's been over in Dick Mack's swearing up and down that he's about to come into money.'

'Can't imagine how. That place of his is falling down around his ears and has been for a long while.'

'Something to do with that nephew of his. He's a right little fecker.'

'Yes, we're not so fond of him.'

'Shotgun man?' ventured Hannah.

'Yeah, that's the man. Ah well, Danny. We ought to be making the best of the weather. Give me your two best kayaks.'

Danny tossed his Biro up and flipped it with a laugh. 'I only have best kayaks.'

Hannah turned to look at the view from the office, leaving the two men bantering and teasing each other as Conor finished the transaction. She'd already decided that she'd buy them lunch later to pay him back.

Thankfully the waves looked gentle, rippling with that sort of soporific swell that promised calm. While she hadn't done any sea kayaking, she was reassured that she'd been through a few gentle rapids and could cope with today's small waves. If the wind had picked up at all she probably would have chickened out.

With helmet and paddles in hand, having changed into wetsuits, they left Danny's basic office and went down to the small, shingled beach area where two red fibreglass kayaks were waiting for them. Hannah wriggled her way into the waterproof spray deck and the neoprene shoes that they'd hired and waded into the shallow water, wincing as the cold water lapped around her ankles.

'All set?' asked Conor, fiddling with the chin strap of his helmet.

'Yup,' said Hannah shortly, trying to hide the tiny sense of apprehension. She was always like this on a new stretch of river or canal at home, but at least here they were in a bay and not the open sea.

As soon as she dipped her paddle in the water, her

muscles working in her back and shoulders, the tension eased and she looked up, squinting against the bright rays of the sun that bathed her face in warmth. High, bright clouds raced across the sky, wispy edges changing shape as they sailed above. The gentle breeze brought with it the taste of salt on her lips and the smell of briny freshness from the sea. She followed Conor, watching his quick, even strokes as they paddled away from the nearby quayside and all the little fishing boats bobbing at their moorings. The air was filled with the ringing and clinking of the metal halyards against the masts teased by the wind like it was conducting some invisible orchestra. Overhead, two irate seagulls bickered, squawking at each with loud indignation, their W-shaped wings flapping as they wheeled and dived at each other.

Once they left the shelter of the little beach, it took more effort to propel the little kayaks forward against the current which was pushing back towards the shore, but despite this it was good to feel familiar muscles contracting and stretching.

Conor slowed and waited for her to come alongside. 'We'll head over that way.' He pointed towards the far side of the bay, marked by an archway of stone just clinging to the supporting rock. It had clearly been worn away over the years, and there didn't look to be many more left from the appearance of the weathered pillar of darkened stones.

Conor, his eyes shielded by his hand, looked out across the bay, scanning as if he were looking for something. They paddled on and Hannah found her rhythm. She'd always loved being out on the water but this was something else, the rolling motion of the sea more hypnotic and beguiling with the ebb and flow of the waves around her. There was an immense feeling of space, unlike being enclosed by the banks of the river, but thankfully she was reassured by the fact that they were in a sheltered bay. The truth was that she preferred her adventure on the safer side.

A tiny bump, almost a nudge, startled her, making her grip her paddle tighter and pay a little more attention to the water instead of the scenery.

'Conor,' she called over, anxiously studying the water below the surface. 'Are there any rocks I should be aware of?'

'No.' He paused and turned to call over his shoulder. 'This is quite deep water.'

That didn't make her feel better.

'Right.' Maybe she'd imagined it and it was just a crosscurrent. Being in the sea was very different from a river or a canal. Actually, being on a canal in comparison was rather dull. To her surprise she was enjoying the exhilaration of the breeze dancing across her face, the dip and pull of the water, and the slide of the kayak through the waves. Her body felt more in tune with the natural motion, riding the swell, anticipating the cyclical up and down.

A seabird dived a few feet away, emerging with an empty beak and screeching before it turned sharply and took flight. She looked down into the water, wondering what sort of fish they had here, and caught sight of a flash of grey. A seal? She sat for a moment just watching and when she looked up, she realised a distance of about two hundred metres had opened up between her and Conor.

She squinted at him out of the corner of her eye, and spotted what looked like a dorsal fin, slowly gliding along parallel to her just a few metres away. As her head whipped round, the shape disappeared. She rested the paddle in front of her and clutched a hand to her rapidly rising chest. They didn't have sharks in Ireland, did they? She must have imagined it. Just the criss-cross of the waves and the current. A bit like those old black-and-white shadowy pictures of the Loch Ness monster.

Suddenly, without warning, there was an explosion of water about twenty-five metres away as a huge grey shape arced out of the water and landed ahead of her. The wash tossed the kayak up and down, as Hannah's heart leaped into her mouth and she gasped, sucking in so much air she almost choked, nearly dropping her paddle. What! Was! That? She gripped the paddle in both hands, terrified she might let go of it. If that happened she'd really be in trouble. Her pulse thudded as she fearfully twisted this way and that, looking all around her. Oh God, where was it? Now holding the paddle in front of her like a barrier, she frantically searched the water, her heart pounding so hard she thought her ears might explode. What was it and was it coming back?

Then she saw the unmistakable shape of a dorsal fin snaking through the water just behind Conor. A shark! It was a shark.

'Conor!' she managed in a hoarse scream as fear paralysed her muscles. She couldn't even lift her arm to point as she recoiled from the sides of the kayak. Oh God, that earlier bump. It could have turned the kayak over easily. The shoreline looked terrifyingly distant. Could the two of them fight off a shark? Perhaps if they doubled up to seem bigger? She tried to remember everything she'd ever known about sharks; it wasn't a lot. They could smell blood from miles away. They had a lot of teeth. Could you fight one off with a paddle? She gripped the handle in her gloved hands. Wasn't there some guy that had once punched a shark on the nose? An Australian surfer?

She'd seen *Jaws*. She could hear Roy Schneider's Chief Brody saying, 'We need a bigger boat.' It didn't get much smaller than a kayak. The fin had disappeared now. She closed her eyes. What if it were underneath them?

'C-Conor. We need to get out of here.'

He executed an elegant turn and slid toward her, a huge smile on his face. 'Did you see him?'

She stared at him. 'See him?'

'Fungie. The dolphin.'

'Dolphin?' she echoed stupidly. 'I thought it was a shark.'

Conor grinned with complete unconcern. 'Sharks don't leap out of the water like that.'

She slumped in her kayak, relief coursing through her. A ruddy dolphin. Of course it was.

'It's news to me that there are dolphins,' she snapped, irritated by his amusement. He seemed to think it was funny. As far as she was concerned while dolphins might have the reputation of being the lovable, cuddly animals of the sea, that didn't mean she wanted to get up close and personal with one. Especially not now she'd seen how big the flipping thing was. It could easily capsize her.

'Only one dolphin. Fungie.' Conor peered around them and suddenly pointed. 'There he is.'

She watched as the dolphin – yes she could see that now – jumped out of the water. Of course it was a dolphin because that was exactly what you expected to see in Ireland. Wasn't the country renowned for its prevalence of dolphins – not!

'Did you know it was here?' asked Hannah, her voice shrill with the hangover of terror.

'Yes.' Conor flashed her one of his trademark megawatt grins, the sort that had clearly, in its TV heyday, garnered fans in their droves but at the moment was intensely irritating when her heart was still trying to beat its way out of her chest. 'He's famous in these parts.'

'And you didn't think to warn me.' Her voice was so tight she could barely squeeze it out over her vocal cords.

'Sorry, I wanted it to be a surprise and I wasn't sure if we'd see him, although most of the boat tours guarantee your money back if you don't spot him.'

Hannah stared at him. 'You knew *that* was in the water.' It was a surprise all right and not a good one. Why on earth had he thought it would be? If she'd known, she wouldn't have stepped within twelve feet of a kayak, let alone immersed half of her body below the water line.

'He's a local celebrity. He's been in the bay for the last twenty years. They think he got separated from his pod and ended up staying here. It's very unusual for dolphins to be solitary but this one swam in one day and never left. Since then, he's been very friendly; he loves interacting with humans.'

'I'll take your word for it,' she said through pinched lips, giving him a baleful glare and looking longingly at the shore. 'Shall we go?'

'Trust me. If we wait a minute and we're lucky, he might put on a show for us. He loves playing with the boats, racing them and teasing the tourists playing hide and seek. It would be a shame to miss it.'

Hannah wasn't so sure about that. She'd far rather have seen him from the safety of a much bigger vessel, say a cruise liner, instead of the one she was currently paddling. She peered anxiously into the water on either side of her. 'What if he capsizes us?'

'I promise you, he's perfectly safe. He's never hurt anyone.'

'There's always a first time,' muttered Hannah as she gave the water another dubious scan. 'Do you think he's gone now?'

She could almost see Conor weighing up the pros and cons of his answer.

'He has gone, hasn't he?' There was a tinge of hysteria in her voice which she hated but which she allowed. Being out at sea with a huge, unpredictable, wild animal was as risky as it got. Her teeth began to chatter and her chin tucked down into her chest. She wanted to go back. Back to the cottage. Back to sit in front of the fire, safe and warm.

His face gentled with concern as he paddled alongside her. 'Hannah, honest to God, he's as safe as houses. I promise you I wouldn't have brought you otherwise. There's nothing to be frightened of.'

Nothing to be frightened of! Hannah shrieked inside her

head. *Apart from capsize them, what if he didn't like them? Dolphins had teeth, didn't they?*

Suddenly the dolphin surfaced right beside them and she jumped before going rigid with tension as the sleek, shiny body glided by, one intent eye watching her before the dolphin sank below the surface again. He was so close she could have reached out and touched him. She watched warily, grateful that Conor had brought his kayak alongside hers. Then, with a shower of water like an elaborate waterfall, Fungie burst high out of the water in a twisting jump, followed in quick succession by two more similar leaps. A moment later he jumped again, completing several flips, then diving below before resurfacing for a third time.

Fascinated in spite of her fear, Hannah marvelled at the strength in the supple body as it spun in the sunshine, its distinctive tailfin silhouetted by the sun. For the next few minutes, he put on quite a show, swimming and leaping in front of the kayaks at a safe distance as if he knew how precarious they were in the little boats.

'He knows we're here,' she said at last.

'Yes. It's difficult to believe, but he loves an audience.'

'And he's never capsized anyone?'

He leaned over again and touched her arm. 'Never. I swear on my mother's life. Granny Bridget's too.'

'Incredible,' she said as the dolphin resurfaced and executed another three leaps and then another two and another three. 'He's amazing.' She laughed as the spray drifted over them carried by the wind. It was impossible to believe that he was putting on such a display just for them and quite the most extraordinary thing she'd ever seen.

After a little while he disappeared and they waited for a moment to see if he'd emerge again.

'Show's over, I think,' said Conor. 'Will we head back? I don't know about you but I'm starting to get cold.'

They began to paddle back across the bay.

'That was… so special. I'll never forget that as long as I… oh! Look!' Next to the little red kayak, the dolphin rose, his beady eye meeting Hannah's for a heart-stopping moment, and then he flipped onto his back and began swimming alongside them, the wide mouth beneath the bottleneck nose grinning at her and its flippers in the air. She smiled in delight, her mouth so wide she could feel the tautness of the skin on her cheeks. 'Hello.' The dolphin disappeared, reappearing a second later almost as if he were escorting her. 'Aren't you gorgeous?' The silvery-grey skin, with water pouring off the surface, looked as smooth as glossed paintwork, the big unblinking eye trained on her. She was so fascinated she forgot to be afraid.

'I didn't even know there were dolphins in Ireland.'

'We get the occasional sighting. And by the way, there *are* sharks.'

'Conor Byrne, a dolphin I can accept but now I know you're pulling my leg.' She gave an anxious look into the water. 'Aren't you?'

At that moment the dolphin flipped back onto his front, circled in front of them and gave one final leap before skimming over the surface of the water towards a small boat heading out into the bay.

'Someone new to play with,' said Conor.

She watched as the dolphin disappeared from view. 'Do you think he's lonely?'

'Who knows, but he's certainly no wallflower, although I've not seen him swim alongside a kayak like that before.'

Hannah's smile held a tiny hint of self-satisfaction. She was imagining it, but she liked to think that Fungie had known she'd been scared at first and had come to reassure her.

What would her parents have thought of this adventure? Would it have been too tame for them? She wasn't sure she'd tell Aunt Miriam and Uncle Derek – at least not the full details; they'd be horrified.

Chapter Eighteen

When they gently beached the kayaks, Hannah tugged off the spray skirt she wore and wormed her way out of the fibreglass body, managing to step out of the boat without too much indignity. She yanked off her life vest and threw her arms around Conor, desperate to share the heady mix of gratitude, delight, and happiness that thrummed through her veins. 'Thank you. Thank you. Thank you.'

From the expression on his face, it was clear she'd startled him but he responded immediately, snaking an arm round her and pulling her as close as his vest would allow. After a moment she pulled back and they both stared at each other, sombre for once. Hannah wondered what he was thinking.

Flashing him a deliberately carefree smile, she said, 'This is wonderful. Being by the sea. It's such gorgeous day.' She threw her head back and let the wind tangle her hair. She looked back over the water, scanning the surface for one final glimpse of Fungie. For some reason she wanted to run along the beach with her arms outstretched and let the wind rush through her open fingers.

'You OK?' asked Conor, the corners of his mouth tilting up as if he were holding back a smile.

'Are you laughing at me?'

'No. You look… different. Happy.'

'I didn't realise I normally look miserable.'

'No'– he batted the suggestion away with an incredulous hand – 'you don't, but you're quite serious even when you're happy, if that makes sense. Today you look happy all the way through.'

She laughed. He'd summed it up perfectly. 'I feel happy all the way through. And something else,' she added, bubbling with inexplicable enthusiasm. 'I feel brilliant.' How could she describe it? Illuminated from inside, like someone had switched on a light except she hadn't known it was dark. Energised. It was as if her batteries had been recharged when she hadn't known they'd needed recharging. The feelings both confused and elated her. For no reason, other than because she could, she sprang forward and turned a clumsy cartwheel on the short tussocky grass next to the shingle beach.

'Inspired by Fungie?'

'Something like that,' she replied, not really understanding herself.

'Fancy some lunch? It's a bit late but they'll still be serving at The Fish Box.'

'Yes.' Hannah realised she was absolutely ravenous.

'It's the sea air.'

And something else, she realised, aware that all her senses seemed to be tuned to everything around her.

Hannah discovered, as they ate lunch in The Fish Box – a gorgeously quaint family run restaurant – that there were indeed sharks in Ireland.

'There are indeed,' said the waitress cheerfully in answer to Hannah's innocent question, 'Are there sharks round here?'

'They're mainly basking sharks – totally harmless. They just eat the plankton. They look a little scary but that's all.' She placed their orders in front of them and Conor gave her a told-you-so grin, his eyes twinkling as he broke off to scoop up a forkful of his crispy chilli monkfish, which looked amazing.

He groaned. 'Mmm, that is good. Thanks, Eimear.'

'We're honoured to have the famous Conor Byrne patronising our humble restaurant.'

'Go away with you.' He turned to Hannah. 'Deidre could cook rings round me.'

'Give my best to your ma. I must away. See you later.' She bustled away with a word here and a word there to the customers sitting at the other tables.

'Here, you must try this.' Conor held up a forkful of the monkfish.

'Wow, that's got a kick.' she said as the hit of chilli reached the back of her throat. 'But it's delicious.'

He leaned forward and wiped a tiny piece of fish from the corner of her mouth, his hand pausing to gently rub under her lip. The touch reignited the simmering warmth dancing in the pit of her stomach and she couldn't help herself touching his salty skin with the tip of her tongue.

He shot her a lopsided, knowing smile, devilment flashing in his blue eyes. This blatant flirtation reminded her of the night they'd first met and a little frisson ran through her. Something had changed between them and they both knew it, even if neither of them had acknowledged it out loud.

With its simple wooden tables and metal chairs, plastic squeezy bottles of tomato ketchup and little glass bottles of malt vinegar and containers of cutlery, The Fish Box might not have offered elegant dining but it made up for it with simple, genuine friendliness and homeliness. There were lots of rosy-cheeked people tucking into huge portions with evident enjoyment while others sat, slightly windblown, with happy faces full of expectation.

As well they might; the menu looked amazing. Hannah had been spoiled for choice before finally opting for a prawn, honey, and chilli stir fry which smelled heavenly. The first bite of juicy prawn and the hot, sweet sauce confirmed that the dish tasted every bit as good as it looked and had her issuing a heartfelt groan of enjoyment. 'That is *so* good.'

'You don't get better fish than here. It's a family concern

– the Flannerys. Patrick, one of the brothers, skippers the family boat, the *Cú Na Mara* and they catch the fish. It comes fresh to the table. They can tell you when it was caught, where it was caught, and even who caught it!'

'Wow, that is impressive.'

'They use locally sourced ingredients and use compostable packaging and even bring sea litter home with them. Deirdre Flannery does all the cooking while her husband and brother-in-law prepare all the fish. Eimear is their daughter and their son runs the place.'

'How brilliant,' said Hannah, looking around the small, packed restaurant. 'Thank you for bringing me here today.'

'Even though I didn't tell you about the big, scary dolphin?'

She scrunched her mouth up. She'd been thinking about that ever since they'd beached the kayaks, buoyed by the thrill of seeing the dolphin at such close quarters in its natural environment. Those twists of its body as it flew through the air, the dynamic movement… It was a rare privilege and one that she'd have missed if she'd known. Shame nipped at her.

'You do know that if you'd told me, I wouldn't have gone in.'

'I wasn't sure. And then when you said you didn't like surprises, I really wasn't sure. I was hoping you'd come round although I thought at first I'd made a terrible mistake.'

'Well, hello. Excuse me for being a little frightened when a huge great fish jumped out of the water! It's not exactly what I was expecting.'

'Sorry.' His sheepish grin as he reached across the table to take her hand made it clear he wasn't that sorry and, if she was honest, he had no need to be.

'You don't need to apologise. Well, maybe a little, as I was flipping terrified at first but now... oh my goodness, how could I have ever missed it? That's something people dream of but never get to experience. He was right there in front of us, communicating with us. And I'd have missed that.'

She'd missed a lot, she realised. A memory slid back. A swimming pool on a campsite in France. It had been the first day of their holiday, a gorgeous sunshine-filled morning that had them all hurrying to the poolside. Mina, impulsive as ever, had immediately made a running jump into the pool, curling up into a ball as she hit the water with an almighty splosh. Her aunt had let out a worried moan before saying, 'It might be deep. You don't know. So dangerous. Oh she's just like— Please be careful, Hannah.' So Hannah had walked around to the shallow end and waded in slowly, rather than jumping in after Mina like her initial instinct. It had set the pattern. Being cautious. Not wanting to upset her aunt. Not wanting to be just like her mother.

'Penny for them.' Conor's warm hand squeezed hers. She liked the feel of it, almost like an anchoring bringing her back but not weighing her down.

'Just pondering on what makes us who we are.'

'Heavy stuff.'

'Sorry. I'm embarrassed to admit that I'm a coward. I really wouldn't have gone in the water if I'd known about

Fungie or the sharks. I'd have been too busy thinking of the potential dangers, what could go wrong.'

'Some might say that's sensible. Not cowardly.'

'Yes but sometimes you can be too sensible. Sometimes you have to take a risk. Do things even though there might be danger because otherwise you miss out on so much.' Now she thought about it, that swimming pool incident had rankled. She could still remember imagining the sensation of flying through the air and breaking the surface of the water with a splash, even though it had never happened. She remembered Mina bobbing up, triumph all over her face, her blonde hair slicked down her cheeks, grinning with delight. Mina, who'd taken a risk staying in Switzerland and ended up meeting Luke.

'I agree. I risked a lot striking out on my own. I had a ball. Got to see New York, LA, led the life of Riley and even though I crashed and burned, I don't regret it. I needed to do all that to find out what it was I really wanted.'

'You don't miss it all?'

'No. I enjoy my cooking far more now without the pressure for perfection, but I also enjoy other things and realising I'm good at other things. In our family, cooking has been the be all and end all of everything. Fergus gets away with it because he's the baby of the family, but there was a lot of pressure on Mairead, Sinead, and me to carry the family badge of honour. To be the next generation of the Byrne cooks.'

'Have you ever said anything... to your mother?'

Conor raised a telling eyebrow.

'Why not?'

He deliberately looked over her head out of the window, his eyes narrowing.

'Because she lives and breathes the place. What would have been the point? She's disappointed enough that I've given it all up. I was the shining star, the one with the Michelin-starred restaurant in Dublin. A brilliant ambassador for Slow Food and everything she believes in. The TV show that attracted millions of viewers in the US and in Ireland. And then I split up from the next big hope, who Ma was grooming for greatness.'

'I'm sure she's not disappointed in you.' Hannah frowned. 'Why did you come back if you think that?'

'It was by choice, originally. I only came home because Franklin, my granda, had a turn – he did all the maintenance originally. I used to follow him around when I was a kid; he gave me my own tool belt when I was six. I knew if he gave up working completely, he'd fade away, but he's too old to do everything on his own so I became his partner, and the more I did, the more I enjoyed.'

'Still keeping it in the family, then.'

'I guess I've always been closer to my grandfolk than my parents. They were the ones that brought us up. Don't get me wrong, I'm fierce proud of what Ma has achieved. She's an amazing woman.'

'She is.' They both took another bite of food as if to fill the reflective silence that had fallen between them.

Hannah could see that the farm and the cookery school were a testament to hard work, dedication, and real vision.

A little bit like the place they were in. Family. Tradition. Authenticity. There was a lot to be said for it. She envied Conor his family background and that sense of generations working together to build something so concrete. She realised with a painful pang, that she really missed her sister.

Sensing that Conor wasn't about to be drawn any further about his mother, she changed the subject. 'My sister would love it here,' she gestured at the restaurant, 'and at the farm. Mina's a real foodie.' During the rest of lunch, Hannah told Conor all about her sister's venture in Switzerland and about the cakes she regularly pictured in their WhatsApp chats.

'She's the adventurous one.'

'And you don't think you are? Coming out to try something brand new in a different country sounds just as adventurous to me. Perhaps you're more like your sister than you realise.'

'No way,' said Hannah automatically, but for the first time she began to wonder. She was the one who had chosen to do a brand-new subject at university, whereas Mina had focused her career on her interests. Doing Law had been a complete leap into the unknown and everyone at work was always slightly surprised to hear that she was a member of a canoe club.

After lunch, they wandered along the narrow streets filled with a mix of touristy and local wares. Hannah relaxed, feeling unusually content as they wandered past pretty painted buildings in an array of colours from rich, deep teal through to dusky red, brilliant blue, and bright yellow. There was wholesomeness about the place, as if the little town was happy to be what it was – both a tourist mecca and a place for locals. There were shops offering a huge selection of Irish wool jumpers mixed among a Spar, a local pharmacy, betting, leather, music and record shops, and sandwiched between each one, it seemed there was another yet another pub, even one that combined drinking with a hardware shop and bicycle hire.

'Come on, I'll take you to Dick Mack's; they have a fine selection of whiskey. We'll take a dram and continue your education in the hard stuff.'

England Hannah would have demurred or at least raised a protest. Drinking in the afternoon! But at that moment, she realised with a faint sense of triumph, she couldn't think of anything nicer. She couldn't remember the last time she'd felt so much at ease with someone – well at ease in some ways. Her body was as taut as harp strings, playing a melody of excitement every time Conor brushed against her amongst the crowds.

Walking into Dick Mack's was a little like stepping back in time and everything a proper Irish pub should be. This wasn't some plasticky tourist copy – this was the real deal. Quaint, battered, and unorthodox. No one else in the pub seemed to bat an eyelid at the cobbler's bench on the left-hand side of the room, where a tall man was making belts, busy punching holes in the leather, while opposite, a traditional bar ran the length of the wall filled top to bottom with dozens and dozens of different whiskeys. Around the walls were shelves, cubby holes, and glass-fronted cabinets filled with everything from books to boots, shoe laces to paintings, and old boxes to wellingtons. A long bench with stools on either side took up most of the centre of the room, while up against the bar, rush-topped high stools were squeezed into the remaining space. On either end of the bar were tiny snugs, almost like confessional boxes with small windows opening onto the bar.

'This is interesting,' said Hannah, watching the man working on the leather belt.

'It's been a bar and cobblers since it opened in 1899 and it's now run by Finn,' he nodded towards a young man, serving behind the bar. 'He's the great-grandson of Tom MacDonnell. The place has been in the family for four generations.'

'Does anyone ever leave Dingle?' she asked, curious rather than critical. How wonderful to belong so steadfastly somewhere.

'Some, but they often come back, and why wouldn't you?' His eyes twinkled. 'It's God's own country.'

She laughed. 'I hate to tell you but I've heard that said about Yorkshire, America, New Zealand, Australia, and Kerala in India.'

'There's still nowhere I'd rather live. Dingle is full of expats and blow-ins from Cork and Dublin, not to mention folks from as far away as Germany and the US. After all, it's twinned with Santa Barbara in California.' He sighed with satisfaction. 'It's good to be home.'

Hannah went quiet for a moment. Could she live in a place like this? She'd never lived anywhere but Manchester. Never even thought about it. Even when her boyfriend, Mike, had moved to London and asked her to go too, she'd never really considered it. Their relationship might have survived, but she'd been too scared to make the jump. To step out of the comfort zone that had cocooned her all her life. Had she shut down possibilities in life? Look at what had happened when she'd actually taken that step. She'd slept with Conor, kayaked with a dolphin and she was learning to cook. Just thinking about these things lit her up inside. This was living. For so long she'd been existing, which had been OK but it had been a black and white sort of life. Whereas now she was living in technicolour with sunshine pouring into corners that she'd left unexplored for most of her life.

'What do you fancy?' asked Conor.

'What do you recommend?' she asked boldly, deciding to live dangerously.

'I think a shot of whiskey is called for, although they do have a microbrewery here and they make an excellent coffee stout.'

'Hey, Conor.' Finn leaned over and shook his hand. 'Good to see you.'

'And you. I hear the brewery's taking off.'

'Yes but we're keeping it local. If people want to taste it they have to get themselves along to Dingle. What'll you be having?'

Conor turned to her, quirking his eyebrow in question.

She scanned the shelves, with the plethora of bottles in every shape and size, and the beer handles on the bar. 'I'll have that one,' she said pointing to the nearest handle.

'Ah good choice. A half or a pint?'

'A pint,' she said firmly as Conor looked at her in surprise.

'Good choice. What made you decide on that?'

'They don't have it anywhere else – it's local. Your mother's rubbing off on me.' She pointed to the sign on the handle. *Dick Mack's coffee stout.*

He rolled his eyes but then he said, 'I'll have the same.'

The barman poured the two drinks and they took them through to another small room with battered wooden benches and scarred tables that suggested a lifetime of being used by generations of drinkers. She wondered at all the people that had sat in this very spot over the years.

She loved that all these people knew Conor, not because he was famous but because he was part of the community. At home, the man in the flat upstairs was called Alastair. He'd once called to borrow some milk, although, never again when he'd discovered she was as hopeless as he was and didn't have any. There was a couple across the hallway who worked even crazier hours than she did. She was pretty sure the woman was called Claire, but only because the man had called out her name impatiently in the echoey corridor a couple of times. Not a lot to show for living there for four years.

She took a sip of the thick, dark creamy beer, both hands holding the unfamiliar pint glass.

'That's very good.'

'Some say it's better than Guinness. They brew it out the back. You should do a brewery tour while you're here sometime.'

She smiled, remembering that Aidan had suggested the very thing and she'd discounted it out of hand at the time.

'I might just do that,' she said, surprising herself. Normally, she'd decline out of habit, without even thinking about it. After all, what did she know about beer? She laughed at herself; she'd know more if she did the tour.

'And I still want to go back to Dublin. I didn't see everything I wanted to.'

'Actually, I've to go to Dublin to sign some papers. You could come with me, if you fancied it. I'll play tourist for the weekend.'

'That would great, if you didn't mind.'

'I wouldn't mind.' He gave her a considering look, as if he'd surprised himself.

There was a brief silence, not quite awkward but Hannah felt the need to fill it. 'I love this place. I can imagine people have been sitting here at this time for years.'

'Some of them literally did. You had to be careful you didn't sit in someone's spot. I remember old Father O'Malley had his own beer glass.'

'The priest?'

'Oh, yes. He liked a pint after Mass. He always said it was a good way of keeping an eye on his flock. I think it was a reminder to folk of his presence and that they should be in church the next Sunday. He was a canny aul soul. The new fella's not quite the same. He's a bit smarter and he has his hair cut more than once a year.'

'The other guy sounds a bit like the old guy from *Father Ted*.'

Conor laughed and took a swallow of beer. 'Father Jack.

Not quite that mad but he was a character and he had a good understanding of human failings. The new fella is a bit too clean and shiny – makes me feel like I've been caught with my hand in the cookie jar.'

She lifted one eyebrow, thinking of the pictures of him with numerous women.

'I've not led a blameless life and I might not go to confession anymore but I hope I do right by people. The newspapers exaggerate.'

'I know that.' Her face crumpled. 'My poor sister ended up in a national newspaper after she went viral on social media.'

'What did she do?'

'Unfortunately, she made a rather public proposal to her boyfriend, who'd got cold feet about their relationship and hadn't bothered to tell her. Or that he was shagging her best mate. A *friend* recorded it and posted it on Facebook – it went everywhere.'

'Some friend.'

'To be fair, it was a mistake. They thought they were posting it privately, didn't realise their settings weren't right and a friend of a friend shared it and' – she lifted her shoulders in a resigned shrug – 'once it's out there, there's no stopping it. Anyway, the newspapers made a right old meal of it, painting her as some manipulative bridezilla who was determined to bag her man, even though in actual fact, he was the one that had discussed the church they'd marry in and what their kids would be called.'

'Ouch. Poor thing.'

'It made me so mad because it just wasn't true! And

there was nothing we could do about it.' She clenched her hand on the table; the frustration still rankled. 'Luckily Mina had left the country by then, so she was oblivious.'

'So you do know then what the papers are like.' He sighed and took a long swallow of his pint before he spoke again, his forehead creased in disgruntled lines. 'I'd be at some do talking to some woman – you know, party talk – "Oh I love your show"', he spoke in a high-pitched American accent, 'And I'd do the polite, "Thank you, that's very kind of you. What do you do?"'

She burst out laughing. 'Conor Byrne, I'm sure you were a lot flirtier than that. I've seen you in action, don't forget.'

He gave her a sheepish grin. 'OK, I might have played along a little but I'd only have to speak to someone and the next thing, the papers were printing that we were having it away with each other. If I'd slept with half the women I'm supposed to have done, I'd be a broken man.'

She giggled. 'I'm sure you would have risen to the challenge.'

'Well, I always do my best.' He winked and she felt the quick stain of a blush rush up her neck and across her chest as her heart did one of those funny loop-the-loop things.

She took a strategic sip of her drink, hoping he hadn't noticed – she really was doing her best to come across as completely cool about things.

'I never said I was an angel.' As he said it, his mouth tipped up in a twisted, devilish smile. She tried to give him a disapproving look but failed miserably and instead huffed out a sigh of resignation. How could she condemn him when she found him irresistible? And nothing was quite such a turn on as someone making it clear that they wanted you too. Conor's direct gaze turned her inside out and when he began to rub his thumb over the soft skin of her inner wrist with slow insistent strokes, she wanted to cross her legs. Each pass over her skin seemed to send a signal direct to her rapidly overheating core.

'Would you like another drink?' The husky question seemed to vibrate through her.

'No,' she said, with a touch of desperation that brought a satisfied nod.

They both knew where things were headed and Hannah had reached a point where she didn't see the need for any further delay. She was the sort of person that, once she'd decided on a course of action, she'd see it through. She might dither before coming to the decision, but once made she was a woman of her convictions. She wanted to sleep with Conor and she couldn't for the life of her think why on earth she'd been fighting it.

As soon as they left the pub, Conor curled his hand into hers as they half ran and half walked back to the Land Rover. As he unlocked the doors, he snagged her hand and pulled her back towards him for fierce, quick kiss.

'Conor,' she laughed up at him, feeling a heady punch of power. He wanted her as much as she wanted him. 'At this rate we'll never get back.'

'True,' he said and with another one of those naughty

smiles, bundled her up into her seat and slammed the door before hurrying around to the driver's seat.

He drove with one hand on her leg, as if he had to keep touching her.

'Are you sure about this?' he asked in a low voice.

'Yes.' Hannah swallowed. 'I'm sure. Are you?'

'Oh yes. I just wanted to give you a chance to change your mind, if you wanted to.'

'I'm not going to change my mind,' she murmured, as his fingers massaged her inner thigh.

'Just don't want things to go off the boil on the way home,' he teased, in a low, throaty voice.

'You are a chef. I'm sure you're quite adept at keeping things simmering.'

'Oh, I am,' he agreed, his hand inching a little higher.

'Don't you think you should concentrate on the road?' she squeaked.

'Where's the fun in that?'

'Staying alive is always good.'

'Spoilsport.' He gave her thigh a squeeze and put his hand back on the steering wheel but not before giving her a look that promised so much more later.

She caught her lip between her teeth, trying to think of an opening conversational gambit but all her senses were humming and she felt too lethargic to try and break the thick atmosphere. Instead, she leaned back against the headrest and closed her eyes, enjoying the feelings buzzing through her body.

When they approached the turning for Killorgally, Conor

wheeled the car up the gravelled track and slammed on the brakes as soon as they hit the car park. He looked at her from the driver's seat, a question in his eyes. She nodded and they both almost hurled themselves out of their respective seats. He caught her hand and they dashed down towards the cottage. Anticipation hummed like an electrical charge between them. In fact, Hannah almost expected sparks to arc and jump where their hands touched. Her breasts felt heavy and between her legs there was a sweet ache; she'd never felt so revved up and desperate in her life. She squeezed Conor's hand and he squeezed back. They exchanged mischievous grins. Hannah loved this. Loved being so open. Nothing shameful or hidden.

He leaned in, dropping her hand to cup her ear and whispered, his words sending a zing of heat straight to the sweet spot. 'God, I want you, Hannah Campbell.'

'I want you too.' She spoke with a natural sultriness she hadn't known she was capable of. She relished this feeling of being all woman. With other men she'd always let them take the lead. Now that Conor had declared his desire for her, it gave her the confidence to be bold. She might not be like those other women but right now and right here he wanted *her*. And it might not lead anywhere but she was done worrying about that. She'd spent too much of her life worrying about the unknown and the unexpected. Today had shown how wonderful the unknown and unexpected could be.

The cottage came into view and they both slowed a little as if now with their goal in view they could afford to take their time.

'Hannah! Conor!' Meredith stepped out in front of them

from the orchard next to the path, followed by Alan. Her face was lit by a lovely, contented smile and she was wearing the cherry-red cardigan that she'd talked about. 'Isn't it a lovely day? We've been to Killarney. What a lovely little town. Do you know it, Conor?'

He nodded dumbly.

'Alan drove me there and we had the most wonderful lunch on the coast. Honestly, Hannah, you should take a drive out that way. It really is glorious, isn't it, Alan?'

He stepped forward. 'It really is. I've not been out this way before but it's such a gorgeous spot. Although you wouldn't want to get stuck behind one of those buses.'

'No,' agreed Conor, succinctly.

'And the views are just spectacular. We had to stop the car a couple of times. It's just breath-taking. I was glad I wasn't driving.' Meredith beamed at Alan. 'Thank goodness you're such a good driver, otherwise I think I might get a little nervous on some of those narrow roads.'

Hannah was tempted for a second to pipe up with, 'Boreens', but thought better of it. She could see Conor shifting from foot to foot with the same frustrated agitation that was killing her.

'And where've you been today? Exploring? Conor showing you the sights?' Meredith's gaze became a little calculating. 'Where did he take you?'

Hannah and Conor exchanged a quick, guilty glance, which was ridiculous because they had nothing to feel guilty about. Well, not yet.

'We've been to Dingle, kayaking.'

'Kayaking. Now that's something I've not tried.' She

glanced down at her stomach. 'Not sure I'd squeeze into the little hole.'

Alan gave an exasperated snort. 'Woman, I tell ye. You're grand as you are.' He turned to Conor. 'There's no arguing with the ladies though, is there?'

Conor nodded.

Meredith laughed. 'Did you enjoy it, Hannah? Very adventurous of you. Gorgeous day for it.'

Hannah was horribly conscious that if she didn't respond to Meredith's tumble of good-natured conversation, she'd appear rude; she genuinely liked the woman and didn't want to cause offence.

'I've done it before but the sea was beautiful.' She glanced at Conor. There was a very faint trace of wariness on his face as if he were daring her to mention the dolphin, which would inevitably prolong the conversation. 'But also quite cold. I'm dying for a nice hot bath to warm me up.'

'Oh, don't let us hold you up.' Meredith's warm, understanding response made Hannah bite her lip. 'You go on. Get warmed up. No doubt we'll see you later. Are you coming to the pub tonight? They've got some more live music on. It'll be quite the *craic*.' She turned to Alan, pleased with herself. 'Did I say it right?'

'You did. The *craic* will be mighty. You're almost starting to sound like a local,' he teased.

'Right, well. We'd best be off,' said Conor, already starting to edge forward.

'Yes, sorry. You go. We'll see you later. Shall we knock for you, Hannah?'

'Er…' she flailed for a moment.

'Come on, leave the poor girl alone,' said Alan, taking hold of her arm.

'Well, Conor, if you feel like coming, don't be a stranger,' said Meredith over her shoulder as Alan finally steered her away.

'Bye,' called Conor, his lips pressed together and his cheeks dimpling as he tried his best to hold the laughter at bay.

'Bye, dear.'

They waited a moment as Alan bore her away before a snort escaped from Conor. Hannah began to giggle.

'Come on,' Conor grabbed her arm. 'Before anyone else appears and wants a blow-by-blow account of the day's activities.'

'She was only being friendly,' said Hannah, with another explosive giggle.

'I know but my balls are turning bluer by the second.'

'Conor!' she said primly, but her dancing eyes gave her away.

'Don't you *Conor* me.' He grabbed her hand and they began to run.

She grinned unrepentantly at him as they raced towards the cottage.

As soon as the door closed behind them, Conor peeled off his jumper in one fluid movement and threw it to the floor, kicking off his shoes at the same time as Hannah ripped off her fleece and then their mouths fused together for what felt like a long overdue kiss. They kissed as they stripped, Conor walking backwards up the stairs, simultaneously unclipping her bra. Every brain cell was shouting *hurry, hurry* as together they stumbled up to her bedroom. They fell onto the bed, rolling over, kissing and giggling as they struggled to remove the last of their clothing. Conor's hands were already racing over her body and all coherent thought left her brain when, finally, they lay skin to skin on the fine cotton sheets, breathless with anticipation and desire.

Chapter Nineteen

'I f Meredith could see you now,' teased Conor, tugging at the sheet draped around Hannah as she sat propped against the pillows in the big king-size bed, with the sun streaming in through the dormer window.

'Oh God, what time is it? I need to text her.'

'You don't want to go to the pub then?' Conor asked with an overly suggestive raise of his eyebrows.

'What do you think?' she retorted, stretching lazily like a cat in the sunshine. She didn't want to spoil the euphoric post-coital mood by having to get dressed and make sensible conversation with people. She could stay here forever, lounging in the pool of sunlight with Conor next to her, both of them relaxed and comfortable in their own skin. He was so beautiful to look at, so at ease with his nudity that she didn't feel the need to cover up either. Conor was delightfully confident and sure of himself. It seemed to give her added confidence, enabling her to follow suit.

'Shall I tell you a little fantasy I've been harbouring?' he whispered in her ear, his hand splaying across her hip.

'What's that?'

'You know my fancy shower? I've been thinking about getting you naked in there.'

'Have you now?' she purred, enjoying playing the femme fatale.

'I have.' He leaned in and touched her shoulder with his lips, trailing hot kisses along her collar bone. 'I've got you naked; now I just need to get you into the shower.'

'And how do you propose to do that?'

He paused for a moment, one finger idly stroking the dip between her collar bone and neck, pretending to give it some thought. 'Well, there's enticement and bribery. I could cook you a nice meal and light a fire.'

'That's a thought,' she replied softly.

'Or…' his eyes darkened and her heart missed a beat at the sultry promise in them. 'I could…'

There was another pause as he stared into her eyes. Then suddenly he leaped out of bed, grabbed her waist, and hauled her over his shoulder. 'I could give you a fireman's lift.'

'Conor Byrne!' she shrieked, beating him on the back and giggling. 'Put me down!'

'You don't really want me to.'

The truth was, she didn't. She was enjoying this light-hearted, playful irreverence. It meant that they weren't taking things too seriously which suited her fine because she wouldn't know what to do with serious. That would be delving into a murky pool that she hadn't signed up for.

In the bathroom he changed tack, gently letting her slide down his front inch by inch. When her feet touched the ground, she hooked her arms around his neck and kissed him on the mouth, a long, deep kiss designed to stir him up as much as he'd stirred her up. Although they'd only just made love, she still couldn't get enough of him. She let one hand glide down his back to cup one firm buttock, pressing him close to her, grinding him against her.

Conor groaned and lifted a hand to caress her breast, his fingers teasing her nipple, eliciting a tense gasp and moan from Hannah. She'd never felt so uninhibited with a man; it was a revelation because it gave her power to explore and to take charge, to demand and to tease.

When they emerged from the shower, they were both still laughing.

'Those tiles were cold,' complained Hannah. 'I'm not sure shower sex is quite what it's cracked up to be in the movies.'

'It was all right from where I was,' he joked with a wink. 'Although you were heavier than I expected.'

'Conor!' She squealed in mock horror.

'Just joking.' He grabbed the front of her towel and pulled her in for a kiss, adding afterwards, 'You're perfect as you are, especially that peachy butt.' His hands slid down to pat her towel-clad bottom. 'And when you wrap those long legs around me...'

'Behave.'

'Why?' His lips twitched and she couldn't think of a suitable answer.

They dressed in lazy, slouchy casual clothes, both in

agreement that they weren't going to the pub this evening. Hannah texted Meredith to ensure that they didn't get any unexpected interruptions. Conor left her to go downstairs and she picked up her hairbrush to tug it through her damp curls.

She frowned as she looked down at the dressing table. The hairbrush was in the wrong place; it was supposed to be next to her detangle hair spray which was next to her tangle teaser comb and next to which was a pile of scrunchies. Mina teased her about being a fusspot which wasn't the case at all but Hannah had a system. It was a standing joke that she could get ready in the morning blindfolded because everything was in its place. She looked around the room, her mouth drying. Had her laptop been moved? She couldn't be sure. Glancing back at the dressing table and her hairbrush, she bit her lip, trying to tell herself she was being paranoid. Goosebumps rose on her forearms. Someone had been in here since they'd left this morning, she was absolutely sure of it.

'Conor,' she called as she lightly ran down the stairs.

'Yes.'

'Someone's been here.'

'What do you mean?'

'Someone's moved my things around.'

'Are you sure?'

'Yes. No, well...' She couldn't be one hundred percent sure. This morning she'd been thinking more about spending the day with Conor than anything else. Maybe she had ignored her usual routine.

Conor put down the bottle he'd just opened and strode

into the lounge, then he went up to his room before coming down to say. 'Nothing's missing and I can't see anything out of place in my room.'

Hannah felt like an idiot but she couldn't rid herself of that creepy gut-instinct feeling. Someone *had* been in her room.

Rather than come back into the kitchen, Conor opened the cottage door and went outside. A moment later he returned, grim-faced.

'Well, someone's been back. There are fresh footprints in the flowerbeds. And I...' he paused, 'I'm sorry, I didn't lock the cottage door when we left. Force of habit. Normally we leave the doors open during the day.'

Hannah nodded immediately and rather ironically felt reassured. At least she wasn't imagining things.

'I'm sorry, Hannah. This shouldn't have happened. In future, I'll make sure the door's locked and if you're here on your own, you must lock the door behind you. I'll tell the staff to make sure everyone keeps an eye out for any strangers and I'm going to get Seamus and Peter to do some regular patrols. This isn't on. We just don't have that sort of trouble out here normally. I don't like it all. I'm calling the guard as well.'

'OK.'

He widened his eyes. 'That's it. OK.'

'OK. I'm a little freaked but I'm trying my best to be cool about it and not turn into a damsel-in-distress who actually needs a hug.'

'Hugs, I can do. Come here.' He wrapped his arms

around her. 'You're still amazingly calm. I can't imagine any other woman taking things this much in her stride.'

She shrugged, desperately trying to be logical and sensible. 'There's no point having hysterics. The horse, or whoever it was, has bolted. I'm creeped out that they were here but they've gone now and it's not like they've left a threat or stolen anything. They came in because they could. Might be kids or something. And like you say, I've got you here.'

'God job I did karate in my youth.'

'Did you?'

'For three weeks,' he admitted before adding more sombrely, 'But Seamus and Peter won't take any nonsense. They might look on the small side but you wouldn't want to cross them.'

She managed a quick laugh, even though she didn't feel like it. The thought of someone being in her bedroom made her feel a bit sick. Having Conor here definitely made her feel better. 'We'll keep the door locked then.'

'You really are amazing,' he said, walking forward and planting a kiss on her forehead. A warm glow spread inside her. She liked being amazing. He didn't need to know she didn't feel amazing inside.

'Would you mind doing the honours?' He nodded towards an open bottle on the kitchen table as he began to slice onions with his usual deft skill. She poured the velvety plum-coloured wine into two large fine glass goblets, admiring their elegant balloons. She'd never been fussy about glasses before but now, being with Conor, she thought he might have spoiled her for ever. Somehow the enjoyment of the wine was so much more in a nice glass.

'Why is that?' she mused holding up the glass to the light.

'Why is what?' Conor glanced up quickly.

'Wine tastes better in proper glasses.'

'It's about being kind to yourself,' he said, laying down his knife and picking up the second glass and chinking it against hers very gently. 'Taking pleasure from those things is a way of celebrating the small things. It's like taking time to cook a proper meal and using the best ingredients. People are prepared to spend a fortune on clothes, make-up, grooming products and yet they stuff all sorts of crap into their bodies.' He lifted his shoulders. 'It doesn't make sense to me.'

'I'd never thought about it before. Not before I came here.' Food had always been fuel to her. A means to an end and, quite frankly, the quicker to prepare the better.

'What's on the menu this evening?'

'A good old-fashioned Irish stew.'

She nodded, slightly surprised and a tiny bit disappointed that he was cooking something that didn't sound that exciting and almost laughed at herself. Clearly she was getting too used to the good life. Once upon a time, someone else cooking for her would have been enough of a treat. But an Irish stew was probably just the thing, as it looked as if the clouds were gathering.

Almost as if he'd read her mind he said, 'There's a storm coming in.'

'There is?' She peered out of the window and saw that the sky had blackened, vanquishing the day's earlier sunshine. That would put off any peeping Toms for the night, but even so she scanned all the areas outside before pulling the curtains. 'Gosh, it's changed quickly. We were lucky with the weather today.' That explained why he'd lit the fire in here, she thought, settling into the little sofa and curling her feet around her, clutching the wide glass with both hands. The fire cast a warming golden glow as the flames coiled and curled in the glass window of the four-legged wood-burner. 'Do you need any help?'

'No, it's an easy dish – the secret is in the cooking.' He turned, his mouth twitching. 'Long and slow.'

She rolled her eyes. 'I presume you're talking about the cooking technique.'

'Of course. It's going to take a while. But I'm sure you like a slow build-up.'

'Conor Byrne, are you being filthy?'

'Not yet.' He shot her that irresistible lopsided smile.

She sipped at her wine, concentrating hard as she tried to analyse the flavour – again, something she wouldn't have done a few weeks ago. Black cherries. Leather? No that couldn't be right.

Conor came over and tapped at the frown lines wrinkling her forehead. 'What's wrong?'

She sniffed at the glass. 'Leather?'

'Yes. That's right. Definite aroma of leather.'

'Really?'

'Really.' He kissed her nose, as if in reward for her obvious delight. 'It's a Barolo from Italy. I get black tea and tobacco as well.'

'Now you're just showing off.'

'Of course.' He went back to the counter and she heard the sizzle of onions. With a sigh she settled back into the sofa, feeling the glow of her slightly windburned cheeks. It had been a lovely day and, she realised with a quick smile, she felt a little buzzed (OK, a lot) from the fantastic sex. The highlights kept popping into her mind and she hugged herself with smug satisfaction. Conor certainly knew what he was doing but he'd also expressed his appreciation in no uncertain terms. She could still hear his groans echoing in her head.

'What are you looking so pleased about?' asked Conor with a teasing lift of one eyebrow.

'Wouldn't you like to know,' she said softly with a quick grin.

'That's going to take a couple of hours,' said Conor, shutting the oven door. 'What do you want to do?'

'Weeell…' she replied slowly.

'God have mercy on me. You've worn me out.'

She laughed. 'I quite fancy standing here, watching you…' she paused suggestively, '… cook.'

'The stew's going to take a while. I thought we could go next door. Light a fire. Make out.'

'Make out? Isn't that for teenagers? Besides, you ought to rest. Build up your strength for later.'

'Later! Hannah Campbell.'

She bit her lip, pleased and surprised by her uncharacteristic boldness. Ireland Hannah was back and she was rather enjoying herself. Although she couldn't quite forget that at some point she was going home and would be England Hannah again.

'Conor?'

'Yes?' He turned at the question in her voice.

'This,' she waved a hand, suddenly shy. She really wasn't that sexually experienced.

'This?' he teased, and she blushed.

'Well, you know.'

'I do.' He came forwards and kissed her on the lips, sitting down next to her on the sofa.

She searched for the words. 'I… I get that it's temporary. I mean, I'll be going home soon and, well, I know you said you didn't get involved with guests…'

He pulled a face. 'Yeah?'

Taking a deep breath, she plunged in. 'Well, I'm… I'm not expecting anything from you. I know it's just a fling thing.'

'Fling things can be a lot of fun,' he said, leaning in and kissing her again. 'We can have a lot of fun in a few weeks.'

He put an arm around her and pulled her closer. 'And this is why I put a sofa in the kitchen. Of course the official reason is that it always seems a sin to rush off to another room after a good meal, almost as if you're turning your back on it.'

'I like that way of looking at it. Seems a shame to light another fire when the wood burner's going so'—he kissed the corner of her mouth—'well. And there are such delicious smells'—she squirmed as he trailed more kisses down her neck—'and it's so lovely in here.'

'You know, you talk too much,' he said, kissing her mouth.

After a while, when both of them came up for breath, he rose and topped up their wine glasses. She turned to face him, snuggling her bottom into the corner, drawing her knees up to her chin and putting her wine glass down on the small table next to her. She needed to regain a bit of equilibrium.

'There's something about sitting in a kitchen. When we used to eat at my sister's there wasn't much room, so we always ended up staying at the table talking. My aunt could never wait to get out of the kitchen. She's not much of a cook either.'

'Why be so hard on yourself? I mean, you're not planning to open a restaurant, are you? Or write a cookbook?'

'Good God no! Can you imagine it?'

'So just enjoy yourself. Have fun learning a new skill. Maybe it will come a little easier if you relax a bit.'

'I don't think I'm very good at relaxing.' It was true; she was always on her guard, always trying to be, not *the* best, but *her* best.

'You managed just fine today.'

She nudged him in the thigh with one of her feet. 'Are you talking about the sex again?'

He caught her foot and began to tickle it. She tried to yank it away. 'No! Don't.' She squirmed under his relentless fingers.

'Ticklish?' He loomed over her and the next thing she knew they were kissing again – not that she was complaining – and she'd somehow ended up in his lap. He handed her her wine glass and they sat snuggled on the sofa as the rain began to spatter against the windows.

'This is lovely, all snug and warm when it's peeing down outside,' said Hannah. 'From this angle I really don't mind the rain.'

'Another reason to make the cottages so cosy. It's not called the Emerald Isle for nothing. You don't get all this greenery without a fair lashing of rain.'

'I'm used to the rain. Manchester is fairly wet. And that's what makes a green and pleasant land.'

She smiled at him, feeling the intimacy of the moment and both of them in complete accord. Conor wasn't as sophisticated and world-weary as she'd first thought, or maybe she was just getting to know the real him, rather than the face he put on for the world.

After the most wonderful dinner of slow-cooked lamb stew with Conor's own twist – aromatic carrots cooked in butter and star anise (he had to tell her what the slightly aniseedy flavour was), soft creamy potatoes, and thick pieces of translucent onions served with warm broccoli and barley pilaf sprinkled with toasted sesame seeds – they retired to the lounge where he'd lit the fire.

'I'm absolutely stuffed! That was delicious.' She still marvelled at how he'd managed to get so much wonderful flavour into what she'd thought of as a rather boring dish.

'You saw how easy it was.' He sprawled lazily back on the corner sofa, stretching and rolling his neck. His jumper rode up and she tried hard not to look at the dark hair on his stomach.

She swallowed and dragged her eyes back to his face with a wry smile. 'Easy, yes. Time-consuming too.'

'And was it worth it?' He tilted his head in that knowing-the-answer sort of way.

'Yes, you know it was.'

He leaned over and kissed her full on the mouth. 'I'll convert you yet.'

'I think you already did,' she murmured beneath his lips, sinking into his arms.

They lay entwined for a little while, listening to the comforting hiss and pop of the fire.

Hannah sighed. 'This is so peaceful. I could stay here forever.' As she said it, something shifted inside her. It had been a passing thought but it seemed to take root. What if she could stay here forever? Not necessarily with Conor but in this place? She shook her head, as if to dislodge the seed of the idea. She needed a big, bad crow to come and peck it away. What a daft notion! She would no more up sticks and move to another country than… than what?

She realised Conor had said something.

'Sorry?'

'I said did you fancy doing a jigsaw?'

'A jigsaw?'

'Yes, those funny little wooden things that all fit together.'

'I know what a jigsaw is, Conor.' She laughed. 'I didn't have you down as a jigsaw sort of person.'

'Oh you can have a lot of fun with a jigsaw.' He waggled his eyebrows in a ridiculously lascivious way that had her laughing.

'I'll take your word for it. I haven't done one in years.'

'They're curiously addictive. I always put one in every cottage and you'd be surprised how often people do them.'

He got to his feet and crossed to one of the wooden cupboards built in on either side of the pretty Victorian fireplace and pulled out a box with a quaint harbour scene on the front.

'That's sweet.'

He opened the box and pulled out a purple drawstring bag.

'And posh.'

'This is a Wentworth puzzle; they're made of wood. Smell.'

Surprisingly, there was the smell of freshly cut wood and as the pieces spilled from the bag, she spotted various shapes – a piece like an anchor, a beach hut, a fish, and even a pair of sunglasses.

'It's gorgeous.' She laughed, picking up another piece shaped like a turtle.

It was also fiendishly difficult, she discovered, as they started with finding the edge pieces. Despite sifting carefully through the box, there didn't seem to be any corner ones.

Once they started, she realised that it really was rather soothing and completely addictive... and that Conor was up to no good. It took her a while to notice that as he reached across her to place a piece, he'd casually skim a hand across her stomach, under her breast, across her breast.

Seduction by jigsaw was definitely a new one on her but she wasn't complaining.

Chapter Twenty

S he was convinced the hens were pleased to see her on Monday morning as they came rushing out of the hen coop.

'Did you miss me, girls?' she asked, as they fussed around her feet, Attila already pecking at her toes as if to say, *get a move on*. Hannah scattered a few scraps to save her feet. 'How are you today? Have you had a good weekend?' She gave herself a little shiver, thinking about just how good her weekend had been. This morning her whole body felt soft and pliable. She'd never look at another jigsaw in quite the same way again, that was for sure.

'Good morning, Hannah.' Adrienne appeared, as if from nowhere in that spooky habit she had.

'Hi.' Hannah's voice squeaked with a touch of guilt, blushing as she thought of waking up with Conor in her bed this morning and the long, slow, lovely kiss he'd greeted her with as she was worrying about her breath. He'd made her coffee and they'd sat at the little patio table, even though it was a little chilly, looking out at the sea, pearl-grey today under a flat sky. It was possibly the best start to any day she'd ever had.

'You look refreshed. Obviously a good weekend,' observed Adrienne, interrupting her wayward thoughts.

'Yes. Yes, it was. Erm… Conor took me to Dingle. To see the dolphin. Kayaking. I had no idea there was a dolphin. We went to the fish place. The family one. It was good. And… yes, Dingle. It's lovely.' The words tumbled out in guilty haste, providing quick bullets of more information than was required while avoiding spitting out the other facts. *We had sex. Several times. Who knew a jigsaw could be sexy? And did you know, that shower is big enough for two?*

'Flannery's Fish Box. That's a grand place. What did you eat?'

Hannah was relieved and amused. Of course Adrienne was only interested in the food.

'I had the prawn stir fry. I love seafood and it was really good.'

'There's nothing quite like really fresh fish. It'll spoil you for anything else. You'll never want to leave.' Her eyes met Hannah's, guileless and open, but her words held a certain weight about them, as if she were declaring a truth. They pricked at Hannah, reminding her of the careless thought of Saturday night – what if she stayed?

'We'll be cooking with fish one week. It's one of my favourite weeks. If the weather's fine, we'll go out on John Malley's fishing boat to see a catch. A day trip.' Hannah could have predicted her next words.

'As you know I like my students to see where food

comes from. We're plenty blessed here with an abundance of seafood. Now, I must leave you; we've another busy week.'

With that she was away in a whirl of today's floaty linen number in chocolate brown, dressed with glowing amber beads, all of which complemented her auburn hair perfectly. It made Hannah feel slightly exhausted but also inspired. How could a woman who'd worked with food for the last thirty or forty years still retain so much enthusiasm? The woman had the energy of ten. No wonder she managed to accomplish so much. She was amazing and it sounded as if she never stopped learning. That was something Hannah could relate to. She loved going on courses at work, learning new things. Although, she had just realised that in fact she was rather conservative in her choice of courses, always sticking to areas that she felt comfortable with. Apart from this cookery course, when was the last time she'd really pushed herself?

She picked up an egg from her basket and held it up to the sunlight, marvelling at its smooth shape and the delicate matt finish of the shell. For the next fifteen minutes she collected the eggs, picking each one up and staring at it thoughtfully. Eggs, she'd decided, were a miracle. Last week's course, although difficult, had really opened her eyes. She'd never really connected food and its provenance before. Standing there in the courtyard with the girls pecking and foostering around her, she felt a deep-rooted satisfaction. This felt right. Finding roots to nature. Her understanding of the world around her expanded and she realised just how limited she'd become in her life. Although she was successful in the usual ways – good job, good salary, owning a home – they were colourless in comparison to the life she was leading here. It was a moment of realisation: she wanted more in life.

Breakfast was in full swing when Hannah arrived with the eggs. Jason and Fliss were bickering about a pool game from Saturday evening.

Izzy rolled her eyes. 'Only they would go out in that weather.'

'It was a rematch,' said Jason with his usual cocky grin. 'And I won, even if Miss Fliss here doesn't agree.'

'You won by default. That man jogged my elbow and I potted the black by mistake.'

'Sore loser.'

'I'll beat you next time.'

'Did you not go to the pub then?' asked Hannah.

'No. Wimped out. Couldn't face going out in that downpour. Meredith invited Alan over and the three of us watched a film on RTE. *Dark Lies the Island*. I'd have suggested you come on over but Meredith said you were planning an early night.'

Hannah remembered the hastily sent text. 'Yes. Stayed in. Did a jigsaw.' Again she reverted to shorthand speak, not wanting to give more away. As an experienced lawyer she always advised clients to say as little as possible. Giving more information than necessary provided openings for questions.

Izzy looked at her quizzically. 'Saturday night? You are wild. You need to get out more. Alan was talking about going to another pub on Friday.'

'Grand.'

'You're starting to sound like a proper Irish person,' she teased.

'I do love the accent. It's so…' She wasn't going to say sexy, which was the first thing that came to mind. She'd been listening to Conor's husky lilt too much. 'It's musical – if that isn't too stereotypical.'

'No, I think you're right. Conor has a lovely intonation to his voice.'

Hannah felt the familiar blush rise again and she focused her attention on the golden yolk of the boiled egg in front of her.

'He's not bad to look at either,' said Izzy, with a quick nudge. 'What's he look like first thing in the morning?'

'What! How—'

'Sharing a place with him.'

'Oh, yes.'

Izzy looked at her more closely and her mouth dropped open in a little 'o' of understanding. She glanced around at the others who were all absorbed in their own conversations before lowering her voice. 'You're not…?'

Hannah couldn't lie to save her life but at the same time she didn't want to admit it. She made a tiny squeak and widened her eyes and she shook her head vigorously. 'No. Of course not.' What was between her and Conor was private and no one else needed to know.

Thankfully, Izzy nodded and murmured. 'OK then.'

Hannah heaved an inwards sigh. She was going to have to come up with a good story for the weekend. Conor had invited her to take a trip back to Dublin with him since he had a business meeting with the family lawyer.

'Are you coming?'

'What?' Hannah needed to focus otherwise she'd give herself away. Izzy was no fool.

'The herb garden. You said you'd come with me.'

'Oh, yes.'

'I am so going to plant a herb garden when I get home, although I'm not sure how it will cope in the snow. I'll have to ask Adrienne what she'd recommend. She's so knowledgeable about the properties of all these herbs. Did you know basil can help with flatulence?'

'Good to know. I'll try to remember that.'

Having gathered several bundles of herbs which were now bucolically arranged in a wooden trug which Izzy carried with a touch of innocent self-importance, they headed to the kitchen for the day's tuition. As always on Monday mornings, their aprons were freshly laundered, hanging on the hooks in the large lobby which served as their breakroom where tea and coffee were served in the mornings and the most delicious home-made cordials in the afternoon. Hannah had become rather partial to pomegranate and rhubarb with sparkling water even though before coming to Ireland she could safely say she'd never even tried pomegranate.

Neat piles of ingredients awaited them at each station when they arrived in the kitchen. Hannah was pleased that Bronagh was back from her holiday and Conor had relinquished his kitchen assistant role. He was back working on his cottage on the other side of the estate. Having him in the kitchen today would be sooo distracting. She wouldn't be able to concentrate on a thing!

'Morning, everyone.'

'Morning,' they all chorused back like obedient schoolchildren.

'Welcome to week four, over halfway through the course and today we're talking cakes.'

Hannah perked up. Cake-baking was what had brought her here, although she was finding it difficult to imagine the triumphant return to the office, bearing a spectacular *Bake Off* showstopper, that she'd once daydreamed about.

'Cake-making encompasses everything from genoise sponge through to French patisserie. Difficult but rewarding.'

Hannah's heart sank. If Adrienne said it was difficult, then it really was difficult.

'The French of course are renowned for their patisserie, but here at Killorgally we like to put our own spin on things. Today we're going to be making eclairs with a whiskey-chocolate glaze and filled with delicately flavoured whiskey cream. We'll also be making millefeuilles with our home-grown raspberries and Irish cream filling.

'Ooh, lovely,' said Meredith. 'I want to serve some extra fancy things when we open the cafe.'

'Patisserie requires precision and concentration.' Was it Hannah's imagination or did Adrienne look very directly at her? 'It also requires attention to detail and very careful measurement of the ingredients.'

'Seriously?' moaned Jason under his breath. 'Load of ef — poncey nonsense.' Fliss tutted but Adrienne either hadn't heard or chose to ignore his grumblings as she began to talk through the process of making the choux pastry for the eclairs. Throughout, Jason sighed, shifted from foot to foot, picked at his nails, and gazed around at the ceiling. Hannah thought if he could have got away with it, he'd have been on his phone the whole time.

'Now, don't forget, you need to shoot the flour into the water and butter and make sure you chop the butter in small pieces so that it melts quickly. You don't want too much of your water boiling away. Getting the proportions right is essential for a good choux.'

'Yeah, yeah, yeah,' muttered Jason beside Hannah. From the corner of her eye she saw Fliss poke him sharply in the ribs.

'Ow!'

'Is everything all right, Jason?' asked Adrienne, giving him a warm smile.

'Fine,' he said, managing to be civil, although he scowled the minute she looked away.

As they all turned to go to their respective stations, Meredith sidled up to Jason and patted him on the shoulder and gave him a quick hug. Hannah was surprised by his gruff thanks before he stomped back to his usual place at the back of the class.

Meredith was a better person than she was, thought Hannah as she made her way to her place, dubiously eyeing the ingredients awaiting her and crossing her fingers that this week she was going to do better. Rather than try and make notes while Adrienne talked, today she'd focused on remembering what she'd said. It was easier, Hannah decided, to make the notes afterwards, when she'd discovered from experience what the possible pitfalls were.

Hannah had always had steady hands, which she found very useful when it came to piping her choux pastry into neat lines for eclairs and for decorating the tops of rum babas with whipped cream. Adrienne was quite right; concentrating on the task in hand and taking it seriously helped. Sadly, Jason hadn't got the same memo that day.

'Oh for fuck's sake,' he muttered and threw down the spatula he was using.

'Oh for God's sake, Jason,' snapped Fliss. 'What's the matter now?'

Hannah winced. The two of them had been sniping at each other all morning.

'I can't get the stupid effing pastry dough into the bag.'

'That's because you need to rest the bag in a glass or something to support it, like Adrienne demonstrated. Typical, you don't give a toss, do you, so don't even try to do things properly.'

'Who made you God around here? If you're so bloody good at cooking, little Miss Posh and know it all, why are on you on this course?'

Fliss turned and clamped her mouth shut, an angry flush running along her cheekbones.

'You're such a stuck-up cow. What makes you think you're better than the rest of us?' he sneered. 'No one likes you. With your hoity-toity ways.'

'Jason.' Meredith's reprimand snapped out like a coiling lasso rope. 'That's not nice.'

'S'true.' He lifted his chin like a boxer, daring her to contradict him. 'Everyone thinks you're a right snob.'

Fliss gasped and as if Jason had scored a direct hit, uncharacteristic tears began to well up in her eyes. She pushed her tray of eclairs way from her and turned and fled from the room.

'Blimey. She's a bit sensitive,' said Jason, warily looking at the others as they all turned to look at him.

'And you're totally insensitive,' said Izzy. 'Why do you always have to wind her up?'

'Me wind her up? She winds herself up. She's always having a go,' Jason said, putting his hands on his hips, belligerent and defensive at the same time. 'Come on, you know what's she's like.'

Meredith shook her head. 'Jason, you've been very unkind. I think you ought to apologise.'

Jason rolled his head and turned towards Alan. He shook his head too. 'Sorry, Son, you crossed a line.'

'But she gets right on my tits.'

'That's your problem,' said Hannah, with a rare flash of sudden intuition. 'Not hers. You can choose how you respond.' The rest of them might have found Fliss a little irritating on occasion but they'd all managed to keep it to themselves. They'd certainly not talked derisively about her in the way that Jason had intimated. Now Hannah felt desperately sorry for the other girl. God, it was almost like being back at school and being the only one not invited to join the new WhatsApp group.

'I choose to call her out,' he said, with a stubborn narrowing of his eyes.

'And you think the way you did it was helpful?' said Izzy.

He shrugged his shoulders and let out an aggrieved sigh. 'God, women. It's worse than being at home.'

'Jason,' Adrienne's cool voice interrupted; she'd been watching and listening to the exchange from the front of the class. 'I think you owe the pot three euros.'

He shot her a dark look but dug into his pocket and stomped towards the jar she held in her hand.

'I think one of us ought to go and find Fliss, make sure she's all right,' said Meredith, looking at Hannah.

'Me?' She looked at Izzy, who grinned.

'I think Meredith's right. It's a job for a lawyer. Someone who's balanced and can see both sides of the argument.' She pursed her mouth in an annoying prim line, belying her smug amusement.

Hannah did feel sorry for poor Fliss. Although she was quite prickly and very sharp-tongued on occasion, there was something underneath all that arrogant bravado.

With a resigned, 'OK, then,' she walked out into the lobby. There was a small cloakroom there which was typically Adrienne-style with soft blue towels, fresh flowers, and gorgeous-smelling soap as well as a pretty blue chaise longue. As soon as she pushed open the door she heard the sound of quiet sobs and there was Fliss, her head buried in her lap, her blonde hair spilling over her face.

She looked up as the door clicked behind Hannah.

'What do you want? Come to gloat?' Her woebegone,

crumpled face made Hannah's heart ache; Fliss looked all of her nineteen years old. The usual sophisticated sheen had been wiped away and she looked lost and defeated.

Hannah sat down next to her. 'No one's gloating. Jason was out of order.'

'No, he wasn't. He was right. I am an insufferable cow. I can't help it. I try to get in before anyone else does, so they don't put me down.'

'Why would we put you down? You're one of the best cooks here. Look at me, dunce of the class – I'm not going to put you down.'

Fliss closed her eyes and her mouth crumpled. 'They do at home. All the time. Cooking's the only thing I'm any good at.'

'And darts. And billiards, I hear.' Hannah gentled her voice, hoping she sounded encouraging and friendly.

'Huh. You want to know why? Comes of growing up with four brothers who are utterly brilliant at everything they do. It's a constant competition and I'm always the loser. Always trying to keep up with them. Ferdy still beats me at darts – he's the youngest VP ever at some American bank; Johnny got straight As at school and a first at Cambridge; Eddie's the explorer – he's conquered Everest, Mont Blanc, and been to the South and North poles, and Barty was head boy at Harrow and is now training to be a QC. I'm the youngest. All I can do is cook. That's why I came on the course, to learn how to be the best.'

Hannah's mouth twitched as she remembered what Conor had told her.

'What's so funny?'

'Nothing. I was complaining to Conor that I was bottom of the class and he said it wasn't a competition. I hate being rubbish. I do understand, a little. At work I'm always the best; it's not nice feeling that you're useless compared to other people.'

'It's not very nice boasting when you are good either,' said Fliss with a hiccough-sob as if she was going to start crying again. 'I can't help it. It's the first time I've ever been one of the best and Jason's so cocky and he's naturally good. He reminds me of my brothers; it all comes so easily to him and then he treats me like they do. I had a rubbish call with my mum at the weekend and I just couldn't brush it off this morning. So I had to get back at him.'

'I don't think Jason is quite as confident as he makes out, you know. I think this is a long way out of his comfort zone.'

'What makes you say that?'

'I recognise the signs.' Hannah's rueful grimace made Fliss frown.

'You? But you seem so together, even when you're having a disaster. It doesn't seem to bother you. I didn't think you cared that much. In fact, I wondered why you were here… unless it's for Conor.'

'Pardon?'

'He's the big attraction. Especially in the cooking world. You know Adrienne married into the family. Bridget was a famous cook and Adrienne married the son and established this place.'

Hannah nodded.

'Well, lots of wannabe chefs think that snagging Conor is

the fast track to success. You must have heard of Polly Daventree – she's got a TV cookery show and three cookery books coming out...' Her mouth turned down. 'Shame he's too old. That would have made the family sit up and take notice.'

Hannah gulped, glad that Fliss was looking down and couldn't see the expression on her face. Conor and Fliss! It didn't bear thinking about. She was far too young for him, and what a shame that she thought that he was the answer to her problems. No wonder Conor had turned his back on the celebrity chef circuit.

'And I've just made a complete idiot of myself.' Her chin wobbled. 'I don't know what to do now. Maybe I should just leave. I don't think I can face everyone again.'

'Don't be silly,' said Hannah, taking her hand and giving it a squeeze. 'I think you and Jason have got a lot more in common than you think. That night in the pub when you played darts, you had a great time. Why don't you talk to him, explain how you feel? He might surprise you.'

'Huh, you think?' Fliss bristled again.

'What's the worst that can happen?'

'He can take the piss out of me even more.'

'Well then, you can go home,' said Hannah. It was a bit callous but sometimes being brutal with people and honest about a situation worked best.

Fliss laughed. 'You sound like one of my brothers. Sorry. I'm much nicer than this normally. I was trying to be confident; instead I just came over as a stuck-up cow. Oh God, I've got to go back and face everyone, haven't I?'

'Yes, but if it's any consolation, Meredith told Jason off. He was rude and unkind.'

'I'm not going to say I deserve it because he was really winding me up. Doesn't he realise how lucky he is to be here? And his boss is paying for him. I had to beg Daddy to let me come. He only coughed up because it was cheaper than me going to uni. Not that I'd have got in anyway after I loused up my A levels last summer. I couldn't bear being compared to the boys; it was easier to completely mess up so they couldn't make comparisons.'

Hannah gaped at her. 'You did badly on purpose?' The idea was complete anathema to her.

Fliss shrugged. 'I couldn't bear it if I tried hard and my results weren't as good as the boys'.' She put on a deep, exasperated voice, '"Oh, Felicity, a B. Perhaps if you'd worked harder, like Johnny, you might have got an A." It's always the same. I don't try at anything these days except cooking – none of the boys can cook to save their lives.' Her eyes glinted with a flash of fierce determination.

'I can understand that. And so will everyone else.' Hannah spoke briskly; she didn't really do emotional scenes and high drama. 'We'll be breaking for lunch soon – why don't you come back in then?'

Fliss shook her head. 'I'm not sure I can.'

Just then, the door opened and Jason walked in, blinking a bit too self-consciously as he took in the feminine décor. 'Nice in here. Not sure about the settee.'

Fliss immediately rolled her eyes. 'It's a chaise longue.'

'Fancy sofa,' he quipped immediately and Fliss managed a smile.

'You say potato…'

'No I say potater,' he said, emphasising his cockney accent. 'I'm sorry, mate.'

'S'OK.' She lifted her shoulders and looked down at her feet.

Hannah wished she were anywhere else but here between these awkward not-quite-adolescents but as she went to stand, Fliss touched her wrist. Feeling obliged to stay, she sighed inwardly.

Now Jason stared at his feet. Hannah glanced from one to the other. Oh dear lord, this could take forever and she was stuck right in the middle.

'Why are you here, Jason?' Hannah asked, trying a different tack.

He walked over to one of the sinks and picked up one of the pretty bars of soap from the basket, tossing it up and down for a moment before he looked at it consideringly and stuffed it into his pocket, a slightly defiant expression on his face.

'Last-chance saloon. If I cock this up, I'm done for.' He sniffed hard and rubbed at his nose. 'The boss sent me here. Caught me tea leafing. It was this or he'd hand me over to the coppers. That would have done it. Already on probation, they'd have chucked me in the slammer.'

Hannah nodded. She'd met quite a few Jasons over the years.

'That was good of him.'

'Yeah, if I'd wanted to learn all this noncy stuff. He was just showing who was boss and that he could do what he wants with me.'

'But you're so good,' blurted out Fliss.

Jason shoved his hands in his pockets.

'You are,' she insisted. 'A natural. Look at Hannah, she really wants to do it and can't.'

'Thanks,' said Hannah, her dry words receiving a quick apologetic glance from Fliss. 'I was thinking more along the lines that your boss could have found a far cheaper way of doing things. Have you any idea how much the course costs?'

'No.'

Hannah named the price, gratified to see Jason's mouth drop open. 'You're shitting me. No!'

'Yes. And there's a waiting list.'

'Fuck me!' He frowned. 'What the 'ell is he playing at then?'

Hannah wanted to bash his head against the sink. 'Perhaps he's trying to steer you onto a better path. He's seen something in you and is giving you an incredible opportunity.'

Jason repeated the sum she'd mentioned before and then turned to Fliss. 'Is that how much you paid?'

Fliss nodded.

He slid down the wall and clasped his knees, his eyebrows working overtime as if they were having their own conversation.

'That's insane. Me. Gawd, I've been breaking and entering since I were knee-high. I were always the small kid they could post through a window to open all the doors. Went to juvie a couple of times. That's where I learned to pick a lock.'

Fliss looked doubtfully at him. 'What about the people you stole from?'

'Didn't really think about 'em too much. We mainly did offices, factories, not houses. Didn't think the chap at the restaurant paid that much attention. He were asking for trouble with a cellar full of wine and what-nots.' He winced. 'I took a couple of cases, sold 'em down the pub.. He weren't cross though, just did that disappointed look, like my old mum did whenever I came home with a bad report.'

'You were lucky he didn't involve the police,' said Hannah.

'Yeah, I was. I'd be inside now.' He looked up at them both and rubbed a hand over his mouth. 'I'm a twat, aren't I?'

'Yes,' said Fliss straight away. 'This course is amazing and you are so bloody lucky to be here. I could... could slap you. Your boss sounds like a really decent bloke and you're pissing about. You know some of the people Adrienne has trained run some of the best restaurants in the world. Look at Conor – you know he's loaded from being a TV chef. His sister in the US is worth a fortune.' Her lip curled. 'You have to work for it, though. It doesn't just fall into your lap. I'm bloody glad I didn't know this course was being subbed by your boss or I'd have been even crosser.'

'What do you have to be so cross about? Silver spoon in your mouth. Daddy paid for you.'

'Yes, he did, but I had to plead with him. I want to be the best. Prove to him and my brothers that I'm good at something. That's why I'm here and it makes me so mad to see you waste the opportunity, because you are good. Really good. And it bloody annoys me.'

'Good job Adrienne's not around. I think you might have just filled up her swear jar,' observed Hannah.

'Her and her frigging swear jar. No idea what that's all about.'

'It's part of her overall philosophy that you shouldn't need to swear in the kitchen. She's trying to take the pressure out of cooking. It's about the quality of the food, not being a showoff,' explained Fliss.

'How do you know that?' asked Hannah.

'I asked her about it. She comes and talks to me while I'm doing the greenhouses.'

'Huh! She talks to me while I'm doing the porkers. Funny things, they are. That Clarence and Pigwinkle always come and try and chew my wellies. Daft buggers. You have to keep 'em in check; they can be quite aggressive but they're all right.'

Hannah tried not to smile. He sounded quite fond of them.

'Good job I'm not a proper villain. I know how to get rid of a dead body now. Pigs will eat anything. Won't leave anything behind.'

'Good to know,' said Fliss. 'Now, are we all done?'

Jason held out his hand and Fliss took it, and the two shook companionably.

'Right, posh totty. Darts down the pub Thursday.'

'Thursday?'

'Yeah, the team are playing away so we can get a look-in

at the board. See if you can beat me again. I'm sure it was a fluke last time.'

'It was not,' said Fliss hotly, nudging him in the shoulder.

'Nah. Beginner's luck.'

'You just wait, Jason. I'm going to beat you hollow.'

Hannah watched as the two of them bumped and barged each other as they left the ladies' room.

'Oh dear God.' This was exactly why she didn't touch divorce law. She couldn't cope with the drama.

Chapter Twenty-One

M uch to Hannah's relief, the others had made their own plans for the weekend and didn't show too much interest when she said vaguely that she might see her old university friends. She and Conor were able to make their getaway on Saturday morning without anyone observing them leaving together. Not that it was a big secret, but she preferred to keep what was going on between the two of them quiet, especially as it was only a temporary arrangement.

The hotel back in Dublin was just as lovely as Hannah remembered and when they walked in, the good-looking male receptionist greeted them with a friendly, familiar welcome almost as if he remembered her from her last visit, which she was reasonably sure he couldn't possibly have done. Conor, of course, was a different matter.

'Mr Byrne, nice to see you again. Would you like to come into the bar for a whiskey while we take your bags up?'

Conor turned to Hannah, 'Do you want a drink now?' He lowered his voice. 'We could revisit the scene of the crime.'

She kicked him lightly on the ankle. 'No, I don't think that's a good idea. You've got a meeting with your lawyer tomorrow. Won't you want a clear head?'

'I'm not seeing him until 1pm. He's a law unto himself. Complete madman. How many other lawyers do you know who conduct meetings on Sundays? So before then, I thought we could have a leisurely breakfast and a walk around Temple Bar. There's a ton of interesting shops and places if you like and then you could come with me to see Patrick. After that we can go straight on to Trinity and we can see the library?'

'Haven't you seen it, like, a gazillion times?'

'Not with you.'

'You're such a smooth-tongued, blarney sort of guy. I bet you've kissed that stone, haven't you? Did you practise that line?'

'Wounding me again, Hannah.' Conor winked.

'I just like to keep you in your place.'

He leaned over and whispered in her ear, 'And where would that place be? On top or below?'

'Conor!' she said in an outraged whisper, feeling the familiar blush ride out over her cheeks.

He simply grinned and turned to the receptionist who was busy printing out sheets of paper. 'We'll go straight on up.'

'Very good, Mr Byrne. You're in the Seamus Heaney suite this time.'

'Grand,' said Conor, while Hannah's mouth opened to say something. A suite. That was fancy, and not what she'd been expecting at all. Last time his room had been similar to hers.

'So will you come with me?' asked Conor as they went up to the third floor in the shiny black lift, as glossy as a grand piano.

'To your lawyer's? I thought it was family business.'

'It is but Patrick is getting on a bit. He's all but retired. I'd… like a second opinion.'

'It's really not my business,' Hannah hedged.

'Don't worry, it's just paperwork to be signed and he's so vague sometimes, it might be helpful if there's anything I want to query.'

Hannah pinched her lips together in thought for a moment. 'Why are you still using him if you're not sure about his abilities?'

'Because we've always used him and he's so close to retiring, we might as well hang on. We've been using his dad and him for sixty years. We might as well hang on until he retires this year.'

The lift came to a halt with a slight hydraulic bump and fall which left her stomach behind for a second, and the doors slid open. At the sight of the carpet with its retro pattern of large honeycomb hexagons, brown against gold, memories of her previous visit flooded back and she smiled, remembering her and Conor, pressed up against the doors, so focused on kissing each other that they'd almost fallen out of the lift. She glanced at him and saw that he, too, remembered.

She still couldn't quite believe she'd been so brazen that night or where it had led. Now look at her. Ireland Hannah was very different from England Hannah and she wasn't sure she wanted to go back to being England Hannah. With a frown, she realised she wasn't even sure she wanted to go back to England, back to her old life. Which was ridiculous. She had a job, a flat, and a life there. *But what sort of life is it?* nagged an annoyingly perceptive little voice before rather shrewishly adding, *And you don't even like your flat that much. The cottage is so much nicer.* Hannah sighed irritably. She couldn't make life-changing decisions based on a flipping cottage.

'Something wrong?' asked Conor as they walked side by side down the corridor.

'No,' she said with a firm snap as if that would help shut down the wayward 'what if' thoughts in her head which seemed to have taken charge.

'Sure?' Conor shot her one of those quizzical, knowing looks that he and his mother seemed to have down to a fine art.

She definitely didn't want to discuss her thoughts with him; they were a little too adventurous and shocking for her to take hold of, let alone explain.

He opened the door to the room and all thoughts were pushed aside by the charming décor.

'Nice, isn't it?'

'Nice!' She whirled to face him. 'It's gorgeous. I love the colours, although I'd never have chosen them in a million years.' She reached out to touch the navy-blue wallpaper with its elegant hoops of copper foil. Then she realised he was teasing her. Of course he was; he was the one with the designer eye.

'Perhaps I should use this wallpaper in my place? With that big window overlooking the sea, there'll be plenty of light.'

'You should. It's lovely.' With a quick pang she realised that she was unlikely to ever see it in situ. The knowledge brought a deadening in her chest, like a sense of loss, which was stupid because you couldn't lose what you didn't have in the first place. Honestly, being in Ireland was making her far too fanciful.

She walked through to the bathroom to escape the thought.

'Whoa!' she said, turning round slowly to take in the full sophisticated glory. 'Nice shower,' she called out to Conor. It was one of those with a dozen dials, levers, and shower heads, except the whole thing was made of some matt-blue finish set into a bronze shimmering wall. The fittings on the rippled glass shower screens were all bronze to match and the sink was a big beaten copper bowl with a large marble stone in the bottom to act as a plug. It was over-the-top opulence which once again reinforced the complete lack of imagination of her own home. She made her mind up there and then. She was going to move. Sell the apartment and find something… well, not as sophisticated as this, something homely, something that offered a welcoming embrace when you came home from work with sofas to snuggle into and handy cashmere throws to wrap yourself with. Perhaps with a garden for chickens.

'I think the interior designer got a bit carried away in

here,' said Conor. 'It makes me feel as if I should only come in here if I'm preparing myself for the Oscar ceremonies or something.'

'It's striking,' Hannah said trying to be diplomatic, although she could see exactly what he meant.

'There's a fine balance between being striking and intimidating, first rule of Byrne's Design. You want people to be comfortable in their homes not scare the bejesus out of them. Coming in here, I'm worried I have to perform like a porn star and do all sorts of clever standing-up things.' His horrified expression made her laugh.

'Standing-up things aren't all they're cracked up to be,' she said, remembering the cold tiles in the shower at the cottage.

'Thank the lord for that. I don't think I'm cut out to be a stud.'

'Really?' said Hannah, with mock disappointment. 'Does that mean I have to find someone else this weekend?'

With a laugh he pulled her to him and gave her what she considered a particularly stud-worthy kiss. 'Or maybe not,' she murmured against his lips.

'I think we should have a drink in the bar before we go out, for old time's sake. Don't you?' Conor suggested as they towelled down. They'd shared a shower, but not before testing out the bed rather thoroughly.

'Where you took shameless advantage of me.'

'*I* took advantage?' She shook her head. 'I still can't believe I did that. It wasn't like me at all.'

'Wasn't it? You were solving what you perceived to be a problem by taking decisive action.'

'Ah, when you put it like that, I much prefer that version of events.' Hannah tucked her towel in at the front and gave him a quick peck on the cheek, ducking out of his reach with a laugh as he tried to pull her in for a kiss. 'If we start all that again, we'll never get out of here.'

'Spoilsport.' Conor pouted and Hannah very nearly succumbed, charmed by his naughty wink.

Sharing a room now seemed like second nature as they got dressed around each other with unconscious ease, although Hannah still took advantage of the dressing-table mirror to ogle Conor's rather fine backside. It was a sight that she thought might never quite get used to, and she had to store them up since this wasn't forever.

The bar was just as she remembered; even the barman was the same. He gave Conor a friendly greeting as they walked in.

'I've got your table reserved for you,' he said and waved to the two armchairs in front of the fireplace where two glasses of red wine awaited them.

Hannah turned to Connor in surprise. This felt like a celebration, almost an anniversary or a proper date.

His mouth quirked in a shy smile. 'I thought it would be nice to remember how we met.'

Lovely, thought Hannah, her heart doing a salmon leap of surprised delight, trying to decide if this was part of his natural charm or genuine thoughtfulness.

They took their seats and Conor raised his glass. 'Hello, I'm Conor.'

'Hannah, nice to meet you.'

They chinked the glasses together and Hannah grew warm as Conor stared at her. 'You're a strange mix, Hannah Campbell. In some ways nothing like I thought you were that night – a bit wild and impetuous – and then in other ways you are. It's almost as if you don't know either.'

Hannah forced a smile, cringing inside as he'd summed her up perfectly. She started things but never let herself go all the way. When it came to it, she couldn't take that final leap of faith.

'Common sense kicks in every now and then,' she said.

'At least it keeps me on my toes,' said Conor. 'You're not predictable, that's for—'

'Conor, darling,' a fruity voice burst between them, exploding like a ripe peach.

They both looked up, having been so absorbed in their conversation that neither of them had noticed this panther of a woman slinking towards them. That was Hannah's first impression: feline and sleek with her glossy black hair that hung in stylish curls tumbling across one shoulder. A slick of pale, glossy lipstick emphasised a wide mouth stretched to full capacity in delight at seeing Conor.

'What on earth are you doing here? What's dragged you away from the back of beyond?'

'You liked it well enough when you were sucking up to my mother.'

'I was not sucking up to your mother. I love your mother.'

'Everyone loves my mother.'

'You know what I mean.' She tossed her glorious mane of hair over her shoulders with classic put-out disdain.

'Hannah this is Polly, Polly Daventree. You might have seen her on the TV.' His next words held a distinct touch of scorn. *'Polly's Pantry – Everyday Food for Everyday Folk.'*

Hannah wanted to melt into her seat and slide out of sight. In black leather trousers that showed off giraffe legs, a miniscule waist, and a white silk shirt tastefully undone to reveal an attractive swell of creamy skin, Polly was drop-dead gorgeous and as rare and exotic as Hannah was down-to-earth and dull. Even her hair behaved itself, the curls beautifully coiled like glossy snakes instead of spiralling out of control.

It brought Hannah up short, like the reins tightening on a runaway horse. Conor belonged with someone like this glamorous woman. Something plummeted in her stomach, as sharp and brutal as a rock falling from a cliff edge, as she realised that she'd started to get too used to living together with him the cottage.

'Hannah?' Conor's voice came from a long way. Her ears buzzed and she came to, with both of them staring at her.

'Sorry,' she said, blinking, hoping Polly didn't think she was rude or weird. 'Hello.'

'Hello there.' Polly's wide, bright smile seemed genuine.

She held out a slim, artistic hand with short and neatly polished nails. 'Nice to meet you. How are you going?'

'Good, thanks,' said Hannah.

'You're English. I love your accent.' Hannah did a double-take. This woman's voice was beautifully lyrical. 'What part are ye from?'

'Er... Manchester.'

'Oh, I've some cousins there.' She laughed. 'But then, I've cousins everywhere. How are you finding Ireland? Are you here for long?'

'I'm just here for a few weeks. On the cookery course at Killorgally.'

Polly plonked herself down on the arm of Hannah's chair. 'Aw, now that's lovely. Isn't the farm just divine. And how's all the family?' She tossed her head, casting a resigned look at Conor. 'Cos he's not about to tell us. Is Adrienne fine?'

'Yes, she's great.'

'And how about Bridget? She'll not be forgiving me for breaking her boy's heart anytime soon.'

'They're all good,' said Hannah, now curious. This woman, for all her scary beauty, seemed friendly and very personable.

'That's good then. And how about you, Captain Grumpy, still mad as a wet hen at me? You can't blame a girl for trying to get ahead. Like you'd ever had to struggle to get known, born into the Byrne cooking dynasty. You've no idea how hard it is for the rest of us. If someone can give us a leg up, why not?'

Hannah pressed her lips together, in reluctant admiration for Polly's unashamed honesty.

Conor scowled. 'How's your television producer boyfriend?'

'Aw you're as cross as an aul stick. His name's Ronan, as well you know. You worked with him for long enough and he's not my boyfriend anymore.' She gave him an uncertain smile. 'We got married last month.'

'Congratulations,' said Conor, his jaw tightening.

'Thank you,' she said with a simple nod, although Hannah noticed she twisted the rings on her wedding finger. Not quite as confident as she seemed in telling Conor. With a brilliant smile that hid a tiny touch of sadness, she turned to Hannah. 'So what do you do? Chef, restaurant owner, food writer?'

'I'm a lawyer.'

'Good for you. Looking for a career change then, are you?'

'No, absolutely not,' said Hannah with a quick burst of laughter.

'Really?' Polly's face registered utter disbelief as she examined Hannah with the intensity of scientist studying a bug under a microscope. 'So why are you at Killorgally then?' A sly smile darted across her face, as if she'd just added two and two and made the requisite five. Her quick gaze veered from Hannah to Conor and back again. 'You don't have to answer that. He's always had quite the fan club.'

Hannah bristled. 'I'd never heard of Conor before I came to Ireland.'

Polly was too startled to be insulted by Hannah's frosty tone.

'You're kidding me. What, never?'

Conor gave her a suspicious look and she glared at him. Seriously? They'd been through all this before.

'Well, I must be away, back to my table.' She indicated over her shoulder at a table of recognisably 'media type' people who were all dressed as if they'd just come straight from a fashion show. 'Nice running into you, Conor. Nice to meet you, Hannah. Good luck with the cooking.' There was calculation in the final words, as if she still didn't believe that Hannah didn't have some kind of ulterior motive. With a gay wave, she departed, leaving behind a weighted silence.

'She was nice,' said Hannah eventually, for want of anything to say.

'Mmm,' said Conor, swirling the wine in his glass before he took a sip.

'She's not nice?' asked Hannah.

'She's ambitious. Knows what she wants.'

'That doesn't mean she's a bad person. People wouldn't complain about a man being like that.' Hannah knew he probably didn't want to hear that, but she'd rather liked Polly's blunt openness. She had one of those naturally bright and shiny personalities that drew people in, even despite the barbs she'd fired at Conor.

'No, she's not a bad person.' He sighed. 'Just not the right one for me, but pride got in the way. It's not very nice realising that someone likes your family more than you.' He gave a rueful laugh. I thought I loved her but I was wrong… I didn't realise it until…'

'Until too late,' finished Hannah.

He gave her an unexpectedly direct look before saying, 'Something like that.'

She faltered, not sure what to say next, as his intent stare focused on her mouth. She stared back at him, her heart almost missing a beat as she studied his handsome face. Then she reminded herself sharply that she was getting carried away. This was a fling thing. They were here for some fun; obviously seeing his ex had brought back some bad memories.

Then he dropped a soft kiss on her forehead, 'Shall we go?'

'Did you want a drink before dinner? We're a touch early,' said Conor as they left the hotel, not quite as light-hearted as normal. The encounter with Polly had left him subdued, and her thoughtful and introspective.

'Why don't you show me a typical Dublin pub?'

'If that's what you want.'

She nodded. 'You can teach me more about whiskey.'

'All right, then. I'm never one to turn down a good drink.'

They walked in uncharacteristic silence, both deep in their own thoughts, until he steered her into an already busy pub with revellers spilling out onto the pavement. Inside, there was a gentle roar of noise punctuated by shouts of laughter against a backdrop of piped fiddle music coming out of four speakers set up in the corners the room.

Conor wove his way through the crowd to the bar, squeezing through a rowdy hen party. The bride, a very pretty girl with the brightest-pink lipstick Hannah had ever seen and glittery sequins around her eyes, wore a very short minidress that possibly had more in common with a belt, a bright-red garter on each thigh, L plates on her back and front, and the biggest, brightest smile possible. Her ensemble was completed by a wayward full-length veil topped by a multi-coloured tiara full of diamonds, rubies, sapphires, and emeralds that looked as if it had been borrowed from a Disney princess. Her hens all wore pink T-shirts with a list of cheeky hen-do dares emblazoned across the chest in white. Quite a few of the tick boxes next to the dares – including 'lick two strangers' moustaches' and 'kiss a stag' – had been messily ticked with what looked like lipstick. Hannah guessed they'd been out for a few hours already by number of ticks on the T-shirts and the unsteady state of a few of them, as they propped each other up. Despite that, she couldn't help smiling at them; they embodied the sort of sheer joy that comes from being totally uninhibited and out to have a good time.

'What'll you have?' Conor raised his voice as he ducked to miss one of the girls' arms as she emphasised something important to her laughing companions.

'Recommend me something. You're the expert.'

As Hannah tried to follow him, one of the hens turned round to the other girls.

'Oh. My. God.'

'What? What?' they called in ragged chorus, like startled rooks.

'It's only Conor Byrne.' She held her hand to her heart. 'And he looks,' she paused and shouted, *'Good Enough to Eat.'*

Hannah remembered belatedly that this was the name of Conor's cookery programme.

'Where? Where?'

The girl pointed. 'And look at that arse. You wouldn't turn down a ride of him, would you?'

'Conduct yourself, Siobhan,' said one of the more sober girls (relative to the others), giggling.

'That's the dog calling the cat's arse hairy, Bernadette Geraghty,' said Siobhan good-naturedly, stabbing at the ticks on the girl's T-shirt. 'Sure you've already kissed three ugly fellas.'

'Thems was dares.' Bernadette waved both hands before squinting with bleary, unfocused eyes after Conor. 'Though you're right, girls. I bet he's great in the scratcher.'

The rest of the girls burst out laughing.

'I saw him first. I'm going to ask him for a kiss,' announced Siobhan, sticking out her ample chest.'

'You're making a holy show of yourself,' said another girl, which Hannah guessed meant she was taking things a bit too far.

Siobhan pushed up her boobs to cheers from the other girls, tossed her hair over her shoulder, and to the avid interest of nearly everyone in the pub now, began to stalk her prey. Well, it was not so much stalking as pouncing the minute she got within a foot of him.

She clamped one hand on his shoulder and he span around. 'Conor Byrne, you look good enough to eat. Fancy nibbling on me?' She let out a cackle of delighted laughter.

Hannah watched in mortified apprehension as Conor's face underwent a rather magnificent transformation.

'Ah, you're very good.' He gave her a full blast of the Conor Byrne thousand-kilowatt charm, those blue eyes crinkling with amused regret, 'But see here,' he nodded his head towards Hannah, holding out a hand to her, 'my girlfriend's quite choosy about where I eat these days but I'm sure I can spare you a kiss.' He gave the woman a peck on the cheek, as at least two of the girls captured it on their phones, obviously making sure the shot didn't include Conor's grip on Hannah's hand. No doubt the carefully cropped picture would be shared on WhatsApp, go viral on Instagram, and be shared a dozen times on Facebook.

Hannah's heart did a funny thunk at the gentle caress of his thumb on the sensitive skin of her wrist as he tugged her closer to him. She was also charmed – not so much at being referred to as his girlfriend, but at the thoughtful way he'd deflected the attention without hurting the girl's feelings or making her feel a fool.

Hannah stayed at arm's length, not wanting to spoil the moment for the other girl who beamed triumphantly and clapped him on the shoulder.

'Now one for the bride,' she shouted as the other girls propelled the girl in the white dress forward.

Everyone else in the pub turned to watch as Conor graciously bestowed a kiss on the bride's cheek.

Within minutes, people were pushing their way forward

asking for selfies and photos for their nieces, sisters, mums and grannies and Hannah's hand was reluctantly relinquished as Conor gave her an urgent look. *Wait for me*, it said. She smiled at him and watched the interactions which Conor bore with his trademark charm, even smiling off the words of an irate drunken man who told him, 'Yer programme's a bag of shite but my mammy likes you. Gis us a photo.'

While he was being mobbed, Hannah made her way to the bar and ordered herself a glass of white wine, figuring it might take some time for him to free himself. She observed his interactions with pride. Although he'd told her he'd eschewed the limelight, he was clearly good at handling it, but it must be exhausting to live with. No wonder he preferred Kerry.

She stood at the bar and sipped her wine, every now and then nodding at him when he caught her eye with an apologetic, rueful wink. Her heart warmed watching him. Conor was one of the good ones.

She sighed to herself. No wonder she'd gone and fallen for him. Fallen in love with him.

Love!

Hannah blinked, hoping the shock didn't show on her face. Falling in love wasn't supposed to happen. She hadn't even been aware of it until this very moment. There'd been no bolt-of-lightning moment. No, instead, the feelings had sneaked in like mist under a door. For a second it was hard to take a breath with the firefly bursting in her chest. *She* was in love with Connor Byrne.

She stood and watched him, her heart fluttering gently.

It seemed as if the whole pub wanted their three minutes of fame by proxy with him and he didn't manage to extricate himself until she'd almost finished her wine and it was very nearly seven o'clock. He made it to her side and took her wine glass, draining it with one quick swallow.

'Let's get out of here while we can.'

As he pulled her through the crowd, the hens started calling out 'Bye Conor,' and then taking up the chant, 'Good enough to eat. Good enough to ride,' and punching their arms in the air.

Hannah giggled once they burst out of the doors into the cool evening air. 'Good enough to ride, eh?' God, she loved this man.

'Don't you start.' He rolled his eyes with feeling. 'God save us from hen nights. They were fluthered. I thought I was a goner in there.' He put his arm around her and kissed her. 'You were supposed to come to my rescue.'

She nudged his arm, delighting in his easy affection. 'You seemed to be handling things perfectly. They all loved you – even the guy who said your programme was rubbish.'

'Tell me about it. He still wanted a picture though.' He huffed out a long sigh. 'At least in restaurants people are a little more circumspect and if I sit with my back to the room, most don't know its me.'

'You didn't seem to mind too much.' He dropped his arm to take her hand and gave it a squeeze as they walked side by side along the pavement.

'You can't. That's the problem. One bad word, one attempt to disengage yourself, and all of a sudden it's all over social media and the press what an arse you are and how it's all gone to your head. Besides, these are the people that have made me. I earned a lot of money, thanks to them watching the shows, thanks to people turning up to my restaurants. Being polite and playing along is a small price to pay, but that doesn't mean I have to like it. Some people do, though. Polly loves it. Loves being centre stage. Wherever we went the press were sure to turn up. We couldn't even go for a walk in the Phoenix Park on a Sunday morning without some photographer turning up. It took ages for me to figure it out. Turned out Polly was the one tipping them off. Even though she knew how much I hated the lack of privacy. That...' Hannah saw him swallow. 'That was a real kick in the teeth. A betrayal.'

'That's...' Hannah paused, not wanting to be bitchy, but there was something about that level of disloyalty that made her want to comfort him. She was furious on his behalf. Polly should have looked after him better. 'That's terrible.'

He pursed his lips before saying with a resigned shrug, 'She wanted the exposure. I was so pissed off, but she insisted things would be better if we moved back to Killorgally. I should'a realised she wanted to establish the next generation of the Byrne family.' A grim smile twisted his mouth as he slowed his pace and they stepped out into the road to avoid a large group of young men.

'What did your mother think?' asked Hannah, slightly horrified.

'She's just pleased that another one of her cooking disciples is going out there, spreading the word.'

'Really?'

'She's never said anything against Polly and they're still in touch. Her view is that we weren't suited and it was better we found out before we got married. To be fair, in some ways, she's right. Why should Polly compromise her career because I didn't want to be in that world anymore?' Despite his non-committal words, Hannah heard the sense of betrayal in his words.

'That's very fair of you, overlooking the fact that she used you.' She gave him a gentle smile.

'Ouch.' He looked at Hannah. 'You have a way of getting straight to the nub of a matter, don't you? That's what I lo— I…' His eyes met hers and she swallowed. The moment extended as they stared at each other and she could see the tenderness in his eyes. Then he leaned forward and gave her a soft, reverent kiss on the lips, his hand cupping her face.

'Sorry,' she said softly, reaching up to stroke his face. Had he been about to say he loved her? Now she really was being crazy. Just because she'd realised she loved him, it didn't mean he felt the same. He'd been bruised by Polly; he'd made it clear he wasn't ready to go down that road again. 'I didn't mean to be that blunt.'

'It's fine. You got it straight away. Mam won't have a word said against her.'

'But not your grandmother.'

This time he laughed with genuine amusement and the moment between them was lost. 'No, Bridget never liked her. She's the seer of the family. She knows things. Some people think Adrienne has mystical powers, but it's really

Bridget. Anyway, it's all water under the bridge now. Good luck to her. Call me a cynic but now she's married Ronan, her broadcasting future is secure. He's a big fella in RTE.' With an ironic chuckle, he added, 'He commissioned my first cookery show, so I guess I owe him something.'

Hannah could tell that despite his apparent indifference, he'd been hurt by Adrienne's support for Polly.

'My aunt was set to take a wooden spoon to my sister's ex's "saggy treacherous little backside" when she heard he'd been cheating on her with her best friend, even though she'd adored the pants off him because he always bought nice wine to lunch.'

Conor grinned at her. 'Adored the pants off him. You're picking up the Irish there. You'll be a local before you know it. I like the sound of your aunt. I think Granny Bridget might have done the same. She pulls that prune mouth whenever Polly's name is mentioned and switches the telly off the minute Polly appears on the screen and curses at the radio if she's ever on there. Granny's a woman who wears her heart on her sleeve.'

'She thought it was hilarious that I'd not heard of you.'

'That probably endeared you to her. She's proud of what Mam's achieved and that Mam has created a lasting legacy, but she doesn't like the fuss and razzmatazz that goes with it all. She likes a simple life whereas Mam was born to be a CEO. I think if she'd grown up in the city she'd have been running some big corporate entity and been the top dog.'

'She's a very impressive woman.'

'That she is, no doubt. And here we are.' They'd rounded a corner and come up on a small, narrow street which had once been a residential road but now a third of the stately Georgian houses had been converted into bars, restaurants, and hotels.

'This place is run by another one of Adrienne's disciples. Their cheese plate is legendary, all sourced from Ireland, from some tiny places. They also do the most amazing colcannon.'

'Colcannon. That's potatoes and cabbage, isn't it?' Hannah's face said it all.

'If you were a peasant back in the eighteenth century. Here it's kale, Yukon gold potatoes, garlic, double cream, rare-breed bacon, leek, and spring onions. I tell you, it's fierce good. They also do a mean Irish stew – not quite as good as mine, but it's not bad.'

'I love your modesty.'

'I have nothing to be modest about,' he said with one of his cheeky winks.

Chapter Twenty-Two

'Are you sure about this, Conor? asked Hannah the next afternoon. They were standing outside a four-storeyed brick-built Georgian townhouse with beautiful wrought-iron balconies, sash windows, and a piano-black glossy door with a big brass door knocker underneath an elegant decorative fanlight. They'd walked through the peaceful environs of Merrion Square and the elegant surrounding buildings to get here and it was like stepping back in time. She could almost imagine a horse-drawn barouche bowling down the street bearing Jane Austen style characters clad in muslins and silks with feather-trimmed bonnets.

'Yes. If Patrick thinks we've got some place else to be, the quicker I can get the business done. Otherwise, he'll blather on for ages and make us stay to watch the racing. All I need to do is sign a few things and Mam wants me to ask him about something.'

'Can't you sign them electronically?'

'He's old school. Too old to change his ways, he says. I think we're his only clients these days.'

Conor raised the knocker and let it fall and they waited until the door was thrown open with gusto.

'Conor. Good man, good to see you. And who's this with you?'

'This is Hannah.'

Patrick held out a plump hand and shook Hannah's enthusiastically as she tried hard not to stare at the bright-orange tie decorated with parrots that he wore with a blue and cream checked shirt under a Harris tweed three-piece suit.

'Come in, come in.' He had one of those loud, booming voices that came straight from the diaphragm, like some aging actor. 'My housekeeper's just made a big pot of coffee.'

Without waiting for them to follow, he headed straight across the big bright black and white tiled hall to a heavy, panelled wood door on the far side.

Glancing quickly at Conor, Hannah followed him into what turned out to be a rather grandly appointed study. Inside was a vast leather-covered desk with two Chesterfield chairs in front of it and a button-backed swivel chair on the other side. It felt a bit like stepping back in time or into a stately home, thought Hannah, gazing at the Adam-style white fireplace on the opposite wall and the leather-bound books with gilt titles lining a whole wall of bookshelves. The small TV just on the corner of the desk was slightly incongruous, especially as it was relaying racing commentary, with the commentator talking as fast as the thunder of the hooves on the grass.

'And Double Trouble is coming up fast on the outside. Leggy Lady is edging up. Grand Design is floundering and it looks as if he's going to do— And Green Swan is closing the gap. Grand Design is starting to fade and it's Leggy Lady, Leggy Lady with one furlong to go and it's Leggy Lady. Leggy Lady wins!'

'Blast it,' said Patrick. 'I shoulda put a bet on – she was fourteen to one.' He stood scowling in petulant disbelief for a moment before pulling out a notebook and a small pencil to scribble on one of the pages. Then, almost as if he'd forgotten they were there, he shook his head and leaned forward to turn up the volume on the television.

Connor gave Hannah a long-suffering grimace, sat down in one of the Chesterfields and invited her to do the same.

'Yes, yes, sit down,' said Patrick.

With half on eye on the TV, he pulled forward a manilla folder, opened it, frowned, and then pulled a second one out from under the first, muttering, 'Ah, here it is.'

He shuffled through the papers inside and then shut the second folder, huffing with exasperation. Standing up, he heaved his bulky body towards a filing cabinet and began rifling through one of the drawers, muttering to himself.

Eventually he pulled a blue folder from the drawer, scratched his head with comical disbelief, put it back, and then pulled out another.

'Ah, here's the little bugger.' He slapped it on the desk.

'Just need your signature on the pages marked. Here, here, and here.'

Patrick slid the folder towards Conor and turned his attention to the television, his head bobbing between the TV screen and the desk, barely paying any attention to Conor who asked, 'And here?'

'Yes, yes,' said Patrick. 'Come on, son.'

Hannah wasn't sure whether he was talking to Conor or the horse.

They talked for a few minutes about the papers which, from what Hannah could gather, were transfers of deeds. Once that was done, Hannah watched slightly fearfully as Patrick wedged the papers back into the filing cabinet, wondering if they would ever reach their official destination.

'Mam wants some advice. Remember our neighbour, Moss Murphy? There's some talk about him getting planning permission to change the farmland into a light industrial estate which Mam is worried will impact on the farm. She's worried he'll want to use the lane to provide access because it's a shared private road. It's his only access to the main road. And it will mean lots of lorries, noise and fumes right by the kitchens and the farmhouse.'

'Hmm, well I don't need to look that one up. He's been claiming shared ownership of that road for nigh on twenty years, even though he knows full well it isn't his. But I'll dig the file out so we can put the dear lady's fears to rest.' He pushed the glasses, which had slipped down to the end of his nose, back up, gave the television a quick, concerned look, and turned to rifle through the files again. 'Should be a property boundary map in here somewhere.' He huffed and puffed as he sorted through one drawer, every now and then turning to check the progress of the next race. According to the commentator they were under starter's orders. Just as he announced, 'And they're off!' Patrick wheeled round, triumphantly holding aloft another file. He darted his gaze towards the screen and nodded before turning to Connor. 'Copy of the deeds. That'll do.'

He squinted down at the paper, in between checking the progress of the race, and Hannah was itching to snatch it away from him and look for herself. There was no doubt about it: the Byrne family definitely needed a new lawyer.

'Hmm, it's not all... Hmm, some of the paperwork... Can't see the boundary map in here – but you know there's a map on the wall in your mother's office... however this is the important bit, pertaining to the private road.'

He ran a chubby finger, with a gold signet ring tightly sandwiched around the flesh, down the page, contorting his mouth as he went. 'Ah, here it is. All good. I remember last time he claimed shared ownership, he soon backed off when your mother asked him for a contribution to repairs. Your dear mother doesn't need to worry.' His smile towards Conor was a touch conspiratorial, as if Adrienne had been making a fuss about nothing and the men knew better than to get excited about such things. Hannah eyed Patrick with irritation. Same old, same old. That attitude of 'women tend to be emotional about these things but it's the men who understand the business issues' was clearly at work here.

'The road is private and owned by Killorgally to the point of the farm, after which the road is then owned by

Murphy. He has right of access along the road but the road belongs to the farm and as such Killorgally is responsible for the upkeep and maintenance of the road. So your mother can rest easy, bless her soul.'

Conor gave a brief nod but Hannah was pleased to see that he didn't collude with Patrick's patronising dismissal of his mother's fears.

'Good. That probably puts paid to Murphy's plans then. Although I'm sure he knows full well who owns the road.'

'Of course he does but he likes to try it on, especially as both families have been living there for the last hundred years. Often longevity provides presumption. It's as well to check these things but people rarely do.' As he spoke he steepled his fingers, nodding gravely while his eyes slid to the TV again.

'Is that everything?' he asked.

'Yes, thanks.'

'Do you fancy a glass of whiskey and we can watch the rest of the racing. I've a good tip for the next race.' Patrick was already reaching towards a decanter filled with amber liquid.

'Sorry, I'm showing Hannah some of the sights but perhaps another time.' Conor rose and held out a hand and they left without being offered the promised coffee that had sat on the side for the whole of the meeting.

As they came down the steps outside, Conor said. 'I know. Don't say a word. We need to get a new lawyer.'

'I can't believe that the deeds documents weren't all together. Have you considered Aidan Fitzpatrick in Tralee? I know I'm biased because I know him, but I've worked with him. I know he's thorough and his attention to detail is second to none. If it were me, I'd have checked the boundaries too.'

'That's down to Mam but I'll certainly mention it. And I'm not too worried about the boundaries. That road's the only access to Murphy's land.'

Hannah held her tongue. After all, it was nothing to do with her, but it niggled her. Patrick should have taken it all more seriously but she didn't want to intrude, especially as Conor seemed a little sensitive about Polly pushing her way into his family.

'Right, let's do something a bit more fun.'

For someone who loved books, the Old Library at Trinity College was quite spectacular and Hannah stared up at the wooden barrel-vaulted roof. There were two storeys with gallery after gallery of book-filled shelves punctuated at the entrance of each by white marble busts of men of letters from Socrates and Plato through to Shakespeare along with former chancellors of the university and even, for some reason, the Duke of Wellington, although when she read the guide leaflet she discovered he'd been born in Dublin. As they walked along the central aisle looking at the exhibition of medieval manuscripts, there was a hushed atmosphere. If the books could talk, what secrets they would have to tell, Hannah thought.

'Something special, isn't it?' Conor murmured in her ear, sending a shiver across her skin.

'It's beautiful.'

'I never get tired of coming here.'

'I can see why. Imagine being a student here back in the day when you could browse these shelves for yourself.'

They wandered, hand in hand, along the aisle, all sixty-five metres of it, according to the tourist information on Hannah's phone. Holding hands seemed a very couple-y thing to do and while she liked it, it also made her feel a little off balance. Conor had been tender and thoughtful, and when they'd made love last night there'd been a difference. Maybe it was because she'd realised the depth of her feelings for him or maybe it was because his feelings for her had deepened. They hadn't talked about when things would come to an end. It was odd; she'd never been in a relationship with an expiry date before and every now and then, as she gazed up row upon row of books which had been here for hundreds of years, she found herself wondering what would happen when the time came to part. Would it be a finite end? No further contact. Would they stay friends? It wasn't a landscape she'd ever navigated before and she had no idea what the etiquette might be. They'd never ever talked beyond the next week. Would they exchange Christmas cards, WhatsApps, be friends on Facebook, send each other emails? She swallowed. Or would it be easier just to cut everything off, severing the connection hard and fast?

Her head hurt.

'You seem miles away. What are you thinking about?' asked Conor, squeezing her hand as they brushed past several display cases on their way towards the queue to see the *Book of Kells*.

She managed a quick smile, even though inside she suddenly felt a little wobbly. 'Oh, you know, there's so much history here.'

'It does make you think, doesn't it?'

She nodded and pushed her thoughts to the back of her mind as he showed her around, pointing out a host of treasures including the original Brian Boru harp, and the proclamation of the Irish Republic in 1916 before they went back downstairs to see the magnificent ninth-century manuscripts of the *Book of Kells*. Although it was atmospheric in a gloomy sort of way in the specially built viewing room, Hannah was a little disappointed that they were only able to see two of the original pages, although that was only to be expected of a priceless artefact. She decided that the Long Library alone had been well worth the visit.

With overloaded brains reeling with history, they left the twilit rooms to return to the bright sunshine of the afternoon in Library Square and walked out of the grounds onto College Street down towards the river.

'One of my favourite facts about the university is that once upon a time students weren't allowed through the grounds without a sword. In fact, myth has it that the rule has never been dropped, so students could still be fined for not having a sword. There's also the one about a secret wine cellar but again I'm not sure how true that is, and another that if students walk under the campanile bell tower they'll fail their exams.'

'Glad I didn't come here then.'

'There were plenty of other bonuses,' he said, idly staring back at the buildings.

'You went here?'

He nodded. 'Brains of the family.'

'Wow. Just think, you trod the same halls as Oscar Wilde, Samuel Beckett, and Jonathan Swift.'

'Not sure that ever crossed my mind while I was here. I was too busy getting acquainted with the black stuff.'

'Guinness?'

'Yep, and it's true. You'll get no better pint than here. I feel bad – I should have left enough time to visit the Guinness Storehouse. You get a fine view of the city from the Gravity Bar they've build on top. But we can have a pint at Mulligan's. And then head down to the river, cross over the Ha'Penny Bridge, come back over to Dublin Castle, and then back to the hotel to pick up the car.'

'I'm going to have to come back to Dublin. I feel like I've barely scratched the surface.' And in that moment, Hannah promised herself she *would* come back. She'd fallen in love with the city, with its elegant Georgian thoroughfares in Merrion Square, the lively cobbled streets of Temple Bar, pulsing with personality and party vibes, as well as the stately grandeur of the university and other historic buildings.

The only problem was, she couldn't imagine coming back without Conor.

Chapter Twenty-Three

'**H**ow was Dublin?'

Hannah jumped and almost dropped the scraps bucket for the chickens. 'Adrienne! Morning. It was… it was great.' Conor had told Adrienne? She hadn't expected that.

'I hear you had a great time. Conor was…' – she smiled in that knowing way – 'most enthusiastic.'

Hannah felt the blush staining her cheeks. 'Although I gather you were less than impressed with Patrick.' Adrienne's mouth pursed. 'He's been with us for a long time and I've a tremendous sense of loyalty, but I think the time has come for us to consider someone younger and more local. I understand you know Aidan Fitzpatrick.'

'I do. I was at university with him and I've worked with him. He's diligent and thorough… and he's a real terrier on behalf of his clients.'

'That's good to know.' Adrienne nodded her head thoughtfully. 'I'll feel guilty about Patrick but we've known for a while his heart isn't really in it.'

'I can imagine, but I think he'll probably be glad not to have anything interrupt the racing.'

Adrienne laughed. 'That's very true. Although going to see him was always a good excuse to visit Dublin. It really is lovely.'

'Oh yes, I loved it. In fact, I love Ireland full stop.' Hannah gazed out over the view, the hens fussing around her feet like a welcoming committee. There was something about this place that had got under her skin. The slower pace of life, the sense of community, and the warmth of the people, from complete strangers to old friends. She felt at home here and as she watched the white crests dancing on a deep-navy sea beyond the rich-green carpet lining the coast where the hills rolled right down the water, stopped by the ragged cliff edges, a sense of peace filled her. She really didn't want to go home.

With a heavy sigh, she said. 'I'm not sure I ever want to leave.' Attila pecked around her feet, as always in search of the juiciest scraps, and Hannah threw her a couple of pieces of apple, feeling like an old hand. She'd come to love the ladies and relished this curious and unexpected sense of belonging. All her life she'd been a city girl but she fitted here.

'Well don't,' said Adrienne, as if it was as easy as that. 'Stay.'

Hannah stared at her. 'I can't.' She watched the hen pecking the food, her feathers bristling and shaking in greedy ecstasy.

'Of course you can't,' agreed Adrienne, with surprising

alacrity, and then she added, 'if you don't want to.' Her expression held a touch of smugness.

The forthright words were like a punch to the stomach and Hannah felt a little winded by them. In that one brief sentence, Adrienne had thrown all of Hannah's well-constructed defences and arguments up in the air, scattering them like the hen's grain on the floor around them. Hannah rolled the ball of one foot on top of a piece of grain, forward and back, irritated and thoughtful at the same time, unwilling to look up.

'If you want something badly enough, most of the time you can make it happen,' said Adrienne with a touch of sharpness.

Did that include making someone love you? The thought darted into her head like a strike of lightning. Hannah looked up and caught Adrienne's eye. Did she know? Or was, 'most of the time', the get-out clause? Could she take a risk? What would Conor say if she told him she was going to stay? Would he think she expected something from him? Did she? That first night after they'd been kayaking he'd made it quite clear that whatever was between them had a sell-by date, but what if it didn't? For the dozenth time she recalled that moment in the bar when she'd thought Conor might say something more. Had that been wishful thinking?

Adrienne looked out over the land and the two of them stood in silence for a minute before she turned to Hannah. 'When I first came here, my husband thought I was mad for wanting to do this,' she said as she swept a hand towards the horizon. 'He humoured me at first until he saw that it was what I really wanted. And I really wanted it. I wanted this land, this way of life to be a legacy for my family. Yes, it was hard work, and when he died it was even harder but I was determined. I made sacrifices, perhaps some might say to the detriment of my children sometimes, but they've been well loved. I might not have been the best mother in the world but, rather selfishly, I knew that they had the best grandparents. I've built them that legacy. It was what I wanted and I've made it happen. If you want to stay in Ireland, what really is stopping you?'

Adrienne held Hannah's gaze and Hannah tilted her chin and stared back. A dozen reasons why she couldn't stay rose to skirt the tip of her tongue but that little voice, the voice of Ireland Hannah, persisted.

What if she did stay? Hannah looked out across the farm. It was such a beautiful place.

'If you wanted, I'm sure we could find you a job. We can still make a cook of you, too.'

Hannah laughed as Adrienne's words trailed off doubtfully.

'Adrienne, that's a lovely offer but you know as well as I do that I'm never going to be a cook. Don't get me wrong, I've learned a lot and I'm coming around to your way of thinking about our food and where it comes from, but I don't have your passion, Jason's skill, Fliss's determination, or Alan and Meredith's love of food. And much as I've loved being here, my job is important to me...' her words died.

'Could you live here?'

Hannah caught her lip between her teeth. What was stopping her? Really?

'It's a… a big risk.'

'Is it?' Adrienne asked with one of her insightful knowing looks. 'What is it you'd be losing?'

Hannah winced, but was grateful for Adrienne's blunt questions. What did she have to lose? Her flat? The place that she slept in rather than lived in. Her job? She'd been headhunted a dozen times in the last year and then there was Aidan. In the short term she could perhaps cover Sorcha's maternity leave. The dazzling thought blossomed in her head.

There was nothing to stop her. She could go anywhere. Why not Ireland? Why not Kerry?

The idea shimmered in her head like an elusive butterfly that she was almost too afraid to reach out and capture for fear of damaging its wings. But what about Conor? How would he react if she decided to stay?

'Ah, look at the time, I must be away and see how Jason is doing with his beloved pigs. If he didn't need to go back and show his boss what he can do, I'd be tempted to invite him to stay too. He has a way with those boys but he has his own destiny to fulfil. He's going to a great chef one day. I feel it all the way to my bones.' She smiled and began to walk briskly away, and then paused. 'You should think about staying. Think about what you have to lose and what you have to gain.' And with her usual cryptic smile, she disappeared.

'Well that was helpful,' said Hannah to herself, shooing

Attila away from her foot. The hen squawked and gave her foot one last jab before striding off to scold and peck at one of the other chickens who'd had the effrontery to attempt to pick up a piece of broccoli in her path. She took her phone out of her pocket and dialled Aidan's number.

Chapter Twenty-Four

'Are you all right, Hannah?' asked Meredith at lunchtime.

Hannah winced. 'Yes. A lot on my mind, that's all.' Inside her head it was like a blinking tennis match, with Ireland and England Hannah battling things out. At the moment, Ireland Hannah was absolutely trouncing England Hannah. Game set and match to staying in Ireland, which was crazy, wasn't it?

Aidan hadn't paused to think about her question as to whether he'd been serious about offering her a job. His actual words were, 'Yes, yes, yes and when can you get your arse down here already to discuss the details?'

He'd even reassured her that a lot of the law was the same, as much of it was set in place when Ireland was part of the United Kingdom until 1922.

'You do seem a bit distracted. I did wonder when I saw you putting the flour in the fridge.' She laughed. 'That's the sort of thing I do but that's thanks to menopause fog, which

I'm pretty sure you're a bit young for. You've all that joy ahead of you.' She rolled her eyes.

'Mmm,' said Hannah, wondering for a minute what she might buy here if she sold her flat in Manchester. She could have chickens. A vegetable patch. A herb garden.

And since when had she wanted a herb garden?

What would Mina think? Stupid question. Mina would be wholeheartedly in favour. And Aidan's enthusiastic response had steeled her nerve. Nerves gripped her gut. What about Conor? What would he say? She felt a little sick, trying to imagine his reaction. Would he be pleased or shocked? Would he still want her? Could she really stay in Kerry if he didn't want her? He'd signed up for a fling thing, not an open-ended thing. But was she forcing his hand if she announced she was staying? That was changing the rules they'd agreed.

When she returned through a grey misty mizzle to the cottage early that afternoon, Conor was waiting for her with a big grin on his face, as if he were harbouring a surprise.

She gave him a tremulous smile back, knowing she needed to talk to him and wondering when the right time would be.

'Good day?' he asked. 'You've finished nice and early.'

'Adrienne gave us the afternoon off as we all did so well and because the preparations for the Orchard Dinner are well under way.' She paused. 'It seems like quite a big deal.'

The dinner was taking place the following evening and tomorrow they would be cooking all day, helping to prepare food for the buffet.

'It's the highlight of the year. I'd liken it to the Byrnes's personal Thanksgiving. You know my sister has just flown in from the States for it. I've never missed it.' He paused and swallowed. 'It's always held the same week as Niamh's birthday and the week my da died.' Clearing his throat, he added with a wry, sad smile, 'Even Fergus gets a haircut and puts a shirt on.'

Hannah wanted to reach out and hug him, but wasn't sure how he'd take it. It hadn't occurred to her until now that the event held considerable significance or how lucky she was that her visit coincided. 'I'm sorry, I had no idea.'

'How would you? It's Mam's personal tribute to my da. Her way of showing him what she's achieved. Lots of past students come to celebrate, from all over the world. Basically, anyone who's ever been here is welcome. At the last count, I think there were seventy-five acceptances. The table will stretch the whole way down the greenhouse. It's quite something to behold.'

'Seventy-five!'

'Small beer to the Byrnes. We've been catering for the five thousand for dozens of years.' He gave her a confident smile. 'And everyone pitches in to help. I have to admit, it's my favourite occasion – like Christmas and every holiday going rolled into one. There's nothing quite like it.' She could see the slight sheen of something in his eyes and could tell from his heartfelt tones that it was something special.

'I feel honoured to be here.'

'I wouldn't,' he grinned at her. 'Don't forget you'll be working just as hard as the rest of us. Mam's not daft. She's got free labour and you know you'll all pitch in because you've fallen under the Killorgally spell.'

Hannah laughed. 'We certainly have.'

'But it's a wonderful occasion. You'll love it.'

'Do you fancy stretching your legs?' he asked with a lightning change of subject.

Hannah rolled her shoulders. Despite being on her feet for most of the day and the miserable late afternoon, a walk on the beach was just what she needed. And it might be the perfect place to tell Conor that she was thinking of staying. He'd come back because he loved it here. Surely he'd understand that she too had fallen in love with the place. Funny, she'd never considered that she might like to live near the sea but now she couldn't think of anything better.

'Yes. Now?' She nodded towards the rain-dotted windows 'Or do you want to wait?'

'Now,' he said.

'OK, I guess we'll have the beach to ourselves.'

'We're not going to the beach,' he said with a teasing quirk to his mouth.

'Where then?' asked Hannah, wrinkling her brow, just a touch disappointed. She might have grown to love the place but she was still a creature of habit; she liked knowing where she was going.

Conor grinned, pleased with himself. 'It's a surprise.'

'You know I don't like surprises.'

'You'll like this one.' He paused with a cocky smirk. 'And you liked the last one well enough.'

'Once I'd got over the shock, yes.'

'Come on. I'd grab your coat. It looks as if it might lash down later.'

'What's this?' She indicated the grey gloomy weather.

'It's only spitting.'

She rolled her eyes. Hannah had already learned the variations of rain, from a 'soft day' to spitting and to lashing – the Irish certainly knew their rain.

In rainproof jackets they set off climbing up the hill beyond the farmhouse, through a wide grassy field edged with the dry-stone walls she'd become so used to. They were an endless source of fascination to her. Miles and miles of them, like haphazard piles of books that magically seemed to fit together to form straight lines traversing the fields, following the contours undulating over the terrain and disappearing into the misty, murky distance. Their surfaces were lichen-patterned and dampened by the fine drizzle that swirled around them. Although it wasn't cold, Hannah kept her head down, focusing on where she was putting her feet.

It wasn't long before Conor tugged at her hand. 'There she is.'

As she raised her head, she saw the large sprawling grey stone building, transformed at one end by a huge picture window and new wooden window frames.

'This is the place you've been working on?' There was a flutter in her chest.

'Yes,' said Conor, suddenly serious and a touch wary. 'Thought you might like to see it.'

'I'd love to,' she said, aware that this was akin to him placing a tiny, fragile baby bird in her hand. Now probably wasn't the time to tell him that she wanted to stay.

She followed him round to the front to the house. A gravelled track ran up across the hill which she assumed led down to the farmhouse in the next valley. She smiled. 'A good distance and out of sight of the family.'

'Exactly.' He winked at her before leading the way to a neat storm porch with a weathered tiled roof and sturdy front door of oak. She could picture it in a few years' time with climbing plants trailing up the posts. He opened the door and she stepped over the threshold into a stone-flagged hallway with a freestanding wooden staircase which wound around the wall up to the next floor, where a long gallery fronted the void which was open to the high ceiling.

'Wow. This is quite an entrance.' She gazed upwards, admiring the wonderful light and the gorgeous sense of space.

'Like it?'

'Love it. It's fantastic.' Her eyes glowed with enthusiasm and suddenly Conor's face broke into a grin. He grabbed her hand and pulled her forward through another solid wooden door.

'Oh my goodness!' Hannah exclaimed as she walked into the room, her eyes swivelling around as she tried to take in the wonderful open-plan space. At one end, a huge kitchen with a breakfast bar dominated the room and at the other the picture window in the lounge created the focal point of the most wonderful view of the sea. There was no furniture yet but she could see it so clearly: long lean sofas arranged in an L shape around the wood burner that had already been installed. She bent down to touch the honey-coloured wide-planked wooden floor, her fingers rubbing along the grooves, and looked up at the A frames holding up the roof. She could imagine being in here, Conor cooking and her curled up with a book, the fire roaring in the burner and her eyes drawn to the rain-lashed windows and the wild sea beyond, feeling snug and warm.

Her heart pinched at the image and suddenly she wanted that more than anything in the world. Could she risk her heart, her life and make it a reality? Should she tell him now? She gnawed at her lip. What was the worst that could happen? *He could tell you he doesn't feel the same, you fool*, shouted the sensible voice in her head, the one that usually took charge. She couldn't bring herself to say anything. Instead she stood and slid an arm around his waist.

'This is incredible. It's such a beautiful space. It's exactly like your design. You must be so pleased.'

'I am but it's nice to hear it from someone else.'

'Your mum really hasn't seen it?' Hannah couldn't quite believe that he'd managed to keep Adrienne away.

He laughed. 'No, not for want of trying. I've had the glass covered up so there was no peeking. I want it to be finished before I show it to anyone but I thought you... Well, it seemed right. Besides, you'll have gone by the time it's finished.' He gave her a perfunctory smile and moved out of her hold. Her chest felt as if it had been kicked. She really ought to tell him that she'd accepted a job with

Aidan. It wouldn't be long before he heard it for himself, if she wasn't careful. News round here travelled fast.

Trying to keep her feelings from showing, she followed him as he showed her around the rest of the house. Thankfully, most of the rooms still needed a lot of work. Some of them were not yet plaster boarded and so the electric wires were hanging down and the waiting copper pipes were ready to be connected to radiators, which meant she didn't have to pretend to be too effusive when her stomach was so tied up in knots. However, there was enough done in the master bedroom, with its corner window that took in the sea view and the range of hills away to the right, to see what it would be like and to increase her longing to stay. From the bed you'd be able to see the sea and through the Velux windows the sun would shine down on you. The en suite shower room was half tiled with simple cream tile bricks, with tubs of grout and sealed boxes of tiles filling one corner of the room. 'No porn star shenanigans in there then,' she teased, even though there was a lump in her throat as she admired the glossy rectangular glazed tiles.

'No, although I'm game if you are.'

'I'd be worried it might be a health and safety issue. I don't fancy finding a tile spacer digging into my bottom.' Pretending to be funny when she felt anything but was getting harder by the second.

'And it's a bit chilly. The heating's not quite finished yet. The boiler's being fitted this week.'

'When do you think you'll move in?'

'Officially it's all supposed to be complete at the end of

October. There's not too much more to be done – there's only the fridge and the cookers to arrive in the kitchen – so I might move in earlier and live with the chaos.'

A dart of alarm shot through her at the thought of Conor moving out of the cottage. It signalled an ending. An ending she wasn't ready for. She trailed a hand down the banister, revelling in the smooth texture of the solid oak, wanting to grab hold of it to anchor her to the spot. She had nothing and everything to lose.

'Conor,' she said in a rush of breath, the words tumbling out without proper thought or planning. 'I'm thinking about staying.'

'Staying?' He looked around at the beautiful hallway and stiffened. She saw him closing himself off, in the sudden straightening of his posture, the tensing of the sinews in his hands, and the almost imperceptible tightening of his jaw. It gave her all the answers.

She nodded, nervous now, wishing she hadn't just blurted it out like that. Wishing she'd rehearsed a proper speech to explain why she wanted to stay. She had a memory of a heated debate in an English class as to whether Elizabeth Bennett's feelings had undergone a significant change when she'd seen Darcy's home, Pemberley. When she'd seen what her life could be.

But Hannah had had to say it, not because the house was so beautiful but because she couldn't imagine a life without him. Just the thought of him being here and her going back home was like a punch to the stomach.

'I've been a offered a job.'

'Let me guess, Adrienne offered you a job.'

'Well, yes she did but—'

'You never mentioned it before. Or should I guess?' he asked with a lazy insolent drawl. 'You're to be another of Adrienne's disciples, are you?' His mouth twisted. 'You've seen the light and you're going to stay. Why am I not surprised?'

'That's not it at all.' She'd certainly come around to Adrienne's way of thinking about food and sustainability, but at the same time, she wasn't worshipping at her feet.

'So you want to stay.'

'Yes I do but—'

'And she's going to make a cook of you. Where've I heard that before? You do realise she does this all the time. Finds a new protégée. Except...' His mouth twisted again. 'You're not a cook. You don't have that drive or passion. You shouldn't listen to Mam. You'll never be a cook.'

If he hadn't added that charming comment, she might have stayed cool, calm, and communicative, but his obvious derision and instant assumption pissed her off mightily. Hannah didn't have much of a temper, but some things, like injustice and unfairness, were immediate triggers and when she blew, she blew. She could feel her face turning red, reflecting the furious boil of her blood below the surface and her fingers developed their own reflexive desire to slap his smug, know-it-all face. He didn't know it all. He clearly didn't know her at all. Didn't know that she wasn't the sort to take short cuts or hitch her wagon to anyone else for an easy ride. All her life she'd worked hard towards her goals. Instead of correcting him, she decided with grim fury that he could think what the hell he liked. He could go screw himself.

'You big, stupid, arrogant, up-yourself eejit!'

As her face burned with fury, she realised the words seemed to have burst aloud and then felt pleased, especially at the slapped-with-a-wet-fish expression on Conor's face.

'What did you call me?'

'I think you heard, you big, fat eejit.' She huffed out a mirthless laugh, too far gone not to say it. 'And to think I thought I was in love with you.'

As soon as she spat the words out, she realised she'd made a grave mistake.

'You're in love with me. What and you're going to move to Ireland and we're going to found the next Byrne dynasty. Now, where have I heard that before?' He glared at her. 'And fool that I am, I thought I was falling in love with you.'

'Well, it's a good job you weren't,' she said, and with a flounce she was excessively proud of, she turned and slammed out of the front door, stomping down the gravel path towards the farmhouse, uncaring whether Conor chose to follow her or not. After the weekend in Dublin, she'd thought there might be something more. Clearly she was as big an eejit as he flipping well was.

Chapter Twenty-Five

A drienne Byrne knew how to throw a party. When they assembled in the kitchen on the following day, she had ten different lists arranged on the workbench in front of her.

'Right, I've organised you into working parties. Jason and Fliss, I'd like you to sous chef for me here in the kitchen. Alan and Meredith, you'll be working with Conor in here too and Izzy and Hannah, you'll be helping set up the tables in the greenhouse and helping everyone else out.'

Hannah let out a huge internal sigh of relief and rubbed at her sore, tired eyes. She hadn't seen Conor since she'd stormed out of his house last evening. He'd not come back to the cottage until after she'd gone up to her room – although that had been at eight o'clock and she'd lain on her bed, her ears pricked, listening out for him, while going over and over their conversation in her head. She still felt sick to her stomach that it had all turned out so badly. But at the end of the day, she hadn't been anything but honest with him. Lying about her feelings, about what she wanted, wouldn't have made any difference in the long term.

When he'd come back to the cottage at about nine o'clock, she'd hidden in her room, holding her breath when she heard his slow steps on the stairs. She didn't quite bury her head under the duvet but it was a close-run thing as she lay there hoping and praying that he wouldn't knock on the door but at the same time wishing he would.

'Phew,' muttered Izzy under her breath, echoing Hannah's relief. 'I was worried about having to cook for all these famous people.'

Hannah nodded. Her biggest anxiety was facing Conor this morning, although she was equally relieved that her cooking would not be receiving headline billing. It might have improved no end in the last few weeks but her presentation skills were still woeful and she certainly didn't have the flair for cooking that marked out Fliss and Jason. They had that star quality. Meredith and Alan were both very good cooks but not as ambitious or driven towards perfection as the other two, although Meredith's presentation was beautiful and she loved her prettifying as she called it. Hannah and Izzy, while now more than competent, were never going to set the world's Michelin star restaurants on fire in the way that the two youngsters probably would one day. It suited her just fine to be a general dogsbody for the day.

Once Adrienne had given her orders for the morning, Hannah and Izzy found themselves carrying bundles of crisp white tablecloths out to the long greenhouse that stretched down the middle of the orchard, separating the apple trees from the pear trees. The entire fifty-foot length had been turfed and a series of trestle tables ranged down the middle.

Despite the sky being overcast, a flat grey that promised a shower or two, it felt quite muggy, so all the windows and vents of the greenhouse had been opened.

'Wow, this is going to be quite something,' said Izzy, clutching the white cloths as she looked all the way down to the end of the greenhouse.

'Ah, there you are, girls,' said Bridget, striding forward to meet them in a pair of teal dungarees, her head bound up in a bright-yellow scarf, looking a little like the grandma of a member of Little Mix. 'You'll help me lay up the tables, all seventy-five place settings.' She took a couple of the cloths and within a second shook one out, letting it billow like a sail as it fluttered down over one of the tables. Hannah and Izzy followed suit and, in no time, each of the tables was covered.

'Right. Next, table decorations. Come with me.' Without breaking her stride, Bridget marched across the field, through the herb garden and the courtyard to the farmhouse kitchen.

'Someone's been busy,' said Hannah, taking in the forest of wildflowers assembled in glass jars on the big pine table.

'Franklin and Niamh were up at dawn collecting foxgloves, hedge parsley, lady's bedstraw, and speedwell.' She pointed to tall pink flowers, blousy white ones, tiny yellow ones and ever smaller pretty blue ones. 'They're to go on the tables, mixed with the candles.' With a nod she motioned to the jam jars on the counters, each with a sturdy, fat candle and twisted with wire handles around the tops. 'Those ones hang from the metal struts in amongst the fairy lights.' She grinned. 'We're big on fairy lights.'

From beneath the table, she hauled out two large flat crates and helped load them up with the flowers. It took five journeys to transport all the flowers and candles back to the greenhouse and Hannah could feel the sheen of sweat coating her forehead. Annoyingly, with each trip, her mind strayed to Conor.

'Are you all right?' asked Izzy as she let out a sigh, not realising she'd done it out loud.

'Yes, fine.'

'Are you sure? Because you keep sighing.'

'Do I?' asked Hannah, injecting her voice with as much innocence as she could muster and adopting what she hoped was a smile rather than a grimace. 'These are heavier than I thought they'd be, that's probably it.'

'Hmm, although I'd still rather be doing the donkey work than making hollandaise sauce for seventy-five.' Izzy led the way into the greenhouse, where the gardeners were now stringing what looked like miles of fairy lights.

'Me too,' said Hannah. 'I'm never going to be a chef.' It was all right for her to say it, but not Conor. He'd been deliberately hurtful and it still stung. Despite that, she couldn't stop loving him or the heart-cramping pain that thinking about him brought.

'Did you really want to be?' asked Izzy. 'I just wanted to learn enough about cooking that I won't poison people and can have a go at things people ask for.'

Hannah laughed. 'No, truth be told, I just wanted to be competent.'

'Well, I'd say you're more than competent.' Izzy propped her crate on one hand as she walked along, setting the jars of flowers at regular intervals. Hannah followed her, placing candles in jars between each flower arrangement.

'I'm going to stay in Ireland,' said Hannah, suddenly.

Izzy nearly knocked a vase over as she spun round to face Hannah. 'For real?'

'Yes.'

'Fantastic. What will you do?'

'Remember me telling you about my friend Aidan? We used to work together in England. He's offered me a job and...' Hannah winced. 'You were the one who said I wasn't a romantic but I think Ireland has changed that.' Putting another candle down on the next table, she waved a hand at the view through the window. 'I can't imagine not seeing this anymore. The thought of going back to work in the city, in an office in a high rise, makes me feel slightly claustrophobic. Which is weird because I've always loved my job – I still do, but...' She laughed at herself. 'I want chickens.' She also wanted a man like Conor in her life, but, she realised with an inward pang, she couldn't do anything about that. She could, however, do something about the chickens.

'Good for you,' said Izzy, clapping her across the shoulder. 'I can't imagine living in a city. I love the castle. I just hope I can make it earn enough money to keep the ruddy place going.'

'I've never imagined living in the country before.'

'I think Killorgally has some magical influence. I'd like to make the castle like this, a place where you feel at home but at the same time also part of something bigger. Coming here has given me so many ideas, especially the way your cottage has been done with those lovely homely touches.'

'Me too. It's made me realise that my flat is not really much of a home. I won't be sad to leave it, whereas, well, the cottage… I will be a little bit heartbroken to leave but,' she smiled at Izzy, 'I can look for my own little cottage.' The thought thrilled her and she was already thinking of the sorts of things that would be on her house-buying shopping list. An open fireplace, a kitchen-diner – or the potential to create one – a front garden and a back garden and a bathroom big enough for a shower with a magic button. A lump chose to appear in her throat as another thought slipped through. Conor would have been able to give her some good advice and suggestions. She ignored it and said, brightly, 'Adrienne has a friend who has a place I can rent for a few months while I sort myself out.'

The rest of the morning passed in a blur of activity as she and Izzy polished the cutlery which was a random selection of antique silver, some of which needed a good clean. While some of the place settings were stored in their original wooden boxes with velvet linings, there were also job lots in open boxes which meant Hannah had to hunt down the different styles to create matching sets. They also had to sort through a pile of neatly ironed linen napkins, some with pretty embroidery, others plain in pastel shades, and more in delicate faded floral prints, and had great fun choosing which of the assorted napkin rings to use.

'What about this?' asked Izzy as she posted a pale-blue napkin through a sea shell-adorned ring.

'Very seaside. I've got a floral theme going on here,' said Hannah, picking out a bright-yellow linen square and a wooden napkin ring decorated with a large felt sunflower.

'You're doing great work,' said Bridget, coming to watch. 'Not a bother,' she added as Hannah's face fell when she realised that the pattern on the handle of a fork and spoon weren't quite the same and had to start sorting through the cutlery again. 'Don't worry if it's not perfect. We've collected everything over the years from antique shops and family hand-me-downs as well as friends donating to us. But it's a nice touch rather than hire them all in from a catering company. Although we do hire in the plates and glasses so that everyone has the same size, otherwise making sure everyone gets the same portions goes a bit skewwhiff.'

An hour later, Hannah stepped back to examine their handiwork.

'Doesn't it look lovely?' said Izzy, following her gaze.

'It looks wonderful.' The table had been transformed and the bright-white cloths highlighted the splashes of colours from the blousy flowers that billowed from their vases and the rainbow cheer of the different napkins. Fairy lights were now strung throughout the greenhouse and the candle jam jars had been suspended from the vent handles. When dusk fell, Hannah could see that it was going to look spectacular.

'Excellent, girls, but there's lots more to be done. If you

can go back to the kitchen, I'm sure Adrienne can find you a hundred and one jobs.'

Both Hannah and Izzy lifted their eyebrows in mock dismay but Izzy probably felt as she did, Hannah decided: that it was fun to be involved. There was such a fizz of excitement about this evening's dinner; the whole of Killorgally was involved and the place buzzed with activity, enthusiasm, and good cheer. All the permanent workers had been drafted in, the two men who looked after the pigs, the other women who worked at the hotel, the gardeners as well as the students who were here picking fruit and working on the farm. They were all familiar faces that Hannah had become accustomed to over the last few weeks and while she might not know their names, she knew what they did and that they were all part of the Killorgally family. Saying goodbye was going to be so hard. Feeling a sudden pinch of pain, she realised she was going to miss them all.

When Hannah and Izzy returned to the kitchen, Meredith was laughing at something Alan had said, Fliss was telling Jason off in teasing tones, while Adrienne and Mairead were busy chatting away while sliding trays of seed-topped bread rolls into the ovens. There was a sense of well-oiled machinery, with everyone doing their part but in a calm, efficient manner with none of the frenetic activity of shouty TV-chef kitchens. Hannah's eyes, with a life of their own it seemed, homed straight in on Conor who was busy chopping like a fiend, occasionally raising his head to make some point to Jason and Fliss. Her heart constricted at the sight of him and, as if he sensed her presence, he immediately looked up and scowled at her.

'Fuck,' he said, bringing his hand to his mouth as a spurt of blood appeared on his thumb.

'Conor Byrne, I heard that,' said Adrienne without turning around. 'That'll be a euro in the jar.'

Jason grinned.

'Ouch,' said Fliss in her usual loud, plummy voice. 'Are you all right?'

'Fine!' snapped Conor, and stalked to the other side of the kitchen, yanking a red first aid kit out of the cupboard and applying a blue plaster.

Hannah felt a little disturbed by the uncharitable pleasure she received from Conor's slip of the knife. She wasn't normally the bloodthirsty type, but she was still fuming with him.

'Ah, Hannah. Izzy,' said Adrienne. 'Has Bridget finished with you?'

They nodded.

'Izzy would you mind helping Meredith and Alan? Hannah, would you ask Conor what you can do to help?' Hannah nodded, her heart plummeting to her feet. She tried to keep an unemotional expression on her face as Adrienne gave her a serene smile. Why was it that she had a feeling that Adrienne had paired her up with Conor deliberately?

Walking over to the bench, Hannah steeled herself for another of his scowls.

'Hi. Adrienne has asked me to ask you if you need any

more help.' The words made it clear she was there under sufferance.

'You can trim the asparagus,' he said without looking up from the cabbage he was shredding with clean, even, lethal slices.

'Yes, chef,' she snapped, annoyed by his rudeness.

He ignored her and she began slicing off the ends of the poor innocent vegetable with uncharacteristic savagery. Wishing all sorts of ills upon him, she applied herself to the mountainous pile of vegetables. Feeding seventy-five people with six asparagus stalks per person amounted to a lot of chopping. She'd been at it for half an hour when he came over and picked up one of the stalks.

'These are too long. They need another inch off the bottom to fit into the steamers.' With that impersonal observation, he turned and walked away. She narrowed her eyes, watching his broad back in his chef's whites and was about to poke her tongue out at him when she realised that Adrienne was watching with interest, her bird-like eyes bright and keen. Hannah's mouth twisted and she ducked her head and began chopping again. Sod Conor Byrne. He was an overgrown kid who needed to sort things out with his mother. He was the one with the problem.

When she looked up next, having redone all the asparagus to the correct size, Conor had disappeared but Adrienne was passing. 'What would you like me to do with these?' Hannah asked.

'Oh, could you pop them in the cold room? We'll store most of the food in there, ready for this evening when kitchen prep starts.'

Hannah picked up the tray and walked from the kitchen into the narrow corridor which led to the cold store, realising she needed to go to the loo. Popping the tray down she retreated and hurried to the ladies', realising that the regular coffee breaks she and Izzy had taken earlier were now making themselves felt. At the sight of the chaise longue, she was tempted to take a seat and bawl her eyes out. Clearly Conor, who had got completely the wrong end of the stick, was not going to forgive her anytime soon. And she didn't feel like forgiving him and his quick assumptions about her. It was a matter of pride, but it also hurt that he couldn't even bring himself to speak to her. What had happened to the friendship and camaraderie that had developed between them in the cottage? Had she really imagined that special moment in Dublin when she'd thought at the very least he was going to say he really liked her? Was it just wishful thinking that she'd hoped he might love her? Which just went to show what an idiot she was, believing in fairy tales.

She glared at herself in the mirror as she washed her hands. *You idiot*, she mouthed.

Chapter Twenty-Six

Thankfully, Conor continued to avoid her in the kitchen for the rest of the day and as the afternoon progressed, things started to get more frenetic. There wasn't time to think, let alone think about him. At three o'clock Adrienne declared that their work was done and that the professionals would take over from here.

'Go rest yourselves and dress up in your glad rags. Tonight's going to be a fine party. You'll want your dancing legs ready. The fun starts at six-thirty. Don't be late now,' she said, still full of energy as always. The woman was a human dynamo still whirling around the kitchen stirring pans, tasting and beaming at everyone and everything. It was, Hannah concluded, wonderful to find the thing that you are so passionate about. She was looking forward to working with Aidan and with the myriad challenges and issues that came up in a local legal practice. Ingrams in the last few years had grown so much that they did much more corporate work, which wasn't half as interesting as dealing with real people's lives. Her spirits lifted at the thought of making a change and taking a risk.

She hurried back to the cottage to get ready, hoping that she wouldn't run into Conor. When she pushed the front door open, closing it very quietly behind her, she listened carefully and heaved a silent sigh. The only movement was the dust motes flitting about in the sunshine that poured through the skylight above the hallway. She peeped into the kitchen which was empty and, feeling like a ninja, she tiptoed across the hall and up the stairs, wincing when the odd one creaked. Conor's bedroom door was closed, but still she crossed the hall to her room as quickly as she could and slipped inside. Relieved that she'd reached sanctuary, she began to strip off her damp clothes. They'd all been running around like lunatics since first thing and her face and skin were slicked with a sheen of sweat. She felt grimy and desperate for a shower. She rolled her eyes. That was out for starters. Instead she'd have to make do with a quick sluice in the bath.

It was only when she grabbed her bathrobe that she spotted it. A solitary shoe lay on her bed. A plain black sensible court shoe, silhouetted against the white duvet like the dramatic front cover of a crime thriller. She'd entitle it, *Death of a Romance*. She swallowed hard and stared at the polished leather. There was a small note with it.

Sorry it's taken so long to return.

The careful placing of the shoe seemed horribly symbolic, a message officially severing the link between her and Conor. It felt like a sad remnant, a wisp of memory from that first evening spent together, as if the last few weeks had been wiped out and that was all that had ever been between them. The apology suggested that he was sorry he couldn't feel the same about her as she did about him. There was a finality about it that kicked her straight in the gut with an angry punch.

A lump lodged itself in her throat and she blinked back tears. Stupid really. Why hadn't she ever realised that falling in love with someone was the biggest risk of all? Moving to Ireland, getting a new job – there was no risk at all. It was a change but it could all be managed. She could afford a house here, there was a job for her, and if it didn't work out she had the experience to get another.

When you fell in love, you had no control over the other person's feelings. It was a huge risk. You opened up your heart and left it unprotected, and who knew that it could be so fragile? Or so easily hurt? Or that there would be a physical ache in her chest? Or that her spirits would drag like chains pulling on her ankles. Bugger. Love hurt. It really bloody did.

An hour later, with her head held high, she slipped on the black court shoes with a touch of defiance and left the house hunched under a large umbrella. Unfortunately, the rain had begun not long after she'd dressed, with no indication of let-up. There'd been no sign of Conor either. Walking up the track in heels through small rivulets of water probably wasn't her best move but everyone was dressing up tonight and she needed armour.

In the early evening light, the greenhouse shone through

the drizzle, its windows giving off a soft, almost magical glow. The sounder of chatter drifted out through the doors and windows as she neared the entrance where the others had congregated, each of them holding a flute of pale sparkling wine next to a pile of abandoned umbrellas.

'Hannah,' called Izzy, immediately snagging a glass from one of the waiters nearby and pressing it into her hand. 'You look gorgeous. Haven't we all brushed up well?'

Hannah pushed her slightly damp curls over her shoulder, grateful that she'd not attempted some stylish up-do. It would have collapsed in the wet weather.

Meredith was in a lovely patterned maxi dress that flowed over her soft curves while Izzy wore white palazzo pants and a silk vest in bright green with a big white pashmina slung around her shoulders giving an uncharacteristically glamorous stamp to her tall frame. Even Jason had abandoned his habitual jeans and she wasn't about to tell him that he looked like one of the waiters in his smart white shirt and black trousers. Alan was the surprise of the night in a very smart grey suit that had a whiff of custom tailoring to it. He looked almost unrecognisable and Hannah wondered what he had done before he retired. Even his posture was different, with a definite touch of corporate heavyweight about him.

Just then, Fliss arrived wearing a very smart cream shift dress that had 'day at the races' written all over it, her face flushed with excitement. 'You'll never guess what I've just seen. Polly Daventree. Here with her new husband. She said she was in the area and popped in on the off chance there might be space.'

Hannah's heart sank. Poor Conor.

'And you'll never guess. Adrienne turned them away. Said there wasn't room.'

'But another two wouldn't have mattered, would it?' said Meredith, straining her neck to look down the table. 'And with this number of people, someone's bound not to turn up.'

'Cheeky cow, turning up uninvited,' chipped in Jason, echoing Hannah's thoughts.

'From what I've heard, she likes to think she's part of the family,' said Alan.

'Adrienne said she was very sorry but it wasn't possible.'

Hannah smiled to herself. Good for Adrienne. It was Conor who needed to know. Polly wasn't part of the family and wasn't about to receive preferential treatment anymore.

'Yes indeed, that was her told,' said a voice as a couple of familiar faces came to stand next to Jason. Seamus and Peter were the head pig men. 'You wouldn't want to mess with Mrs Byrne. Flighty little madam, that Miss Daventree.' Seamus grinned and turned to Jason, 'Evening, young fella,' said Seamus. 'Remember, Pigwinkle, Clarence, and Porker will still be expecting you in the morning.' He wagged a stern finger at Jason. 'So don't be getting fluthered tonight.'

'No, Grandad,' said Jason to Seamus, with a cheeky wink.

'As long as you're ready in the morning.'

'I'm not a lightweight,' said Jason. 'I wouldn't let my pigs down. Still partial to me bacon though.'

'Jason!' said Izzy.

'What? It's like Adrienne says, better to eat a happy pig than an unhappy one.'

It wasn't quite what Adrienne would have said but Hannah guessed it was close enough. He caught her eye and winked as they were guided by a young waitress through the greenhouse doors to a table a third of the way down.

Jason grinned as he sat down in his chair. 'And it's better to eat quality than cheap. See, I'm on message.' He puffed out his chest and pointed both thumbs at himself before adding, 'Although I'm not sure what my boss is going to say, but it's his call. He sent me 'ere at the end of the day. So he's gonna hafta put up with the consequences, isn't he?'

'Just out of interest, Jay, who is your boss?' asked Alan who had sat down next to him.

'Jeremy Dalmer.'

Everyone stared at him. Even Hannah had heard of Dalmer's, the exclusive Mayfair three Michelin-starred restaurant.

'Get out of here,' said Fliss.

'Straight up,' said Jason, looking a little uncertain as they all stared at him. 'What's the big deal? He pees standing up, like the rest of us.'

Fliss arched an eyebrow.

'You know what I mean. He's just a bloke. Runs a restaurant.'

'Jason,' said Fliss. 'There are only seven-three Michelin star restaurants in the UK. I suspect he's extremely fussy about where his bacon comes from. Are you telling me you're working in the kitchen of one of them?'

'Yes,' he said sliding out of his chair. 'I'm off to get myself a beer. I'm not so keen on this fizzy stuff.' As he walked over to the bar set up on the other side of the table, Meredith and Alan both began to laugh at the look of absolute shock on Fliss's face as she sat back in her chair, her eyes goggling. She shook her head muttering, 'I don't believe it. I don't believe it.'

'Jason doesn't realise he's born,' said Meredith. 'But how lovely that a man like that has taken someone like him and invested in his future. Giving the boy a chance.'

Hannah shot her a sharp glance, wondering if she knew about his previous misdemeanours. 'It's all right, he told us all about it at the weekend. Talking of which…'

Everyone's gaze turned towards her and she felt her face turn pink, just for a change. Would she ever grow out of this unfortunate ability to blush at the slightest thing?

'Yes, Hannah. Dublin. With Conor,' said Izzy.

'He had to go to Dublin on business. He offered me a lift.'

Meredith smiled gently and leaned forward. 'And I'm a flying pig. I've had two daughters – I'm not stupid.'

'And you've got that recently shagged glow,' added Izzy.

Now it was Alan's turn to blush and put his hands over his ears. 'And I've got two daughters and I don't think I want to hear this.'

Hannah's face turned even redder, which shouldn't technically have been possible but apparently was. It seemed her tongue had stuck to the roof of her mouth and she wasn't able to deny or confirm anything. Izzy and

Meredith were grinning at her but with that 'give it up' expression which she knew meant the Spanish Inquisition if she didn't volunteer something.

Alan sighed. 'I think I'll get a beer too.' He rose to his feet and set off to the bar, but not before Hannah saw him giving Meredith a none too surreptitious wink.

'Come on,' said Izzy, turning to Meredith. 'I told you there was something going on. You only have to see the way he looks at Hannah when he thinks no one is looking at him and you,' she turned to Hannah, 'can't take your eyes off him either. We've all had bets as to what's going on in that little cottage of yours.'

Hannah tried to keep her face bland. Their timing was terrible and all she could do was be honest. 'I really don't want to talk about it,' she said stiffly.

Meredith smiled, oblivious to the fractured pain in her voice. 'Don't worry, dear. Izzy is teasing you. Jason and Fliss are oblivious, although I think Adrienne has her suspicions.' Hannah closed her eyes. Of course Adrienne did. She seemed to have the sight or something.

Izzy, however, had noticed Hannah's discomfort and said brightly. 'Oh, look, isn't that sweet. They've tied balloons to Niamh's chair. It's her birthday tomorrow.'

Grateful for the change in direction of the conversation, Hannah looked along the table at the metallic golden balloons bobbing around the chair. All the family were gathered around the girl, including Conor. Hannah slid her eyes away quickly before he spotted her, instead focusing on the growing pile of presents in front of Niamh as various guests detoured to visit her. The excitement was evident in her bobbing up and down and beaming at everyone as she earnestly thanked them all.

'Isn't that lovely,' said Meredith. 'She's such a happy, helpful little soul. I can't wait to have grandchildren. Such a little poppet and so grown-up for her age.'

'She's going to be twelve,' observed Alan. 'If she's anything like my girls, twelve going on eighteen already.'

'Really?' said Izzy. 'Gosh I thought she was younger than that because she's so small. Twelve.'

Twelve. Why did that number niggle at Hannah's brain? Niamh was small because she'd had difficult start in life. Conor had said so, she remembered it quite clearly. Something to do with Murphy's fence. Hannah felt as if she were swimming towards something hidden in the mist. Her brain insisted there was something there but she couldn't quite grasp it. Murphy had put the fence up when Niamh was born.

Twelve years ago.

Throughout the meal she was distracted and then, just as coffee was being served with the most delicious hand-made chocolates, it popped into place. The last piece of the jigsaw. Hannah dropped her chocolate as she narrowed her eyes and then unearthed her phone from her bag.

Aidan picked up on the first ring.

'Hannah what can I do for you? Please don't tell me you've changed your mind.'

'What's the law on squatters' rights and landownership in Ireland?' she asked, straight to business. 'In England if you annexe a piece of land and the landowner does nothing about it, you can claim it after twelve years. Is it the same here?'

Aidan took his cue from her serious tone and it was just like they were back at work together. 'Yes it is. Why do you—'

'Thanks Aidan.' She clicked off her phone and realised that everyone around the table was looking at her. 'Houston, I think we have a problem.' She caught her lip between her teeth. Of course, Murphy's fence made perfect sense now if he was trying to annexe that piece of land but why would he do that? What did he have to gain? It seemed a perfectly innocuous piece of land. Not big enough for a geological find. Too small to mine. What was special about it?

'What?' asked Fliss, for once looking intrigued rather than disinterested.

'Something that's been bothering me for ages. But I need to check something.' She looked at her watch. 'In law if someone takes over a piece of land by fencing it in or appropriating it in some way, if the landowner doesn't object or do anything about it, you can claim the land as your own after twelve years. I think that's what Adrienne's neighbour, Murphy, is trying to do.' There wasn't much time if Niamh's birthday was today. It meant the twelve years was up at midnight.

'Right,' said Alan, his eyes sharpening. 'But what would this Murphy gain from that?'

'I'm not sure.' Hannah thought for a minute and glanced down the table where Adrienne and the rest of the family were gathered around Niamh, who was starting to open her presents. She could hardly interrupt them with a vague half-cocked idea. 'But there's something and I'm just not seeing it properly.' What was it about that parcel of land that was important to Murphy. Why go to the trouble of refencing it so recently? She tried to picture the land and where it was. She really needed to see that boundary map. 'I need to get into Adrienne's office asap but I don't want to disturb them until I know I'm not making something out of nothing.

'Why Adrienne's office?' asked Fliss.

'Because there's a boundary map on the wall in there, which might explain something. The office is probably all locked but I really need to see it.'

Jason rose. 'I can get you in there.' He wiggled his fingers. 'Lock-picking skills.' There was silence round the table and he rolled his eyes. 'If it's an emergency.'

'Oh, it's an emergency all right,' said Hannah. She looked at her watch again. Ten to nine. There really was no time to waste.

'Fine, I'll get you in.'

'But, Jason,' wailed Fliss. 'You said yourself you could go to prison.'

'I didn't know you cared,' he said with a cocky smirk.

'I don't, you—'

'Don't worry. I'll take any flak if we get caught,' said Hannah, looking over at the family. They looked absorbed as Niamh unwrapped presents. She didn't think anyone would even notice she had gone. 'In fact, you don't have to stick around. Just get me in there.'

'Do you want us to come with you?' asked Izzy.

'No, it's best if as few of us get into trouble as possible if I'm wrong. You stay here.'

She and Jason hurried into the rain, and she had to pick her way carefully across the slippery cobbles of courtyard to the dark and silent building. 'I didn't dress for being a cat burglar,' she said as Jason took her arm when she almost stumbled. 'Thanks for this, Jason. I really don't want to get you into trouble.'

'No problem. You're solid, Hannah. You wouldn't be doing this if it weren't important.'

She turned to him. 'Thank you, Jason. That's a really nice thing to say.'

'No probs. I… Well, it's been good this course. Getting to know posh people. You're all right.'

Hannah laughed. 'I'm not the least bit posh.'

'Not as posh as Miss Fliss, but you know what you're about. Educated. Smart, even if you can't cook for bleeding toffee.'

She sniggered at his forthright declaration.

'Thanks, Jason. I've improved at least.'

'There is that but if I were you I'd stick to lawyering.'

'Don't worry, I intend to, but you should definitely stick to cooking and not burglaring… apart from tonight. I think your boss is going to be seriously impressed when you get back.'

Jason grinned. 'Yeah, I think so too. It's quite a feeling, you know. Being good at something. I've never been good at anything before.'

'I know what you mean.' Hannah nodded. She'd taken a risk in trying to learn to cook. It wasn't her thing and she'd never be brilliant at it, but at least she was prepared to give it a go now. It seemed that if you took the risk and failed, it didn't matter as much as she'd always thought it might.

When they reached the office door, she tried it, hoping that it might be unlocked but it wasn't. Jason had disappeared around the corner of the building. She tried the handle again, just in case, and then followed him. Here, the shadows of the farm buildings loomed with gothic intensity as a lone security light created hollows and dark pools and the slash of rain was almost silver. Wiping the water from her face and pushing aside her wet fringe, she blinked at Jason who had turned on the torch on his phone. She saw his teeth, white and grinning like dayglo dentures.

'Here you go.' He pointed to the window, and the open bottom sash. 'No point making life hard for yourself. Always check the windows first.'

'I'll remember that next time,' said Hannah, her heart pounding a little at the enormity of what she was about to do. Although she wasn't stealing anything, breaking in somewhere was still nerve-racking. Crossing her fingers inside her pockets, she prayed that they wouldn't get caught.

Jason had no such qualms and had already slipped inside. Glancing around quickly, guilt wrapping itself round her like a boa constrictor, she took a deep breath and clambered awkwardly over the sill.

'What you after?' asked Jason, suppressed excitement in his voice. Up to this point he'd been remarkably uncurious.

'You're enjoying this, aren't you?'

'Always was a bit of a thrill. Not so much if you get caught, mind.'

'If anyone comes, you get out. In fact, stand by the window just in case.' She didn't like to point out that someone was just as likely to come in through the door.

'Don't be daft. They're all out having a good time. They won't be back for ages.'

Hannah wasn't so sure. Didn't Niamh have school in the morning? God, her hands were shaking.

She switched on her own phone's torch function and cast its dim light over the walls at the shadowy pictures.

'You after a painting?' asked Jason.

'Not to steal it,' she snapped.

'All right, keep your knickers on.'

'Sorry. I'm a bit edgy.'

'Stands to reason. Smart bird like you. The first time's always the worst.'

'There isn't going to be a next time. I'm looking for a map. I want to check something.'

Jason shone the beam from his phone on the opposite wall.

'Like that one?' he asked with a cocky drawl.

'Yes,' said Hannah. 'Brilliant, that's it.' She crossed to the wall, shining the light on the old map. 'Hell. I can't see properly.'

It was much larger than she'd expected and a little too high on the wall for her to get a clear view. 'Damn.' She glanced over at Jason.

'I'm going to have to take it down. Would you mind helping?'

'Sure. You got gloves?

'I'm only looking at it, not stealing it,' she hissed, feeling a little sick now. Together they manoeuvred the map off the wall and laid it on top of the rather messy desk. Hannah peered down at it, trying to get her bearings but the beam wasn't strong enough to cast enough light to enable her to see what she was looking for. She glanced towards the window. 'I'm going to have to put a light on.'

'That's risky,' said Jason. 'But you're in luck. These are good curtains.' Without being asked, he drew the heavy red velvet curtains.

She took in a deep breath and switched on the light, then went back to the map. With her fingers she traced the familiar landmarks. 'This is the house. The cottage. That's the path down to the sea.' She squinted, trying to find the boundary line of the estate. It wasn't terribly clear and it took a while for her to find the pale-yellow line that ran over the field boundaries around the house and down to the sea. At the same time, she was trying to remember where Murphy's fence was.

'Gotcha.' She said, shining her torch beam on the odd dogleg boundary line.

'What are you looking for? Buried treasure?'

'Not quite, but it could be quite a pot of gold for someone. I need to think.'

If this was the boundary line, Murphy's fence was a clear incursion and it had puzzled her for ages as to why he would put a fence there but now she could see it. If Murphy owned that little pocket of land it would give him access to the main road. But he didn't own the land; it belonged to the Byrnes – or rather it did until midnight.

'You're talking in riddles,' Jason said when she explained.

'See here,' she pointed and then a door slammed somewhere inside the house.

They both froze, lifting their heads like startled birds poised to take flight.

'Shit!' said Jason.

'Quick, get out of the window.'

He was already halfway across the room when he turned to look at her. 'Come on.'

Hannah shook her head. 'No, it's all right. First offence. I'll get away with it.'

He pulled an anguished face and she could see he was torn between not wanting to leave her to face the music on her own and understanding the logic.

'Go,' she hissed, flapping her hands and urging him towards the window.

Footsteps marched crisply down the slate floor outside. As quick as a weasel into a tunnel, Jason slid through the gap between the sill and the sash and vanished into the shadows.

There was no time for Hannah to turn off the main light or even attempt to hide so when Conor opened the door, she was waiting quietly, while he jumped.

'Hannah, what—' he said, puzzled at first and then rallying. 'What the hell are you doing in here?'

She heard the suspicion in his voice. He clearly still thought the worst of her.

He glanced down at the desk and the map precariously balanced on top. 'What are you up to?'

'Solving what I perceived to be a problem by taking decisive action,' she snapped, her voice trembling as she repeated his own words back to him. 'Trying to do the right thing even though I'm not sure you deserve it.' She paused, deliberately dredging up the most hurtful thing she could. 'But I'll do it for Adrienne rather than for you.' She stabbed a finger at a spot on the map. 'Murphy's fence. That piece of land will give access to the main road from his land.' Those beautiful new bifold doors from his kitchen-diner windows looked out over Murphy's land. It was probably that very view that might be spoiled.

'Yes, but it's our land.'

'Only until midnight.'

'What do you mean?'

'Niamh's twelve today. You said the fence went up when she was born. You have never challenged Murphy's right to ownership of that land, which he's claimed by putting up the fence. In law, after twelve years, like squatters' rights, it becomes his because you've never challenged it.'

Conor moved quickly and came to stand by her side to study the map. 'Say that again.'

She flinched at his casual closeness. He'd dressed up for the evening in a crisp blue cotton shirt that highlighted those deep-blue eyes of his and she could smell the familiar aftershave that she'd smelled on his pillows when she'd shared his bed. She tamped down the sudden hollow longing.

'In law, if someone claims land and it goes

unchallenged, i.e. you don't make them remove the fence, it becomes theirs.'

'But he can't.'

'He can unless you insist the fence is taken down tonight.'

Conor frowned. 'But Murphy's away. He's gone to County Antrim to the sheep auction.'

Hannah thought for a moment. 'Then we need to take the fence down. Without damaging it.' She looked at her watch. 'Tonight. By taking the fence down, you are challenging the right of it being there. That should stand up in a court of law. If you damage it, he could make a complaint against you, but the imperative is to get it down.'

Conor turned and looked out of the window.

'In this weather? In the middle of the Orchard Party?'

'Yes.'

Chapter Twenty-Seven

'Everything all right?' said Jason, appearing at the window.

Conor jumped. 'Where did you come from?'

'Lookout.' Jason lifted his shoulders in a cheerful, unrepentant shrug.

'We need a plan,' said Hannah. 'Jason, are you in?'

'What, taking the fence down?'

'You were listening?' asked Conor.

'I might have been. Sounds like we need a bit of a crew pulling together.'

Hannah nodded, thoughtfully. 'But we don't want to spoil Adrienne's party.'

'If a few of us sneaked out, she wouldn't notice.'

'Excuse me,' interrupted Conor. 'This is my family's problem the two of you are talking about.'

'Yes,' said Hannah, 'And they're celebrating a birthday as well as it being Adrienne's big night. No one will miss us, but they'd miss all of you.'

'Not me.'

'The great Conor Byrne.'

'There'll be nothing great if Murphy gets his way. I'd never forgive myself. Besides, the party will be over in an hour.'

'Let them enjoy it. There'll be enough of us. Jason, go and round everyone up. They're going to need to change as it's raining cats and dogs out there.'

'We'd say, raining stair rods,' said Conor with a sudden devilish grin. 'It's wet. And I like a woman who takes charge.'

Hannah glared at him, ignoring this, and peered out of the window. 'Stair rods? That's an understatement.'

'I'd say pissing it down but I'd probably have to put a euro in the jar,' said Jason.

'Let's meet at the cottage as soon as we can.' Hannah was already planning. 'We're going to need some tools.'

'I've got some in the truck,' said Conor. 'There are more in the workshop. I'll round some up and meet you at the cottage.'

Going their separate ways, they parted outside the door of the office, leaving Hannah to pick her way down the track to the cottage, bitterly regretting the vanity that had forced her to wear the shoes. She'd wanted to show Conor that she was indifferent to him leaving the shoe for her.

Jason must have impressed the urgency upon everyone because five minutes after Hannah had changed and pulled on a pair of wellies, he and Fliss appeared, dripping, at the front door.

'This is a bit of an adventure,' said Fliss cheerfully. 'Saving the day.'

'It's a bit grim out there,' Hannah said apologetically. 'Sorry to drag you away when it was so cosy in the greenhouse.'

'No matter,' Fliss shrugged. 'Let's face it, we'd all do anything for Adrienne, wouldn't we? Oh, quick, come in.' Fliss beckoned Alan, Meredith, and Izzy into the cottage from the porch, as well as Seamus and Peter who, it transpired, had insisted on getting on the act.

'Moss Murphy and his crowd are a bad seed – gombeen men the pack of them,' said Seamus, shaking the rain from his cloth cap, as he stepped into the cottage in dark overalls and heavy-duty boots.

'Bad cess to them,' said Peter.

The grumbling between the two of them stopped when the lights of Conor's truck appeared outside.

They made a motley crew, trooping down, rustling along the path in rain-slicked waterproofs and wellies, armed with an assortment of tools, but there was an air of underlying excitement as if this was a great adventure. The rain had found its way inside Hannah's coat and an insistent trickle made its way down her neck, pooling into her bra but, fired up by the determination to right a wrong, she tugged at the hood and marched on beside a silent Conor. She was grateful for his silence because she felt uncomfortable in his presence. She'd practically told him – she *had* told him – that she was in love with him but she wasn't about to apologise for it. If they both ignored it, she could hold her head up high and pretend it meant nothing.

'Hannah?' he said, just loud enough to be heard over the wind and the rain.

'Mm,' she said noncommittally.

'I owe you an apology. Mam told me that you've got a job here. That you're going to be a lawyer.'

'I already am a lawyer,' she snapped. She wasn't going to let him off the hook.

'I jumped to conclusions and I'm sorry.'

'So you should be.'

Conor lapsed into silence. 'You're not going to make this easy for me, are you?'

'Make what easy?'

'Do I need to grovel?'

'I've no idea what you're talking about. You've apologised.'

'So that's how you're going to play it?' Annoyingly he grinned at her and then reached for one of her rain-soaked curls and pushed it off her forehead.

She scowled at him and stepped back, annoyed by his confidence.

'And here you are rescuing me again? I might need to keep you around.'

'*You*? Might need to keep *me* around?' She spoke with scorn. 'I promise you, my decision to stay has nothing to do with you and everything to do with me.'

Conor's grin widened. 'Even better.'

'What did you say?' That stung. Clearly he didn't care about her.

'That's been my problem. The women in my life wanted

Killorgally and Conor Byrne, celebrity chef, more than they wanted me.'

'Poor you.' Did he honestly think that she was going to forgive him and let him saunter back into her life, back to a temporary relationship? She wanted all or nothing. No half-measures.

'Yes. I did feel sorry for myself about that for too long. I took up with the wrong women. You're different.'

'You betcha,' said Hannah. 'And I'm not interested anymore.'

'What?' Conor's surprise was almost comical.

'I deserve more than a fling. I'm staying in Ireland for me. Not you.'

That had taken the wind out of his cocky, confident sails and she slowed her stride, allowing Izzy, Jason, and Fliss to catch up with her. Conor looked back, the expression on his face puzzled and she felt a tiny spike of satisfaction. He was used to women falling at his feet. Well, this one wasn't going to.

The fence loomed up out of the driving rain and everyone naturally huddled around Conor and Hannah as the wind swirled into their faces.

'We need to get the fence down but without damaging any of the posts and rails,' shouted Conor over the wind howling around them. Everyone in rain-slicked coats and hoods nodded, their torches bobbing, looking rather like a group of dementors. 'They all need to be neatly stacked on the other side of the boundary.' Conor pointed to the dry-stone wall that marked the separation between Murphy and Byrne land. He consulted with Seamus and Peter for a moment as they studied the fence, tugging at the rails nailed to the posts, working out the construction.

'OK, it's probably best if we organise into groups. Seamus and Alan, Peter and Jason, Fliss, Izzy and Meredith. Me and Hannah, we'll prise the rails off and the rest of you carry them over to the wall.'

If Conor thought he was going to win her over by pairing up with her, he had another think coming. Ignoring her glower, Conor directed everyone to different sections of the fence. 'Once we've got a few off, we'll start trying to loosen the posts. Luckily, Murphy and his nephew obviously believed this fence didn't need to last too long, so they never bothered cementing the posts in.'

Hannah followed him to their allotted section and he handed her a claw-footed hammer to start pulling the nails out. Her fingers slipped on the handle several times and she bruised and scraped her knuckles on the rough wood but she didn't say a word, just kept working, hunched into her coat.

'You all right?'

'Fine,' she replied, ignoring the curl of longing at the concern in his voice. This was the perfect way to halt things between them. Somewhere along the line she'd realised she wanted a proper relationship. One without a pre-agreed expiration date.

They pulled the first rail away and immediately set to work on the second.

'Are you going to give me the cold shoulder all night?' he asked as they moved onto the next set of rail.

'Who benefits the most from this?' responded Hannah, with a roll of her eyes and a sigh.

'What do you mean?'

She ripped out a nail with perhaps more force that the poor thing required, accidentally pinging it across the field. 'Any building on Murphy's land is going to ruin the view from your new house. Do you think I want to be out here in the pouring rain?' She gave an angry yank at a second nail which screeched against the wood as the plank yawned away from the post and fell to the ground. She wanted to pick it up and bash Conor around the head with it. Knock a bit of sense into him.

'You've made assumptions from the very first time we met,' she said, marching onto the next post as Izzy scurried forward to collect the wood, darting anxious glances at them both. 'You assumed that I knew who you were, that I want to be a cook, that I'm here to get in with Adrienne, that I've designs on your house.' She whacked the back of the post with an almighty swing to loosen the plank from the upright. It popped out straight away and fell with a thud into the sodden grass. She took another swing at the lower rail and that popped out with one blow. She was on a roll and already striding to the next post. Conor dodged out the way as she swung again.

'I'm not like Polly Daventree. I don't want anything from you. I'm my own woman with my own successful career and you're too stupid to see that.'

Conor caught her by the shoulders. 'If you'd just slow down and give me a chance to explain.'

'To explain what? Conor, I knew you were a chancer the

first time I met you. I've always known I'm not the sort of woman you would keep. Yeah, I'm pissed off that you thought I was using you, but let's face it, I've never been in your league.'

'What the hell are you talking about?'

'I'm safe, sensible Hannah Campbell, who lives by the book and doesn't take risks. You're Conor Byrne – you've lived all over the world, dated models and actresses. An exciting, glamorous life. I don't compare to that.'

'Now who's being the eejit?' He gave her a gentle shake and then to her surprise kissed her. It was a gentle, coaxing kiss, his hands sliding up her wet face. 'Why do you think I left the shoe on the bed?'

'To be done with me.'

'Don't you believe in fairy tales?'

'No.'

'There really is no romance in your soul, is there?'

'No.' She really didn't believe in fairy tales.

His thumbs stroked her cheekbones. 'I thought that perhaps the prince returning the shoe to Cinderella might say something.'

Hannah stared at him incredulously. 'I think your romantic gestures need some work.'

'Oh for the love of God, woman.' He hauled her against his chest and kissed her again, this time with a thoroughness that left her reeling. 'I love you, all right. I didn't want to. Didn't plan to and I've been fighting it all the way. You caught me by surprise when you said you were staying because I realised that I wanted that more than anything and it shocked the hell out of me. I panicked, OK.

Because I'm an eejit. Actually, I think you said I was a "big, stupid, arrogant, up-yourself eejit". And you might have had a point.'

'You love me,' said Hannah, dazed by the words. 'You can't.'

'Why can't I?'

'Because people like you don't fall in love with people like me.'

'What arrogant, up-yourself eejits can't fall in love with smart, beautiful women? Darn it, that's a shame because I just did.' He flashed his Conor grin at her.

'Do you ever take anything seriously?'

His face sobered and he trailed a finger down her neck. 'I take this seriously. I want you to stay in Ireland. I want you to be here in the winter. In the spring. In the summer, and all the way to next autumn. I want to share all the seasons of Killorgally with you.'

'Excuse me,' said Jason. 'I'd say get a room but we need to get this bugger down.'

Hannah turned around and realised that everyone had stopped to watch them. She felt her cheeks burn until she spotted Meredith and Izzy grinning broadly at her and even Fliss who rolled her eyes had a smile on her face.

They were moving onto the last few posts when there was an angry shout.

'Hey! Hey! What do you think you're doing?' Hannah recognised him immediately. This had to be Moss Murphy's nephew. His face was so screwed up with incandescent fury that his features seemed to blur like a crumpled tissue.

Running and almost tripping in what looked like

oversize wellies, he stormed up to Seamus who was shaking one of the posts loose. 'Get off that. That's my property.'

'Aye, fella, Niall Flanagan, isn't it? The post is yours. Not the land,' said Seamus, relinquishing his hold of the post quite calmly. Flanagan was left holding the post, clearly not knowing what his next move should be.

Conor strode over and Hannah, secure in her legal knowledge and buoyed up by a remnant of anger at their initial confrontation, followed.

'Flanagan, is it? You're most welcome to your fence. We've put it on *your* land. All neat and tidy. Doing you a favour, like.'

Flanagan's mouth bunched as if he wanted to spit tacks and then his eyes zeroed in on Hannah.

'You. The lawyer. This is your doing. I knew I should have kept a better eye on you.'

Hannah stared at him, a chill coming at the memory of how frightened she'd been that night. 'It was you. You were the one in the garden. At the window. You came into the cottage.'

Flanagan gave her a sullen glare. 'I wasn't doing any harm. Just wanted to find who you were and what you were about.'

'Why?'

'You said you were a lawyer. I thought maybe the Byrnes had guessed what—'

'That you were playing to steal their land from under them.'

'They've got loads; they wouldn't have missed this small

bit. We've a right to make money too, you know. Bloody Byrnes are making a fortune. It's not fair. And everything would have been all right if you hadn't stuck your nose in.' He sneered. 'I should have tried a bit harder to frighten you off.'

Conor's fists bunched and he took a menacing step towards him, before saying in a growl, 'You stay off our land, Mr Flanagan. If I catch you trespassing again, I'll be calling the guards. But if I find you within ten foot of the lawyer, I'll beat the living daylights out of ye, so I will.' Conor's accent had thickened and the violence in his voice resonated in the dank air.

Hannah shivered. She had no doubt that Conor meant every word and from the expression on Flanagan's face, he wouldn't be troubling them ever again.

Drawing himself up straight, Conor added, 'And I'll be speaking to your uncle in the morning to remind him just where the boundaries of our land lie. You'd be most welcome to look at the map I'll be sending over.' He turned away, deliberately putting his back in Flanagan's face to make it quite clear that the business was over. 'Let's finish up here, lads and lasses. Our work is done.' He put his arm around Hannah and steered her away. She didn't normally go in for all that He-Man stuff, believing that she could stand on her own two feet, but, just this once, it was rather nice to feel that her man would go into battle for her.

Flanagan retreated, watching balefully as the last post was removed and handed over the wall to him.

'All done,' said Conor, with a shark-like smile. Flanagan looked a little sick. 'You'll not be accessing the road this way. If I were you, I'd give up on your grand property developing plans and head back to Dublin.'

With a nod he turned and was flanked by Seamus and Peter.

'Nicely done, boyo,' said Seamus. 'The aul sleeveen thought he was gettin' one over on us. Murphy won't be up to his tricks anytime soon.'

'He will not,' agreed Peter, chuckling to himself. 'That was mighty.'

Conor gave Hannah a rescue-me grimace but she just grinned back and fell into step next to Izzy. There was time enough to catch up and she wanted to relish this fizzy feeling inside as she gave him covert glances, still not quite believing that he'd said he loved her. Did that really happen? She'd always thought falling in love was a gradual slow-build, and when she'd tumbled off the cliff edge, it had never occurred to her that Conor might do too. She was still coming to terms with it and knew she had a silly smile plastered across her face. Conor *loved her*. What were the chances? If she'd had the chance to think about it, it wasn't a risk she'd ever have taken.

'You OK?' asked Izzy, her freckled face covered in rain and strands of hair plastered to her cheeks but her face stretched in a teasing smile.

'Yes,' said Hannah, unable to hold back her grin. 'A bit knackered and my hands feel like they're full of splinters.'

'Hannaaaaah! You're not going to talk about that kiss?'

Hannah pinched her lips together but she couldn't hold the happiness in. 'Nothing to talk about,' she said but her eyes told another story altogether.

Izzy wasn't deterred. 'I knew something was going on. Meredith and I said there was. Alan didn't agree. Merry's going to be pleased to tell him he was wrong. It was almost as if the air pressure dropped when the two of you were in a room together.'

'It did not,' scoffed Hannah.

'Did, so. Are you going to tell me how long it's been going on?'

Grazing her lip with her teeth, Hannah toyed with telling her the truth but then at the last minute, decided not to. Some things were best kept private. So instead she said evasively, 'It just developed in the cottage.'

'And that's all you're saying.' Izzy tucked her arm through Hannah's. 'Well good for you. He seems to be a good 'un.'

'He is.'

Izzy shivered. 'It's not every night you stand in the pouring rain pulling down fences but I have to say it's been fun.'

'Jason certainly enjoyed it,' said Hannah with a wry smile.

'If he doesn't make it as a chef, there's a job in demolition with his name on.'

'I have to admit,' said Meredith, chipping in from the other side where she and Alan were walking arm in arm, 'I feel a terrific sense of achievement. A bit like Robin Hood,' she glanced at Alan, 'or Maid Marion. Or should that be Matron Marion.'

'You're not that old,' he muttered, nudging her before

muttering something in her ear to which she laughed in delight but didn't share with the other two.

Izzy exchanged a smile with Hannah. Alan and Meredith seemed so well suited; it was difficult to believe they hadn't always been a couple.

Out of the gloom, like a pistol shot, Adrienne's voice rang out, 'Conor Byrne! What in the name of Jesus, Mary, and Joseph is going on?'

Chapter Twenty-Eight

Adrienne strode towards them, her Driza-Bone coat flapping like bat's wings, flanked on one side by Bridget in a bright-red sou'wester hat, pink polka-dot wellies and a floor-length see-through mac over her party dress with Franklin and Niamh in matching cagoules on the other, followed by Fergus who held an outsize umbrella which wasn't doing anything to protect him from the rain at all.

'Uncle Con. Why d'ye leave the party?' asked Niamh.

'It's a long story but it's done. Come on, let's get out of this rain and I'll tell you what's been going on.'

'Did you find the prowler?' asked Bridget, skipping along as she tried to keep pace with Conor's long strides. Everyone followed up the path to the cottage without invitation. It seemed they all wanted to join in and take credit for their part in the drama – all except for the two pigmen who waved goodbye.

'Some of us have an early start,' called Seamus.

One by one they entered through the porch, draping wet coats on the hooks and the doors, and discarding shoes and boots so that there was a haphazard pile that would take some sorting to match up the pairs. Hannah grinned at the sight. This place felt like home, and everyone in it like family. The thought of it lit a warm glow in her heart. This was what she'd been looking for and she hadn't even realised it. A community of her own. With sudden confidence, she knew that she could build one here, in Ireland with her old friends, her new friends, and Conor. It might not last for ever but it was worth taking the risk to find out.

Conor caught her eye, nodded towards the kitchen and the two of them fought their way there through the crowded hall.

'I think it's hot whiskeys all round,' he said, going straight to one of the cupboards and pulling out a whiskey bottle.

'An excellent idea, Conor,' said Bridget who'd bustled in behind them and began reaching around him to take mugs from the other cupboard.

Hannah took a step back as the two of them swung into action, with Adrienne materialising and joining in. It was the proverbial well-oiled machine with the three of them elegantly manoeuvring around each other. Conor sliced wedges of lemon and pierced the flesh with clove and Bridget spooned out brown sugar into all the cups and mugs that Adrienne had gathered from every corner of the kitchen. Amazingly there were twelve which was just enough for all the people that had now crowded into the kitchen as well. Fergus, with Niamh on his knee, Franklin, and Meredith had squashed themselves into the sofa by the wood burner, which Alan was lighting, while Izzy, Fliss, and Jason took kitchen chairs.

At last, with boiling hot water poured into the mugs of whiskey, lemon, sugar, and cloves, the drinks were doled out. With hot whiskey to sip and the fire roaring in the wood burner, everyone quietened. It felt like story time as Conor looked around the room. 'Sláinte.' Everyone chorused, 'Sláinte,' back to him and took a sip.

'Ah *uisce beatha*,' sighed Franklin. 'Water of life.'

'It certainly is,' said Adrienne, closing her eyes for a moment before turning a fierce gaze on Conor. 'Now, are you going to tell us what kept you from the party?'

'You know Moss Murphy's been bragging about making his fortune?'

'Yes, but you told me yourself, from Patrick, that he has no access. The bottom half of the road is ours.'

'Ah but the aul devil realised he could get access through the bottom field onto the main road.'

'How?' asked Bridget indignantly. ''Tis our land and has been forever.'

Conor turned to Hannah. 'Would you like to explain?'

'In law, if someone helps themselves to a piece of land and the landowner doesn't object or claim it back, after twelve years it legally belongs to them. Moss Murphy put the fence up twelve years ago and because you never took it down or asked him to, legally he could claim that you hadn't objected.'

'That bastard,' spat Bridget.

'That'll be a euro in the jar,' said Jason, folding his arms and leaning back in his chair with an ever so slightly smug expression.

'Twelve years?' echoed Franklin. 'The sneaky shite.'

'And another one.' Jason grinned.

'I'll fecking kill him if I get my hands on him,' said Adrienne, her face reddening. 'And before you say it, Jason, I'll put ten euros in the jar because I've a feeling I'll be using a lot of bad language before morning. How dare that bastard try and steal from under us.'

'It's OK.' Hannah held up a calming hand. 'We took the fence down before the twelve years was up.'

'How do you know?' asked Fergus from the sofa.

'Because,' Bridget nodded, tapping her nose, 'I recall clear as day. Murphy put that fence up the day Niamh was born, when we were all at the hospital. And she'll be twelve in a little over fifty-eight minutes.'

'Happy birthday to me,' said Niamh, taking furtive sips of her hot whiskey. Hannah wondered if she was hoping that no one had noticed she had one.

'Exactly,' said Conor. 'And we've Hannah to thank for realising it.' He pulled her towards him and put his arm round her, placing a kiss on her cheek.

Adrienne beamed and whispered loudly to Bridget. 'I knew it.'

'No you did not. You do talk nonsense sometimes.' Bridget rolled her eyes.

'What, you're shagging Hannah?' said Fergus suddenly.

'Fergus Liam Kenneth Byrne. Wash your mouth out with

soap and in front of Niamh,' said Adrienne but her eyes were dancing just a little.

'Thanks, little brother. I think some people might call it *walking out with*.'

'I don't mind,' said Niamh stoutly. 'She's much nicer than Polly.'

'That she is,' said Bridget with a smug smile.

'Which reminds me,' said Conor. 'I had a very irate text from Polly accusing me of poisoning you against her.' He raised quizzical eyebrows at his mother.

Adrienne winced. 'She wasn't over pleased when I refused to let her gatecrash the Orchard Party. I'm not sure she could believe it when I had Seamus throw her out.'

'Polly was here?' Conor stared incredulously at his mother.

Adrienne shrugged. 'She wasn't invited. I certainly wasn't going to give her preferential treatment.' She met his gaze. 'Not anymore.'

'About time too,' said Bridget.

Hannah had to smile, as much at the others avidly watching the family in action as the family themselves. She couldn't blame Polly for wanting to be part of this.

Conor and his mother exchanged a small smile.

'Right, well, now that we've all warmed up, I for one am ready for my bed,' said Bridget. 'And we should let these two have some peace and quiet.' With that she stood up and like a well-trained sheep dog began to chivvy everyone out, interrupting each time someone began a new conversation.

At last, everyone had filed out and Hannah could hear their good-natured chatter disappearing into the night as

Conor waved them off at the door. She slumped into the sofa and drained her hot whiskey. Exhaustion suddenly rolled over her, as well as a touch of shyness now that she and Conor were alone. She closed her eyes for a moment and when she opened them Conor was standing in front of her, obviously holding something behind his back.

'What are you up to?' she asked.

'So suspicious,' he tsked, shaking his head with a mischievous smile.

'I might have fallen in love with you but I haven't completely taken leave of my senses. You have that up-to-no-good air about you.'

'Moi?' He shuffled on the spot.

'Yes, you.'

He ducked down onto his knees and dropped something to the floor. The next moment, he lifted one of her feet, sliding her foot into a shoe. She lifted her leg and looked at the black shoe she'd once abandoned.

'Last time, I got this wrong. The shoe fits. It's part of a pair. I'd like us to be a pair. Two. Together. I love you.'

She laughed, although inside, her heart tingled at the tender words and the warmth glowing in his eyes. 'You know romantic gestures are wasted on me, right?'

With a mock-mournful sigh, he shook his head. 'There really is no romance in your soul, is there?'

'Sorry,' she grinned unrepentantly up at him.

'So I had to come up with something practical to win your heart, as you completely misunderstood my gesture with the shoe.'

'It wasn't exactly obvious.'

'In my head it was. The handsome prince returns the shoe to his love.'

'Mmm. Or the bounder gets rid of the last piece of evidence.'

Conor laughed. 'We're going to have to work on your sensibilities, *mo grá*. But I have something for you.'

He reached under the sofa for a manilla envelope that he must have put there while she'd had her eyes closed.

'What's this?'

'You could open it and find out.'

'I don't like surprises, remember?'

'You'll like this one.'

'So confident, so cocky.'

'That's me. Now, are you going to open it or sit here and call me names all night?'

Kissing him on his nose, she slid a finger under the flap of the envelope and pulled a couple of sheets of A4 paper from the envelope, really puzzled now.

Law Society of Ireland

Then the bold heading beneath.

Certificate of Admission England and Wales

Her eyes stumbled to the first line below.

This form is for use by the following qualified lawyers who wish to apply to go on the Roll of Solicitors in the Republic of Ireland:

She lifted her head, her eyes meeting Conor's. It was the application form to practise in Ireland.

'When did you print this off?'

'Earlier this evening, before the party. I want you to stay,' he said softly. 'More than anything.'

Hannah smiled mistily at him, holding the sheet of paper. 'Now this is what I call a romantic gesture.'

Acknowledgments

A huge thank you to all my wonderful readers who continue to travel to each new destination in the Romantic Escapes series. If it weren't for your support I wouldn't be in the lucky position of being able to make stuff up for a living.

Special thanks go to my lovely friend, Alison, who accompanied me on my trip to Ireland and insisted we went out on a boat in Dingle Bay on a cold grey November day to see Fungie the dolphin. It was a truly magical experience and I wouldn't have missed it for the world. Sadly Fungie is no longer with us but I hope his mention in the book is a small tribute to the joy he gave to so many visitors.

Ireland is the most wonderful place and I hope you enjoyed the trip. I've only touched on a tiny fraction of all there is to see and do, so apologies for all that I've missed.

Thanks go to my amazing writer friend, Donna Ashcroft, who helped so much with this book. It's no lie to say that without her writing would be a lot less fun and an awful lot harder than it already is. I also thank the 'Party People' messenger gang, fellow authors, Phillipa Ashley, Bella Osborne, Darcie Boleyn and Sarah Bennett who keep me sane and cheer me on. Thanks guys, you're the best!

And last but by no means least, my wonderful agent Broo, for always believing in me, and Charlotte Ledger, quite simply an amazing editor and an all-round star. Thank you, lovely ladies, for making me shine.

ONE MORE CHAPTER

One More Chapter is an
award-winning global
division of HarperCollins.

Sign up to our newsletter to get our
latest eBook deals and stay up to date
with our weekly Book Club!
<u>Subscribe here.</u>

Meet the team at
<u>www.onemorechapter.com</u>

Follow us!
 @<u>OneMoreChapter</u>_
 @<u>OneMoreChapter</u>
 @<u>onemorechapterhc</u>

Do you write unputdownable fiction?
We love to hear from new voices.
Find out how to submit your novel at
<u>www.onemorechapter.com/submissions</u>